The Osiris Ritual

A Newbury & Hobbes Investigation

George Mann

First edition

Proudly published in 2009 by
Snowbooks Ltd.
120 Pentonville Road
London
N1 9JN
www.snowbooks.com

Library Hardback ISBN: 978-1-906727-031
Slipcased Hardback ISBN: 978-1-906727-444

A catalogue ⟨...⟩ ⟨...⟩ ⟨...⟩ ⟨...⟩ Library.

Print⟨...⟩ ⟨...⟩ et

Dedication

For Emily May Irene Mann

Acknowledgements

Thanks, as ever, must be extended to Emma Barnes and Liz Gorinsky for continued support. Also to Gordon Fletcher for superb pedantry, and to Jonas Eyles and Craig Caithness for goading him in the pub (and for making me feel better about losing every round of golf to them both). Mark Hodder kept me busy with inspirational reading matter, and Michael Rowley and Mark Newton debated the meaning of life over a number of excellent curries. Lou Anders shared in all of the highs and lows. And Fiona, James and Emily put up with me spending long hours locked away in the study when I really should have been doing something else.

About the Author

George Mann is the head of a major SF/Fantasy publishing imprint. He is the editor of *The Solaris Book of New Science Fiction* and *The Solaris Book of New Fantasy* and the author of *The Mammoth Encyclopedia of Science Fiction* (Constable & Robinson), *The Human Abstract* (Telos), *The Severed Man* (Telos) and *The Child of Time* (Telos, with David J. Howe). His short stories have appeared in venues such as *Black Sails*, *Apex Digest*, *Triquorum* and an anthology of Doctor Who stories. He lives near Grantham with his wife, son and daughter.

Chapter One

London, February 1902

George Purefoy was running late.

The young reporter hurtled down the street, his notebook clutched tightly in his hand, dodging out of the way of the other pedestrians, who eyed him warily as he raced by like some crazed animal, pursued by an invisible pack of hounds. His sand-coloured hair stung his eyes where it whipped across his face in the driving wind. His dinner suit was crumpled and now, to top things off, it had started to rain. The biggest assignment of his career to date, and things had already started to go terribly wrong.

Purefoy skipped around a red post box, narrowly missed colliding with an elderly gentleman in a top hat, and finally flung himself – at speed – around a bend in the road. There, in the distance, was Albion House, the home of Lord Henry Winthrop. The street outside the house was bathed in bright yellow light from the glare in the windows, and even from here, a good hundred feet away, the noise of the party spilled out to form a cacophony of chatter in the otherwise quiet London evening.

Purefoy, catching his breath, slowed his pace to a steady walk. He attempted to regain his composure, smoothing his jacket and straightening his tie. Rain pattered lightly on his face. Other guests were still arriving at the big house, and whilst he was most definitely late, it didn't look to Purefoy like he had missed the main event. At least he hoped not: his career as a reporter depended on it.

Purefoy had made his way here, across town from the office, for *the* society event of the year, to cover the return of the explorer and philanthropist Lord Henry Winthrop from his expedition to Egypt, and more, to attend the grand unveiling of his greatest find: the mummified remains of an ancient Theban king. There had been a great deal of fanfare about the success of the expedition over the last few weeks, accompanied by wild claims from Winthrop that the mummy was a unique specimen; found still wrapped in its finery, it was said to bear strange markings that were unfamiliar to any of the experts he had consulted at the British Museum. It was the talk of London, and tonight, Winthrop planned to unwrap the bindings of the long-dead king before a select audience of guests.

Much to the chagrin of his fellow reporters, Purefoy had been offered the assignment to cover the event for *The Times*, following the success of his recent piece about the revenant plague and the government conspiracy to hide the fact that it was still spreading unchecked through the London slums. He'd set off in plenty of time, of course, first picking out his best suit and selecting a brand new notebook from his pile. But then the ground train he was on had shuddered to a halt a few streets away, and word had spread throughout the carriages that a spooked horse had caused a cart to overturn, spilling its cargo of rags and bones across the tracks up ahead. Knowing that he didn't have much further to go, and sure that waiting for the engineers to clear the tracks would cause him to miss the party, he had taken matters into his own hands and instead set out on foot. Now, uncomfortable, damp and late, he was starting to wonder whether the assignment itself was actually more of a curse than the blessing it had at first appeared to be.

Purefoy quickened his step and made his way along the street towards the party. Grand houses loomed over him from both sides of the wide street. This was a London as unfamiliar to him as the slums he usually found himself writing about. The people who lived in these enormous mansions moved in circles entirely outside of his experience, and he found himself feeling not a little nervous at the prospect of having to hold his own with a crowd of such gentlemen, lords and ladies. Nevertheless, he was certainly anxious to see what Lord Winthrop had brought back with him from the Middle East, and more specifically to bear witness to the unrolling of the Pharaoh himself.

He stopped at the bottom of the steps to let a lady in a billowing, cream-coloured dress – who had just stepped out of a private carriage – enter the party before him. She offered him a gracious smile as he stepped to one side to allow her to pass. He eyed the butler by the front door as the man checked the lady's invitation and showed her inside. Judging by the standard of the servants, Purefoy was starting to feel a little underdressed. He checked his suit again, conscious that he was more than a little crumpled and damp. Sighing, he patted his pockets and located the invitation card. Then, warily, he mounted the steps and presented the card to the older, balding man, who looked Purefoy up and down and raised an eyebrow before examining the card he'd been handed. There was a brief pause.

"Ah, yes sir. With *The Times*. Won't you come this way?" It was as if the man's entire demeanour had changed upon seeing the invitation. Purefoy gave him a quizzical look. He couldn't tell whether the butler had altered his previously haughty attitude because of his respect for the newspaper, or because, upon realising that Purefoy was a reporter, he had somehow lowered his expectations. Either way, he supposed it didn't matter all that much. He followed the butler in through the grand porch, which was impressively decorated with a series of stained-glass panels and Minton tiles, and stepped through the inner door that the butler held open for him on the other side. A moment later he was standing in the grand hallway, where the party was already in full swing.

Purefoy gazed on in amazement. It was like nothing he'd seen before, in all of his life. An enormous staircase dominated the space, its sweeping banisters curving up to form a large gallery that looked down upon the bustling hall. Glass cabinets had been erected at regular intervals all around the tiled floor, filled with the most wondrous gilded treasures from the tomb of the mummified king. People milled around these cabinets, cooing appreciatively, drinks in hand, courting one another with sidelong glances and averted gazes. Purefoy almost laughed out loud. It was like every cliché he could have imagined, and more sumptuous and extravagant than even those. The women floated around in the most magnificent dresses of coloured silk, brandishing their drinks like weapons. The men looked austere in their formal attire, and clustered together in little groups, talking in hushed tones. *This*, Purefoy thought to himself, *is all of London society, here together in one room.* He didn't know whether to be giddy or appalled at the thought.

Feeling a little lost, Purefoy cast around for anyone he recognised. There were faces he'd seen in portraits and photographs, but no one it would be proper for him to approach at a party, at least without a formal introduction. Up on the gallery, he noted Lord Winthrop himself was resting against the balustrade, surveying the scene below. He was sporting a wide grin. When he spotted Purefoy looking, he offered the reporter a little wave, and then pushed himself away from his perch and began making his way along the landing towards the stairs.

Purefoy had met Lord Winthrop only once before, the prior week, when the lord had visited the offices of *The Times* to discuss an exclusive on the story with the editor. He seemed like a gregarious sort of chap, with a welcoming manner, but Purefoy was not so naïve as to miss the fact that the only reason Winthrop was making a beeline towards him through the party was because his inflated ego compelled him to entertain the reporter who would be providing a write-up of his event for the morning edition. He smiled and held out his hand as the lord approached him, the other guests turning to see who their host had decided to grace with his presence.

"Mr. Purefoy! A pleasure. Are you enjoying the party?" Lord Winthrop was a tall, stocky man with broad shoulders, a long, greying beard and a receding hairline. He carried his weight around his jowls and his waist, and his voice was friendly but with an overbearing boom.

Purefoy smiled. "Alas, I've only this moment arrived. An accident in the road meant I had to finish my journey on foot. I trust I haven't missed the main event?"

Winthrop patted Purefoy easily on the shoulder. "Not at all, my good man. Not at all. It's been four thousand years since the Theban was confined to his bandages. I'd say there is no imperative to rush, wouldn't you? Now, let's get you a drink..." Chuckling, Winthrop gestured towards the row of statues situated along the back wall, to either side of the huge staircase. Purefoy watched, fascinated, as one of the statues stepped down from its perch, collected a tray of drinks from a nearby table, and made its way jerkily towards them. Purefoy had assumed the statues were part of the display, items brought back from the expedition by Winthrop and his team. The one coming towards them looked every bit the part: a flawless, life-size replica of an Ancient Egyptian statue, replete with carved headdress and blank, staring eyes.

Winthrop laughed when he saw the young reporter's expression. "Dear boy, haven't you seen one of these new Ottoman automaton devices?"

Purefoy shook his head.

"Why, they're all the rage. Much better than those terrible British things we had last year. No, these truly are wondrous machines. Look here." He waved at the device as it came closer, and Purefoy stood agape as Winthrop took a flute of champagne from the proffered tray. "Brass framework of unsightly cogs and things underneath, but a porcelain veneer over the top, designed to order. I had these ones made up in the style of the twelfth dynasty. Remarkable, aren't they? Just like living statues."

Purefoy accepted the glass of champagne from Winthrop and took a long sip. "Indeed they are. Very impressive." He watched as the bizarre creation made its way back through the crowd, returned the tray to its place on the table and climbed back on to its pedestal beside its fellows. He studied it for a moment, unnerved by the manner in which it had so easily blended once again into the background, becoming nothing but another immobile exhibit. He repressed a shudder. Purefoy turned to Winthrop, who he realised had been talking at him for some time.

"...and there is Lord and Lady Buchanan, talking to Sir David and his wife. Oh yes, and there's Sir Maurice Newbury, examining some of the ushabti idols in that glass cabinet over there. Yes, perfect, I should say. You should meet Sir Maurice right away. Come on. I'm sure he'd be delighted to meet a man from *The Times*."

Winthrop led him through the crowds towards a man who was standing alone beside one of the glass cases, examining the items on display inside. The man was wearing a thoughtful expression and the glass of champagne he was clutching in his left hand appeared to be untouched. He looked up, distractedly, as Winthrop and Purefoy approached, and smiled when he recognised his host. He came out from behind the cabinet, giving Purefoy the opportunity to see him properly. He was dressed in a fitted black suit with white shirt and bow tie. His hair was jet black and swept back from his forehead, and his emerald eyes glittered above a hawkish nose. Purefoy guessed he was in his mid-thirties, but could have been older. He extended his hand and Winthrop took it firmly.

"Lord Winthrop. A pleasure to see you again. I trust you are well, following your return from the Middle East?"

Winthrop nodded vigorously. "Well enough, Sir Maurice, well enough. I see you've been admiring my little collection."

"Indeed. Quite a find you had out there in the desert, Henry. I'm particularly intrigued by the markings on this series of four ushabti figures. They seem very unusual –" He stopped, suddenly, looking up to see Purefoy standing off to one side, sipping at his champagne. "Oh. How terribly impolite of me." He stepped over towards Purefoy and extended his hand. "Please, forgive me...?"

"Purefoy. George Purefoy."

"Please forgive me, Mr. Purefoy. It's just I get a little carried away when I find myself surrounded by such exquisite objects as these."

Purefoy laughed at the man's obvious embarrassment. In truth, it was Lord Winthrop's faux pas for not introducing them, but Purefoy took it as a measure of the man that he accepted the error on himself. "Not at all, Sir Maurice. It's a pleasure to meet you."

Winthrop clapped his hands together with a hearty laugh. "Capital! Maurice – Purefoy here is a reporter with *The Times*. He's going to be writing a piece about tonight's little soirée for the morning edition."

Newbury offered Purefoy a sly, knowing grin. "Indeed? And have you decided yet how you intend to approach your piece?"

Purefoy glanced awkwardly at Winthrop, who smiled at him expectantly. He cocked his head to one side in thought. "I don't believe I have, as yet. I think it rather hinges on the centrepiece." He paused, glancing around at the gathered crowd. "I'm sure it will be a spectacular revelation for us all."

Winthrop stepped forward and clapped him – a little over-zealously – on the back. "Don't doubt it, dear boy! Don't doubt it for a minute. Now, I really must attend to Lady Worthington over there. She looks a little lost amongst the canopic jars. I'll leave you in the capable hands of Sir Maurice, here." He trailed off, his attention already across the other side of the room. Purefoy stepped aside to let him pass, and smiled as Winthrop's exasperated voice boomed loudly behind him. "Lady Worthington... Over here, my dear."

Newbury leaned in towards Purefoy. He lowered his voice to a conspiratorial whisper. "Lovely old chap, but quite lost in his own magnificence, if you know what I mean."

Purefoy chuckled. "Precisely."

"Of course," Newbury looked momentarily troubled, "you won't print that, will you?"

Purefoy shook his head. "Indeed not, Sir Maurice. Your commentary is safe in my hands."

Newbury laughed. "Excellent to hear it!" He sipped at his champagne. "Now, have they given you any notion about what's *really* going on in this room?"

Purefoy frowned. "I'm not sure that I quite understand."

Newbury grinned. "I'll take that as a no." He beckoned Purefoy forward. "Stand here for a minute. Tell me what you see."

Perplexed, Purefoy edged forward until he was standing beside the glass cabinet that Newbury had been studying a few moments earlier. Newbury gestured to the crush of people. "Out there. What do you see?"

"I see a crowd of people, all dressed in their finery, here to see the unrolling of a four-thousand-year-old mummy from Thebes."

Newbury laughed again. "I thought that's what you'd say."

"Why, what do you see?"

"I see a crowd of people desperate to be seen, all dressed up for an ancient dead man. I see no one who is truly interested in whatever it is they'll find under those ancient bandages, or the items on display in the cases in this hallway. No one here gives a damn about Egypt or Winthrop's expedition. London society is nothing but a game, Mr. Purefoy, and a dismal one at that. It's about being seen, about showing one's face at the appropriate functions. That's why all of these people are here tonight, and that's precisely why Winthrop invited them. He likes the pomp."

"Then why are *you* here, Sir Maurice, if you find it all so tiresome?"

Newbury smiled. "Ah, now that's a question. I could tell you that I'm here because I have an academic interest in the subject. Or that I'm very much intrigued by the reports I've seen filed at the British Museum about the expedition and exactly what it is they found out there in the hot sands. Or even that I enjoy the thrill of seeing ancient artefacts uncovered for the first time in millennia. But in truth I'm sure I'm just as bad as the rest of them, here to drink my complimentary champagne and strut around before the gathered society commentators like a peacock."

Purefoy chuckled. "Now I know you're telling the truth."

Laughing, they both took another sip of their champagne.

"Now, see those three chaps over there, standing together in a huddle?"

Purefoy strained to see over Newbury's shoulder. "Ah, yes. I see."
Three middle-aged men in top hats and black coats were standing by
the doorway into the drawing room, gesticulating passionately, deep
in the middle of what looked like a heated debate.

"Well, their story is something entirely different. Those are the
other members of Winthrop's expedition. They were the men who
helped him pull all of these wonderful things out of the ground, and
I'll wager they're about to help him unwrap the old priest, too."

"Priest? I thought it was a Pharaoh?"

"Hmmm. Well I suppose that makes it a little more sensational,
doesn't it?" Newbury raised an eyebrow. "It's clear from looking at
a handful of the items on display here that the character beneath
those wrappings was never a king. And what is more, I'm inclined
to believe that there is a very good reason why the tomb had lain
undisturbed by grave robbers for so long. I'm sure there must be
something about the nature of the burial that Winthrop is not telling
us. Anyway, we're about to find out. Here's our host now..."

Purefoy turned to see Winthrop taking up a position at the foot of
the grand staircase. The man clapped his hands together loudly, three
times, and a hush fell over the assembled crowd.

"Lords, ladies and gentlemen. Welcome. I hope your glasses are
all suitably charged. We are about to begin the process of unrolling
the mummified remains of our Theban king. If you would care to
take up a position in the drawing room, my associate Mr. Wilfred
Blake," at this, Winthrop gestured towards the group of three men
that Newbury had pointed out earlier, "will be delighted to explain
the process to you as we perform the task. We begin momentarily.
Thank you."

There was a brief smattering of applause, and then the room
started to bustle once again as people began making their way

towards the large, white double doors that led into the drawing room. Purefoy turned to Newbury, who swiftly downed the last vestiges of his champagne and beckoned the reporter towards the door. "Come on. Let's make sure we get a good spot."

Tucking his notebook into his jacket pocket, Purefoy found a small side table to abandon his unfinished drink and followed Newbury around the rows of glass cabinets and on towards the drawing room. All the while, society veterans bearing dispassionate expressions milled around him, as though this next stage of the evening was something that they had to bear, like a burden, in order to carry on with their socialising and drinking. Newbury, on the other hand, seemed keen to get both himself and Purefoy to the forefront of things, and when they finally crossed the threshold into the large drawing room, it was little effort for them to establish a position near the head of the table.

Purefoy took a moment to examine his surroundings. The curtains had been pulled shut against the twilight, and the room was dimly lit by an array of flickering gas lamps, casting everything in a warm, yellow glow. Dark wooden bookshelves lined the far wall, filled with musty old tomes that Purefoy couldn't distinguish from one another in the half-light. People were forming a wide circle around a long, central table, whispering to each other in subdued voices. Purefoy savoured the moment as he took his place beside Newbury.

The item that dominated the room, of course, was the funeral casket of the Ancient Egyptian; laid out on the table, the large wooden coffin was shaped in the rough form of its occupant and was a truly wonderful sight to behold. Every inch of it was covered in the most intricate patterns and designs, and it was clear to Purefoy that the craftsmen who had tooled the object had been masters of their art, all the more impressive for the fact they had lived around four thousand years in the past. Gold leaf shimmered in the warm light of the gas lamps, whilst blue ink and inlaid precious stones finished the effect. Hieroglyphs were etched in long black columns over the torso and legs of the casket, and on top of these, other, more unusual symbols had been painted in splashes of red, obliterating much of the original script. The red ink had faded somewhat, however, so it was clear the markings were historical and had not been affected by Winthrop and his men during the course of the expedition.

Purefoy leaned in to examine the face that had been carved into the wooden lid. The eyes stared blankly at the ceiling, giving away nothing about the casket's occupant. It was so heavily stylised that he was unable to get any real impression of what the person had truly looked like in life.

Newbury leaned over to whisper in his ear. "Have you ever been to one of these things before?"

Purefoy shook his head.

"Well I hope you're not squeamish. Fascinating stuff, though. Truly fascinating. I think we're in for a surprise." He raised his eyebrow once again and offered Purefoy a confident smile.

Purefoy glanced around. The other guests were huddling in behind them now, clutching drinks, their faces gleaming in the wan light. Purefoy folded his arms behind his back, and waited.

A moment later a hush rippled through the gathered throng of people as the four members of the expedition filed into the room. They had each shed their suit jackets and hats, rolled up their shirtsleeves and donned leather gloves and smocks. Winthrop and Blake were first to step up to the table, whilst the other two men cleared a space for them, asking the audience to stand back to make room. Winthrop was carrying some sort of bizarre contraption, which a moment later was proven to be a mechanical visual aid, like a pair of spectacles attached to a wire framework that fitted neatly over his head. Lenses clicked down before his eyes, and he fiddled with a tool on either side of the device to adjust their focus. Thus prepared, Winthrop approached the casket, whilst Blake skirted around to the head of the table, readying himself to address the audience. He cleared his throat, and the susurrating voices of the crowd gave way to silence.

"I advise those of you with weak hearts or fragile constitutions to momentarily avert your eyes. Our first task will be to free the lid from the casket, and whilst we expect to find only another, smaller casket inside, we have no way of knowing how accurate our assumptions may be." His voice was thin and nasal, and he delivered his speech with an impeccable precision. Purefoy looked him up and down. The man was slim, drawn and clean-shaven, quite the opposite of the burly Winthrop. His blond hair was brushed back from his forehead in a neat side parting and his eyes were a piercing blue. "There are many things about the burial of this ancient king that are inconsistent with other contemporary burials in the same region." Blake stepped nearer to the casket and waved his hand to indicate the splashes of red paint that had been hastily daubed across the engraved hieroglyphs. "For example, we have no understanding of the nature of these red markings, but suspect them to be a magic ward of some type, a warning to anyone in the afterlife who may happen upon the spirit of the person contained within the casket. Of course, any such concerns are moot – nothing but superstitious nonsense – but it nevertheless serves to suggest that there may be more irregularities contained within the casket." He gave a dramatic pause. "None of our assumptions can be trusted. We hope to discover more as we proceed."

Newbury glanced over his shoulder at Purefoy with an unreadable look on his face.

Blake approached the casket, taking his place opposite Winthrop, who had moved around to the other side of the table. They both placed their hands on the lid of the casket, and together they proceeded to test the seal.

The two men worked the lid back and forth, but after a couple of minutes it became clear that it was stuck fast, warped with age, grime and decay. Unperturbed, Winthrop took a three-inch blade from the pouch in the front of his smock and set about running the knife along the join, hacking away at the seal in an effort to work the lid free. Purefoy noticed Newbury wincing as flakes of gold leaf and four-thousand-year-old hieroglyphs fell to the polished floor by their feet.

It didn't take Winthrop long to complete his rather brutal assault on the seal, and a minute or two later he had resumed his position opposite Blake as they prepared to lift the lid. Purefoy edged closer, anxious to get a good view of whatever they would find inside.

Winthrop grunted as he wedged his fingers underneath the rim of the seal. There was a splintering crack, followed by a loud *sigh*, as the two men heaved the lid free of the base. They placed it hastily on the table. Dust plumed into the air from within the shell of the casket, undisturbed for millennia. Purefoy wrinkled his nose. There was a dry odour from within the wooden coffin: the scent of ancient, foetid decay.

The four men from the expedition hurried forward to crowd around the casket, and Purefoy found it hard to see what was going on as they gestured to one another excitedly, clearly animated by their find. He edged around the table, feeling uncomfortable as the press of people behind him became more pronounced, each of the guests straining to see over the others. When he did finally manage to get a good look, he nearly gasped aloud with surprise. The contents of the casket were magnificent. Another coffin, decorated in shimmering black and gold, lay inside the outer shell like a Russian doll, perfectly designed to fit within the larger casing. The decoration was impeccable: beneath the thin layer of dust it was so bright and glassy it could almost have been new. The inner coffin itself had been carved out of a dark hardwood and inlaid with generous bands of bright, yellow gold. The face seemed slimmer and more feminine than the visage on the outer casket, and its eyes had been set with deep red gemstones that reflected the warm glow of the gas lamps. Once again, the torso was covered in a spidery pattern of white hieroglyphs and symbols that, to Purefoy, seemed as exotic as the entire experience of being there, in the drawing room of the grand house, watching the scene unfold before his eyes. He was more than a little awed by the experience.

He glanced at Newbury, who was leaning over the casket studying the ancient markings. He looked thoughtful. Purefoy was just about to ask him what had caught his attention when Winthrop stepped back from the table and clapped his hands together to garner attention. "Lords, ladies and gentlemen! You are in the presence of a truly magnificent find!" Winthrop's excitement was clearly genuine. "The inner casket is like nothing we could have expected. The black and gold decoration is highly irregular. Please, take a moment to enjoy the sight before we continue with our unrolling." He urged the others back from the edge of the table and waved a handful of people forward to take a look. Blake and the other two members of the expedition – Purefoy considered he would have to elicit their names by the end of the evening for his article – moved away reluctantly and stood off to one side, whispering to one another with some urgency, as many of the guests came forward to peer into the open casket of the dead man.

Purefoy caught Newbury's attention, keeping his voice low. "So, tell me, Sir Maurice, do you know if this is quite as irregular as Lord Winthrop has cause to make us believe?"

Newbury furrowed his brow. "Indeed so. It's quite the most singular casket I've ever seen. The black and gold decoration is most unusual. And the fact that the occupant has been rendered anonymous, by virtue of the complete absence of any cartouches bearing his name on the inner or outer caskets, is particularly strange. There's certainly nothing like it in the annals of the British Museum." He smiled. "Didn't I tell you we were in for a surprise?"

Purefoy nodded. "I can't deny it." He looked around. People were beginning to mill around amongst themselves once again, and the hubbub of chatter had noticeably increased. Newbury had been right; most of the people in the room had feigned a minimal amount of interest in the contents of the casket, but left to their own devices had reverted to conversing with their neighbours. He searched for Winthrop, and eventually spotted the lord by the fireplace, deep in the middle of a heated discussion with Blake.

Newbury leaned closer, smoothing the front of his jacket distractedly. "I suspect this has thrown them into something of a quandary." He nodded in the direction of the bickering men, who were still dressed in their leather smocks and bizarre headgear. "I'd wager that Blake wants to halt proceedings so that they may spend a little more time making a study of the inner casket, whilst Winthrop is anxious to give his guests a good show. If I know anything at all about the man, he'll make a point of continuing with the performance."

"Yes, I rather think he'd prefer to destroy the thing than allow his guests to leave unsatisfied."

"Well, Mr. Purefoy. I do believe you have the measure of the situation. I wonder. Do you –"

"Well, really, Winthrop! This is unbearable. I shall have no further part in it!" Newbury was cut off abruptly when Wilfred Blake, raising his voice above the din, exploded at Winthrop, who was now leaning against the fireplace, his face unreadable behind the mechanical spectacles which he still wore over his eyes. The room was silent as Blake, his shoes clicking loudly on the tiled floor, turned about and made a hasty exit from the drawing room, his disagreement with Winthrop apparent to everyone in the room.

Winthrop stepped forward, his hands wide apart in a placating gesture. "Let us continue with the task in hand. Arthur?" He beckoned to one of the other men, who readily stepped forward to adopt Blake's place. Winthrop turned to the sea of faces. "We shall now extract the inner casket from the outer shell, before exposing the mummified remains of the king inside."

The two men closed on the casket base and, reaching inside, fumbled around until they had a grip on the snugly fit inner coffin. Their eyes met, and Winthrop counted to three before wheezing with the strain as they lifted the weighty coffin out of its former resting place. There was a collective gasp from the audience as the true magnitude of the casket's beauty became evident. The two men carefully laid the object on the table beside the base, and then set about making themselves some more room to work by replacing the outer lid on the base and moving the larger casket to a spot on the floor behind them.

Winthrop ran his hands gently over the top of the coffin. There was no denying how impressive it was. The thing seemed to radiate an aura all of its own, capturing the attention – and the imagination, Purefoy assumed – of the assembled guests, many of whom had forgotten their idle conversations and were now watching with apparent interest.

Winthrop looked up at Arthur. "Are you ready?"

Arthur nodded.

They both ran their fingers along the seal between the coffin lid and base. Then, with a brief glance at the gathered crowd, Winthrop slid his fingers into the gap and together the two men lifted the lid. This time it came away easily, and Purefoy found he was holding his breath, transfixed.

In truth it came as something of an anti-climax after the grandeur of their earlier find. As Winthrop and his man laid the casket lid carefully to one side, Purefoy was able to see into the coffin. There, amongst a bed of decayed reeds, was a human figure, bound in yellowing linen bandages, only the very tips of its claw-like fingers exposed for the world to see. The bandages were covered in an archaic scrawl that Purefoy did not recognise, black, faded runes that appeared to have been inked onto the linen before the body was wrapped.

Winthrop took no time to ponder his next move, or to concern himself with any sense of decorum that Purefoy felt may have been appropriate in the handling of the dead. He reached directly into the coffin and scooped out the withered body, fetching it up into his arms and then, as Arthur moved the coffin shell out of the way, placing it down upon the tabletop. He turned to Purefoy, smiling. "Now, let us see how our ancient king exited this world."

Taking up the same blade he had used earlier to break his way into the outer casket, Winthrop made a slit into the wrappings along the right side of the mummy. Then, taking up a fistful of bandages, he began to peel away the layers, discarding the wrapping casually to the floor. Purefoy was appalled, and almost started forward to challenge the lord in his mistreatment of the ancient artefact, but remembered himself at the last moment and was able to bite his tongue. Layers of crumbling linen fell away.

Soon enough, Winthrop had exposed a large expanse of the mummy's wax-like flesh, part decayed and browned with age. It had taken on the appearance of beaten leather, hardened with exotic compounds and age. Winthrop had also extracted a number of small trinkets from within the wrappings: small jewels and talismans, a number of blue ushabti icons and a disc of gold, engraved with a series of intricate hieroglyphs. All the while, Newbury had stood watching on the sidelines impassively.

A few moments later, Winthrop had unrolled everything but the head of the long-dead Egyptian. It was clear now that the body had been imperfectly preserved: the flesh had decayed around the ribs, exposing the bones, and the hands were nothing but bony protrusions with the last remnants of human tissue still attached. Sweating, Winthrop straightened his back and rubbed his hands together. It was clear he was now so involved in his task that he had almost forgotten about the multitude of people that stood around him, watching his every move. When he spoke, it was barely a whisper. "Now, we look on the face of our Pharaoh for the first time in four thousand years."

He gripped a loose flap of linen and began slowly unrolling the wrappings around the mummy's head. After a moment it became evident that the cadaver still maintained wisps of thick, black hair on the crown of its head, as locks of the stuff fell loose as the bandages came away. No one spoke as the final strands of the linen were unravelled, finally revealing the Egyptian's face.

A woman screamed. Winthrop gave a visible shudder and stepped away from the mummy. Purefoy looked on in horror. There were shouts from the back of the drawing room.

The dead man's face was a twisted visage of terror and agony. He was screaming, his mouth wide open in a silent, millennia-long cry. His features had been perfectly preserved, his eyes stitched shut with coarse threads, his brow furrowed in intense pain.

Newbury looked round at Purefoy, the shock evident on his face. "My God. He must have been mummified alive."

Purefoy felt bile rising in his gullet. He looked away.

Winthrop had removed his headgear and was standing back from the table, a deathly pallor to his cheeks. People were talking anxiously all around them. The other man from the expedition came forward and hurriedly covered the mummy with a white sheet. Arthur fetched Winthrop a brandy from a cabinet beside the fireplace. Guests began to spill back into the hallway, where the automatons were waiting with more drinks.

Newbury put a hand on Purefoy's arm. "Come along, dear chap. I think the party's over for tonight." They followed the other guests as they filed out into the grand hallway, Purefoy glancing back over his shoulder to see Winthrop shakily consuming his brandy in one long draw.

He turned to Newbury. "Not quite what I was expecting, I must admit."

Newbury smiled. "Nor I. Yet I can't help thinking that all of the clues were there. It was evident that there was something unusual about the burial, and now we have a mystery. There has to be a reason why that man was mummified alive." He met Purefoy's gaze, his eyes gleaming. "I do enjoy a good mystery, Mr. Purefoy."

Purefoy smiled. "Well, I think that's enough excitement for me, Sir Maurice. And I have an article to write for the morning edition." He glanced at his pocket watch. "I think I should be on my way."

Newbury nodded. "Very well, Mr. Purefoy. I suspect I shall do the same. It's been a pleasure to meet you. I'll look out for your article in

The Times." He extended his hand, and Purefoy took it firmly.

"Likewise, Sir Maurice. I do hope we meet again."

Newbury smiled. "Good evening then." He turned and disappeared into the crowd.

Purefoy, an empty notebook in his pocket and a head swimming with images of the screaming dead man, straightened his jacket, took one last look around the thronging crowd and made his way slowly towards the exit and the street outside.

It was still raining. He hunched against the downpour, and set off for home. It was going to be a long night.

Chapter Two

The station concourse was bustling with people. Newbury watched as they rushed from pillar to post: men dressed in black and grey business suits and long, billowing coats, brandishing hats and folded umbrellas; ladies standing in little huddles under the shelter of the impressive roof, attempting to avoid the inclement weather that was gusting in through the open doors, spattering the marble floor with fat droplets of rain.

Newbury stood on the platform, a copy of *The Times* tucked neatly under his left arm. He tapped his foot impatiently. Around him, the air was infused with the sharp tang of oil, heated by the machinations of wheels and gears as trains screeched in and out of the station. Engines sighed easily at other, nearby platforms, their carriages slowly disgorging passengers onto the concourse. Steam hissed from pressure valves, fogging in the cold, damp air. He'd been there for thirty minutes, waiting for his quarry, and to his dismay had discovered a distinct lack of interesting distractions.

Whilst waiting, Newbury had been considering the events of the previous evening, mulling over the details of the things he'd seen, trying to ascertain what it was, specifically, that had made him uneasy about Winthrop's unrolling of the Theban mummy. It was certainly more than the revelation that the man had been mummified alive – much more than that – although the scene had indeed left him with a sharp sense of disquiet. And more also than the sheer lack of respect shown to both the dead man and the intricate craftsmanship of his casket. Newbury had been appalled by the manner in which Winthrop had attacked the unrolling like a stage performance, but this in itself was nothing new or surprising; he'd seen any number of such events in the past, and had chosen to attend the party fully cognisant of what he expected to see. No, it had more to do with the unfamiliarity of the decoration – the black and gold casket, the strange hieroglyphs – coupled with the manner in which the man had died. There was more to the dead man's story than was immediately obvious.

Newbury had pondered on this for a short time, before instead deciding that it was really far too early to be contemplating anything other than breakfast. Now, his stomach growling, he was growing impatient, keen to be done with his task. He checked his pocket watch. It was nearly half past seven. The train would be arriving soon.

He had made his way to Waterloo Station that morning to meet another agent, a man who was returning to London after spending a number of years undercover in St. Petersburg. He had no idea what this agent looked like, or, indeed, the man's real name. All he'd been offered was a codename, "Caspian", a carriage number, 3b, and instructions to meet the man from the train and escort him immediately to the palace. It was certainly one of the more sedate tasks he had been required to carry out on behalf of the Crown, and he wondered briefly why one of Her Majesty's footmen couldn't have performed the task to equally adequate effect. Yet, he admitted to himself begrudgingly, he *was* intrigued to discover more about the mysterious man. It was certainly no surprise to him to learn that Her Majesty had been managing agents abroad, in territories outside those of the Empire, but he had no notion of why the man's identity had to be protected in such a way, at least from another agent. Not only that, but it perplexed him why the man would choose to travel so far by rail, rather than airship. It must have added days, if not weeks to his journey, mostly spent in cramped, noisy accommodation. Perhaps that was what the man had grown used to in Russia, living undercover and shrugging off the veneer of wealth. He wondered how difficult the agent would find it to readjust to life back in London after so many years away, steeped in the routines and society of another culture. Of course, the thought was entirely redundant. He knew nothing of the man.

He looked around, sighed, and then took his copy of *The Times* from underneath his arm. He shook it open and gave the headlines a cursory glance. Smiling, he realised what he had failed to spot earlier that morning when he had scooped the paper up off the silver tray in his hallway. The main headline read: THE MYSTERY OF THE SCREAMING MUMMY, and the article beneath it was attributed to Mr. G. Purefoy. The front page! Newbury chuckled to himself. Purefoy had done well.

He gave the article a brief scan. The slightly sensational tone of the piece grated against his more literary sensibilities, but he could tell immediately that it was an excellent example of the journalistic art. It was insightful and made mention of many of the same observations that Newbury himself had noted during the course of the evening. He was impressed by Purefoy. The boy would make a good agent, one day. He appeared to have an eye for detail. Newbury resolved to mention it to the Queen next time he had cause to request an audience. Not that he had time to take on an apprentice.

He looked up from the page to see the train screeching into the station. He folded the paper away under his arm once more, and watched as the enormous green engine juddered to a halt before the buffers, the carriages clacking together noisily as the train slowly came to rest. He edged along the platform as the thin wooden doors of the carriages began to swing open, spilling passengers onto the concourse. The agent would be waiting for him in the appointed compartment.

Dodging the sudden press of people who were clamouring to take their leave of the platform, Newbury paced alongside the row of carriages until he located the correct number. It was a first class carriage, near to the front of the train. He could see little through the grimy windows, which had obviously been spattered with mud and dirt during the course of the journey. Dark shapes moved around inside as people attempted to find the quickest route off the train. First waiting for a young lady in a flowing yellow dress to step down onto the platform, Newbury mounted the step and hauled himself up into the carriage.

The lobby area was small, and the carriage itself was divided into three separate compartments that branched off from a long passageway, each of them with their own windows and interior doors. The carriage was panelled in a dark wood, and whilst it appeared comfortable enough, there was a sour odour in the air that Newbury found difficult to place. Bringing the back of his hand to his face to stifle the smell, he shuffled along the passageway, glancing in at an empty compartment as he passed by. He assumed this was the room that had been occupied by the lady in the yellow dress. He wondered what she had made of the smell.

Beside the empty compartment was another, identical room, although the blinds had been lowered over the windows and glass-panelled door. Newbury double-checked the small brass plate beside the door handle. The legend read: 3b. He rapped his knuckles loudly on the wooden frame. There was no reply. He tried again, and this time didn't wait for a reply before turning the handle and pushing the door open to step inside.

"Hello?"

The small room appeared to be empty, save for two long, leather seats that faced each other across the compartment, and the overhead racks for storing luggage. Both were vacant. Newbury glanced from side to side, wrinkling his nose. The smell he'd encountered upon entering the carriage was much stronger here, a lingering stench like foetid, rotten meat. It made him gag involuntarily and reach for the handkerchief in his jacket pocket. He used it to cover his mouth and nose. It did little to disguise the overwhelming smell. He wondered what could have caused such a foul odour. It was as if a dead animal had been left in the compartment to rot, or had only just been removed upon arrival at the station, its musty stink still circulating in the stale air.

Newbury edged further into the small room, looking for any obvious sign that he had somehow missed the man he had come to the station to meet. There were no notes or items left behind for him to collect. He wondered if the man had already found his way off the train and was waiting for him on the platform. That would be a distinct break with procedure, but the man *had* been working alone in Russia for a number of years. He could hardly be expected to follow protocol to the letter. Whatever the case, if Newbury did find the man waiting for him on the platform, he hoped that he wouldn't have to spend long in his company if he were carrying with him the article that had generated such an offensive smell.

Shrugging his shoulders and coughing into his handkerchief,

Newbury stepped out into the passageway and clicked the door shut behind him. He was relieved to get a measure of fresh air, although the foul stench had left a thick, cloying taste at the back of his throat. Sputtering, he made his way back to the lobby area, hopped down to the platform and glanced from side to side in search of the other agent. The concourse was nearly empty. A few stragglers were still edging their way towards the station exit, porters humping luggage behind them as they drifted towards the row of waiting cabs on the other side of the main doors. Rain was drumming loudly on the roof overhead.

No figure stood on the platform awaiting Newbury. He paced up and down, growing increasingly infuriated. There was no sign of the man known as "Caspian"; no note left in the compartment, no luggage, and no clues as to what may have become of him. Her Majesty would not be amused. Newbury could only assume he'd somehow missed the man, and that he'd set out to make his own way back to the palace.

Frowning, but resigned to abandoning his abortive mission, Newbury quit the platform and made his way briskly along the concourse. The rain was still blowing into the station on a fierce wind, and he cursed himself for forgetting his umbrella. Using his copy of *The Times* to shield his head from the worst of the weather, he dashed out into the street in search of a hansom cab, intent on making his way to his office at the British Museum. There, he would construct a brief missive to the Queen, detailing the bizarre circumstances of his morning and seeking clarity on what his next move should be, if any. And then, he promised himself, he would finally make time for breakfast.

Chapter Three

"**M**orning, Watkins."

"Good morning, sir."

Newbury, still damp from being caught in the shower outside
Waterloo Station, nodded politely to the doorman as he made his
way up the steps at the front of the British Museum. The building
was a magnificent edifice of grey stone, redolent of a classical Greek
structure, with towering Corinthian columns and bizarre effigies
carved in relief along the roofline in long, decorative friezes. The
dreary morning didn't show the wonderful architecture off to its
best, Newbury thought, as he looked up to note with dismay that
the sky was almost as grey as the building itself. It was going to rain
again shortly.

Watkins held the door open for him, and Newbury smiled as he
slipped inside.

It was still too early for the public to be milling around the exhibits,
and the place felt deserted as he crossed the lobby, his shoes clicking
loudly on the polished marble floor. He'd abandoned his copy of *The
Times* in the back of the cab, but his fingers were still stained with
streaks of dark ink that had run when he'd used the newspaper as
a shield against the rain. He'd have to wash and dry off before he
prepared his note for the Queen. He coughed, still hacking on the
grotesque smell that seemed to have lodged in his nostrils and throat

following his bizarre experience on the train. He hoped a pot of Earl Grey would help to clear the disgusting scent.

Newbury made his way to the private staircase that led down towards the bowels of the enormous building, where his office was located, hidden amongst the dusty stacks of the archives and the administration offices of the museum managers.

A few minutes later, having passed along a network of winding corridors, he came to the door to his office. He straightened the front of his jacket and pushed on the handle. The door swung open to reveal a small room, lit by a series of hissing gas lamps. He stepped inside, clicked the door shut behind him and began shrugging off his damp jacket to hang on the coat stand in the corner.

"Ah, Sir Maurice. I trust you had a pleasant evening?"

Newbury turned to see his secretary, Miss Coulthard, emerging from the adjoining room, where he and his assistant Miss Veronica Hobbes kept their desks. Miss Coulthard was a diminutive woman in her early thirties, with dark, brown hair tied up in a tight bun. She was dressed in a long grey dress and matching woollen cardigan. She was not conventionally pretty, but she was one of the most reliable people that Newbury knew, and he admired her for her dedication and resolve.

"Pleasant enough, thank you, Miss Coulthard. An interesting diversion." He draped his jacket on the coat stand and rolled his shirtsleeves up to his elbows, leaving dirty smears of ink on his white shirt. "I fear this morning has been entirely less successful, however." He raised an eyebrow with a sigh.

Miss Coulthard gave him an appraising look. "Tea?"

Newbury laughed. "It's almost as if you can read my mind, Miss Coulthard. Thank you. Tea would be delightful." He turned as if to head into the other room, and then stopped by the edge of Miss

Coulthard's desk. "May I enquire as to the health of your brother, Miss Coulthard? Is he making a smooth recovery?"

Miss Coulthard nodded. "As expected, Sir Maurice. The doctor says he'll need a few more weeks to get his strength back, but his memory is returning, slowly but surely."

Newbury smiled. "Delighted to hear it." He regarded his hands. "Ah, excuse me for a moment." He crossed to the sink in the corner of the room and, taking up a cake of soap, began scrubbing away the newsprint stains. Then, grabbing a towel from the rack beside the sink, he made his way to the adjoining room, leaving Miss Coulthard to set to work with the kettle.

Newbury hovered on the threshold for a moment, watching his assistant at her desk as he dried his hands. She was lost in a stack of papers, a look of concentration furrowing her brow, and if she was aware of his presence she was choosing not to let it distract her from her task.

Miss Veronica Hobbes had been working with him for over three months now, and had already saved his life on more than one occasion, both physically and, he considered, emotionally too. She was a most excellent woman; full of the energy and spirit of the modern age, an embodiment of progress, of equality, and of the future. She was pretty, too; brunette, in her early twenties, and full of life. Her features were well proportioned and feminine, and her eyes were a deep, arresting blue. She had a sharp mind, and an even sharper tongue.

Newbury cleared his throat. "Good morning, Miss Hobbes. I see you're still hard at work on that mystery of yours."

Veronica looked up, offered him a warm smile, and then returned to her reading. She spoke whilst her eyes followed the lines on the page before her. "Indeed. I believe that I'm making good progress, too. I have a potential suspect."

"Excellent. I look forward to hearing all about it. Just as soon as we have tea, and I've dashed off a short missive to Her Majesty."

At this Veronica looked up again, leaning back in her chair to regard him. She seemed to see him properly for the first time. "You're damp, Sir Maurice. I take it this morning's outing did not progress as planned?"

Newbury shook his head. "Quite so. In fact, I'd go as far as saying it was an unmitigated disaster. The gentleman I was tasked with escorting to the palace did not arrive for our rendezvous. The circumstances were most peculiar. But I won't go into it now. I'm much more interested in hearing your news." He dropped the towel on the edge of his desk and moved around to find his chair. "Now, where did I put those note cards...?" He fumbled with the many piles of paper that cluttered his desk.

Veronica laughed. She opened her draw and withdrew a sheaf of small white note cards. "Here. Take one of these."

Newbury smiled and accepted the proffered stationery. "My thanks." He lowered himself into his chair, took up a pen and inkwell, and began to write:

Majesty,

Agent by codename "Caspian" did not attend rendezvous as expected. Please advise if further action is required.

Yours,

Newbury

He gave the note a cursory glance, considering whether he should elaborate on the strange circumstances and the disturbing smell he had found lingering in the appointed compartment. He decided against the idea. After all, it was clear that Her Majesty knew more about the situation than he did, and he knew that she would just as soon summon him to the palace if she had any cause for concern. He resolved not to make any plans for the following morning. He'd likely have to cancel them, anyway, when the summons from the palace arrived. He folded the card into an envelope, which he retrieved from a tray on his desk. Then, still holding it in his hand, he leaned back in his chair and stared thoughtfully at the wall.

"I take it you've seen this morning's edition of *The Times*, Sir Maurice?"

Newbury grinned, blinking away his reverie. "Yes, indeed I have. I've just washed half of it down the sink." Veronica frowned, not catching his meaning. He chose not to elaborate. "I met the reporter at Winthrop's place, actually. Decent sort of chap. The piece was a little sensational for my liking, though."

"It certainly sounds as if it was an interesting evening, whatever the case. Are you planning to involve yourself in the mystery? Of the screaming mummy, I mean." Veronica delivered this with her usual, casual aplomb, but it was clear to Newbury that she was fishing for something. He smiled.

"I doubt it's really a case for the Crown. I did think I might call in on old Peterson this afternoon; just to run a few things past him, to be doubly sure it's not of interest. But I suspect it's probably one for Winthrop to worry himself with. I never was an expert on the Egyptian arts, anyway." He searched Veronica's face for signs of disapproval. There were none. "Besides, I doubt Peterson will have much to add, either. He's more of a traditionalist. If he'd been interested in the find he'd have been there last night alongside me."

Veronica laughed. "Come now, Sir Maurice! Admit that you're rather taken with the whole affair. It sounds as if there's a story to be had from it. You could write a paper on it."

"Well, I..." There was a high-pitched whistle from the adjoining room. Newbury slapped a hand on his desk. "Ah, good. Time for that pot of Earl Grey." He stood, brandishing his letter to the Queen. "I'll ask Miss Coulthard to have this couriered directly to the palace. And then you can tell me all about your missing girls."

Veronica nodded, clearly amused. Newbury felt his cheeks flush. He circled his desk and went in search of Miss Coulthard. He needed his morning tea. And, he reminded himself, he still hadn't found time for any breakfast.

†

"So tell me about your suspect, Miss Hobbes." Newbury was sitting behind his desk once again, sipping at his tea. He was watching Veronica intently. She placed her sheaf of papers on the desk and folded her arms. She met his gaze, her face serious.

"*Potential* suspect, Sir Maurice. The man might not have done anything wrong."

"So it is a man?"

"Yes."

"And?"

"And he's a travelling stage magician. He operates under the disappointingly unoriginal *nom de plume* of 'The Mysterious Alfonso'."

Newbury smiled around the rim of his teacup. "Oh dear, that is rather fanciful. So tell me, how is this travelling magician associated with the missing girls?"

"He's not. Well, at least not directly. But there are a few too many coincidences to easily rule out his involvement. Firstly, the dates and locations of his travelling stage show coincide exactly with the dates and places that the girls went missing. And secondly, many of the families of the missing girls reported that the last thing the girls did before they disappeared was attend a travelling show. They were never seen again."

Newbury studied Veronica's face. She was clearly passionate about bringing the case to a successful conclusion. She'd been on the trail of the missing girls ever since Sir Charles Bainbridge, Chief Inspector at Scotland Yard and a close friend of Newbury's, had brought the case to their attention.

A string of young females, aged between seventeen and twenty-three, had been disappearing from towns all over the Home Counties, and as yet, no one had been able to piece together any pattern. It had been going on since Christmas, and the disappearances showed no signs of abating. Many of the families were declaring witchcraft, and it was for this reason that Bainbridge had stopped by to seek Newbury's advice. Newbury, however, had felt that there was no evidence of supernatural wrong-doing, and was himself engaged with an entirely different case involving an infestation of ghostly spirits at a manor house in Cambridgeshire. Veronica had been aiding him on the Huntington case, of course, but for some reason had been unable to put aside her desire to help Bainbridge solve the mystery of the missing girls. Convinced that there were never any supernatural elements involved in the case, she had set to work looking for patterns in the web of disappearances, and since the successful conclusion of the Huntington case she had spent almost every waking hour at her desk, looking for clues in the statements and police reports. Newbury, of course, had been given other assignments to contend with, but he had allowed Veronica to pursue her quest, and now, it seemed, she had finally found something that resembled a lead.

"Are you planning to call on Sir Charles?"

Veronica frowned. "Not yet. Not until I know that the man is definitely involved. It wouldn't do to set Scotland Yard on him unnecessarily."

Newbury placed his teacup down on its saucer with a clatter. "I'm not convinced that is the wisest course of action, my dear Miss Hobbes. We can't have you putting yourself in any danger. This is a police matter. Besides, how do you intend to go about proving this magician fellow is actually involved?"

Veronica smiled. "That's easy. He's here in London. It's my intention to attend his performance this evening."

Newbury looked thoughtful for a moment. Then his face cracked into a wide grin. "Well, Miss Hobbes, you find me at your disposal. I fear I am without a dinner date for this evening, and I've always enjoyed the theatre. Would you mind terribly if I escorted you to the show?"

Veronica laughed. "Indeed not. I have two tickets." Her eyes glittered. "If you can bear to tear yourself away from your Ancient Egyptian mystery, it would be a pleasure to be escorted to the event."

"Then we shall take it in together. A most satisfactory resolution." He glanced at his pocket watch. "But now, I suspect old Peterson will have found his way to his desk, and I rather think it would be opportune to catch him before he allows himself to wander off again."

Veronica laughed. "I knew you wouldn't be able to resist!"

Newbury shrugged. "Well, we can't just leave that young Mr. Purefoy to sensationalise the whole affair in the national press, can we? Someone is going to have to set the record straight. I doubt very much it will be Winthrop." He got to his feet. "Until this evening, then?"

Veronica nodded. "Until this evening."

Smiling, Newbury set off to find Claude Peterson, one of the British Museum's foremost experts on Ancient Egyptian ritual. He had a notion to question the man on the strange carvings he had seen on some of the ushabti statues the previous evening, and to see if Peterson found any significance in the red markings on the outer casket of the mummy.

Then, later, he would return to his Chelsea lodgings to prepare for an early evening trip to the theatre. He wondered what bizarre treats *The Mysterious Alfonso* would have up his sleeves, and whether he would prove to be forthcoming in his interview. The case of the missing girls was certainly disturbing and had entirely consumed Veronica these last few weeks. He hoped for the sake of all involved that she had finally found her man, and that soon they would be able to bring the episode to a tidy conclusion. Most of all, he hoped that whatever it was that had caused Veronica to become so emotionally embroiled in the case would be resolved at the same time. He missed her companionship. And her support.

Chapter Four

The Archibald Theatre in Soho transpired to be rather more bohemian than Newbury had been expecting. In fact, it was so far removed from the austere splendour of Drury Lane that he could hardly bring himself to consider it a theatre at all. Nevertheless, there was a stage – which, considering the condition of the rest of the building, he assumed had been erected specifically to accommodate the new show – and an auditorium, of sorts, to seat the raucous crowd. The rest of the facilities were a little basic, to say the least, and it was clear the interior decor had seen better days. The floor was sticky, the seats uncomfortable and the smell almost as unpalatable as the stench he had encountered at the train station earlier that day. The space was dimly lit by a series of gas lamps mounted in a row along the rear wall, and whilst the venue was sizeable enough, the conditions still felt cramped and uninviting.

With a sigh, Newbury surveyed the audience around him. The crowd was comprised of a mix of both men and women, workers who had spilled out of the factories and cookhouses just an hour or so before and were now engaged in quaffing extraordinary amounts of gin and heckling the magician with a continuous stream of jibes and cheers. For his part, though, the magician appeared to revel in all of the attention, responding to the cheers of his audience with increasingly impressive sleights of hand. So far they had seen a host of elaborate illusions, ranging from a bunch of flowers being pulled out of a sleeve, to card tricks, to doves being made to disappear and reappear beneath a red silk sheet. The Mysterious Alfonso was a consummate performer who had clearly spent years perfecting his act, and even longer learning how to engage the crowd. His thick Italian accent added a sense of the exotic and his little flourishes at the end of each trick – a roll of the arm followed by a brisk bow to the front row – showed clearly that he understood how and when to give his audience a cue to applaud. Duly, they showered him with praise.

Newbury leaned back in his uncomfortable seat. The show was impressive, yet it offered him nothing that he had not seen before, and whilst he sat in the midst of the noisy audience, jostled from side to side by the people around him, he found himself growing impatient. He was keen for the show to be over so that he and Veronica could attempt to get backstage and interview the showman about his possible connection to the missing girls. He shook his head. He was starting to think like Charles.

He studied Veronica for a few moments. She appeared to be increasingly enraptured by the magician's trickery, and had allowed herself to be carried along by the audience, applauding loudly at each appropriate juncture and generally accepting the show for the entertainment it was. Newbury envied her that. He simply didn't have a mind that would allow him to enjoy such trivial pursuits without first attempting to analyse exactly *how* the trick had been carried out, what the basis of the illusion was, or how his eye had been tricked into believing something contrary to what had really occurred. He knew the tricks were nothing but illusions – as complex as they may be – and that was enough to dispel any sense of enjoyment for him. There was nothing truly mysterious, arcane or occult in what he was seeing down on the stage. Added to that, he was surprised that Veronica should engage with the show in such a way, given the reason for their visit to the theatre; unless, of course, she were feigning enjoyment as a means of gaining access to Alfonso after the show.

Newbury's attention was pulled back to the performance. Alfonso had wheeled out a large, coffin-shaped contraption on a trolley and had placed it in the very centre of the stage. It reminded Newbury somewhat of the Ancient Egyptian casket he had seen the previous evening, although this contraption was hewn from plain wood and lacked the gaudy decoration of the Egyptian artefact. Not only that, but Alfonso's box also had a series of thin slits cut into it at regular intervals along the sides and lid.

The magician moved around to stand behind the box, lifted his top hat and gave a dramatic sweep of his arm to silence the audience. A hush settled over the theatre. Newbury glanced at Veronica, whose eyes flashed in the low light.

"Ladies and gentlemen! The time has come. This is what you have come from miles around to see, no? The Mysterious Alfonso offers to you his death-defying sword box!" The magician smiled a toothy grin as the crowd began to cheer again, loudly. He waved them quiet once more. Slowly, as if to punctuate his next few words, Alfonso began to tug his white gloves from his hands, extracting one finger at a time, keeping a watchful eye on the audience all the while. "Now... do I have a volunteer?"

A few tentative hands went up around the room. Alfonso seemed to consider his options, scanning the audience with his outstretched finger. After a moment he settled on a young woman in the second row. She was blonde and pretty, and wearing a pale blue dress. The men to the left of her all stood to allow her to pass. She made her way slowly through the row of seats and approached the stage. Alfonso came forward and took her hand as she mounted the steps, helping her up so that she could take her place beside him. He twirled her around on the spot, showing her off with a wide smile, as if to suggest that she wasn't a plant and that there was nothing unusual or untoward about her person. The crowd clapped appreciatively. Next, Alfonso led the woman forward, towards the coffin-shaped box at the centre of the stage. He left her there for a moment whilst he fetched a small stool, which he placed on the wooden boards before her. Then, lifting the lid to reveal the interior of the box, he stood back and encouraged her to climb inside.

The woman looked nervous. She peered over the lip of the box as if she suspected there might be something hiding within. Then she glanced back over her shoulder, searching out the face of her companion in the crowd. Newbury watched the man wave at her to continue. Hesitating, the woman stepped up onto the stool and, holding her skirt so as not to trip, she lifted first one leg and then the other into the box, until she was standing inside it, towering above Alfonso and shaking visibly. Newbury wondered what was going through her mind. Gulping at the air, clearly terrified, the young woman sank to her knees and then lay down inside the open casket, disappearing from view. Alfonso acted quickly. He took the lid he had removed just a few moments before and lifted it back into place, being careful to ensure a snug fit. The audience was almost silent with anticipation. Even Newbury found himself leaning forward in his seat, straining to see what Alfonso would do next.

The magician moved off to the left-hand side of the stage, where a young female stagehand – dressed in a most revealing costume of feathers and sequins - had wheeled on a large wooden rack filled with glittering swords. Alfonso stepped up to this and drew one of the blades. He held it high above his head, showing it off to the crowd. It reflected brightly in the dull light. Then, moving back to stand before the box containing the woman, he slapped the flat edge of the blade against the casket, causing it to clang noisily. Next he took the sharp end of the blade between his thumb and index finger and held it aloft, trying to flex the metal. The audience continued to watch, fully enraptured.

Alfonso moved the casket around a little so that the crowd could see what he was about to do next. He took the point of the sword, found one of the thin notches that had been cut into the sides of the coffin-shaped box, and thrust the blade into it with all his might. The tip of the sword exited the box on the other side through another of the pre-cut slits. Alfonso pushed the blade home until the hilt of the sword was resting against the side of the box.

There was a gasp from the audience. Alfonso didn't hesitate to soak up their admiration. He went back to the rack of swords, took another blade and proceeded to repeat his actions, first proving to the crowd that the blade was real, and then pushing it through the box – and, supposedly, the woman inside it – until its tip was clearly protruding from the other side. He did this again and again until the rack was empty and there were at least ten of the blades perforating the box. Finally, frenetic and short of breath from the exertion, he mounted the stool, placed the tip of a blade against the lid, and thrust it downwards through another hole, so that it slid through the box and burst out of another hole in the base. There was no way the woman inside the box could have survived.

Alfonso climbed down from the stool and stood before the audience. Panting, he rolled his shirtsleeves up to his elbows. The audience were silent and agog. Smiling, Alfonso kicked the stool away and grasped hold of one end of the box. It was still resting on the low trolley on which he had earlier wheeled it across the stage, and he spun it around for the audience, offering them a view of the casket from all sides. Newbury frowned. It was not at all clear what had happened to the woman. There were no obvious trapdoors in the base of the box, and if she *had* dropped out through a small hatch in the bottom she would have been easy to spot. The only explanation was that she was still inside the box, but Newbury found that hard to believe. The swords had certainly looked real enough, and he couldn't see how Alfonso could have missed her when he inserted the blades, no matter how much precision he had used when cutting the guide holes prior to the event.

"Impressive, isn't it?" Newbury turned to see Veronica leaning in towards him, a smile on the curl of her lips.

"Most definitely. I'll admit I was growing a little impatient with the performance until this most recent development. I haven't a notion of how he has effected the woman's escape from the box. It's really quite intriguing."

Veronica laughed. "Perhaps there will be chance to ask him after the performance has finished. If we're not taking him into custody, that is."

Newbury nodded. "Quite so." He paused. "Look, he's about to get her out again."

They both turned back to see Alfonso removing the swords with abandon, sliding them out of the box and dropping them noisily to the stage. It took him only a moment before all of the blades had been extricated. He hesitated before the box. Then, with one last, grand gesture, he swept the lid from the top of the casket and stepped back, allowing the final scenes of his act to play out before him. There was a gentle cough from within the box, and then the woman sat up, looking around at the audience, her eyes wild with disorientation. There was a roar from the gathered crowd. The front rows stood, their applause deafening. Newbury smiled as he watched Alfonso enjoying the adoration of his fans. The man was definitely growing on him.

Alfonso returned the stool to its place beside the box and helped the young woman to step down, seeing her back to her seat in the second row. The female stagehand came out onto the stage and began collecting up the swords, sliding them back into their housings in the wooden rack. When she had finished, Alfonso, smiling and nodding his appreciation to the audience, made his way back to where he'd left the open casket on the stage. He replaced the lid and then pushed it off to one side, allowing it to roll away on its castors. He turned to the crowd. "One more?" They roared again, loudly. Alfonso waved them to quieten down. "I shall warn you, though. This is no trifling feat of illusion." His voice dropped to a staged whisper. "This time I offer you the chance to glimpse some real magic." There was another cheer. Alfonso approached the very front of the stage. He threw his arms wide. "Then I find myself in need of another volunteer."

This time hands shot up all across the theatre. Newbury turned to Veronica, and was appalled to see she was also offering herself up as a volunteer, her hand raised high above her head. "Miss Hobbes! I feel strongly that this is not the safest course of action to pursue. We came to this place expecting to find a villain."

Veronica turned to meet his gaze, but kept her hand raised in an effort to be seen from the stage. "And that is exactly what I intend to do, Sir Maurice. We need to get close enough to see how his illusions work." Her whisper was strained. She clearly didn't want to be pressed further. Nevertheless, Newbury felt he had no choice.

"Really, Miss Hobbes. I must insist that you lower your hand. I cannot sit by and allow you to put yourself forward for such a dangerous enterprise, especially given the fact that you yourself are investigating this very man in connection with a series of missing women. I would be foolish to allow it. I quite understand your desire to bring this matter to a close, but I will not be responsible for allowing *you* to become one of your suspect's many victims. Will you desist?"

Veronica drew a sharp breath and lowered her hand. "I will." She broke his gaze and returned her attention to Alfonso, who, whilst Newbury and Veronica had been debating, had chosen a volunteer from the audience and was in the process of helping her up onto the stage. Newbury glanced at Veronica once more, unsure of her reaction, and then leaned forward in his chair to observe the goings-on that were taking place at the front of the theatre.

The volunteer was once again a young woman, this time with raven-dark hair and a lilac dress. She seemed more confident than the previous volunteer, and, from what Newbury could gather from her manner, happy for the attention she was receiving. Alfonso stood her in the very centre of the stage. He bade her to remain still. Then he circled her, looking her up and down from all angles, as if studying her carefully, weighing her up with his eyes. He glanced up, catching sight of his stagehand standing off to one side, and beckoned her forward. She hurried over to him, handed him a red silk sheet, and then edged away again, smiling at the audience as she disappeared from view.

Alfonso turned to the audience. "Watch closely." He unfurled the large red sheet and then draped it over the woman, spreading the edges out neatly so that they pooled on the floor around her, completely covering her from head to toe. Then, with barely a moment to catch his breath, he snapped his wrist and swept the sheet away again, flicking it up into the air in a bold dramatic flourish.

The woman was gone.

The crowd took a moment to react. The woman had completely

vanished. There was not a trace of her to be seen. One minute she had been there, clearly evident beneath the thin silk sheet, the next she had entirely disappeared. There had been no sound, no sign of any movement. It was as if she had simply been swept up into the ether like an errant spirit.

Someone started to clap. Others followed. Soon the entire audience was standing, applauding the magician, who lingered just a moment longer on the stage, before offering a sweeping bow, collecting his hat and then exiting stage left. The audience continued to clap, even after the final curtain was drawn.

Newbury turned to Veronica. He had to shout to make his voice heard over the clamour of the audience. "*Now* I'm impressed."

Veronica nodded, a knowing look in her eye. "It's what happens to her next that concerns me."

Newbury smiled. "That, Miss Hobbes, is what we are here to find out." He glanced over his shoulder. "Come on, let's see if we can make our way around this crowd. I can't imagine it will be too difficult to find our way backstage."

Veronica rose to her feet. She was smiling. "Thank you, Sir Maurice."

Newbury grinned as he offered her his arm. "Always a pleasure, Miss Hobbes. Always a pleasure."

Chapter Five

As Newbury had anticipated, it was not difficult for the two of them to find their way backstage. Newbury was without doubt the best dressed man in the house, and after speaking in hushed tones with the wizened old man who was standing guard – sentry-like – on the artists' entrance, the two Crown investigators soon found themselves admitted to the private area at the back of the theatre, passing themselves off as wealthy patrons who wanted to congratulate Alfonso on his excellent performance.

The Archibald Theatre was a small venue, and it was soon clear to Newbury that most of the space had been reserved for the paying guests. The conditions behind the scenes were cramped and dirty, and if the front of the house was dilapidated, the backstage area was ready to be condemned.

Newbury and Veronica found themselves in a short, narrow corridor, which terminated in an artists' exit to the street behind the theatre, and contained a number of mildew-stained doors that opened into dressing rooms along either side. The wooden floorboards creaked alarmingly as they walked. Newbury noticed that Veronica was lifting the hem of her yellow dress ever so slightly to avoid letting it trail on the dirty floor. Crossing to one of the open doorways, he peered into an empty dressing room with a grimace. The room had not seen use for some time, and had been allowed to become run-down and mouldy. The walls were slick with damp, the floorboards peppered with rodent faeces and other, indescribable dirt, and the furniture had been piled up in one corner and was covered in a thick film of dust.

"It astounds me that the theatre can function in such a decrepit state." Veronica wrinkled her nose as she joined Newbury in the doorway of the abandoned room. Her eyes were shining in the low light. She seemed full of energy and life, excited at finding herself here, in the midst of another adventure. Newbury couldn't help but smile; the thrill of the chase was upon her.

He nodded in agreement. "Quite. I fear the halcyon days of this particular establishment are long behind it."

There was a sound of coughing from one of the other rooms along the corridor. Veronica turned her head. Newbury looked over her shoulder. There was no one in the doorway, but it was clear which room the sound had come from; the door had been propped open and a light was spilling out into the corridor, causing shadows to flicker ominously up and down the walls. They made their way towards the light. Newbury hesitated in the doorway and rapped loudly, three times. He couldn't see the occupant from where he was standing by the doorjamb, but what he could see of the room suggested it saw more frequent use than the dressing room he had seen just a moment before. Bills were pasted all over the walls, gaudy posters advertising events that had long since moved on to other, more salubrious venues: strong-man acts, dancing girls, magicians from the Far East. A dressing table was pushed up against one wall, a top hat resting before the discoloured mirror, a sepia photograph of two women tucked into one corner against the glass. A dove fluttered its wings in a domed cage hanging from the ceiling. It looked uncomfortable in the small cage.

"What is it?" The man's voice was gruff and unexpectedly English.

Newbury stepped across the threshold and into the room. Veronica followed behind him. The man – whom Newbury immediately recognised as Alfonso – was lounging in a chair, dressed in his shirtsleeves and trousers and smoking a long cigarette, on which he puffed luxuriously. Smoke plumed from his nostrils. He looked up at Newbury, a dour expression on his face. "The show's over. I think you must have taken a wrong turn." He returned to studying his boots.

Newbury smiled. All sense of the man's Italian accent had gone, replaced by a Home Countics drawl. "On the contrary. I sought you out in order to offer my compliments, Mr. Alfonso. My name is Sir Maurice Newbury, and this is my associate, Miss Veronica Hobbes."

At this mention of Newbury's honorific, the magician seemed to snap to attention. He glanced at Veronica, seeing her properly for the first time. "Sir Maurice. Please forgive me. I'm sure you will understand that a venue such as this does not frequently attract clientele of the genteel variety." His face cracked into a wide grin. He shifted his feet from where they were perched on a stool and stood, offering Newbury his hand. Newbury took it and shook it firmly. "So, what on earth attracted you to the Archibald this evening?"

"You, Mr. Alfonso. I hear your show has been causing quite a stir in the Home Counties and wanted to see it for myself."

"Really? Well, thank you for taking an interest. And how did you find it? I hope it wasn't a disappointment?"

"No. Not at all. It was most impressive. I was particularly taken with the card tricks. I've been studiously attempting to work out how you managed to effect them all so easily."

Alfonso grinned. "Ha! Parlour tricks. It surprises me that a man of your distinction should be so taken with such trivialities."

Veronica laughed. Newbury was pleased to see that she had taken his cue. "Well, I for one was struck by how successfully you made that girl disappear. I am quite in awe of you, Mr. Alfonso. She seemed to vanish in a puff of smoke!"

Newbury feigned ignorance. "Yes, indeed! But tell me, what happened to the poor girl? You didn't make her reappear again afterwards? How did you pull it off? I do hope she hasn't disappeared forever!"

Alfonso smiled, shaking his head. "Sir Maurice. I'm sure you don't really expect me to give away my secrets, do you? I've worked for many, many years to develop my act. Many have tried to impersonate it. So far, none have succeeded. I intend to carry the secret to the grave."

Veronica frowned. "But what of the girl?"

Alfonso laughed. "The girl? She's probably on her way home by now. My assistant will have given her the fare for a cab." He waved his cigarette. "Now, I'm afraid I really must press on. I have another show to prepare for the morrow, and the act rather takes it out of me." He looked from Newbury to Veronica and back again. "I appreciate your kind words."

Newbury nodded. "Of course." He took Veronica's arm as if to lead her from the room. Then, just as they were about to turn their backs on the magician, he paused. "How long do you intend to continue your run at the Archibald, Mr. Alfonso?"

"Another week, Sir Maurice. Then I'm taking the show north to Manchester."

Newbury met his gaze. "Excellent. In that case, I'm sure we'll meet again. Good night."

"Good night."

The two investigators took their leave.

†

Outside, the fog had descended on the city like a thick, woollen blanket, smothering the streets and diffusing the light so that everything seemed to lose its definition, becoming hazy and soft around the edges. Newbury sniffed. The air was damp with the grey miasma. He adjusted his hat and scarf, and then offered Veronica his arm.

The two investigators stepped out onto the cobbled road, pausing to close the door behind them. The artists' exit opened directly onto the street at the back of the theatre. They had taken advantage of the private door, slipping out in order to avoid the crush of people who, even now, would still be spilling out of the front of the theatre following the end of the show.

Newbury glanced from side to side. He could hear horses whinnying in the murky fog, somewhere off to the left. It was likely there were still a few hansom cabs patrolling the area, hoping to pick up fares as the theatregoers stumbled into the night and found themselves drunk and in need of transportation home.

He looked to Veronica, who was bracing herself against the cold. She shivered. "Well, 'The Mysterious Alfonso' wasn't quite the wretch I had anticipated. What did you think?"

He shook his head to indicate the conversation was better left until they were safely out of earshot. "I think that, in places such as this, even the walls have eyes and ears. Let's find ourselves a cab."

Huddling against the chill, Veronica nodded her assent. They edged along the road, following the curb to ensure that they didn't wander too far off track in the thick, wintry fog.

There was a sob from somewhere just to the right of them. A woman's sob, soft and stifled.

"Hello?" Veronica broke away from Newbury, trying to locate the source of the crying. "Hello?"

Newbury followed her. The sobbing sound came again. "Veronica. Over here." He approached the shape that loomed out of the fog. It slowly resolved into the form of a young woman, leaning against the wall of the theatre, clearly distraught. He stepped closer, putting a hand on her arm. "My dear. Whatever is the matter?"

The woman looked up. Newbury almost started in surprise. She had a spill of long, dark hair and she was wearing a lilac dress. She was pretty, young, and her cheeks were stained with tears. It was the girl from the theatre, the woman who had disappeared during the show. She looked confused, her eyes searching Newbury's face for the answer to some undisclosed question. When she spoke it was with another sob. "Where am I?"

Veronica, who had moved over to stand beside Newbury, offered her a concerned but quizzical look. "You're outside the Archibald Theatre. You were there to see a show, a magician. Don't you remember getting up to go on stage?"

The woman bit her bottom lip apologetically and shook her head. She sniffed and wiped her eyes with the backs of her hands. "I'm... I'm not sure. I don't remember." Her voice was a whimper. Her accent was thick and telling; she was from the East End.

Newbury leaned closer, trying to catch the scent of gin on her breath. He wondered if she were simply drunk. She didn't smell of alcohol, however. She seemed sober, but terribly confused. And there was the hint of something else, some chemical he found difficult to place. He frowned. "Are you able to recall your name?"

She nodded. "Miss Annabel Myers."

"And do you have an escort this evening, Miss Myers?"

"Yes." She gave another sob. "My brother, Jimmy. He should be around here... somewhere." She looked from side to side, but it was difficult to make out anything in the cloying fog.

Veronica smiled, warmly. "Miss Myers. Do you have an address we could see you too? I suspect that, even if your brother is searching for you now, he won't get far in this fog. If we were to see you to your home, I'm sure he would be relieved to find you there upon his return."

The woman stifled her tears. "Yes." And then, more resolute: "Yes, that sounds like a good idea. I live at my father's house at twenty-six Nelson Street, Shoreditch." She looked down at the palm of her hand, which she held up towards Veronica. Resting there was a smattering of small coins. "I think someone handed me this for my fare. I'm sorry..." She hung her head. "I'm so confused."

"Put your money away, Miss Myers. I'll fetch us a cab."

"Thank you...?"

"Sir Maurice Newbury. And this is my associate, Miss Veronica Hobbes."

"Thank you, sir." Miss Myers looked utterly bemused.

"Don't mention it. Miss Hobbes, I shall return momentarily with a cab." Newbury made his way towards the sound of horses, somewhere up ahead of them by the side of the road. Behind him, the two women were soon enveloped by the thick, tubercular blanket of smog.

✝

The house in Shoreditch had been everything that Newbury had been expecting: run down, dirty: a pile of red bricks leaning awkwardly against its neighbour for support. The cab ride had proved uneventful, and Miss Myers had been able to tell them very little about Alfonso and the method by which he had caused her to disappear on stage. Her memory of the event was erratic and impressionistic, and all she kept telling Newbury and Veronica was that she was terribly confused, and remembered feeling as though she had somehow been squeezed into a box that was too small to contain her. The next thing she remembered was being found by the two investigators in the street, with the vague recollection that someone had pressed money into her hand and turned her out into the foggy street.

Newbury had waited in the cab whilst Veronica had shown Miss Myers to her door, and then they had set out for Kensington, so that Newbury could escort Veronica home to her rooms just off the High Street. With all this talk of missing girls, and the continuing threat of the revenants prowling the streets, Newbury was keen to ensure his assistant made it back to her home in safety. That, and the fact he was keen to discuss his impressions of the evening's events with her.

He glanced up at her, watching as the motion of the cab caused her to rock from side to side in her seat. "So, to answer your question, Miss Hobbes: I think our 'Mysterious Alfonso' was every bit of the wretch you anticipated him to be."

Veronica frowned. "So you believe him to be guilty, then?"

Newbury shrugged. "All the evidence suggests not. The girl was found to be fine – if a little confused and disorientated by her experience – and he had provided her with the cab fare home as he suggested. But I do feel there is more to the man than meets the eye. I'd like to know what sort of trick he's using to pull off that disappearing act, and what's more, why it should leave the volunteer feeling so lost and unwell. I have a suspicion she was rendered unconscious, probably with some kind of chemical compound. It certainly bears more investigation."

Veronica nodded. "Indeed. I wonder if it is the process itself that is causing the girls to go missing. By that I mean – do they stumble out of there disorientated and with no memory of the preceding events, and then wind up getting themselves lost, or worse?"

Newbury looked thoughtful. "Or perhaps some of them are simply rendered unconscious during the process, and then don't wake up at all? But we must also consider the possibility that Alfonso, or whatever his real name is, may not be to blame. There is always coincidence to consider."

Veronica raised an eyebrow in a parody of Newbury. "Mmmm. Coincidence indeed."

Newbury laughed. "Yes, you have me there, my dear Miss Hobbes." He glanced out of the window. Kensington loomed out of the fog. "Shall we talk further in the morning?"

Veronica nodded. "I'll wait for you at the office." The cab juddered to a halt as the driver reined in the horses. Veronica got to her feet. "Did Peterson have any thoughts on your mysterious screaming mummy, by the way?"

"Very few. He suggested it was probably some sort of elaborate punishment, that the poor chap was probably mummified alive for some terrible crime he'd committed. Other than that, the markings are unlike anything he's seen before."

Veronica smiled. "Well, I'm sure tomorrow will bring with it some fresh ideas." She clicked open the cab door and moved to step out.

"Oh, and Miss Hobbes?"

She turned to look over her shoulder, framed for a moment in the open doorway of the cab. Newbury couldn't help but feel stirred by her beauty. He felt the impulse to reach out to her, but fought it back.

"Yes?"

"Assure me you won't place yourself in any unnecessary danger."

She nodded. "Good night, Sir Maurice."

"Good night, Miss Hobbes."

The door snicked shut behind her, and a moment later Newbury rocked back in his seat as the cab rolled away towards Chelsea, and home.

Chapter Six

Morning brought with it a laudanum fug that would have proved debilitating, if not for Mrs. Bradshaw's revitalising breakfast of bacon, eggs and Earl Grey tea. Newbury, wrapped in his blue velvet dressing gown, sat heavily at the table, wincing at the sunlight that was streaming in through the dining room window. Outside, a frost had settled, clearing the fog, and people were already beginning to bustle along the streets, their carriages creaking loudly, their animals yapping and chirping, their steam engines firing noisily as they careened along in ground trains and other, stranger, steam-powered vehicles. The last two months had seen a proliferation of new devices: bizarre, single-person carriages that barrelled along at great speed, bowling everyone and everything over in their wake. They were smaller than a hansom, but far larger than a bicycle; squat, fat little things on four wooden wheels, into which the driver lowered himself, leaving his head and shoulders exposed to the elements. Newbury was a huge supporter of progress, but he didn't believe the city was ready for the coming transport revolution that these new devices seemed to foreshadow. Aside from that, they were damn ugly, and a nuisance, too. Perhaps Veronica was right, after all. Perhaps there was a very real need to slow things down, to stop the world from rushing too hastily towards the future. Or perhaps he was just feeling dour and hung-over.

He been taking more risks recently, with the laudanum, and he knew he was playing a dangerous game. He'd even visited an opium den, just over a week ago, a place at the back of a coffee house, known to its clientele as "Johnny Chang's". It was a nauseating place, full of Chinese sailors and fallen gentlemen, but the heady aroma of the opium and the promise of relief at the end of the pipe had proved too tempting, and he had allowed himself to wallow there for most of an afternoon, buried in a sea of silk cushions. Chasing the dragon was something new to him. Until that point a week ago, he had experimented only with laudanum, measuring it out into glasses of red wine and imbibing it in the comfort of his own home. But the ritual of the pipe was exotic, bewildering and, somehow, more appealing. He planned to purchase one of the devices for use in his apartments. He preferred to indulge himself in private.

Newbury understood that others could not appreciate his craving for the opiates, that both Charles and Veronica saw it as a weakness to be overcome. But to Newbury it was much more than that, more than just the need for a physiological intoxication. It helped him to think, to see the world from a different perspective. It was during his opium hazes that he often found the solution to a case, or made a connection where previously he had seen none. The drug allowed him to retreat into the crevices of his own mind, and what he found there was often illuminating. It lifted the shades of perception, opened his eyes to things that others would deem impossible. It enabled him to trust his instincts. Without the opium, he feared he would not be half the detective he was, and that troubled him beyond regard for his physical wellbeing. So he continued to indulge, keeping his practices hidden from the world. The opium was at the epicentre of a maelstrom of need and desire. It was fuel for his mind, but poison for his body.

For a moment, Newbury considered going back to bed. He allowed himself to entertain that fantasy for a few minutes, knowing full well that it was never truly an option. He had to meet with Veronica for a start and besides, he was fully expecting to receive a summons to the palace to discuss the missing agent, "Caspian", and whether or not Her Majesty had any intention of pursuing the matter further.

Regardless, his mind was also exercised by the mystery surrounding the Theban mummy. He'd spent the evening reading through his library of occult tomes, searching out any references to irregular mummification practices in Ancient Egypt, but had found nothing that could help him to identify what it was that Winthrop had uncovered in Thebes. Unperturbed, he had dashed off a note to Aldous Renwick, a long-time correspondent and a master of occult literature, describing the circumstances and asking his friend to examine his own library on the off-chance that he might be able to throw up something different. For the time being, both of Newbury's mysteries had stuttered to a halt. Whilst he waited on others, he would do all he could to help Veronica bring her own matter to a close.

Downing the dregs of his tea, Newbury forced himself to stand, flinching as the movement caused a brief explosion of pain in his temples. He sighed, cursing under his breath. Then, swooping up another piece of toast from the rack, he made his way with trepidation towards the washroom, where he planned, if at all possible, to make himself reasonably presentable.

†

A short while later, following a wash and a shave, Newbury had dressed and was feeling more like his usual self. He had donned one of his black suits, with a white collar and red cravat, but he knew from catching a glimpse of himself in the cheval glass that the black rings beneath his eyes betrayed his tiredness, if not the reason for it. He hoped he could hide it from Veronica. He couldn't bear to think that she could consider him weak.

It was just after nine o'clock, and Mrs. Bradshaw had cleared away the debris from breakfast, leaving a small silver tray on the table containing his post for the day. He eyed it from across the room, immediately recognising the heavy, vellum envelope that lay atop the pile. So, he'd been right about the summons. He collected the small pile of letters and took them through to the drawing room, which adjoined the dining room through a single door. In the corner of the room, sat atop its little wooden perch, the brass owl that he'd inherited from Lord Carruthers trilled noisily and fluttered its metallic wings.

Casting the rest of the pile on the coffee table, Newbury searched out his letter-opener – a small blade he'd picked up in India, with a handle shaped like the head of a tiger – and slid it underneath the gummed fold of the envelope from the palace. The vellum tore readily, and inside there was nothing but a small note card, printed neatly in the perfect handwriting of one of Her Majesty's administrators. He withdrew it and held it up to the light.

Newbury,
You are expected at the palace forthwith.
Victoria R.

He turned the card over in his hand, smiling. Perhaps now he'd find out a little more about "Caspian" and the reason for the man's failure to rendezvous at the station the previous day. Miss Hobbes, he feared, would have to wait a while longer. He placed the card on the bureau beside the letter-opener. Then, taking a moment just to steady himself, he fetched his coat and hat from their place in the hallway, and set out to see his employer, Her Majesty the Queen.

†

"Well, Newbury?"

Her Majesty had not kept him waiting for long. He had taken a cab directly to Buckingham Palace: one of the loud – but fast – steam-powered vehicles that Veronica detested so readily. Sandford, the aged butler who now waited on the Queen's small coterie of field agents, had been waiting for him by the side entrance and had guided him in, taking Newbury's coat and hat and hurrying him along the secret passageway to Her Majesty's audience chamber.

Newbury stood before the monarch now, trying to make her out in the shadowy half-light of the room. She was sat, as ever, in her life-giving chair, the pumps and bellows wheezing noisily as they artificially inflated her lungs, heaving her chest back and forth alarmingly as they forced her to breathe, artificially sustaining her life. Tubes coiled from the bags of strange-coloured fluid that were attached to a metal frame above her head, pumping preservatives, saline and other, more unusual compounds into her bloodstream. Her chest was covered by a swathe of black crinoline, but Newbury could see where the tubing snaked from the tanks at the back of her chair, up under her arms and into her chest, just below the breasts. Victoria was the Empress of half the world, and she clearly wasn't going to give it up without a fight. At least not whilst she had the marvellous machines of Dr. Fabian to keep her alive indefinitely.

When she spoke again, her voice was a husky, gritty rasp. "Where is our man, Newbury?" She offered him a reproachful look.

Newbury took a deep breath. "Your Majesty, I attended the rendezvous as requested. The agent codenamed 'Caspian' was not in the appointed carriage, nor did he make himself known to me on the platform. All I was able to glean from the experience was that the person who had inhabited compartment 3b was carrying with them some item or creature that smelled distinctly as if it were carrion."

Victoria raised an eyebrow. She wheeled forward in the chair, the wooden rims creaking against the marble floor. Her hands were shaking with the effort. "Newbury. Let us make the situation clear to you. You must locate this man, 'Caspian', and bring him to the palace forthwith."

Newbury tried to hide his exasperation. "As you wish, Your Majesty. To do so I fear I will need some more of the details, however..."

Victoria laughed, a wet, spluttering laugh. "Very well." Her face became serious. "This is a difficult assignment, Newbury. It may have repercussions for both you, personally, and for the Crown."

"How so?"

"That will no doubt become clear as you continue. For now, all you need to know is that the man you are looking for was once an agent named William Ashford."

Newbury frowned. "Ashford? I thought he died years ago, before my time? I've heard stories of the man."

Victoria gave the approximation of a shrug. The machinery groaned with the movement. "It was all a long time ago, Newbury. Ashford *was* killed, five years ago, in a manner of speaking. But he was rebuilt by Dr. Fabian as an instrument, and a blunt one at that. He has been living a half-life undercover in St. Petersburg, but now, for some reason, he has returned, contrary to our instructions. Another agent in Russia was able to warn us of his intended return."

"So Ashford is rogue? Why would he risk returning to London, and why should he travel so far by train, rather than airship?"

"Ashford is no longer a man, Newbury. Not in the sense that you would understand. He is an anomaly, neither living nor dead, but trapped somewhere in between and full of vengeance. His sense of what is right and wrong no longer equates to our own. We believe he has returned to seek revenge on those who plotted his downfall. He travels only by land and sea, for the altitude of an air-going vessel would affect the workings of the machines that sustain him." She paused, meeting Newbury's gaze. "You must find this anomaly, Newbury, and bring it to heel. One does not allow such things to travel freely about the capital."

"Quite so, Your Majesty. Quite so. I shall attend to it directly."

"See that you do. Put all else out of mind. Ashford must be foremost in your thoughts."

Newbury nodded. "There is just one other thing, Your Majesty, that I would prevail upon you for."

Victoria nodded her consent for him to go on.

"A boy. George Purefoy. He's a reporter for *The Times*. I have a notion that he deserves our attention. He could make an excellent agent, given time, perhaps."

Victoria waved a dismissive hand. "Later, Newbury, later. There will be time enough for taking a young apprentice under your wing. For now, we urge you to focus on the task at hand. Go to it."

Newbury watched as the Queen rolled back in her strange, mechanised chair. The darkness enveloped her. He turned to leave.

"Oh, and the Hobbes girl." Her voice called out from the shadows.

He looked back, but Victoria remained shrouded in darkness.

"Veronica?"

"No. The younger one. We have considered your request and have decided to oblige. She will be moved to a new facility. More information will be forthcoming. We suggest you do not involve the family until arrangements have been made."

Newbury grinned. "Thank you, Your Majesty. That is most excellent news."

Victoria's hissing laugh echoed around the dark, cavernous room. "We do what is necessary. As do you, Sir Maurice." She coughed. "Now go and deal with Ashford."

"As you say."

Newbury crossed the room and stepped through the door into the passageway that would lead him back to Sandford, the waiting room and the cold London morning outside. It seemed Veronica would have an even longer wait on her hands; whilst Her Majesty had given him a little more to go on, Newbury still felt he was only hearing half of the story, and that, if he were to uncover a little more information about Ashford, he'd be able to bring the case to a much swifter resolution. Not only that, but her talk of Newbury's personal stake in the assignment had left him feeling more than a little uncomfortable. He had no idea how an agent from five years ago could have any bearing on him, or the nature of the repercussions that she had referred to. But he did know someone who might: Sir Charles Bainbridge. Charles had been an agent for many, many years and would likely remember Ashford. He may even have worked with the man on a number of assignments. Whether he knew the truth, or, like Newbury, had been led to believe that Ashford was dead, Newbury had no idea. But he knew that he needed to find out. He would head directly to Scotland Yard and speak with Charles. For now, it was the only lead he had.

Chapter Seven

"Ashford, you say? It's a long time since I last heard that name."
Sir Charles Bainbridge, Chief Inspector at Scotland Yard, moved about behind his desk, shuffling papers, a flustered expression on his face. He was older than Newbury, just over fifty, with greying temples and a big, bushy moustache. He was dressed in a grey suit, with a white starched collar and black neck tie. He glanced up at Newbury, who was sitting in a chair off to one side, watching his friend as he went about his business. "Why do you ask?"

Newbury stroked his chin thoughtfully. He hadn't really decided how to put it yet. "Her Majesty has asked me to find him."

Bainbridge nodded and looked down at the stack of papers in his hands. Then, realisation dawning behind his eyes, he dropped the papers into a heap and looked back at Newbury, before lowering himself into the chair behind his desk. "Newbury, William Ashford has been dead for over five years. What on earth are you going on about?"

Newbury nodded. Clearly Bainbridge wasn't aware of Ashford's remarkable second life. "Indeed. That, apparently, is the received wisdom on the matter. But it transpires that there is more to Ashford's death than meets the eye."

Bainbridge looked confused. "Stop talking cryptically and get on with it, Newbury."

Newbury gave a curt nod. "You start. What can you tell me about Ashford? What sort of man was he, and how did he die?"

Bainbridge sat back in his chair. "He was a good man, I'll venture that much. I knew him fairly well. He was married, with two children. A boy and a girl, if I remember correctly. He was a good agent – hard, but fair. He always had the best interests of the Empire at heart."

Newbury nodded, glancing out of the window. In the yard below, a group of uniformed men were readying a police carriage. He turned to meet Charles's gaze. "So how did he die?"

"It was a nasty business, Newbury, and not something I care to remember."

Newbury furrowed his brow. It was unusual for Bainbridge to be so reserved. "Come on, Charles! This is important." He banged his fist on the table with impatience.

Bainbridge sighed. He leaned forward in his chair again. "What do you know of Dr. Aubrey Knox?"

"Not a great deal. Former agent. Lost in action about the same time as Ashford. It's never really come up."

"There's an explanation for that, Newbury. It's never come up for a reason."

"Go on."

"Knox was a genius. A brilliant man, who, like you, had a fascination with the occult sciences. He was one of the shining lights of Her Majesty's secret circle; he had proved himself to be a reliable, loyal subject for over ten years, and his service record was impeccable. He took on many of the same sorts of cases that you take on now: anything strange, psychological, paranormal, supernatural. He had a depth of knowledge surpassed by none in the Empire, yet he didn't crave personal recognition. He wrote no papers, attended no lectures. In many ways he was the perfect agent; quite brilliant, but quiet, effective, and unassuming."

"What happened to him? Is it all tied up with Ashford?"

Bainbridge nodded. "It was midway through eighteen ninety-six. June, I think. There was a botched assignment. I'm not sure of the details, but something went wrong. Something that everyone expected to be an easy job. Somehow, somewhere in the aftermath, it was brought to the attention of Her Majesty that Knox had been pursuing his own interests. He'd become obsessed with the practice of the occult. Agents were sent to his laboratory in Ladbroke Grove. They discovered that he'd been experimenting on human subjects: waifs, whores, paupers. No one knew what he was trying to do, but we were all appalled by it. It wasn't just the work of an enquiring mind. You should have seen the place, Newbury. It's burned into my mind. The things he'd done... he should be damned to hell for all eternity. Anyway, a warrant was issued for his arrest. Ashford was given the case. He was told to find Knox and bring him in, whatever the cost."

Pausing, Bainbridge stood, crossed the room and collected two brandy glasses from a shelf by the door. He reached into a cupboard and searched out a plain glass decanter, from which he removed the stopper and sloshed an ample measure of brandy into each glass. He returned to his desk and handed one of the drinks to Newbury. He looked pale. "Bit early, I know..." He shrugged. His tone changed. "Now, Newbury, you must understand that Ashford was very much unlike you or I. His disposition was entirely different. Put him in a room with a foreign agent and he'd make them talk, without even batting an eyelid. He was the sort of man who could bring down a network of criminals with sheer brute force. Simple, but effective. 'A tool', Her Majesty would call him, for when we needed 'something a little stronger'. But he had no experience of the occult, no sense of what he was getting himself into with Knox. And Knox, for his part, knew how to play him." Bainbridge sighed. "Ashford tracked Knox across the country for months, finally cornering him back here in London. But Knox was expecting him and had laid a trap. No one is sure exactly what happened to Ashford, but his body was found mangled in an abandoned warehouse near the docks, ripped apart, as if he'd been torn open like a paper doll. Knox was never heard from again."

"So he got away? No one went after him?"

"Plenty of people went after him. But no one ever found him. He disappeared. I wouldn't be surprised to learn that Her Majesty still had people looking for him now, all over the world. But poor old Ashford was buried a few days later, and I had to break the news to his wife. It was a sorry business indeed."

"So why have I never heard of this before?"

"Because, Newbury, you were brought in to replace him. In many ways you're the same sort of man: brilliant, dedicated, effective. But even the very best of men are fallible. Don't think that I don't know about your fondness for the laudanum, for a start."

"Look, let's not get into that now."

Bainbridge took a long draw on his brandy. "The Queen is worried. Not because she doubts you, you understand, but because she's seen it before. Knox left a bad taste in her mouth. In all our mouths. She's concerned that, one day, you may drift too close to the line, that the allure of the occult is too strong, not just for you, but for any man."

Newbury gripped the arms of his chair. "God damn it, Charles! That's ridiculous. How can she equate me with a man like that? I have a mind to head back there now, to have it out of her myself!"

Bainbridge slammed his drink down on his desk with a bang. "Don't be a fool, Newbury! Didn't you hear what I said? It's precisely that sort of behaviour that Her Majesty is trying to avoid." He stood, looking down at his friend. "Newbury, we've been friends for a long time. Listen to me when I tell you this. Stay away from this. It'll do you no good. Ashford is dead, Knox is lost, and you, my friend, are one of the finest men I know. It wouldn't do to mix yourself up in this business. The Queen has nothing to fear. I've told her that myself. She's simply trying to protect you."

Newbury looked up at Bainbridge, resignation in his eyes. "I'm afraid it's not that simple, Charles. Ashford isn't dead, at least not in the way you think he is."

"What?"

"The Queen told me herself, just this morning. It's all starting to make a horrible sort of sense. After what happened at the docks – after they found Ashford's shredded remains – Dr. Fabian took the body to his laboratory and *rebuilt* him. He's still alive, but he's barely human. Her Majesty said he is 'a blunt instrument' and 'no longer a man in the way that I'd understand it'. He's been living undercover in St. Petersburg for five years. Now, for some reason, he's gone rogue. He's probably somewhere in London as we speak. Her Majesty thinks he's returned to wreak vengeance, that he's probably half mad. She's charged me with bringing him in."

Bainbridge flushed red. He looked flustered. "My God..." He grabbed for his glass and downed the rest of his brandy in one long gulp. "It seems that I don't know everything, after all."

"I'm beginning to think it's an epidemic." Newbury took a pull on his own brandy. "Do you think he's come looking for Knox?"

"Perhaps. I don't know. Knox hasn't been heard of for years.

There could be other reasons."

"Such as?"

Bainbridge shrugged. "All I know is that the Ashford I knew would never go rogue. Not without a damn good reason. Perhaps he's on to something. Perhaps he's following a trail. Or perhaps he really has lost his mind."

Newbury nodded, slowly. "Perhaps. Being half-dead for five years, trapped in Russia without his family. No one could blame him." He placed his empty tumbler on the edge of Bainbridge's mahogany desk. "Will you help me, Charles? I don't even know where to begin."

The Chief Inspector looked pained. "Newbury... I can't. I have no time. I'm about to head out to the scene of a murder. A high-profile one, too. A lord has been found dead in his home. I need to attend to it before I can think of anything else."

Newbury smiled. "Of course. Can I ask – what are the circumstances?"

"It's all rather rum. Lord Henry Winthrop, found dead in his drawing room at Albion House. He held an extravagant soirée on Tuesday evening, something to do with a mummy unrolling. He'd just returned from an expedition to Egypt. It looks like a bungled robbery, according to the chaps on the scene. The burglar may have been disturbed by Winthrop: there's not a great deal missing. We're wondering if someone scoped the place out during the party and tried to come back the next day."

Newbury was already on his feet. "Charles! I was there. Two nights ago, at the party. I spoke to Winthrop. My God..."

"What! Then you could be of use to me on the scene. Can you talk me through what happened there?"

"Of course. I may even be able to point you to a suspect. There was a heated exchange at the party between Winthrop and a man named Blake. Wilfred Blake. He left under a heavy cloud."

"Good man! Come on, grab your coat. The carriage should be ready and waiting. Once we've got this nasty business out of the way I can help you with Ashford, assuming that he doesn't show his hand in the meantime." Bainbridge strode over to the coat stand in the corner and collected his overcoat, gloves and cane. Newbury followed suit. He couldn't help but wonder if, somehow, Winthrop's death would prove to be connected to the mystery surrounding the screaming mummy. But it was not enough of a distraction to quell the rising feeling of disquiet that gripped him, tightly, in the chest, every time he considered Bainbridge's words: "The Queen is worried... even the very best of men are fallible."

He knew that feeling only too well himself.

Together, the two men set out for Albion House.

Chapter Eight

Veronica stood on the gravel path at the foot of the sanatorium building and tried to will herself to smile. It was mid-morning, and the journey to Wandsworth had been fraught with chaos. The progress of her hansom had been arrested at the scene of a terrible accident, in which a small, steam-powered vehicle had exploded, sprinkling the driver in a bloody mess across a residential square, leaving debris scattered over the road and frightened horses bolting in every conceivable direction. Many cabs, including her own, had been dragged half-way across the neighbourhood, and Veronica would not have been surprised to learn that these errant vehicles themselves had been the cause of further accidents. Thankfully, her driver had been quick to get his spooked horses under control, and had soon arranged for a swift detour to avoid the inevitable delays that awaited them in the other direction.

In truth, however, Veronica knew it was not this that had left her feeling so dejected. Sir Maurice had failed to make their appointment once again that morning, and whilst she knew that she shouldn't blame him – wrapped up as he was in the whole "screaming mummy" affair – she couldn't help but feel a little slighted that he should choose to spend his time worrying about a musty old corpse rather than aiding her with a serious investigation.

Then, of course, there was Amelia. Last time she had visited her younger sister, a week earlier, Veronica had found the experience almost unbearable. Amelia was growing weaker and frailer with every passing day. It was as if her sporadic seizures were somehow draining the life out of her, stealing her vitality, as if she was suffering from some kind of wasting disease that was slowly dragging her towards death. Veronica couldn't bear to stand by and watch that happen. She cared for Amelia too much.

She stared up at the building. It looked foreboding, deserted. The airing courts were empty, and a thick, rolling mist lay heavy on the gardens. The clock tower disappeared into the milky sky above the entrance. She couldn't put it off any longer. Sighing, Veronica walked decisively towards the sanatorium, her boots crunching noisily on the loose gravel.

†

Inside, the reception area was a remarkable counterpoint to the misty solitude of the sanatorium grounds. Here, there were signs of life in plenitude. A nurse sat behind the reception desk, a vacant expression on her face; a doctor strolled purposefully along the corridor, his shoes clicking on the tiled floor; the sounds of patients in their rooms, suffering from any number of terrible mental afflictions. Veronica always felt disconcerted by the sounds of the inmates. Their keening, shouting, wailing and babbling was a constant background noise, disturbing and inescapable. It left her feeling edgy, as if she was surrounded by fear, and it was this, if nothing else, that made her wish that Amelia could be found a more salubrious environment in which to heal. She was certain that her sister's surroundings were adding to her slow decline. Veronica blamed her parents for that, for washing their hands of the "embarrassment". They had insisted on having her committed. What she needed was love, and to be treated like a real person, not someone who needed to be hidden away from society, or else a puzzle that was proving difficult to solve.

Distracted, Veronica turned to see Dr. Mason, Amelia's physician, approaching across the reception hall. He looked tired, worn down by his work. He was dressed in a smart black suit with a white collar, although he had evidently removed his tie and had forgotten to replace it. He was swarthy, with dark hair swept back from his forehead, in his fifties, and when he spoke his voice was filled with relief. "Miss Hobbes. I'm glad you've come. I've been trying unsuccessfully to reach your parents for a week now."

Veronica frowned. "Dr. Mason, I do not pretend to follow their movements. I fear I am no better equipped to locate them than you. Perhaps they are visiting Father's cousin, in Paris." Her expression softened to one of concern. "Why? Is there news of Amelia?"

Dr. Mason looked pained. It was evidently bad news. "Your sister is gravely ill, Miss Hobbes. I fear you must prepare yourself..."

Veronica gave an involuntary, wracking sob. *Prepare herself...* Then things had become even more desperate for Amelia. Quickly, she gathered her composure, but her voice was thin and reedy when she spoke. "How long?"

Dr. Mason shook his head. "I cannot answer that, Miss Hobbes. Two or three months would be my estimate, judging by the rate of her deterioration."

Veronica realised she was clenching her fists so hard that her fingernails were biting into the flesh of her palms. "Is there nothing you can do?"

The doctor looked shame-faced. "I can make her comfortable." He wouldn't meet her eye.

Veronica blinked away stinging tears. "Where is she?"

"This way. I'll take you to her." He set off along the corridor, and Veronica trailed behind him. She dabbed at her eyes, attempting to regain her composure.

A few moments later, after following the doctor through a seemingly endless warren of blank, sterile passageways, they stopped before a door. "She's in there. She may be asleep." He turned, glancing back the way they had come. "I'll give you some time alone. Try not to tire her too much. And do your best to stay buoyant." He coughed once into his fist and then, smoothing the front of his suit, he left her there, standing outside the door. In a moment his echoing footsteps had dissolved into the ever-present cacophony of voices.

Steadying herself, Veronica reached for the handle and pushed the door open, stepping into the room. It was small, with space for only a single bed, a chair, and a bedside table. It was lit only by a single lamp, and the curtains were drawn shut over the window.

On the bed her sister lay slumped, almost entirely subsumed by the pillows and blankets. Her raven-black hair spilled out all around her face, and she looked painfully thin, emaciated by her inability to eat. Her eyes were sunken pits, and her face was gaunt. She was only nineteen years old, but could easily have passed for a woman twice her age. To Veronica, though, she was still beautiful. She offered her brightest smile as Amelia turned to look at her, startled by the sound of the door clicking back into place.

"Sister, don't think I don't realise what people see when they look at me." She offered Veronica a hard stare. "I'm dying. Degenerating. And the doctors don't understand why. I've seen myself in the mirror." Her face softened. "You don't have to hide your dismay."

Veronica crossed to her bedside. "I don't hide anything from you, Amelia."

"Then why are you standing there trying to pretend that everything is normal?"

"You know why."

Amelia shrugged. "I'm not scared, Veronica. It's nothing new. People die every day. It's the same for us all. Life is simply one long fight towards death. I've come to realise that all we learn from life, all we truly learn, is how to die with dignity. I intend to do just that."

"My God, Amelia..."

"Do you believe in God, sister? I mean really, truly believe in him?"

Veronica hesitated. Her voice was a breathless whisper. "I... no. I don't. At least not in the way you mean. I –"

"It's alright," Amelia cut in, her voice faltering. She turned her head on the pillow so that she was looking at the panelled door. "Neither do I. I don't have the capacity to imagine an afterlife."

Veronica sucked in her breath. "Amelia, that's a terribly stark view of life."

"It's a terribly *honest* view."

"And that's what you want? For everything to end?" Veronica couldn't keep the scorn out of her voice.

Amelia tried to sit up. She turned to meet her sister's gaze. "No! That's not what I want. Quite the opposite. I *want* to live. I'm not ready for it all to end. Not yet. But all the same, I recognise the end is near."

Veronica shook her head. "Don't you dare stop fighting this, Amelia!"

Amelia smiled and allowed herself to sink back into the folds of the pillows. "Veronica, I have no intention of giving up without a fight. Now," she beckoned her sister closer, "will you come here and let me look at you properly? I want to hear all of your news."

Veronica stifled another sob. She knew she needed to be strong for Amelia. Later, when she was at home, in the darkness. Then she could allow herself to cry.

She propped herself on the edge of the bed, taking up her sister's hand, and realising, surprised, that in the intervening seconds Amelia had drifted off into unconsciousness. Sighing, she brushed Amelia's long, dark hair away from her forehead, and watched her breathing, an overwhelming sense of sadness in her heart.

†

"Amelia, I have to go. I have to be somewhere. But I'll be back soon, I promise." Veronica's voice was a gentle whisper. She had sat by her sister's bed for over an hour, and it was only now that Amelia had begun to stir.

Amelia blinked up at her sleepily. "The missing girls?"

Veronica offered her a quizzical look. "Yes... How did you...? Have you started to remember the content of your visions?"

Amelia gave an almost imperceptible nod. "A little." She propped herself up on her elbow, yawning. She looked suddenly serious. "Veronica, I've seen terrible things. Nightmarish things. A man with no face, looming out of the darkness. Horrible screeching sounds. And spinning. Always spinning, around and around, like I'm trapped on a carousel, unable to focus. I have no idea what it means."

Veronica couldn't bear to look Amelia in the eye. She studied her own hands instead, turning them over, following the map of folds and tributaries described by her pale skin. "It may not mean anything, Amelia. It may be your mind attempting to heal itself, is all."

Amelia clenched her fists dramatically, gathering bundles of the bed sheets. When she spoke, her voice was hot with anger. "Not you, Veronica. I can't stand it if you begin spouting their rhetoric, too. You know better than that. Tell me you don't think that."

Veronica placed a placatory hand on her sister's arm. "I don't think that, Amelia. Not for a minute. But I hate what your... condition is doing to you."

Amelia nodded, silently. Veronica knew that she hated it too.

"I really have to go now, sister. I'll come back as soon as I'm able."

Amelia smiled. "I know you will."

Veronica placed Amelia's hand carefully on the bed and got to her feet. "Take care, Amelia."

Without looking back at the thin shadow of the woman who lay on the bed behind her, Veronica opened the door and stepped into the hall. Dr. Mason was nowhere to be seen, called away, she presumed, to attend to another patient. It was probably for the best. Veronica couldn't imagine dealing with the man now. Instead, she needed to throw herself into the case. Crying wouldn't help her sister. And out there, somewhere, were missing girls that she *could* help. She needed to do that, for herself, and for Amelia.

Drawing her coat around her, Veronica set out. Whether she could count on Sir Maurice's assistance or not, she would solve this case. And in the meantime, she would consider how best to aid her dying sister.

Chapter Nine

The police carriage pulled to a sharp halt. Newbury looked out of the window.

Albion House was once again bustling with people, but it was an entirely different sort of bustle than the one he had witnessed just a couple of evenings before. Gone was the impressive flock of lords and ladies, who had fluttered around on the front steps like preening birds, all dressed in their elaborate finery; replaced instead by an army of uniformed constables with grey, tired faces and expectant looks.

A large crowd of onlookers had gathered on the pavement outside of Lord Winthrop's house, each of them attempting to catch a glimpse of whatever gruesome mystery was hidden behind the shuttered windows. The bobbies were doing their best to marshal this unruly crowd, keeping them back from the scene and ignoring their pleas for information. Newbury guessed there would be half a dozen reporters in the mob. He wondered if one of them was Purefoy.

Newbury edged forward in his seat, leaning over to open the carriage door, but before he could it swung open, as if by its own volition, and a man's face peered in. He was wearing a full, black beard and his eyes were a shining sea-green. He looked official in his grey woollen suit and bowler hat. Newbury grinned: a wide, welcoming grin. "Inspector Foulkes. How unfortunate that we seem only to meet on occasions such as this."

The man glanced at Newbury and nodded sullenly. "Indeed, Sir Maurice. Unfortunate is the word. My job would be so much easier if people would only desist from killing each other." His moustache twitched. He glanced at Bainbridge. "Sir Charles, we haven't touched anything inside. What would be your preferred course of action?"

Bainbridge sighed. "I'd *prefer* to be back in my warm office shuffling papers. But I suppose we should get to it. We'll go inside and take a look." He climbed to his feet, leaning heavily on his cane and muttering beneath his breath. "This cold weather will be the death of me."

They stepped down from the carriage into the crisp London morning. The horses were sweating profusely, their breaths fogging in the cold air. Newbury looked up at the house. It seemed quiet; different, somehow. He supposed it was simply the lack of lights and noise coming from inside, the fact that last time he'd been here, it had seemed warm and inviting, full of bustle and excitement. Now, instead, it seemed cold and dreary, and Newbury knew that inside, all that awaited him was the stink of death and corruption. His mood darkened. Winthrop had been rather a buffoon of a fellow – a buffoon with a great deal of money to throw at his hobbies – but whatever had happened to him in there, it was unlikely he deserved it.

Glancing back at Charles and Foulkes, Newbury mounted the steps and made his way up to the grand entrance. There was no butler to show him in, this time, but one of the uniformed officers pushed the door aside to let him pass. Newbury nodded his thanks and stepped into the porch. Nothing there had been obviously disturbed. There were no signs of forced entry. The stained-glass panels of the inner frame were still perfectly intact, beautifully refracting the light. He turned the handle on the inner door and pushed it open, stepping through into the grand hallway on the other side.

Immediately, it was clear that something devastating had occurred. Where there had previously been an arrangement of tall glass display cases, perfectly placed to allow people to move easily amongst them, there was now only a sea of glass: a shattered wave of splintered panes, broken frames and ancient artefacts, a landscape of devastation writ small. A few of the display cases were still standing, partially smashed, like buildings towering mournfully over the wreck of a city.

Newbury heard Bainbridge step through the door behind him, his cane clicking noisily on the tiles. There was a pause. "Good God! What a mess."

"Hmmm." Newbury rubbed a hand over his chin, thinking. He stepped further into the room. "This is no bungled robbery, Charles. I'm sure of it. This destruction was systematic. Whoever did this was looking for something specific, and they created this chaotic scene to throw us off the scent." He approached the nearest display case, his feet crunching on broken glass. "Look at this." He beckoned Bainbridge over to examine one of the artefacts that was still in situ, a necklace resting on a small black stand. "Ancient gold, inlaid gemstones... Charles, this piece is priceless. Why would they leave it here? Anyone – even the most common of thieves – would think to snatch this up on their way out of the door." He glanced at the ruination by their feet. "There's more of it there, too. A fortune's worth of ancient treasure. Whoever did this left most of the valuables, but took the time to smash the displays, regardless. What were they looking for? What didn't they want us to see?"

Bainbridge shrugged. "You tell me, Newbury. You were here. You saw the displays intact."

Newbury shook his head. "I didn't have time to look in any real detail. I remember noticing an unusual ushabti figure, over here..." He stepped over a heap of broken panes towards another partially intact display case. "I only recall seeing it because the inscriptions were so out of the ordinary. Most of these things carry a particular passage from the *Book of the Dead*. This one was inscribed with something different, something I'd never seen before." His voice was subdued, almost a whisper. He studied the remnants of the display. The small statuette was gone. He looked up at Bainbridge. "It's gone."

Bainbridge shrugged. "It could be anywhere in that mess, Newbury. It doesn't mean anything." He shook his head. "And I suppose that was the point of the exercise. It's going to take us days to work out what's missing. We'll have to match the artefacts to Winthrop's inventory, one-by-one, before we'll have any idea of what the killer has taken. Assuming Winthrop even *had* an inventory."

Newbury nodded, looking around himself at the mess. Behind him, he noticed all of the strange, Egyptian-like automatons were still frozen in silent vigil on their pedestals behind the staircase. There was no sign of Winthrop's body. He caught Bainbridge's attention. "Where *is* Winthrop?"

"In the drawing room." Bainbridge sighed. "Come on. Let's get it out of the way. I'm told it's not pretty."

Newbury clambered out from the wreckage of the displays, being careful not to slice his hands on the broken glass. He followed Bainbridge silently across the hallway, towards the double doors that led to the drawing room.

The room was still shrouded in darkness, the heavy curtains pulled across the windows, just as they had been the last time Newbury had visited the room. It took a moment for his eyes to adjust to the gloom. Bainbridge coughed. There was a dry, musty odour, and Newbury realised immediately that the familiar smell originated from the exposed remains of the mummy, which was still laid out on the long table, just as it had been two nights before. Rolls of unravelled linen bandages surrounded it like a bed of ornamental reeds.

At first, Newbury couldn't see where Winthrop's corpse had been left. There was nothing by the fireplace, or by the bookcase on the far wall. He frowned and looked over at Charles, who was staring, dumbfounded, at the empty casket of the mummy, which lay on the floor beside the table. Newbury followed his gaze.

Winthrop's body had been carefully placed inside the shell of the casket, his arms folded across his chest in an obscene parody of the mummy's burial pose. His throat had been slit, and blood had pooled behind his head, forming an oily, congealing puddle of red. His mouth was set in a terrible rictus grin.

Newbury crouched down beside the wooden coffin. "Someone has a ghastly sense of humour, Charles."

"I'll say. Poor sod. We mustn't let the press get hold of this."

"Quite." Newbury reached down and turned Winthrop's head slightly from side to side. The gash across his throat yawned open like a second mouth with the movement. There was blood everywhere; matted in Winthrop's beard and hair, soaked into his clothes. Gritty arterial spray had spattered the floor around the coffin, too. It had been a quick, effective murder. Not the sort of thing Newbury would expect to see as the result of a burglary. "Charles. Have you seen the precision with which his throat has been cut? This is not the sort of wound one would expect from your average ruffian. This is not a bungled robbery. It's an execution. And it's very much in the style of one of Her Majesty's agents."

"No, Newbury. I absolutely refuse to believe it. Why would Ashford do such a thing? What possible motivation could he have for murdering Winthrop in such a manner?"

Newbury stood, wiping the blood from his fingers with his handkerchief. "I have no idea. But it's clear from what Her Majesty said that Ashford is disturbed. And you've received the same basic training in the combative arts as I have, Charles. You know as well as I do that this is a textbook assassination."

Bainbridge shook his head, the distaste evident on his face. "I don't like it, Newbury. Ashford was a good man. And the grotesque way in which this body has been posed..."

"It's been a long time, Charles, and a lot of water has passed under the bridge. Ashford has been in Russia for five years, living hand to mouth. We have no idea what he's been through, what vile practices he's learned. He isn't the man you once knew. From what I gather, he isn't even a man at all. For all we know, someone else could be guiding his hand. He may have defected."

"Still, Newbury, we have to consider all of our options. There remains Blake, and the –"

There was a loud crash from out in the hall, the sound of glass shattering on marble. Both men rushed to the door, Bainbridge hefting his cane, ready to take on the intruder.

A young man was standing amongst the wreckage of the display cabinets, a sheepish expression on his face. His hair was sand-coloured, his eyes a bright, shining blue. He was dressed in a brown suit and tie, and he was clutching a notebook in his left hand. Bainbridge started forward, but Newbury put a hand on his arm to hold him back.

"It's alright, Charles. This is Mr. George Purefoy, a young reporter from *The Times*."

"Good afternoon, Sir Maurice." Purefoy grinned. He stepped out from amongst the pile of debris and came towards the two men, his hand extended.

Bainbridge lowered his cane. "What is the meaning of this? This is the scene of a crime, Mr. Purefoy. You have no right to be here. I consider this a case of trespass."

Purefoy dropped his hand. "Ah... well, I..."

Newbury stepped forward. "Mr. Purefoy, how did you happen to find your way onto these premises?"

Purefoy clearly didn't know where to look. "An open window around the back." He glanced at the floor.

Newbury raised an eyebrow. He looked at Charles. "Perhaps that's the entrance used by our murderer? We should take a look."

"Murderer? So it is murder, then?"

Newbury smiled. "Do you think, Mr. Purefoy, that the Chief Inspector and I would be here if it were not?"

"I'm not sure what to think, to be truthful, Sir Maurice. Would you care to elaborate on your role in the matter? As I understand it you're an academic with an office at the British Museum?"

Newbury laughed. "You're bold, Mr. Purefoy. I'll give you that. And if you don't want Sir Charles here to have you charged with trespass, I recommend you be on your way forthwith."

Purefoy nodded. "I think I have enough for the time being."

Bainbridge coughed into his fist. "And I suggest you think carefully before you commit any of it to print, young man. I don't want to hear any of this liberal nonsense about 'the people having a right to know'. This, Mr. Purefoy, is a murder investigation, and I expect you to respect that before you go rattling off your nonsense for the front page. It's difficult enough as it is to catch a villain these days, without having the details splashed all over the morning edition." It was evident that Bainbridge was feeling flustered by the appearance of the young man.

Newbury put an arm on Purefoy's shoulder and guided him to

the door, avoiding the spilled fragments of glass as they walked. He lowered his voice. "Three things you need to be aware of, Mr. Purefoy. Firstly, if you're going to sneak around at the scene of a murder, it's preferable not to get caught. Secondly, there are more professional agencies at work in this Empire than simply Scotland Yard and Her Majesty's military. I belong to one of them. Thirdly, Winthrop was murdered because of his connection to the mummy he brought back from Thebes. Now, when you write about this morning's events, you will refrain from printing any details of the murder or any mention of Sir Charles or I." He looked the young reporter in the eye. "I don't expect to catch you like this again."

Purefoy took Newbury's hand and shook it firmly. "No, Sir Maurice. I don't expect you do." He pulled on the door handle and, without looking back, stepped out into the foyer and the street beyond.

Newbury turned back to Bainbridge. "One day, Charles, that boy will make an excellent agent."

Bainbridge shook his head, exasperated. "One day, Newbury, I'll have a notion of what goes on in that mysterious head of yours." He leaned heavily on his cane. "Now, what of Winthrop?"

Newbury ran a hand over his chin. "I'm not sure what else there is to say. Until we have a notion of what has or hasn't been taken... it's just another despicable murder of a society gentleman. You need to talk to Blake, of course. And I need to find out where Ashford is hiding. I can't help thinking he's at the heart of it, somehow."

"I usually trust your instincts, Newbury, but this time I can't help feeling that you're on the wrong track."

Newbury sighed. "Time will tell, I suppose, old man. Time will tell." He turned up the collar of his coat. "Dinner? There's a new chef at the White Friar's. Excellent *Pigeons a la Duchesse*..."

"What? You're leaving?"

Newbury looked pained. "There's little more I can do here, Charles, and I promised Miss Hobbes I'd assist her with this damnable situation of the missing girls. You have Foulkes. Have him and his men turn the place over. Then meet me at my club at seven and we'll talk it over. I need to give some thought to this situation with Ashford, too."

Bainbridge waved his cane at the door. "Very well. Tonight. Seven o'clock. I imagine I'll be needing a brandy."

Newbury laughed. "I imagine we both will." He inclined his head in farewell, and then quit the house, relieved to be putting some distance between himself and the horribly brutalised corpse of Lord Henry Winthrop. He had no real notion of what Ashford could be up to, or why he should have executed Winthrop in such a horrendous manner. He needed to uncover the significance of the missing ushabti figure and the strange engravings he'd noticed during the party. He also needed a way of discovering where Ashford was hiding, and what his connection to Winthrop might be. Most of all, he needed time to think. And he knew a place where he could find it.

First, he would call on Veronica at the office, to explain how he had found himself detained, and to make arrangements to assist her the following day. Then he would pay a visit to Johnny Chang's.

Chapter Ten

Newbury emerged at the top of the stone staircase to find the light was already beginning to wane. It was windy and cold – so cold that his breath fogged before his face – but the warm haze of the opium high was enough to dispel the effects of the bracing weather. The street was busy, criss-crossed with people coming and going, shutting up their store fronts and retiring to their homes for the evening. Newbury checked his pocket watch. It was nearly half past five. He'd need to head directly to the White Friar's if he wanted to keep his appointment with Charles.

Newbury blinked as a ground train rolled by, its large, iron wheels groaning beneath the considerable weight of the engine. Steam billowed from a wheezing funnel. Carriages clattered along behind the huge machine, filled with passengers making their way home from any number of manufactories and offices, their faces dour after hours spent relentlessly pursuing an incalculably small wage. The driver looked cold and exhausted in his open-sided cab. Newbury shivered. He hadn't been near one of the vehicles since his encounter with the man posing as "the glowing policeman" a few months earlier. He'd sustained serious injuries fist-fighting with the man on the roof of one of the trains, and now, any time he found himself in close proximity to one of them, he couldn't help but recall the fate of the other man, his head cracked open on the cobbles after Newbury had caused him to tumble over the side. It was no more or less than the man had deserved – Newbury knew that – but the look of horror on his face as he fell to his death was something that would stay with Newbury forever. Such, he supposed, was the life he had chosen to live.

Sighing, he pulled his coat a little tighter around his shoulders, and set out, hoping the crisp air would help to clear his head before dinner.

He had called for Veronica after leaving Winthrop's house earlier that afternoon, but found she had already left for the day. A small, terse note printed in her immaculate handwriting had been waiting for him on his desk:

Sir Maurice,

I have taken leave to visit Amelia in your absence. I trust I shall see you in the office tomorrow morning so that we may continue with our investigations.

Miss Veronica Hobbes

It pained him to think that he had let her down. Moreover, it pained him to consider the missing girls and their plight. He knew, in his heart, that they were probably already dead, slung into the Thames like broken ragdolls or else dumped unceremoniously into hastily dug graves somewhere on the east side of the city. But he had a job to do, and presently Her Majesty considered it necessary for him to curtail the exploits of the rogue agent, William Ashford. It didn't sit well with Newbury to consider that the life of a lord should take precedence over the lives of innumerable working-class women, but he also knew that he wasn't yet in full possession of the facts. He didn't know what Ashford was looking for, nor what he was capable of. He might yet pose an even greater threat. And besides, it wasn't just a matter of bringing him in for the death of Winthrop. It was a matter of stopping a traitor – a traitor who knew everything about the innermost workings of Her Majesty's operations – from doing any more damage, at the very heart of the Empire itself, no less.

So, instead of chasing after his headstrong assistant, Newbury had retreated to the clandestine haven of Johnny Chang's, where he had passed the afternoon in a heady opium dream, cogitating on all of the disparate threads of the case, searching the annals of his mind for a possible solution. A part of him could see the hypocrisy in that line of thinking, but he knew himself better than that. The drug had enabled him to relax, to recede into his own quiet world, where his instincts could come to the fore and he was able to seek a different perspective of the chaotic mess of leads and clues and mysteries that faced him. And, as a result, he had formulated a plan. He knew how he was going to deal with Ashford. He was going to lay a trap. All he needed was a little –

Newbury turned sharply at the sound of a scuffed heel from close behind him. He made a fist in his gloved hand, expecting someone to be upon him at any moment. His breath became shallow, his heart hammering hard in his chest. He spun around on the spot, seeking out his assailant. But there was no one nearby. The street behind him was almost deserted, the bustle of earlier gone, as if the shopkeepers and passers-by had simply melted away into the shadows. Now, there were just a handful of people on the other side of the road, heading in the opposite direction.

Newbury glanced from side to side. The shadows of the terraced houses loomed large and uninviting, a few gas-lamps giving off an amber glow in the wan evening light. The wind whistled ominously through some nearby railings.

Perplexed, Newbury carried on walking. He had the sense of

someone there, on the periphery of his vision, but each time he looked back over his shoulder he could see no evidence that he was being followed. He wondered if it were the opium, playing tricks with his mind, causing the shadows to come to bizarre, hallucinatory life. Worse, he knew better than most that the shadows of London *did* contain creeping things that were better avoided; things that lurked in the darkness, preying on the ignorant and unwary; things from children's nightmares, fashioned from both the flesh and the spirit, or more recently, from the steam-powered manufactories of men.

Newbury shuddered, and then laughed at himself for allowing his mind to run away with him. It was clear the opium was still influencing his thoughts, much more than he had anticipated. He was not used to partaking of the drug in such a way, to such an extent, and had underestimated its effects. He took a deep breath, trying to cleanse his lungs. Everything that was happening had a dream-like quality about it, as if he perceived the world through some sort of hazy filter. He relished the feeling, the loss of control, but he also knew how dangerous that could be for a man in his position. Absently, he hoped that Charles would not be able to discern his condition over dinner.

There was another sound from behind him, this time over his right shoulder. Cautiously, he carried on walking so as not to give away the fact he had noticed. This time he was sure it was no hallucination. He'd heard the sole of a boot scuffing against the road. On his left was the dark frontage of a furrier's shop, the window display filled with shop dummies dressed in all manner of animal pelts, fashioned into coats, hats, scarves and more. Slowly, he approached the window, feigning interest. He studied his reflection in the glass. He looked pale and drawn, with dark rings beneath his eyes. He put it out of mind. Newbury watched for a moment, looking for signs of the person who had been following him. Sure enough, a moment later he caught a glimpse of something moving in the reflected scene of the street: a large, hulking shape, bigger than an average man, its face hidden beneath the cowl of an ominous hood. It was shrouded in a thick, black cloak. Newbury spun around, quickly, hoping to catch the creature off guard, but just as before, there was nothing to see. The street was deserted. He heard footsteps padding away, up ahead, in amongst the shadows. Whoever had been following him had clearly realised he was on to them, and wasn't ready to make themselves known.

For a moment, Newbury considered giving chase, but he knew he wasn't up to a fight, and besides, he had to be across town to meet Charles. But this new development altered things, altered the plans he'd been conceiving. Perhaps he wouldn't need to go after William Ashford, after all. Perhaps Ashford was coming after *him*.

He needed to clear his head.

Slowly, Newbury set off, heading in the same direction as the footsteps. He hoped that Ashford – if it were, indeed, Ashford – was not lurking in the darkness up ahead, waiting to pounce on him as he made his unsteady way towards Piccadilly. He kept his hands free as he walked, ready to defend himself if the situation arose.

After a few hundred yards, however, Newbury allowed himself to relax. It seemed that the mysterious figure had bolted when Newbury had caught sight of him in the shop window. His fingers were growing numb in the biting cold, and although it wasn't far to Piccadilly, he decided that he would hail a cab at the next available opportunity. Further ahead, the road opened out into a large set of crossroads, and the thoroughfare there, even from this distance, seemed busy with people and vehicles. He quickened his pace, knowing that he would be likely to be able to employ a hansom at the junction.

A shadow passed overhead, and Newbury looked up to see the

dark underbelly of an airship sweeping low over the city, a rope ladder trailing, forgotten, off the port side. He watched it drift lazily across the sky, the growl of its engines a gravelly counterpoint to the sharp, biting howl of the wind. He dropped his eyes to the road ahead and stopped, with a start.

The hooded figure was standing by the corner of the road, about a hundred feet away, regarding him steadily, its face hidden beneath the wide, shadowy cowl of its cloak. The black fabric trailed in the wind, billowing up around its legs. Beneath the hood, from somewhere within the pool of darkness that hid the person's face, a small, round, bluish light flickered like a blinking eye. It was a menacing sight, and caused Newbury to give an involuntary shudder. There was little else that Newbury could discern from this distance, other than that the man – for, given the figure's size and bulk, it had to be a man – was wearing black leather boots and matching gloves. It *had* to be Ashford.

Newbury broke into a run, charging towards the solitary figure, his head bowed against the driving wind. The man remained stationary, watching, silently, as Newbury dashed towards him. Newbury had no idea what to expect, no notion of what he was letting himself in for. In his present state he knew he wouldn't be able to put up much resistance if Ashford was angling for a fight, but he couldn't turn down the opportunity to tackle the rogue agent and get the whole matter quickly resolved.

Gasping, he flung himself forward as if to grapple the hooded figure, only to see him side-step around the corner at the last moment. Newbury caught hold of the wall, stopping himself from pitching over. He heaved against the brickwork, pulling himself around the corner after Ashford as if to continue the chase, but, bizarrely, the other man was gone.

Newbury, dumbfounded, glanced from side to side, looking for the means by which Ashford had made his escape. There were no obvious alleyways or doorways he could have dashed into, no ladders or vehicles by which he could have effected his disappearance. Just a series of dreary shop-fronts and red-brick walls. He looked up. The sky was a leaden canopy overhead, but there was no sign of Ashford atop the nearby buildings, either. He hadn't somehow managed to scale the wall. The man had simply vanished.

Panting, slowed by the opiate in his veins, Newbury fell back against the wall, attempting to catch his breath. There was a foul stench in the air, a rancid, carrion tang that made him splutter in disgust. Bile rose in his throat. The smell was immediately familiar, and there was no mistaking it. The man in the hooded cloak had most definitely been his quarry.

Newbury looked around, frustrated. Was everyone now able to simply disappear at will? Or was Ashford just fleet of foot, and Newbury, in his disorientated, half-delusional state, simply didn't have enough of a grip on the situation to be able to keep up with him? One thing was certain, though. Ashford was either teasing him, or was trying to tell him something. Either way, the end result would be the same. Next time they met, Newbury would be ready.

Sighing, he pushed himself away from the wall and checked his pocket watch again. He was late for Charles. He looked along the street. A hansom cab was trundling slowly in his direction. He stepped out in the road and waved his arm to hail it over. He needed to get to the White Friar's Club before Charles gave up on him. They had much to discuss.

Chapter Eleven

"You're late." Bainbridge's bushy grey moustache twitched as Newbury approached his table, a severe look on his face. "It's only by the good grace of Foster that I managed to get in at all." He indicated the butler on the door, who was standing by the door jamb, an implacable look on his face. "I'm not a member here, you know. I wish you'd had the foresight to –"

"Not now, Charles."

Bainbridge frowned. "What do you mean, not now? What the devil have you been up to, man?" He lowered his voice so as not to be overheard. "Indulging in that blasted vice of yours, judging by the look of you. It's a despicable business, Newbury. You look terrible." He folded his arms and leaned back in his chair, studying Newbury's face as he awaited a response.

Newbury waved his arm and dropped into a chair opposite his friend. There was resignation in his voice. "As I said – not now, Charles." He looked up and caught the attention of one of the waiters, who stepped forward, smiling, to take an order of drinks. "Usual, please, Williams." He glanced at Bainbridge's empty glass. "And whatever Sir Charles is drinking."

The waiter offered a polite nod of his head. "As you wish, sir." He retreated to the bar to place their order.

The White Friar's was a gentlemen's club on Arundel Street, and a second home for Newbury, who often visited the place to conduct meetings, dine with associates or friends and to otherwise escape the oppressive pressures of his life as an agent of the Crown. The club itself was a haven for literary types: writers, artists and intellectuals, and frequently Newbury left the establishment feeling invigorated, as much due to the stimulating conversation as the fine selection of brandy. The dining room, in which he had found Charles, was a smallish room, panelled in dark oak and furnished with a smattering of round tables, which were each large enough to accommodate five or six people at a time. A fire roared in the grate on the far side of the room, causing shadows to dance haphazardly over every surface like mischievous pixies, and the murmur of conversation from the adjoining lounge was a constant background hum. The room was filled with the pleasant scent of roasting meat, wafting through from the kitchen.

It was quiet that evening, however, and aside from Charles and himself, there were only two other diners making use of the room, huddled over a table in the corner, deep in the midst of some deep, philosophical debate. Or so Newbury liked to imagine. Other than this, a small army of waiters and servants kept a watchful eye on the patrons, keen to cater to their every whim.

Newbury ran a hand over his face. He looked at Bainbridge from beneath hooded eyelids. He was coming down from his opium high. "You can save the lecture for another day, Charles. I apologise for my tardiness."

Bainbridge leaned across the table towards him, toying with his fork. "Newbury." His voice was firm. "You're the only friend I have left in this Godforsaken city. I won't lose you, not to something so ridiculous as that dreadful Eastern weed."

Newbury smiled, a sad, knowing smile. He stared at the fire.

When, a moment later, he looked back at Bainbridge, he didn't meet the other man's eye. "What are you drinking?"

Bainbridge sighed. "A tolerably good Cognac. But my belly is in dire need of sustenance. Let's order some ruddy food."

Newbury grinned. "Yes, in a minute. I need to talk to you first."

Bainbridge looked concerned. "What's happened, Newbury?"

Newbury unfolded his napkin and, placing it on his knee, looked up at his friend. "Don't be alarmed, Charles. I need some more information regarding William Ashford, is all. I've been wondering: what became of his family after he died?"

Bainbridge shrugged. "They were moved. To a house near Cheapside. Dreadful place. It was one of the worst things I've ever had to do, Newbury, telling that woman her husband had been killed, and then, to compound it, that she and her family were being uprooted as a consequence. She broke down on my shoulder. Begged me to let her keep the house. But I had my orders." He fingered the rim of his empty glass. "Now, to learn that it was all a lie. Well, it casts things in a different light, doesn't it?"

Newbury furrowed his brow. He'd rarely seen Bainbridge in such a reflective mood. "I'm sure those things were done for the right reasons, Charles. It's been five years." He paused to accept his brandy from the waiter. "Do you think Ashford will go looking for them?"

"Wouldn't you?"

"I suppose that's what I'm getting at. I imagine that's as good a place as any to start my search."

Bainbridge shook his head. "No. You mustn't, Newbury. Don't go dragging up the past. Ashford may well be looking for his family – and I feel sorry for the man, I truly do – but the last thing his wife needs is to know that he's been alive all this time, turned into some sort of half-mechanical monster. Besides, he'll never find them.

And even then we're assuming that the family is still there, in that Cheapside hovel. As you say, it's been five years. They've probably moved on." He lowered his voice. "God knows, I hope they have."

Newbury took a pull on his brandy. He felt fingers of warmth spreading down through his chest as the alcohol banished his chill. It was clear that something about this case had touched a nerve with his friend. "Very well, Charles. I'll look elsewhere – for now. It may not be necessary to search him out, anyway."

Bainbridge leaned back in his chair. He took up the dinner menu. "How so?"

"I believe I find myself in the midst of a game of cat and mouse, and I'm unsure which of us is enacting which role – the hunter or the hunted."

Bainbridge looked up from the top of his menu. "Stop speaking in riddles, Newbury."

Newbury laughed, for the first time that evening. "I have reason to believe that Ashford has been following me. I encountered him in the street earlier this evening, but he gave me the slip."

"What? Where?" Bainbridge was frowning.

"Not far from here, as I made my way over to meet you. I had the curious notion that I was being followed, but for quite some time I was unable to ascertain by whom. I thought it may have been... well, I thought it may have been my mind playing tricks on me."

"But it was Ashford?"

"I believe so."

"Well, why the devil should he be following *you*?"

"A good question, Charles, and one for which I intend to find an answer. With any luck, this may not turn out to be the protracted affair I had initially feared." Newbury regarded the menu on the table before him. "Venison and creamed potatoes, I should say."

"Well, just be careful, Newbury."

Newbury offered his friend a sly look. "Of the venison?"

Bainbridge shook his head, exasperated. "Look, the Ashford I recall was a decent man, but having seen Winthrop today... I don't know any more. Just look after yourself. I'll help however I can."

"So, you've changed your mind about the nature of our suspect, have you, Charles? Does that mean Wilfred Blake has an alibi?" Newbury offered the Chief Inspector an amused grin.

Bainbridge nodded. "Indeed. And a solid one at that. He was in the company of a lady, dining out in full public view. He cannot be considered a suspect for the murder." He sighed again. "It looks like you may be right about Ashford, unless we have a foreign agent in our midst, someone who knows our ways."

"It's possible. But unlikely, I think. The simplest explanation is often the correct one, Charles, and here we have a rogue agent loose in London, and a corpse with all the hallmarks of a swift, purposeful execution. I do not think it is too much of a stretch to assume that we know the identity of our quarry, if not his motivation."

"Perhaps." Bainbridge drummed his fingers on the table. "Now, however, I believe I must eat, or I shall waste away to nothing and you shall have to find yourself another dining companion."

"Well, that, of course, would never do!" Newbury, laughing, turned and gestured for the waiter, Williams, to return to their table to take their order. His stomach was growling, and his head was finally beginning to clear. Soon, he'd need sleep. But first, he needed food, drink and the company of a good friend.

Chapter Twelve

THE CURSE OF THE SCREAMING MUMMY

BY MR G. PUREFOY

DEATH AND DESPAIR SURROUND THE DISCOVERY OF THE MYSTERIOUS "SCREAMING MUMMY", AS LORD HENRY WINTHROP IS FOUND DEAD AT HIS ALBION HOUSE MANSION, ONLY TWO DAYS AFTER RECEIVING SOCIETY VISITORS FOR A GRAND UNROLLING PARTY. WHILST SCOTLAND YARD STRUGGLE FOR LEADS, TALK OF AN ANCIENT CURSE IS RIFE AMONGST THE OTHER MEMBERS OF THE EXPEDITION, NOW FEARING FOR THEIR LIVES.

TURN TO PAGE 3 TO READ THE FULL STORY.

Newbury dropped the morning newspaper on the table with a hearty laugh, causing his housekeeper, Mrs. Bradshaw, to jump with a start and nearly miss the teacup she was pouring into, sloshing a small amount of the pungent brown liquid into the saucer. Newbury eyed her warily as, clearly flustered by the experience, she swept the offending china up into her arms and left the room, her only acknowledgement of the entire incident a short "tut" under her breath as she stomped out into the hallway. Newbury couldn't help but smile.

Reaching for another slice of toast, he scanned the front of the newspaper again with a chuckle. Purefoy had taken him at his word, anyway. When he'd told the boy to desist from sharing any details of the murder, or mentioning him or Charles by name, the reporter had evidently concocted some sort of elaborate story to explain away the lack of facts. Newbury wondered if the young man wouldn't be better off turning his talents to the writing of fiction. He clearly had an eye for it. Still, Newbury supposed it would sell newspapers, and besides, Purefoy had done him a favour. At least this way the public had something trivial and sensational to focus on, rather than dwelling on the more disturbing fact that a rogue agent was on the loose somewhere in the city. If the real details of the case had been splashed across the front page that morning, he supposed he and Charles would have been hauled up before Her Majesty with any number of her own difficult questions. At least this way most people would dismiss the story as supernatural claptrap, assuming it was just another botched robbery, of the type they read about almost daily in the assorted national press. With luck, Purefoy's actions would enable him and Charles to continue unimpeded with their investigations. He made a mental note to thank the young reporter at the next available opportunity.

Newbury had left Charles in the doorway of the White Friar's the previous evening, having retired to the drawing room after dinner to enjoy a conversation and a pipe. It hadn't been late, but Newbury had known that, after the trials of his day, he would have been ill-advised to make a night of it. Sure enough, upon returning to his Chelsea home, he had slept for a good nine hours, and was currently sitting at his breakfast table in his red silk dressing robe, picking at the remnants of the morning's feast. He could always rely on Mrs.

Bradshaw for a hearty breakfast, no matter what time of the day he actually found himself in need of it.

Pushing the newspaper to one side, Newbury turned his attention to the small silver tray of post that Mrs. Bradshaw had brought up with his tea. Idly, he flicked through the smattering of envelopes, ignoring anything that looked like correspondence from abroad. He was expecting a number of letters from Venezuela, pertaining to a private matter involving his deceased father, but he could deal with those later, when the whole Ashford matter had been resolved. Reaching the bottom of the pile, he gave a brief exclamation, pulling free a small white envelope that had been scrawled upon in black ink. The handwriting was scratchy and ill-formed. A large, oily thumbprint blighted the otherwise crisp envelope in one corner, and there was no stamp upon it, suggesting the letter had been sent round to the house via courier.

Leaning back in his chair, Newbury used the edge of his index finger to tear the envelope open and unfold the short note he discovered inside. As anticipated, it was a reply from his old friend Aldous Renwick, barely legible and smudged where Renwick had not waited for the ink to properly dry. He angled it towards the window so to see.

Newbury,
Come to the shop immediately. I have the information you require.
AR

Short, but pointed. Newbury sighed. Another detour, but clearly one he could not avoid. If Renwick had put his finger on the mystery of the screaming mummy, it could help to make the circumstances surrounding Winthrop's death far clearer. Not only that, but it might explain Ashford's motive for enacting such a horrific execution in the first instance.

Newbury looked up to see Mrs. Bradshaw returning with a fresh teacup and saucer. "Ah, Mrs. Bradshaw – perfect timing." He dropped the letter onto the table beside his plate. "I'll take my tea whilst I dress."

"Very good, sir." The housekeeper placed the china on the table and began pouring another cup.

Newbury stood, dabbing the corners of his mouth with his napkin. "Thank you, Mrs. Bradshaw. Another excellent breakfast." He collected his cup and saucer with a smile, and began making his way towards the hallway. Then, on second thoughts, he paused, hovering in the doorway. "Oh, and Mrs. Bradshaw? If I could prevail on you to send for a hansom forthwith, it would be very much appreciated."

The Scotswoman nodded with an exasperated sigh, and began noisily collecting up the remaining bowls and plates without another word.

Laughing, Newbury sipped at his Earl Grey and made his way hastily to his room to prepare for the day ahead.

†

"Miss Hobbes. I daresay I did you a disservice yesterday, and I'm fearful I'm about to do it all over again." Newbury was framed in the doorway that separated his and Miss Hobbes's desks from the rest of the small office, still attired in his hat and coat. It was early, and he'd made his way directly to the museum after finishing his daily ablutions and dressing in his usual black suit. He offered his assistant an earnest look, awaiting her response.

"No need to apologise, Sir Maurice – I saw the morning edition of *The Times*. I gather you're contending with an ancient curse now, amongst other things?" She offered Newbury a wry smile. She was dressed in a smart grey frock with a matching jacket, and her hair was tied back from her pretty face.

Newbury laughed. "Well, quite so. You know how these things go: a murder in the night, an ancient curse before breakfast. All in a day's work." Veronica grinned. "In all seriousness, however, I find myself terribly preoccupied by this Winthrop situation. I believe it somehow ties up with that missing agent I was intended to meet at the station the other morning."

"So it's *not* a curse then?" It was clear she was toying with him.

"Not in the supernatural sense of the word, no. But it feels somewhat like a curse, I assure you." He adjusted his collar ruefully. "I admit I'm finding it difficult to give my attention to anything else. I must attend to a small matter this morning off the Tottenham Court Road. Perhaps you could accompany me there, and then together we can go on to Soho and attempt to locate the lodgings of this 'Mysterious Alfonso' character?"

Veronica shook her head. Her expression grew serious. "I'm afraid there has been a further development since we last spoke. Another missing girl. This time I'm convinced there's a clear link between the disappearance and the theatre. The girl was last seen in attendance at the show, volunteering for the disappearing act. She hasn't been seen since, and she failed to return home that evening. There's little room for doubt."

Newbury looked thoughtful. "Yes, I see your dilemma. But I must insist, Miss Hobbes, that you do not, under any circumstances, confront this man on your own."

Veronica frowned. "Sir Maurice, I'm quite capable –"

"Yes, yes. I rather think it's not a matter of capability, Miss Hobbes, but one of safety. Whilst you are in my employ, you are in my care. I understand how frustrating it must be to have to sit by and wait for me to deal with this damnable Ashford thing, but really, I must insist that you will not commit yourself to any dangerous course of action in my absence."

Veronica had fire in her eyes, but she nodded in agreement. "I plan to visit the family of the missing girl this afternoon, to obtain a better understanding of the circumstances. I thought it wise to gather some further evidence, no matter how circumstantial, before we decide to tackle Alfonso himself, once again."

Newbury smiled. "An excellent plan, Miss Hobbes." He paused. "Then perhaps, this evening, we could make an appointment to meet for dinner...? You could fill me in on your findings and we could plan ahead to our next encounter with the dubious magician."

"Very well." Her lips curled into a smile. "Where shall we meet?"

"I'll call for you, at Kensington, around seven. Does that suit?"

"It does."

"Excellent. Then for now, I'll be on my way." He lifted his hat from his head. "Until this evening, Miss Hobbes."

"Until this evening, Sir Maurice."

He turned as if to make an exit from the office. Then, recalling an errand, he stopped by the door and pulled a slip of cream-coloured paper from his pocket. He crossed to where Miss Coulthard was sitting behind a new, broad mahogany desk. She looked up from amongst unruly piles of paper. "Sir Maurice?"

"Miss Coulthard. As busy as you are, I wonder if I may trouble you with one additional burden." He held the piece of paper out between two fingers with a smile. Miss Coulthard accepted it, the hesitation evident on her face. She unfolded it and examined the contents. On it was scrawled a woman's name and the word "Cheapside" in Newbury's loose hand. "I need you to find an address for this woman, as soon as possible. She may have moved location at any point in the last five years. Can you do it?"

Miss Coulthard nodded. "Of course."

Newbury grinned. "You really are a treasure, Miss Coulthard. My thanks." And with that, he bid her good morning and took his leave.

†

Aldous Renwick's bookshop was, upon first appearances, not unlike any of the other small emporiums that were to be found amongst the winding side streets that branched off the Tottenham Court Road. It sat nestled between a small general store and a haberdashery shop, its windows piled high with gaudy works of modern fiction, bound in leather or bright paper wraps. It was a cold, crisp morning, and Renwick had placed a small table outside of the door, a smattering of penny papers and cheap mystery stories on display, their covers fluttering in the light breeze. The legend above the door read simply: BOOKS.

Newbury had discovered the place many years ago, when engaged in the hunt for a rare Venetian treatise on the occult. A mutual acquaintance had tipped him off that Renwick may be able to source such a work, so, after due consideration, he had paid the man a visit. Renwick had found the book, too, along with many other archaic tomes in the intervening years, and although Newbury had paid dearly for them, he appreciated the discreet manner in which the man carried out his business. Renwick was one of the most learned men that Newbury knew, with a particular knowledge of esoteric literature, and as such Newbury had found numerous occasions to pay him a visit over the years. Today, it appeared, was one such occasion.

Stopping momentarily to glance at the cover of a tattered copy of the *Union Jack*, Newbury turned the doorknob with a gloved hand, allowing the door to creak open loudly on its hinges. He stepped over the threshold. Inside, the shop was filled with a cornucopia of books and periodicals, all piled high in huge stacks or pressed tightly onto bulging shelves of dark, heavy wood. There appeared to be no method in the way in which the various volumes had been scattered, chaotically, around the room, but Newbury had every suspicion that Renwick would be able to swiftly put his hand on any title that a given customer might request. Newbury, smiling, mused that the interior of the shop was ordered somewhat as erratically as its owner's mind, and that, in all probability, one was a close reflection of the other.

Newbury looked around for the man he had come to see. The shop was devoid of life. There was a musty odour about the place, that Newbury immediately identified as that of old books, and he filled his lungs with it, enjoying the familiarity of it. He called out. "Aldous? Are you there? It's Newbury here. I received your note this morning and came forthwith."

There was a banging sound from somewhere behind one of the bookcases. Newbury approached it, warily. Sure enough, there was a dull, repetitive thudding sound, like the turning-over of an engine, which seemed to be coming from the other side of the wall. "Aldous?"

The banging ceased, momentarily, and then was followed by a muffled shout, coming from the same direction. "I'll be out in a moment, Newbury. Bear with me." The voice was sharp and high-pitched. Newbury smiled. The banging returned, and whilst the other man kept him waiting, Newbury turned his attention to the spines of the nearest stack of books. Many of the titles were old, but distinctive and in excellent condition. There was everything from a monograph on the nature of steam power in the horticultural industry, to Dickens novels, to bound collections of *Blackwood's Magazine*, and more. It was a bibliophile's dream, but Newbury knew that, in reality, Renwick's real treasures lay in the back room, beyond sight of the casual book-buyer.

A moment later Newbury became aware of the sound of another man coughing, fitfully, and then the door behind the counter – previously concealed behind a collage of gaudy posters – swung open and Aldous Renwick stalked in, his hand outstretched in greeting.

Aldous Renwick was one of the most unusual characters that Newbury had the pleasure of calling a friend. He bore all the hallmarks of a caricature. He was rough around the edges: unshaven, with a wiry, bristly chin, a wisp of chaotic white hair, and yellowed fingers from the excessive smoking of cigarettes. He had a tendency to wear a worn leather smock over a stained white shirt, open at the collar, and his left eye had been replaced by a remarkable mechanical device that whirred and clicked disturbingly when he looked around. It was not as elegant as something designed by Dr. Fabian, but then Renwick was only a civilian, after all, and clearly valued function over the aesthetic. Newbury had no idea if the false eye was elective, or the result of some earlier, undisclosed adventure. Whatever the case, Newbury had long wondered over the sanity of his friend, and was as yet undecided as to whether the man was actually mad, or simply had a degree too much insight into the darker side of the human psyche.

He came forward to meet Renwick, clasping his outstretched hand in his own. "Good to see you, Aldous. How the devil are you?"

The bookseller chuckled, his good eye twitching with an alarming nervous tic. "A darn site better than Lord Henry Winthrop, from what I gather!"

Newbury sighed. "Well, I don't think I can contest that." He met the other's gaze. "I received your note."

Renwick studied him, his strange mechanical eye whirring in its socket. It protruded from the empty cavity with the look of a magnifying glass, not unlike the sort of tool used by jewellers to examine precious stones. But this device, Newbury knew, was wired directly into Renwick's brain. Absently, he wondered if this had been the cause of his nervous tic, or worse, his generally neurotic demeanour. A glass plate fixed into the end of the device turned slowly as the mechanical eye drew its focus, and deep inside, down in the dark depths of Renwick's skull, a pinprick of orange light wavered and blinked as information was transmitted to his visual cortex. All of this had been explained to Newbury, of course, some time ago, but it never failed to both fascinate and unnerve him, on every occasion he spent time in Renwick's company.

"The note. Yes. Lots to discuss." Renwick wheezed noisily and raised his fingers to his lips, as if expecting to find a cigarette smouldering there. He looked disappointed when he realised there was not. He looked back at Newbury. "Tea?"

"Yes..." He hesitated. "Well, actually – it depends. What exactly do you mean when you say 'tea'?"

Renwick laughed; a dry, crackling laugh. "Don't worry, old friend. I know you too well by now to offer up any of my usual concoctions. I have a tin of Earl Grey in the back room. Let me finish up in the workshop and I'll set a kettle on the stove."

Newbury grinned. "My thanks, Aldous."

The other man rubbed his hands on the front of his apron. He nodded. "I'll just lock up the shop. You go on, through here..." He turned and pushed on the concealed door, which swung open once again, and ushered Newbury through to the back room.

Newbury stepped over the threshold, taking care not to miss his footing on the step down. The large room on the other side of the door was cast in a dim half-light, the only illumination coming from a flaming Bunsen burner and a strange glass orb in one corner, which flickered with a violent storm of bright electrical currents. On the workbench in the middle of the room, a series of bulbous glass flasks and connecting rods had been set up, and an unusual pink liquid was bubbling over the Bunsen's flame, the vapours being siphoned off into another nearby flask. The dull thudding noise continued, and Newbury realised that the device responsible for the sound – a large iron box on the floor, with two protruding levers, a trail of thick cables and an unmarked dial – was a generator of some description, powering the electrical orb in the corner. Aside from this, other bizarre, assorted props were heaped in piles upon the floor or stacked haphazardly on the shelves that lined every inch of available wall space: unusual masks, vials filled with unaccountable specimens, strange African idols and assorted components from any number of mechanical devices. Newbury smiled. It reminded him somewhat of his Chelsea study, although here there was a far greater selection, in far greater disarray. Yet it was the other contents of Renwick's shelves that held the real attraction for him. Here, in the back of this small shop, was perhaps the finest collection of occult and esoteric literature ever amassed under one roof. The library far diminished Newbury's own, not insignificant, collection. He'd spent hours here before, browsing the shelves, amazed at the rare editions that Renwick had somehow been able to amass. There were copies of an ancient Hermetic treatise thought lost in the sacking of the library at Alexandria, rare Venetian tracts on summoning evil spirits, and details of arcane rituals attributed to the lost druidic tribes of Prussia. It was a delight to behold, and one of the best-kept secrets in the Empire. Unlike the more sedate tomes that lined the shelves in the front of the shop, of course, these exquisite volumes were not for sale. But, as Newbury had learned over the years, Renwick was a genial fellow, and for the right person asking the right question, he could be a marvellous repository of rare and unusual knowledge.

Renwick stepped through into the room and clicked the door shut behind him. He looked around absently for a moment, and then crossed the room, pushing past Newbury unceremoniously, and set to work putting a kettle on the small stove.

Newbury examined the back of the door, which was carved with all manner of intricate runes and wards. He recognised a number of them. The six-fingered hand in a circle was intended to prevent witches crossing the threshold. He shook his head. The room, like Renwick, was the embodiment of a contradiction. The juxtaposition of the progressive science – the generator, the electrical orb, the artificial eye – seemed to sit ill beside the more supernatural preoccupations that seemed to concern the man. Science and the occult. In truth, Newbury had no real notion of where one stopped and the other began. Clearly Renwick was intent on exploring that boundary, and judging by the protective wards he had chiselled into the doors, walls and floor, he was taking no risks, either.

Renwick set the kettle to boil, and then turned and waved Newbury in the direction of a chair, which was covered in a heaped pile of papers. "Take a seat, man. You may be here for some time."

Newbury smiled, and bending low, scooped the debris from the seat and placed it by the foot of the chair in a neat pile on the floor.

He lowered himself into the chair, dropping his coat over the back and resting his hat on the white porcelain head of a phrenology bust that sat on a low table beside him. He watched Renwick as the other man crossed to his still, used a pair of tongs to remove the flask of bubbling pink liquid from the heat, and poured a measure of the stuff into a blue coffee cup, before returning the vessel to the flame. He blew gently on the hot liquid, and then took a long draw, swallowing it down with a hearty gasp. He placed the empty cup on the workbench beside him, and turned to Newbury. "Right. Your screaming mummy."

Newbury chuckled. He had no idea what the pink concoction contained, but he was sure it had a large measure of alcohol in it, whatever else. He met Renwick's strange, glowing gaze. "So tell me, what have you found?"

Renwick's mechanical eye seemed to refocus on the Crown investigator. His other eye continued to twitch nervously. "I believe I know the identity of your mysterious dead man. A priest, who served the Pharaoh Thutmose I at Thebes, around fifteen hundred years before Christ."

"Go on."

"His name was Khemosiri, 'the black Osiris'. You do know the story of Osiris, don't you, Newbury?"

Newbury shrugged. "I have a rudimentary understanding of the myth. But go ahead – enlighten me." He sat back in the chair, intrigued, his fingers forming a steeple on his lap.

"Osiris was the king of the Land of the Dead. He stood in judgement over the dead, having supplanted the god Anubis as the overseer of the afterlife. To an Ancient Egyptian noble, the afterlife was everything: the chance to live forever beyond the physical world. Osiris was the god who straddled the two realms, who ultimately decided their fate.

He enabled their resurrection after mummification." Renwick paused as he collected his tongs and poured himself another measure of the pink liquid. He nursed the coffee cup in his hands as he continued. "Osiris was unique in the Egyptian pantheon, however. The myth tells of how he was murdered by his brother, Set, first drowned and then cut into thirteen pieces and scattered throughout Egypt. Osiris's wife, Isis, was able to find twelve of these parts, however, and with a singing spell she learned from her father she was able to effect a resurrection. The lovers enjoyed congress, in which their son, Horus, was conceived, and shortly after Osiris died once again and became king of the Land of the Dead."

"Fascinating. A resurrection spell. And so the mummy – Winthrop's mummy – was known as 'the black Osiris'?"

"I believe so, if it is indeed him. Khemosiri has long been considered apocryphal, a footnote in the story of Thutmose I; a cautionary tale, if you will, to ensure adherence to the core belief system of rebirth in the afterlife." Renwick crossed the room to one of his tall bookcases, removed a dusty cat's skull from where it was resting in front of a neat row of books, and pulled down a leather-bound volume. He flicked through it purposefully, and then, finding the page he was looking for, crossed the room and handed it to Newbury. "Here. This is the only contemporary reference to Khemosiri that survives."

Newbury examined the page. It was a copy of a long document written in hieratic script. The accompanying footnote explained it was the record of the trial of a priest, found in the tomb of an Egyptian noble at the turn of the nineteenth century. Newbury handed the book back to Renwick. "What does it say?"

"It basically sets out the case against one of Thutmose's priests, who is accused of blasphemous behaviour, for attempting to extend his life in the physical world and avoid the judgement of Osiris. It claims he had perfected an 'Osiris Ritual', a means by which to effect this longevity, but all records of the actual ritual are lost." Renwick shrugged. "It seems this particular priest wasn't a true believer in the eternal resurrection of the spirit. Either that or he didn't want to give up all his earthly possessions."

Newbury smiled. "So what happened? What makes you think there is any connection between this story and the mummy lying in Winthrop's dining room?"

"Ah... well that's due to the punishments that were enacted upon the priest, and the description you gave me of the casket. The document here lists the horrifying sequence of measures that were carried out to ensure that the priest suffered a very full and real death, in both the physical world and the afterlife. He was essentially obliterated from history." Renwick looked up at the sound of the kettle whistling on the stove. He set the book down on the arm of Newbury's chair and made his way over to where he'd laid out a teacup and strainer. He continued talking as he worked.

"First of all, the man was stripped of his true name, and all records of this name were purged, from his house, his family, and his temple. They even destroyed a royal stele that mentioned the priest by name. No stone was left unturned. Without a name, an Egyptian soul was not permitted to cross into the afterlife, you see. It was only after his death that others began to refer to the now nameless man as Khemosiri."

Renwick coughed loudly, fetched around for his pouch of tobacco – which he found amongst the flasks and vials on the workbench – and began rolling himself a cigarette. Then, after allowing the tea a sufficient time to brew, he handed Newbury his cup of Earl Grey, the cigarette drooping from the corner of his mouth. "Next he was sentenced to be mummified alive, his body preserved as a warning to those who may have been harbouring similar notions or persuasions."

Newbury shook his head. "You should see the expression on his face, Aldous. It's like nothing I've ever seen before. He must have suffered terribly."

"I don't doubt it." Renwick's face was grim. "Do you know what they did to people during the mummification process?"

"Yes, I'm quite well aware of the procedure." Newbury frowned. "I can imagine what they did to him. It's barbaric."

"Hmmm. Well, that wasn't the end of it. The list goes on. It was decreed that once the priest's name had been erased and the mummification process was complete, a curse was to be written upon the linen bandages that covered his body, and he was to be interred in a black and gold casket, which itself would be painted with wards and warnings. His tomb would then be hidden at an undisclosed location so that thieves would not accidentally stumble upon the cursed remains."

Newbury sat forward in his chair. "That matches the description of the mummy almost perfectly. I think you're right. I think you have our man. How the devil did you put your finger on it?"

Renwick grinned. His glass-fronted eye shimmered in the harsh electrical light of the orb. "A half-remembered tale, is all. Your letter provoked a memory. I found the book and, upon rereading the hieratic script, realised Khemosiri was your man."

"I wonder why Peterson didn't see it."

"What, at the *British Museum*! Newbury – as I mentioned, Khemosiri is a footnote, a reference in a long-forgotten document that most professionals would dismiss as naught but fiction. Only specialists such as you or I, with a deep interest in the occult, would place any value in such a story, and not for its historic significance, either."

Newbury looked doubtful. "What? You believe that Khemosiri really did find a means of extending life beyond the natural span of a man?"

Renwick laughed. "Of course not. I believe that *he* believed he had. And others believed him, too. The Pharaoh, of course, and the priests that committed him to such a terrible fate. But more than that. He was said to have a coterie of followers, others who subscribed to his beliefs, who aided him in his bizarre practices. When the military men purged his home, they found no records, no trace of the so-called 'Osiris Ritual'. No one knows for certain, but it's thought that his followers had secured his secrets, and that they were buried with him, hidden, somehow, inside his tomb. His followers planned to resurrect him, to give Khemosiri new life, just as the original Osiris had been brought back from the dead by his beloved Isis. But most of that is nothing but speculation and myth. We have no proof either way."

"Other than a corpse that proves that they did not achieve their goal."

Renwick laughed. "Quite so." He took a long draw on his cigarette, watching the smoke plume lazily around him as he exhaled. "That wasn't the point I was getting at, though."

Newbury nodded. "Indeed. I understood your reasoning. If there were others who believed in the ritual *then*, there may be others who believe in the ritual *now*."

Renwick's lips curled in a satisfied smile. "Exactly so. The man who killed Lord Winthrop may have been looking for the secrets of the ritual. I doubt very much that Winthrop himself had an understanding of what he'd found."

"No. He didn't." Newbury leaned back in the chair, resting his chin on his fist. It was impossible to second-guess Ashford's motives.

He'd spent five years living a half-life in St. Petersburg, kept alive by the machines that Dr. Fabian had installed inside his broken body. Had he turned? Was he working for the Russian government? Or had he spent the time looking for ways to regain the life he'd once had, turning to the occult in desperation? Perhaps he thought this "Osiris Ritual" would somehow restore his body to its former state. Only finding him and bringing him in would provide Newbury with the answers.

Newbury looked across at Renwick. "Do you know of anyone else who might have a notion of this link? Between Winthrop's mummy and the tale of Khemosiri, I mean."

Renwick looked thoughtful. He considered his answer for a moment. "No. I might have named you, if the circumstances had been different. But I can think of no other, in London, at least, who would have access to the necessary texts. It's not the sort of thing one would happen across in an academic journal." He paused, rapping his knuckles on the workbench. "You might consider discussing the matter with Wilfred Blake, one of the men who aided Lord Winthrop during the expedition. I doubt he'll give you anything new, but I understand he has an appetite for all things mystical."

Newbury raised an eyebrow. "Indeed?" That certainly shed a different light on the man he'd seen arguing with Winthrop during the unrolling party. Perhaps his ironclad alibi wasn't as secure as it had at first appeared to the Yard? He'd taken the liberty of obtaining Blake's address, along with those of the other members of the expedition, from Charles the previous evening. He'd been considering paying Blake a visit that afternoon, and it now appeared he had another good reason to do so. He downed the remains of his tea and leaned forward, placing the empty cup and saucer on the workbench. "Thank you, Aldous. I believe you've been of great service to me today."

The other man chuckled, sprinkling the ash from the end of his cigarette carelessly onto the floor. "Never any trouble, old man." He sighed. "There is one thing you could do for me, though."

"Name it."

"Can I see it?"

Newbury smirked. "I'm sure it can be arranged. Just as soon as Winthrop's funerary arrangements are finalised."

Renwick nodded in appreciation.

Newbury stood, collecting his coat and hat. On an afterthought, he turned towards Renwick. "What of Aubrey Knox?"

Renwick seemed to freeze on the spot. He turned slowly to offer Newbury a wary look. "What of him?"

"He casts a long shadow, is all."

Renwick looked somewhat relieved. "Knox is gone, Newbury. He's not mixed up in this. If he were, I'd smell it."

Newbury gave one short nod of acknowledgement. "Thank you once again, Aldous. I can find my own way out."

Renwick was already fumbling with his tobacco pouch, intent on rolling himself another cigarette. He didn't look up again as Newbury, bracing himself for the cold, clicked the inner door shut behind him and took his leave.

Chapter Thirteen

Arbury House, Regent's Park, was exactly the kind of respectable, middle-class address that Newbury expected a successful bachelor such as Wilfred Blake to keep. It was a large, austere building, a Georgian edifice: square, with tall sash windows and a feature entrance. It was, Newbury considered, a fine example of the less ostentatious architecture of a time that had now passed. These days, it was difficult to avoid the horrors of the neo-gothic, and one risked facing gargoyles and other grotesques at every turn.

Clearing his throat, Newbury examined the row of brass address plaques on the wall, and then rapped the knocker with three sharp bursts. He stepped back onto the street, awaiting the attention of the doorman.

To the casual passer-by, Arbury House had the air of a large townhouse about it, but on closer inspection it became apparent that the house was in fact divided into a number of smaller – but no less desirable – apartments. Wilfred Blake, Newbury gleaned from the address plaques, had taken up residence in apartment number six.

Newbury waited for a moment longer, and then stepped forward and rapped the knocker again. This time he called out. "Hello?" There was no response. "Hello?" Shrugging to himself, Newbury tried the handle. It turned. He pushed the door open, surprised by the weight of it, and stepped inside, clicking it carefully shut behind him.

If the exterior of the house had seemed impressive, the hallway proved even more so. The foyer was expansive and well lit by a series of large sash windows in the south wall. The afternoon light spilled through these in long, lazy shafts, picking out the dust motes that swirled chaotically in the air. The floor was tiled in black and white Minton, and a huge staircase curled up to the next floor, and beyond. It was startlingly quiet, save for the barely audible strains of someone playing a violin elsewhere in the building. There was no sign of any doorman.

Newbury searched around. He could see the stairway to the basement levels, and doors to apartments one to five. Blake's residence was obviously on the first floor. He took to the stairs, admiring the portraits that lined the wall as he climbed. The people represented there were obviously members of the owner's family, going back, he guessed, over a hundred years. Their baleful faces watched him as his footsteps rang out on the marble steps.

The first floor landing was a mirror image of the hallway below. The staircase continued up to a second floor, and a series of doors, all painted royal blue, suggested that the floor plan of the apartments on this level matched precisely those of the apartments beneath. Newbury crossed the landing towards the door marked with a brass number "6". A few feet from the door, however, he stopped short. From the angle of his approach he could see that the door had been left slightly ajar. Stepping carefully across the landing, walking on the balls of his feet to ensure that his footsteps were not heard, Newbury edged closer to the door. He stopped just before the threshold, hovering in the hallway. The door stood open by just a couple of inches, but it was enough to cause Newbury to hesitate. Why would Blake have left the door open in such a manner? More likely, an intruder wanted to ensure a quick getaway without the need to fumble with a lock. He put his head close to the opening and listened. There were sounds of someone moving around inside: papers being shuffled, drawers being opened.

What if someone had broken into Blake's apartment? Newbury realised he would have to tread carefully. He was unarmed and alone, and he hadn't told anyone where he was going that afternoon. If he found himself in a difficult spot, he'd only have his wits to get him out of it.

There was a gust of sharp, cold air from along the hallway, and Newbury stepped back from the door, glancing to his left. Along the landing, past the row of doors that led to the other apartments on this floor, was a large window. This window, he assumed, looked out over the back of the house and the streets below. The netting that covered the window was billowing luxuriously in the breeze. Someone had lifted the sash.

Taking care not to make any sounds, Newbury walked to the end of the landing and examined the window frame and ledge, holding the netting back from the frame with his right hand. It was far too cold for someone to have opened the window for air. He ran his other hand around the frame, looking for signs that it may have been forced from the outside. It didn't appear to have been forced, and the catch was perfectly intact.

Holding on to his hat so as not to lose it to a sudden gust, Newbury leaned out over the window ledge. To his surprise, the drop on the other side was only a few feet, terminating on a small roof terrace that must have been accessible from one or more of the apartments themselves. Beyond that, the building was buttressed by a number of other, single-storey buildings, with only a network of thin alleyways between them. If someone planned to use this window as an escape route – or, indeed, a makeshift entrance – it would not have been difficult to get away over the rooftops and from there, down into the relative anonymity of the backstreets of Regent's Park. He considered climbing down to take a better look. He glanced back in the direction of Blake's apartment. He was conscious of the fact that there was still someone poking around inside, and it wouldn't do to let them get away unchallenged. The window could wait. The likelihood was that whoever was in the apartment – assuming it wasn't Blake himself – was responsible for opening the window anyway.

Newbury crept back to the door to apartment number six. Steeling himself, he gently pushed on the open door, hoping that the creak of the hinges wouldn't betray his presence to the person inside. He realised he was holding his breath as he tried not to make a sound. The door caught a little on the deep pile of the wine-coloured carpet on the other side, but Newbury was able to side-step into the hallway beyond.

The apartment appeared to be well furnished and clean. The hallway comprised a long corridor, with three doors stemming off it and a small table just behind the door, its surface covered with a scattering of unopened letters. The first thing that struck Newbury, however, was the rank stench. An all-pervasive odour of rotten meat and decay filled the hallway, assaulting his nostrils and causing bile to rise in his throat. He knew immediately the source of that smell. Ashford. He must be the one in the other room.

Newbury edged along the hallway, staying close to the wall. He could see into the room at the far end of the corridor, which appeared to be a kitchen. He paused, listening for sounds of movement. Just as before, it was clear that someone was rifling through Blake's belongings, in the room just behind where Newbury was standing, his back to the wall. It must have been the drawing room.

Newbury moved across the hall, switching sides so that he was facing the door into the drawing room, his back protectively to the wall on the other side. He shuffled a little closer, until he could see through the open doorway into the room beyond. From the angle he'd achieved, he had a fairly good view of the back half of the room. There was a large, cold fireplace, stark in its simplicity, a large mirror in a gilt frame over the hearth, a busy mantelpiece covered in photographs and statuettes, and the corpse of Wilfred Blake, sprawled messily on the floor. Newbury almost gasped aloud. Blake was still dressed in his evening wear, a black suit and white shirt. But the white shirt was spattered with a spray of dark, arterial blood, turning it a dirty crimson. More of it had pooled on the floor beneath his head, matting the back of his hair. His face was turned so that Newbury could see the gaping, silent mouth and the milky eyes which had rolled back in their sockets. His throat had been cut, roughly, with a blunt blade. His body was surrounded by scattered papers and Ancient Egyptian artefacts which had been cast unceremoniously to the floor during the killer's frantic search. This time, Newbury mused, there hadn't been time for ceremony. Blake, unlike Winthrop, hadn't even been given that honour.

Newbury felt his ire rising. The person on the other side of the wall – Ashford, he was sure – was pacing back and forth. Newbury knew from his brief encounter with Ashford that he was a big powerhouse of a man, but Newbury had the element of surprise. He hoped that would be enough. He had no idea what Dr. Fabian may have done to upgrade Ashford's rebuilt body, but he was certain he was about to find out.

Quietly, Newbury removed his hat, placing it on the floor beside him. He flexed his neck and shoulder muscles. Then, before he allowed himself time to reconsider, he pushed away from the wall, propelling himself forward into the drawing room to face Ashford, and, quite possibly, the fight of his life.

Chapter Fourteen

The streets of Soho were, as was typical at this time in the afternoon, bustling with people, as Veronica made her way from the bus stop towards the Archibald Theatre. She was dressed in a smart mauve jacket, with matching culottes and a white blouse. Her hair was pinned back beneath a small mauve hat that completed her professional ensemble. She'd come directly from the home of Miss Rebecca Irlam, the most recent of the missing girls, where she'd spent the last two hours consoling the girl's mother and digging around for any information that may help to put her on the trail of the girl's abductor. As anticipated, the details were sketchy, but everything the girl's mother had told her matched what was written in the police report, of which Veronica had managed to obtain a copy from one of Sir Charles's young protégés. Sometimes, being an attractive young woman had its advantages.

The girl had attended the performance of "The Mysterious Alfonso" the previous evening, where, with her fiancé, she had taken a seat in the stalls and enjoyed the ensuing show. The last anyone had seen of her was when she had volunteered for the disappearing act at the end of the show, when she had made her way up onto the stage before the large, gathered audience, and been vanished away by the illusionist. The pattern was exactly the same as that witnessed by Veronica and Newbury earlier in the week. Yet something was fundamentally different. This time the girl had not made it home at the end of the performance. Her family and fiancé had searched frantically for her in the hours that followed, but there was no sign of her whatsoever. The police had been called and Alfonso had been taken away for questioning, but a cursory search of the theatre had thrown up no leads. Alfonso himself had assured the men at the Yard that he had seen the girl into a hansom cab – much as he had assured Veronica and Newbury earlier in the week – and without evidence he could not be held accountable.

Veronica, however, felt differently about the matter. For some time now she had suspected that there was a connection between the events at the theatre, and not only the disappearance of Miss Rebecca Irlam, but a string of girls throughout the whole of the Home Counties where Alfonso had toured with his illusionist show.

Veronica had come to Soho alone, expressly against the wishes of Sir Maurice. She knew she was playing a dangerous game, that she risked exposing the truth about her situation. She found herself wishing – as she did most days – that she were able to reveal the truth to Sir Maurice: that she, herself, was also an agent of Her Majesty Queen Victoria, and that she was quite capable of managing a case of her own. She was fully aware of the risks, and saw nothing unduly dangerous about her choosing to tackle Alfonso on her own. If he proved difficult, she had the wherewithal to incapacitate him and call for the police.

Telling all of this to Sir Maurice, of course, was out of the question. Her Majesty had specifically forbidden it, and besides, she was already abusing her duty to the Crown. She could hardly claim that she had fulfilled her primary mission, of late: to keep a watchful eye on Sir Maurice. She had been entirely absorbed in the case of the missing girls. Something about the case, something about the manner in which the girls had been plucked from their daily lives, seemed to strike a chord with her. It made her blood boil.

Perhaps, in some way, it reminded her of her sister, Amelia, who had been wrenched away from the family home at a crucial age, only to be deposited in a series of increasingly bleak sanatoriums, where she had been left to suffer in isolation. Perhaps that was the root of her obsession with the case. Nevertheless, Veronica knew that the police were getting nowhere, and whilst Sir Charles was tied up with the Winthrop situation, Sir Maurice aiding him, all she could do was press on. She hoped to bring the matter to a conclusion before any more girls found themselves "disappeared away" by the errant magician. It pained her to lie to Newbury, of course, and she recognised that it drove a wedge between them, a barrier that prevented them from ever being truly honest with one another, but she could see no other satisfactory recourse. One day, she knew, the truth would come out, and she only hoped that it would not result in Sir Maurice losing all trust in her, or pushing her away. She couldn't bear that. She cared for him too much. She was, she reminded herself, only acting in his best interest – in the best interest of the Empire, no less – but in the back of her mind she knew, honestly, that Sir Maurice would not see it that way. It was a betrayal. A betrayal of the most gentle kind, but a betrayal nonetheless. She tried to put it out of mind.

She arrived at the theatre. It was clear immediately that the place was closed. A number of bills had been pasted on the windows, informing any potential theatregoers that the evening performance had been cancelled. Inside, the lights in the lobby appeared to have been extinguished. Frowning, Veronica tested the door. To her surprise, it was open. Glancing from side to side, Veronica crossed into the dimness of the foyer. There was no sign of the commissionaire. No sign, either, of any people manning the kiosks or ticket booths that ran around the edges of the lobby. Like the rest of the now-dilapidated theatre, the lobby had once been grand, a reception hall worthy of receiving even the most auspicious of visitors. The floor was a stunning white marble, although it was now covered in a patina of dust and dirt, caused by the tread of innumerable boots. Tall Corinthian-style columns stood proud on either side of the archways that led through to the theatre proper. The ticket booths on Veronica's left were now cast in darkness, with shutters pulled low to obscure the glass partitions. To her right, a number of small kiosks had been set up to sell food and drinks to the hungry patrons, but were presently silent, like small, abandoned islands in the murky light.

Veronica drew a deep breath. She almost turned on her heel and left, assuming the theatre to be empty, but then, from somewhere inside the auditorium, she heard a number of faint clanging sounds. She still hoped to find and confront Alfonso before the day was out for, if he too had somehow disappeared, the trail would grow cold.

Quietly, so as not to disturb whoever was at work in the main theatre, Veronica approached the entrance to the stalls, sweeping aside the heavy velvet drape and peering into the dimly lit arena on the other side. The darkness, Veronica thought, had a kind of texture to it, an oppressive air. The empty stalls and seats were like a sea that stretched out before her, unmoving. She gave an involuntary shiver. The only sign of life in the entire auditorium was a man – Alfonso – who stood on the stage, spot-lit by the harsh glow of an electric lamp. He had a frustrated look on his face, as he tried, over and over, to insert a sword blade into his upturned hat. Clearly, he was practising a new illusion for his act.

Veronica stood in the shadows at the back of the hall, observing what was happening on the stage. She realised she was holding her breath. She studied Alfonso as he made another attempt. His top hat had been upended on a small, round table that rested on the stage. She could see clearly between the three wooden legs. There appeared to be nothing underneath it, although Veronica fully expected the table to be rigged in some way. Alfonso raised a sword, placed the point of it inside the brim of the hat, and gave a sharp thrust, downwards. This time it appeared to work. The blade slipped down inside the hat until only the hilt was standing proud, still held firmly in Alfonso's right hand. The blade itself, however, was nowhere to be seen. As far as Veronica could see, it had not pierced the tabletop. She could see nothing between the legs of the small table. It was rather a marvellous illusion, Veronica considered, and whether it was effected with a collapsible blade, or, as she had at first suspected, a simple trick of the light, she could not say. Most likely, the blade had passed through a notch in the table, and was simply not visible from the angle in which the audience were able to view the stage.

Alfonso stepped back and rubbed his hand across his chin, thoughtfully regarding his handiwork. He smiled. Veronica took this as her cue to approach. Making no attempt to hide her presence, she descended the stairs at the back of the hall and passed along one of the aisles, her boots echoing loudly on the wooden steps. Alfonso turned to watch her approach, a surprised look on his face. He clearly wasn't expecting any visitors. Veronica was a picture of professionalism. "Good afternoon, Mr. Alfonso. My name is Miss Veronica Hobbes. You may recall we met earlier in the week?"

Alfonso narrowed his eyes and offered her a disdainful look. "Indeed. I recall your visit. But Miss Hobbes, unfortunately it seems that this evening you have wasted a trip. The theatre is closed. I fear I must ask you to leave."

Veronica smiled. "Ah, well. I'm afraid it's not quite as simple as all that. I have some further questions for you, regarding Miss Rebecca Irlam."

"Who?" Alfonso furrowed his brow. Then, as if realisation had suddenly dawned on him, he nodded in acknowledgement. "Ah, yes, the girl who went missing from the theatre on her way home last night. A sad affair. I've already given all the information I have to the police." He waved his hand dismissively. "Now, I'm sure you'll understand that I'm a busy man. If I can ask you to be on your way..." He turned away from her, examining the hilt of the sword, which was still protruding from the brim of the hat on the table.

Veronica stepped closer to the stage. Her eyes were hard, and they gleamed in the harsh electric light, as she mounted the small set of steps that led to the platform where Alfonso was standing. She hadn't noticed on her previous visit how high the stage itself was raised from the floor. She regarded the magician. The set of her jaw was firm and unyielding. Her blood was up. "Mr. Alfonso. For what reason has the show been cancelled this evening? I should have imagined it represents a great deal of lost revenue. Surely you are not ending your run at the Archibald prematurely? It appears to have been a magnificent success."

Alfonso looked sheepish. "Something like that," he muttered under his breath. Veronica stepped forward, closer to him now. "Look, Miss Hobbes, I assure you that the disappearance of this woman has nothing to do with me!" He was flustered now.

"Ah, so you *didn't* make her vanish on stage last night, then?"

He was growing increasingly agitated. "Not *that* disappearance. The one that happened later, after she had already left the theatre."

"It sounds like you're splitting hairs to me." Veronica put her hand on her hip. "Mr. Alfonso – or whatever your real name is – I suggest that quite the opposite is true. That you had everything to do with the disappearance of Miss Rebecca Irlam, as well as any number of other young women, such as Miss Cordelia Fletcher, Miss Jane Eyles, or, indeed, Miss Sophia Caithness. Girls you spirited away from towns all over the Home Counties before bringing your illusionist show to the capital. Can we forgo the pretence now, Mr. Alfonso?"

Alfonso looked shaken. He stepped back, edging away from Veronica. "Look, I really must ask you to leave now. I'm afraid I cannot help you with your enquiries." It was clear to Veronica that she had him cornered. The guilt was evident in his eyes, written in the signs of panic that had suddenly gripped him. "But surely, you were here just the other evening, Miss Hobbes? You saw a young lady disappear on stage and enquired of her wellbeing after the performance. Did she not make it home safe and well?"

Veronica smiled. "Yes, and that's the clever part, isn't it? They don't all disappear. That would be far too obvious, and you are much cleverer than that. Any number of young women have taken part in your disappearing act, whisked away before a large audience. And many of them you set free, to minimise suspicion." She paused. "What is it that you are looking for? What makes you choose one girl as a victim, over another?"

Alfonso glanced nervously from side to side, unsure how to respond. He stepped backwards, stumbling as the back of his knee encountered the large wooden rack of swords that had been placed on the stage as part of his act. He jumped as the rack clattered noisily to the floor. He glanced down at the mess around his feet. Then, realising that his options were swiftly diminishing, he reached down for one of the swords and came up again in a crouching position. Without hesitation, he swung the sword deftly in Veronica's direction.

Veronica moved quickly. She'd been trained for this sort of situation. She leapt backwards, away from the tip of the blade, as it swept past her in a wide arc, narrowly missing her breast. Alfonso grinned. He stabbed forward, and Veronica twisted away, causing his thrust to fall short. It was immediately clear to her that Alfonso was no brawler. He was lacking the finesse, the confidence. She stepped forward, grasping hold of Alfonso's outstretched wrist with her right hand, twisting it hard and causing him to yelp and release the sword, which clattered loudly to the floor. With her left hand, she jabbed out, striking him sharply on the chin. He staggered backwards, but Veronica, still retaining a grip on his sword arm, did not allow him to push away, returning for another quick jab to his face. By now, panic had entirely gripped the magician, and he must have realised he was fighting for his life. If Veronica was able to prove his connection to the missing girls – of which she had no doubt – Alfonso would surely swing from a taut noose.

Alfonso kicked out hard at Veronica's ankles, attempting to unbalance her. The blow struck home, but Veronica was too deft on her feet to tumble. She danced away, releasing her grip on his arm and wincing at the smiting pain of the blow. She kept her eye on Alfonso, trying to judge his next move. A change had come over him. He looked desperate, animalistic, even. His mouth was set in a grim sneer, his dark eyes seemingly boring holes right to the back of her skull as they met each other's glare. Shuddering, Veronica skipped forward and aimed a blow at the man's chin. She was fast, and she struck home, not giving him any chance to respond. His head twisted awkwardly to one side with the force of the impact. Blood was trickling down his chin from a split lip.

Veronica stepped back. She knew she needed to bring him down quickly, incapacitate him so that she could call for the police. Alfonso, however, was not giving up easily. He was like a cornered bear, and he lashed out, his bony fingers clawing at her face. She felt his nails biting painfully into her cheek, and she gasped as he raked them across her face, drawing bloody welts. Drawing ragged breath, she battered his arms away and kicked out at him in an attempt to maintain some distance. If she let him in too close, she feared he may manage to overbear her. She caught him forcefully in the upper thigh and he fell back, stooping low and cursing loudly. "You filthy whore!"

Veronica rushed him as he was still bent low from the blow to his leg. She drove her fist hard into his gut. He creased, choking as the wind was driven out of him, doubling over at the waist. He clutched at his belly. Veronica saw her chance. She clutched at the straggly hair at the back of his head and brought her knee up, connecting resoundingly with his face. His nose burst with a sickening crunch, spreading a fountain of dark, red blood into the air and staining her culottes. Alfonso gave a pitiful wail and sank to the floor. He was panting, spitting blood, pawing at his broken face. Veronica stepped back, looking down at the sorrowful wretch. Alfonso looked up at her. He was giggling like a lunatic.

"What? What is it?" Veronica was disconcerted by the sudden outburst. There was no reply, other than more of the insane laughter. She could only conclude that his mind had finally broken under the strain. She cast around, looking for a length of rope or fabric she could use to bind him whilst she fetched the police. She stepped towards the round table at the centre of the stage, where Alfonso's upturned hat and sword were still in situ. The pitch of the man's bizarre giggling increased. The noise was like insects crawling up and down her spine; like nails being dragged across a dry blackboard. She gave an involuntary shudder. Still, she had him, finally, and as soon as she had bound him and arranged for the police to detain him, it would be over. No more missing girls.

She examined the hat, glancing back at Alfonso to ensure that he hadn't decided to risk his chance to escape whilst her back was turned. He was still clutching at his bleeding face, but he glowered back at her, almost expectantly. She had the feeling she was somehow missing something. Then, with one sudden, unexpected movement, he flung himself to the right, slamming the heel of his hand down hard against the wooden stage. He must have hit a pressure paddle, for, to Veronica's astonishment, the ground beneath her feet suddenly gave way, and before she could react – before she could even fling her arms out to brace herself – she was falling.

She landed – hard – feeling her legs give way beneath her. The hatch in the stage through which she had fallen clicked tightly shut above her, throwing her into impenetrable darkness. She could still hear Alfonso's mad laughter echoing in the auditorium above. Veronica tested the space around her. She was encased within some kind of casket or coffin-shaped box. It was made of rough, untreated wood, and it splintered against her palms as she slapped at the sides of it, frustrated and scared. She thrashed out in every direction, trying to find some means of escape. But the box would not give.

She kicked, testing the floor, and she noticed that there was something at her feet. She reached down, as best she could in the confined space. Cloth. Bundles of heavy cloth. She frowned in the darkness. And then, with rising panic, she realised what they were: the rags had been soaked with chloroform. There was no mistaking the sickly-sweet perfume of the drug. She didn't have long before the fumes would overwhelm her.

Something creaked beneath the box, and Veronica felt it judder. She fell awkwardly to one side. The box began to move. She could feel it rolling downwards, further underground. It must have been on castors, triggered by the introduction of her weight. This was clearly the mechanism that Alfonso had used to cause the women to disappear during his act. The chloroform explained why the girls who were later freed were left dazed and disorientated. And the girls who weren't freed... Veronica tried not to think of that.

She had no idea what to do. She was trapped beneath the stage, trapped in a narrow wooden box that was creeping inexorably towards an unknown destination, where Alfonso was likely waiting for her, his motives still unclear. This time, there was no one to save her. She cursed herself for not listening to Sir Maurice. Nobody knew she was there. She had to face facts. Her time was running out. If she didn't find a way out soon, she'd likely die in the casket, or worse. She called out, knowing it was a useless endeavour. The only person there to hear her was her captor.

The floral scent of the chloroform became overbearing. Veronica felt her senses fogging. She knew she had to fight it, knew that whatever happened, she couldn't allow herself to be overcome. She had no idea what Alfonso may have in store for her if she did. She gasped for breath. But her fate, under the circumstances, was inevitable. The casket continued its slow descent.

Soon, darkness overcame her.

Chapter Fifteen

Newbury barrelled around the corner of Blake's drawing room, fully expecting to be confronted by a large man, clad in a thick black cloak, rifling through Blake's belongings. What he actually found, however, was a younger, more diminutive fellow, dressed in a brown corduroy jacket and slacks. The other man turned, startled, when he heard Newbury burst into the room.

"Ah! Sir Maurice! Thank goodness you're here. I was about to send for the police."

"Purefoy! What the devil..." Newbury lowered his guard, but only fractionally. He glanced at the corpse on the floor, spattered in blood, and then back at the young reporter.

Purefoy looked sheepish. "I... I can explain!"

Newbury regarded him. Could it really be that this young man was mixed up in these murders? He thought it unlikely. But Newbury had now found Purefoy hovering at the scene of two of the crimes. What was his connection to the dead men? Newbury couldn't, at this stage, discount his involvement. He hoped it was only a journalist's instinct that had led the reporter to the murder scenes. There were questions that needed answers. "Mr. Purefoy, this is the second time I've encountered you in less than salubrious situations. I think it is time we had another of our little discussions." Purefoy nodded, a serious expression on his face. "So, tell me – how do you come to be in the apartment of a murdered man, searching through his belongings in such a manner?"

Purefoy dropped the sheaf of papers he was holding onto the rosewood writing desk that stood against the far wall, and crossed the room, coming to stand before Newbury. Blake's belongings were scattered everywhere: everything from fine antiquities to old editions of *The Times*.

"Did you make this mess?"

"No! Not at all. It was like this when I entered the apartment. I found the place in this terrible mess. The killer was evidently searching for something, just like he had been at Lord Winthrop's place."

Newbury sighed. "Hmmm. Let's just slow down a little, before you jump to that kind of conclusion."

"What conclusion?" Purefoy looked a little bemused.

"That the person who murdered Lord Winthrop is the same person responsible for... this." He grimaced as he glanced down at Blake's body, on the hearth before the fireplace just a few feet from where he was standing. He cleared his throat, a thoughtful look in his eyes. "So, tell me, what was the purpose of your visit?"

"I came to interview Wilfred Blake – about the expedition, you understand. And Winthrop's murder. I wanted to see if he had any comments. If he felt his own life might have been in danger..." He trailed off as he realised the weight of his own words. He met Newbury's unwavering gaze. He sighed. "To be truthful, Sir Maurice, I hoped to discover whether Mr. Blake had any real notion of what had happened to Lord Winthrop."

Newbury couldn't help but smile. Perhaps he had been right about the boy, perhaps he did have the necessary instincts to make it as an agent of the Crown. He resolved to find out. "So, carry on."

"Well, I arrived around ten minutes ago. I had Blake's address from the offices of *The Times*. We'd interviewed him before, in relation to the Theban expedition. I made my way here by ground train from Westminster, and approached the building in plain view. Finding there was no commissionaire on the door, and that the door was open, I entered and made my way to Blake's apartment. Until that point I had no reason to suspect that anything was wrong." He paused for breath. The story was spilling out of him at a remarkable rate, and Newbury had to pay close attention to decipher the stream of gabbled words. "When I got here the door was slightly ajar. I knocked, but received no reply. I hesitated on the threshold, trying to discern the best course of action. It was then that I became aware of a banging sound from somewhere inside. I pushed on the door, and to my surprise a large chap, whose face was obscured by a thick black cloak, came charging out of the apartment, slammed into me, knocked me to the floor and hurtled away down the landing. I called out, but he didn't stop, and a moment later he slipped out through that open window and onto the rooftop beyond."

Newbury noticed that Purefoy was holding his right arm awkwardly by his side. If his story was to be trusted then he must have been hurt in the fall, when Ashford had pushed him to the ground. "So, what, didn't you think of following him, or calling for the neighbours?"

Purefoy didn't know where to look. "I..." Newbury could tell he was embarrassed to speak the truth. "I fear my reporter's instinct overtook me. That, and the fact I was concerned for Mr. Blake's wellbeing. I pushed my way into the apartment and found him, like this." He indicated Blake's corpse. "It was a shock. I'll admit that much."

Newbury nodded thoughtfully. "Did you touch the body?"

Purefoy shook his head resolutely. "No. Not at all. I even started out to find the police. But then I got to thinking. Who was the chap in the black cloak, and what was it exactly that he'd been looking for? I was taking a look through the items he'd strewn around the place when you burst in a few moments ago."

Newbury sighed. It sounded like a believable tale, and his instinct was to trust the young reporter. Nevertheless, he couldn't discount the potential that Purefoy was somehow involved.

Purefoy filled the silence that had grown between them. "So, Sir Maurice, do you have any understanding of who that man could have been? The man in the cloak, I mean?"

Newbury nodded. "I do. I do indeed." Purefoy looked at him expectantly. "His name is William Ashford," Newbury said. "And he's a dangerous man."

"A foreign agent?"

Newbury frowned. "You could say that." His voice was grim.

"And what of the stench? He carries a rank odour if ever I encountered one."

"Ashford is... not the man he once was," was all Newbury offered in reply. In truth, he still had no real notion of where the foul smell originated. He presumed it must have something to do with the dubious work that Dr. Fabian had carried out on the man.

Purefoy looked curious. "What did he want, with Winthrop and Blake? What is he looking for?"

Newbury was unsure how much to tell him. He hadn't yet decided to what degree the reporter was involved in the murders, and besides, for all Newbury's theorising, much of his information was nothing but supposition. "Something to do with the expedition. Something they found. It's all connected with that screaming mummy we saw back at Winthrop's party. There were secrets buried with that ancient priest. Secrets that Ashford appears anxious to get his hands on."

Purefoy nodded. "So what next?"

Newbury glanced down at the contorted cadaver on the floor. "Next we examine the body."

†

"Turn up that gas jet over there, Purefoy. It's too dark in here. Oh, and see if you can find some brandy."

Purefoy looked perplexed. "Do you intend to use it to clean the wound?"

Newbury looked up from the body. His face was serious. "No. I intend to drink it." Purefoy chuckled and set about his tasks.

Newbury was kneeling by the corpse. It was a bloody mess. The man's throat had been entirely gouged out, ripped open with a blunt instrument, such as an old penknife or letter-opener. It was different from Winthrop's murder, executed with less finesse, but just as effective. Newbury was convinced that whoever had committed the murder had a hand in both deaths. The motivation was clearly the same: the victims had something the killer wanted.

He walked through what he supposed had happened in his mind's eye. Winthrop had been grabbed from behind, his throat slashed rudely from right to left. His body had been dumped unceremoniously on the floor and left there to bleed out on the oil cloth. His formerly white dress shirt was now stained a deep crimson, and his eyes stared blankly at the ceiling, as if searching for an absent god. They were developing a milky, glazed appearance, and Newbury, shuddering, reached over and closed the lids with his fingertips. It was a dubious kind of rest, but Newbury could not stand the cold, accusing glare any longer. He couldn't help thinking that he should have somehow warned the man earlier. He resolved to take it up with Charles. The other members of the expedition had to be protected.

Newbury rocked back on his haunches. The problem, he mused, was not in identifying the nature of the killer, for he was already convinced that Ashford was the culprit, but in tracking the man. Ashford knew how to disappear. That much was clear to Newbury. His quarry had spent years living undercover in one of the most dangerous cities in the world. An agent could not live through an experience like that without gleaning at least a handful of new tricks. Even putting that to one side, Ashford had once been an agent for the British Crown, and as such, he had received at least the same measure of training as Newbury himself. If Ashford chose not to show his hand, Newbury knew that he could be in for a very long game of cat and mouse indeed.

He glanced over his shoulder, looking to the door. He hoped that brandy would come soon. His skin was starting to crawl and he was beginning to sweat: symptoms, he knew, of his addiction. Hopefully, the alcohol would help to take the edge off, for a short while, at least. He listened out for Purefoy. He couldn't hear the boy. For a moment he almost panicked, thinking that he may have allowed Purefoy the perfect opportunity to slip away, but a moment later the reporter reappeared from the hallway, bearing a large tumbler and a wide grin. "Here you are, sir. I hope that helps take the edge off." Newbury looked at him suspiciously. *He couldn't possibly know... could he?* Newbury accepted the glass, regardless. He didn't have time to concern himself with the matter.

Purefoy leaned forward, resting his hands on his knees and examining the corpse with inexpert eyes. "So, what of the body?"

Newbury followed his gaze. He could see no real harm in making Purefoy aware of the details. He'd given the young man plenty of opportunities to trip himself up, and so far he had only managed to reward Newbury's faith in him. He was perceptive and inquisitive, and could prove to be a great asset in helping to bring Ashford to justice. He continued to stare at the body whilst he talked. "Assuming that none of this is going to end up in the morning edition..." He paused, waiting for Purefoy to nod his agreement before continuing. He indicated Blake's devastated throat. "His throat has been cut from behind, the perpetrator using his left hand to slash from right to left. It was a brutal murder, and the killer showed no respect for his victim. Nevertheless, it was an efficient execution. Whoever it was wanted Blake dead, and he achieved that goal swiftly and without emotion. It's not unlike Lord Winthrop's death, in many respects, aside from the ceremony. The killer had time to place Winthrop's body where it would have maximum effect – a calling card, if you will. Here, he had no such luxury and was forced to leave Blake's body where it fell." He took a long draw of his brandy, feeling the warmth of it spreading, most welcome, throughout his body. "I don't believe the killer came here specifically to murder Blake. I think Blake is almost irrelevant to the equation. The killer – Ashford – wanted something that Blake had, and Blake, unfortunately, just found himself in the way."

Purefoy looked taken aback. "My God..."

Newbury empathised with the sentiment. "Quite. Quite so."

Newbury sunk another measure of his brandy, and then placed the empty glass on the mantelpiece. He glanced around. Items were strewn all over the place. He didn't know where to start. If Purefoy's testimony was to be believed, the reporter had disturbed Ashford mid-search, and whatever he was trying to find could still be there, buried somewhere under the mess.

He leaned on the fire surround, considering his next move. The grate beneath was cold, well stocked with coal. But something about it struck a sharp note of discord. There! Buried in the coals to the far right of the grate was something small and metallic. He stooped closer to see. It was long and thin, the pommel and guard of a small silver blade. Purefoy moved round to stand beside him. "What is it?"

Newbury smiled. "The murder weapon." He reached into his breast pocket and produced a white, monogrammed handkerchief. "The killer has abandoned the knife in the fireplace."

Purefoy crouched down to take a closer look. "Yes. Yes, you're right!"

Newbury pinched the handkerchief between his fingers and reached down, withdrawing the blade from where it jutted inconspicuously between the coals. It was covered in blood and gritty, black dust. It was about five inches long, from its tip to its hilt, and fashioned from fine silver. Newbury turned it over in his hand and regarded it carefully. "It's an antique. A letter-opener." He glanced over at Blake's desk, but the leather writing surface was so buried in Ashford's mess that he was unable to tell if that was where it had come from. "I think Ashford must have simply grabbed the first thing to hand. It shows incredible resourcefulness. Not as though that's any consolation for poor old Blake, here."

"Do you think the police will find fingerprints? Something to help us confirm the identity of the killer?"

Newbury shrugged. "I don't suppose we will, no. Ashford's too clever for that. And besides, he knows we're on to him. He'll have to try a different tactic, now. Fingerprints won't help us find him." Newbury looked thoughtful. "I wonder where he was going when he bolted through that window? Those rooftops could lead him anywhere."

"Assuming he found what he wanted, of course."

Newbury turned towards Purefoy. "How so?"

Purefoy gestured around the room, both of his arms outstretched. "Look at this place. He's turned the apartment upside-down looking for... whatever it is that you think he's looking for. It could be I disturbed him before he found what he wanted." He shrugged. "I don't know. Perhaps he'll return when he thinks it's safe. It depends very much on how much he needs what was here. And, judging by the state of Blake, I'd say it seemed as if he needed it very much."

Newbury was impressed. "Good thinking, Purefoy. It's certainly a possibility." Newbury bent low and placed the letter-opener neatly on the floor beside the body. He folded his handkerchief – which was now filthy with blood and coal – away into his trouser pocket. It wouldn't do to leave the murder weapon at the scene, wrapped in one of his personal, monogrammed items. Not that he feared the police would in any way consider him a suspect, but he didn't want to set them accidentally down the wrong path. He brushed himself down. "Come on, Purefoy. There's little else we can do here. We need to inform the police. Sir Charles and his men will be here like a shot." He turned and left the room, Purefoy following closely behind.

†

On the landing, Newbury stopped and looked back over his shoulder to ensure the reporter was following. "Before we take our leave I want to have a look at that rooftop, to see if Ashford left any traces behind in his haste." He ushered Purefoy out of the apartment and then clicked the door shut behind him, testing it to ensure it was secure. He didn't want any of the neighbours accidentally stumbling across such a terrible scene.

At the end of the landing, the window was open, just as Newbury had left it. A cold breeze was gusting in from outside. He could hear the sounds of distant traffic: horses, ground trains and carriages, all clattering along the busy thoroughfares of the city. Newbury brushed the netting aside and leaned out, taking another measure of the drop to the rooftop below.

"Here, hold this." Newbury slipped out of his topcoat and handed it to the reporter. Then, grasping hold of the edges of the wooden frame, he placed his knee on the windowsill and hauled himself up, propelling himself through the opening and down to the roof below. He landed in a squat. Rising to his full height, he looked back to see Purefoy following suit. His topcoat was draped over the window frame. Newbury chuckled to himself. The young man was incorrigible. He supposed the coat would be lost, now, and he'd have to explain to Charles why it had been left behind at the scene. Thankfully, Newbury knew many of the inspectors at the Yard, and they in turn were aware of the services he had provided over the years in helping to bring a variety of criminals to justice. Newbury regularly left traces of his presence behind him at crime scenes, but a mixture of police incompetence and Newbury's reputation meant that such matters were disregarded and he was seen as being above suspicion.

The light was fading now, and a wispy mist was beginning to settle on the rooftops. The moon was peeking out behind grey clouds: a bright, shimmering orb, hung low in the sky like a curious Chinese lantern. In the distance, airships soared lazily over the city. It was early evening, and soon enough the night would draw in. Newbury, feeling the bite of the cold, looked around, trying to spot any trace of the rogue agent. The roof terrace stretched away in both directions. It had once been grand, affording an admirable view of the urban spread of the capital, but it was clearly now in disuse. A row of large plant pots abutted the wall, the flowers inside them now choked by weeds and fumes from the steam engines that traversed the streets below. A small rail ran around the outer edges of the terrace, there, Newbury presumed, to prevent people from accidentally tumbling to their deaths. Two old wooden chairs, rotten through, had been abandoned in one corner, surrounded by the spent ends of expensive cigarettes that had been cast haphazardly from the window above. They were scattered, too, across the paving stones upon which Newbury now stood. There were no signs that the terrace was ever used by the current inhabitants of the house.

Newbury, stooping low, examined the ground beneath the window, near to where he had landed. In the dusty mulch there was a clear footprint, where a large, booted foot had made an impression as its owner had dropped heavily from above.

Newbury moved to one side to allow Purefoy to see. He pointed to the boot print. "There, look. It's a fresh print. Someone definitely jumped down from this window, earlier this afternoon." He glanced surreptitiously at the reporter's shoes, just to be sure of his earlier judgement. Purefoy was wearing smart brogues, and his feet were at least two sizes smaller than those of the man who had left the print. Newbury smiled. Ashford, then. He had definitely come this way. Purefoy's story appeared to be credible. He could now, without doubt, place the rogue agent at the scene of Blake's murder. Not only that, but he was close to ruling out Purefoy's involvement in the matter. His instinct told him to trust the young man. He decided to follow his gut.

Newbury scanned the surrounding rooftops. In the hazy light it was like a rich landscape, punctuated by innumerable chimneys, belching dark, foggy clouds into the sky. The horizon was like a microcosm of all of London: industrial buildings, terraces, slums and large mansions, all clustered together in an unlikely arrangement.

Then, about two hundred yards away, on another, lower rooftop, Newbury saw his prey. Or rather, he saw two glowing, red pinpricks of light, emanating from where Ashford's eyes had once been. They were staring out – unwavering – from behind a large terracotta chimney pot. They were unmistakable, even in the fog and the gloom. The rest of the man was obscured by the shadows. "There he is!" Newbury exclaimed, pointing across to where the rogue agent was lurking.

Purefoy couldn't see. "What! Where?"

But Newbury wasn't waiting. He rushed to the edge of the terrace, looking across at the intervening gap between Arbury House and the building behind it. There was a gap of around six feet between the two rooftops, with no clear run-up, and only a small ledge on the other side of the iron railings from which to make the jump. Below, there was only darkness and swirling fog. If he missed his footing and pitched into that... all that awaited him below was death, dashed across the uneven cobbles and lost amongst scattered piles of refuse and human waste.

He glanced back at the bizarre, red eyes of his enemy. They seemed to bore into him, urging him on. He had no time to consider. Grasping hold of the top of the railing, he swung one leg over, trying to avoid impaling himself on the rusty fleur-de-lys that crested the ironwork. He climbed down cautiously onto the ledge on the other side. There was little room to move, and his left foot slipped, causing him to grasp hold of the railing once again to maintain his balance. Crumbling brickwork shimmered down into the grey darkness. He didn't hear it strike the ground. His heart was hammering hard in his chest. He was sweating, too, feeling an intense, burning desire for the narcotic that sustained him. He gripped the railing, fighting the urge to climb back onto the relative safety of the roof behind him.

He heard Purefoy run over to stand beside him, on the other side of the railing. "Sir Maurice! You're not going to..."

Newbury paid him no heed. If he thought too long about what he was about to do, he simply wouldn't do it. Keeping his head up, to avoid looking down at the sheer drop beneath him, Newbury examined the other rooftop. There was a small, decorative stone lip that ran around the edge of the roof. At least, he mused, if he misjudged the jump, he'd have something to attempt to catch hold of. He had no idea how Ashford had got across the gap, or, indeed, why the man was still lurking in the shadows when it was clear that he had been spotted. Perhaps he didn't expect Newbury to successfully leap across the two rooftops to confront him. Whatever the case, this was the best opportunity Newbury had yet encountered to bring the man to justice, and he planned to do it before any more people died. Assuming, of course, that he wasn't about to kill himself.

Coiling like a spring to get as much power into his legs as possible, Newbury pounced. He flung his arms out as he sailed across the alleyway, keeping his eyes fixed on the point where he intended to land. He almost made it, but a trailing foot caught the stone lip and sent him sprawling. He slammed down hard onto the other roof, only just managing to get his arms up in time to protect his head. His elbows smarted from the blow, and he'd knocked the wind out of himself. He lay on his front for a moment, breathless, before rolling onto his back and sitting up. He took a moment to regain his composure. Then, not wanting to provide Ashford with a chance of escape, he clambered to his hands and knees, and then to his feet, gasping as he finally managed to pull the cold, damp air down into his lungs. He turned, fully expecting Ashford to be rushing him across the terrace. But he was still there in the shadows, still watching. Newbury could make no sense of the man's motivations.

He heard a crash beside him, and, surprised, turned to see Purefoy landing neatly on his haunches and breaking into a forward roll to cushion his landing. He came up standing beside Newbury, a wide grin on his face. They looked at each other, something wordless passing between them. An understanding. And then Newbury set off, bolting across the rooftop towards the glowing lights that represented his murderous prey. Purefoy's footsteps fell in behind him.

As he drew closer, Newbury watched the shape of Ashford resolve in the dim, foggy light. He made no attempt to conceal himself. He was dressed as Purefoy had claimed – as he had been when Newbury had last encountered him – in his flowing black cloak, hulking beside the towering chimney stack. His red eyes seemed to track Newbury's progress across the rooftop. Newbury skidded around a skylight, and then realised, with shock, the reason why Ashford had not yet taken flight. He was rushing headlong towards the lip of another building. Newbury had misjudged the distance in the fog. Ashford was waiting on the next rooftop. It was too late to stop. He was already careening towards the drop, which yawned open before him like an ominous chasm. There was no railing this time, only the same decorative lip that had caused him to trip on the other side. He didn't stop. Reaching the edge of the building he leapt up onto the lip and propelled himself forward, flinging himself through the air so that he hurtled across the gap and landed at a run, stumbling slightly but managing to maintain his momentum. His arms wheeled as he tried to maintain his balance. He didn't have time to congratulate himself for the manoeuvre, however, as something seemed to change with Ashford. As Newbury darted between the chimney stacks that peppered the roof, Ashford turned and began to flee.

Ashford's legs seemed to drive him forward at a phenomenal speed. He was like a blur, as he shot towards the other end of the building. Newbury's legs pumped hard at the ground as he attempted, ineffectually, to keep up.

There was a terrified cry from somewhere behind him. Newbury, torn, skidded to a halt, glancing back over his shoulder. He realised almost immediately what had happened. Purefoy hadn't seen the gap between the two rooftops until it was too late, and had failed to clear the opening. A lump rose in Newbury's throat. He was labouring for breath, not used to the exertion. Turning, he rushed back towards the alleyway. He knew he was allowing Ashford to get away, but if there was any chance...

Newbury scanned the line of the building as he ran, but everything was shrouded in cloying, yellow fog. He called out.

"Purefoy?"

There was no reply.

Newbury came to a halt a few feet from the drop. He searched the terrace around him. Empty. There was no sign of the young man. The roofline opposite was also clear.

Purefoy, it seemed, was nowhere to be seen. Newbury, drawing ragged breath, could only fear the worst.

Chapter Sixteen

Hesitantly, Newbury approached the lip of the building. He couldn't see any sign of the other man. He called out. "Purefoy? Purefoy! Are you there?" He was panicking now. He didn't know how he could live with the responsibility if the reporter had fallen to his death.

There was a grunt from down below, somewhere in the fog. Newbury knelt on the edge of the building and leaned over, searching, urgently, for the source of the sound. "Purefoy? Is that you?"

"Here..." The voice trailed off, and Newbury heard the sounds of something soft and heavy banging against metal. There! He leaned over as far as he dared. An iron staircase resolved in the fog. It was an emergency stairwell, attached to the side of the building. And, dangling from it, twisting and turning, clutching on by only one hand, was Purefoy. He seemed dazed, as if he may have caught a blow to the head in the fall. Blood was smeared in a long line across his cheek. Newbury knew the situation was precarious. One slip and the reporter would be dead. He called out to him.

"Purefoy! Focus. Use your other hand. Hold on!" Purefoy seemed to respond to this. He eased himself around so that he was facing the brickwork, and swung his left arm up, trying to catch hold of the ironwork. His hand, however, did not seem able to find purchase, and he slipped, dangerously, crying out as he lurched awkwardly from side to side. Newbury feared the motion would cause him to lose his grip altogether as he swung wildly over the alleyway below. "Stay there. I'm coming for you."

Newbury stood, surveying the scene beneath him. The fog was thick here, and it obscured his view. He knew the iron stairwell would have a small platform, just to the right of where Purefoy was hanging, and knew also that it couldn't be far below the lip of the building itself. But it was difficult to see. Past Purefoy, he could make out the indistinct shape of a railing, but little else. He'd have to take it on faith. Edging along the lip of the factory, he drew a deep breath. If he missed, they would likely both wind up dead in the gutter below. He hadn't planned on *this* when he'd decided to visit Wilfred Blake that morning, and he wondered, absently, what Veronica would say if she could see him now.

Newbury judged he was standing above the metal platform. Purefoy had once again disappeared into the syrupy miasma. Below, all Newbury could see was a swirl of grey. He took a deep breath. He couldn't put it off any longer, and he couldn't let Purefoy fall to his death. He closed his eyes, flexed his shoulders, and jumped into nothing.

His feet clattered against the metal rungs, but the platform was higher than he'd imagined and it was this that nearly toppled him over the side of the railing as he fought to get his balance. Frantically, he scrabbled to get a grip, grasping hold of the iron bars as he slipped and slid on the slick metal. Finding his feet, he heaved a brief sigh of relief, and then rushed immediately to the left-hand side of the platform and sank to his knees, searching for Purefoy between the metal bars. The reporter was still there, clinging on for his life. Newbury thrust his arm through the grate, and reached down to grasp Purefoy by the wrist. The reporter's other arm was still dangling uselessly by his side, and he seemed unable to gain enough leverage to swing it up to try for a better hold.

"Here! Use my arm. Pull yourself up."

Purefoy stared back at him with panicked eyes. He was breathing quickly, and the strain was starting to show. Newbury tried to keep him focused on the task at hand. "Don't look down. No! Purefoy! Keep your eyes on me." Newbury heaved, trying to give the boy a better chance of grabbing hold of the stairwell with his other hand. Purefoy struggled, his feet kicking frantically as they sought something solid upon which to gain purchase. Instead, the result was to pull alarmingly on Newbury's arm as Purefoy swung out wildly, and Newbury felt his shoulder burning as he took the other's weight, his arm fully extended, his face pressed uncomfortably against the hard metal bars.

"Oh God!" Purefoy exclaimed in terror as Newbury's grip slipped and loosened, and he slid a little further towards the alleyway below.

"I have you." Newbury fixed his gaze on the other man. "I *have* you. Now pay attention. You need to get your other arm up here, right now!" Newbury was gasping for breath and struggling to gain leverage. The instructions registered with the young man, however, and, with Newbury still hanging on to him by his left wrist, he managed to get a grip on the iron frame with his right hand. "Good. Good! Now, I'm going to let go and reach over to grasp hold of your collar. We'll heave you over the top. Hold on!"

Newbury waited a moment to be sure that Purefoy was not going to fall, and then scrabbled to his feet, leaned over the rail and used both hands to grab fistfuls of the boy's jacket. "On my mark. One, two, three..." He grunted as he lifted the reporter up, bodily, by his clothes. Purefoy was quick to get his feet into position, jamming them through the bars of the rail to support himself. A moment later, he swung over the top of the railing and collapsed beside Newbury on the cold platform, both of them struggling for breath. He stared with wide eyes at the drop beneath him. His eyes passed wordless thanks to the Crown investigator.

Newbury patted him on the shoulder. "You need to thank your tailor, dear boy." He wheezed as he tried to regain his breath. "That's an excellent jacket you have there."

They both laughed out loud, relieved, as they rubbed their aching joints. After a few moments, still gasping, Purefoy turned to Newbury. "Ashford?"

Newbury shrugged. "I'm in no doubt that he got away. Once I've regained my strength I'll head up there to take a look, see if there are any other clues that may help us to pick up his trail."

Purefoy looked sheepish. "I..."

Newbury interjected. "Best left unsaid. It's not necessary. Not at all."

Purefoy nodded gratefully.

After a moment, Newbury, who had been slumped on the platform, his back to the railing, climbed to his feet and regarded the building before him. Here, the metal stairs became a short ladder that terminated just below the lip of the roof. He shook his head, cursing that he hadn't noticed the ladder from above. Taking hold of the rungs, he levered himself up, leaving Purefoy where he was, still panting and nursing his sore arms on the platform below. It was a short climb to the roof, and he was soon able to pull himself over again. He made a mental note of where the ladder was, scuffing the gravel with the edge of his shoe in case he needed to find it again in the fog.

Newbury looked around for signs of Ashford. The fog was

thickening, but even so, he was shocked to see, a little further along the rooftop, the familiar red eyes of the augmented man staring back at him. Newbury could barely believe it. Why had he waited? Perhaps he wanted to be sure that Newbury and Purefoy were gone? Perhaps Purefoy had been right, and he intended to head back to Blake's apartment before Newbury was able to alert the police? Regardless, he couldn't waste the opportunity.

"Ashford!" The other man's head turned, and Newbury could no longer see his face beneath the darkness of his cowl. "Ashford, we must talk." Newbury rushed forward, and as he drew closer, the situation became quickly apparent. Ashford was perched on the corner of the building, his heavy cloak draped over his shoulders, giving him an ethereal, formless appearance in the foggy darkness. Across from him, the buildings to the side and rear were both taller – at least a storey higher than the factory on which they were standing – and the leap across to either was impossible, even for an augmented giant such as Ashford. Newbury smiled. He had him. He knew, this time, he had him. Digging deep for every last reserve of his strength, he thundered forward towards his quarry.

Ashford seemed to respond to this with an air of calm acceptance. He turned away from the approaching Newbury, stepping up carefully onto the raised lip of the roof. He seemed to be judging the distance to the bottom of the alleyway, far below, but Newbury knew there would be nothing to see but a thick river of fog. Ashford inched closer to the edge.

Suddenly, Newbury got a measure of the man's intention. Ashford meant to jump. He bellowed across the roof. "No! Don't do it, man! You'll fall to your death!"

Ashford, however, seemed not to hear him. With one last glance over his shoulder, the rogue agent leapt suddenly into the air.

Newbury darted towards the edge of the building, in time to see Ashford's black, fluttering cloak billow out like some obscene wing, as the man soared out into the gap between the two buildings, plummeting down into the milky abyss. Surely the drop would kill him?

Newbury gave an involuntary wince at the sound of Ashford impacting against the cobbles below. There was a sickening *crunch* – as of metal striking stone – a cry of pain, and then silence. Newbury sighed. It was over.

Newbury turned back towards Purefoy and the metal stairwell. He'd have to recover Ashford's body, first to verify his death, then to keep the matter out of the papers and the police reports. He kicked at the gravel, frustrated. He wanted to know *why*. What had driven this man – this former agent – to such murderous lengths? Had he really believed the secrets of Khemosiri would have granted him a new life? Newbury doubted that very much. But desperate men are often driven to desperate measures. He hopped down from the lip at the corner of the factory roof. Then, to Newbury's amazement, he heard the sounds of someone shifting around in the alleyway below. There was a groan, followed by the ringing of tentative footsteps as Ashford, unseen due to the thick shroud of vapour, evidently climbed to his feet and continued on his way.

"Oh no, you don't!" Newbury rushed along the edge of the building, looking for some means by which he could quickly descend to ground level and continue his pursuit. If he lost Ashford now, he knew he risked losing him forever.

Below, bolted to the side of the building, Newbury spotted the top of an iron ladder, similar to the one he had ascended a few minutes earlier, and smiled with grim satisfaction. Another stairwell. The platform would be fixed to the wall, a storey below. He glanced behind him. Purefoy was watching him from across the rooftop, nursing his bloodied hands where they had been torn clinging to the iron railing. Newbury weighed up his options. Did he risk the jump? Or did he waste valuable time on the ladder? He knew, with steady resolve, that there was only one answer to that question. He didn't look back to see if Purefoy would follow. Hopping up onto the stone lip, Newbury casually stepped off the side of the building, his body tautening as he prepared for the drop to the platform below.

This time, Newbury was ready for the impact and did not lose his footing, instead using his shoulder to take the brunt of his fall. It smarted painfully where it smashed against the hard railing, but he used the momentum to fling himself forward, tumbling down the first flight of stairs. He knew he would be black and blue with bruises by the morning, but he barely registered the knocks and scrapes as he dived headlong down flight after flight of metal steps towards the ground. His hands rasped on the worn metal as he slid from one storey to the other, his chest burning with the exertion.

All the while, the prickly need for opium was like a constant pull. He could feel his body craving the stuff. Once this was over, he promised himself, once he'd brought Ashford to justice; then he would attend to his own needs. For now, the needs of the Empire were far greater than his own.

In a matter of moments Newbury hit the ground, breaking into a roll to cushion his fall. Climbing to his feet, he glanced up at the side of the building to see if Purefoy had followed, but everything above was veiled in dense mist. Here, at ground level, it was beginning to pool, pulling a thick, yellow curtain across the city, but it was still wispy enough to allow Newbury to get his bearings. He took in his surroundings. The alleyway stank of raw sewage and rotting food. It was filthy, strewn with detritus, and outlet pipes gushed steam and dirty water onto the cobbles, drawn from the innards of the surrounding buildings. A feral cat was mewling loudly, somewhere out of sight. Newbury attempted to dust himself down, to little avail. His suit was covered in a layer of grime from the chase across the rooftops and his roll across the greasy cobbles. Mrs. Bradshaw would be delighted.

Newbury glanced from side to side, searching for signs of Ashford. The rogue agent had reached the other end of the alley now, his back to Newbury. He was clearly in no hurry to get away. Newbury grinned. Ashford hadn't heard him on the stairwell, and had incorrectly assumed that Newbury would be unable to continue his pursuit, following his leap from the top of the factory. It was an advantage that Newbury desperately needed. If the man could drop four storeys onto cobbles and survive to get up and walk away, then Newbury needed all the help he could get. In a fight, he didn't fancy his chances against such a monster.

Newbury set off after the hulking form of the former agent, keeping pace. He needed to ensure that he didn't inadvertently give Ashford a chance to lose himself in the warren of backstreets that criss-crossed this district of Regent's Park. The light was almost gone now, and without his topcoat, Newbury could feel the damp air penetrating his clothes, filling his lungs like a cold compress. Nevertheless, he crept along the alley, clinging to the shadows, keeping Ashford locked in his sights.

They came to the mouth of the alleyway. Here, the street opened up in both directions, and directly ahead, across the main thoroughfare, the alley appeared to continue in a straight line for miles, disappearing into the dense fog. The street lamps had been diminished to nothing but diffuse, radial orbs that hung in the sky like a bizarre constellation, giving the air around them a tactile, almost physical quality. Newbury shivered. The cold air was damp and his face felt slick with moisture. The thoroughfare was busy; Newbury could hear the brisk chatter of people, the clatter of horses' hooves, and the rude firing of numerous steam engines to his left. To his right, a street vendor was expounding the virtues of the latest edition of *The Evening Standard*.

Newbury lurked for a moment by the corner of a butcher's shop, watching Ashford as he stumbled along in the darkness. Perhaps the fall had caused more damage to Ashford's rebuilt frame than Newbury had at first imagined. If he could surprise the man from behind, he might have a chance of taking him down. He needed to act.

Newbury broke cover, dashing forward to make a leap for the other man. Too late, he realised there was a broken wooden pallet in the road, abandoned by a market trader and hidden by the low-lying vapour, and he lurched to one side to avoid colliding with it. His foot scuffed noisily on the paving slabs as he righted himself.

Ashford came to life. He spun round to catch sight of the Crown investigator charging him from the rear. Newbury could see no measure of emotion in Ashford's cold, red eyes; indeed, he had yet to properly catch sight of the man's face, concealed as it was beneath the dark cowl of his cloak. But he knew there was steel and darkness behind them. He considered the fact that he was potentially rushing headlong towards his own death.

He was surprised, therefore, when Ashford turned on his heel and fled, somehow managing to spring at least two foot into the air with each stride, his legs pumping furiously as he bounded along the thoroughfare at an incredible speed. He clearly wasn't spoiling for a fight.

For the slightest of moments, Newbury stood, rooted to the

spot, mouth agape in amazement. Whatever Dr. Fabian had done to Ashford, he was clearly now more machine than man. No human being could ever propel themselves along at such a pace.

Newbury, realising that he'd soon lose Ashford in the fog if he failed to act, took after the man, careening along the street behind him, dodging out of the way of other, confused pedestrians as he ran. He left a young man sprawling in his wake, but had no time to stop to help him to his feet. Newbury's lungs burned, and his muscles ached. And, with mounting frustration, he watched as Ashford gained more and more distance with every stride.

Realistically, Newbury knew that he could not keep up. He considered his options. If he continued to run, he would surely lose sight of Ashford. The man seemed tireless, and Newbury was already feeling the strain of the exertion. Ahead of him, a hansom cab clattered along the road, and for a moment Newbury almost decided to leap aboard. But he knew the horse and driver would still be no match for the reconstructed man. He glanced over his left shoulder.

There, by the side of the road, a young man was attending to one of the new steam-powered automobiles that had so taken London by storm during the prior months. It was a bizarre contraption. Balanced on three wheels, with a pear-shaped body and a fat rear end that housed a small furnace and water tank, the vehicle was in practice a miniaturised version of the steam-powered hansoms of which Newbury made frequent use. Inside the pear-shaped body was a deep pit, into which the driver would lower himself, and which also contained a series of panels and pulleys by which they would operate the steering mechanism. Early on, Newbury had considered obtaining one of the strange vehicles, but *The Times* had reported on a growing number of fatalities involving the contraptions, and over time, far from feeling a mounting temptation to adopt the new form of transportation, Newbury had grown to see them as a menace. Nevertheless, he needed a means by which to keep pace with Ashford, and as far as he could see, there were no better options available to him at that juncture.

The furnace of this particular vehicle was well stoked, for it was belching black smoke from its twin exhaust pipes. The man, who Newbury presumed to be the owner, was dressed in a smart black suit with matching leather gloves, and had a pair of flying goggles affixed to his brow, pushed up onto his forehead whilst he regarded his machine. Newbury skidded to a halt beside him. The man looked up, startled at the appearance of the detective.

"In the name of the Crown, hand over that vehicle!"

"What? I... er..." The man looked flabbergasted. "Certainly not!" He looked Newbury up and down, unsure how to react to this dishevelled man in front of him, who, thick with the detritus of his rooftop chase, was claiming to represent Her Majesty Queen Victoria. Newbury stepped forward and gently pushed the man to one side. He swung his legs up and over, into the control pit of the vehicle, and began fiddling with the controls, searching around for the lever that would propel it forward. He could see Ashford gaining ground in the distance, and he wasn't about to let him get away. He was sweating profusely from his run. Wiping his brow on his sleeve, he fiddled with a pair of matching brass handles and felt the front wheel turning from side to side beneath him. The steering mechanism, then. Next, cranking a lever with a sharp jolt, he set the vehicle into motion. It lurched forward, nearly knocking its owner to the ground. The man was shaking his fist and bellowing for the police, but Newbury chose to ignore the outburst. He didn't have time to engage in an argument with the man, nor to attempt to prove his credentials. The man would be suitably reimbursed for his trouble. Probably.

The engine roared and smoke billowed like a black stain from its rear end. The vehicle stuttered forward again, and then hopped fifty yards along the road in short, jolting bursts. Frustrated, Newbury glared after Ashford. He knew that time was running out.

By this time the owner had gathered a fair crowd of onlookers, and a brief glance over his shoulder warned Newbury that a uniformed bobby had joined the fray. More distractions he could do without. He concentrated on deciphering the controls. Tentatively, Newbury eased back on the accelerator lever – which he assumed opened some sort of pressurised steam valve – and the vehicle kicked into a forward roll. The wheels clattered bumpily against the cobbled road, and he was jarred awkwardly as he continued to slowly adjust the lever to introduce more speed. At the last minute, he grasped for the brass steering knobs and swung the contraption out of the path of a middle-aged woman who was crossing the road before him, apparently oblivious to the rush of the oncoming vehicle. He slewed wildly to the right, and then, jamming the controls sharply to the left, he was able to bring the contraption back under some semblance of control. Other pedestrians dived out of his way as he called out to them, hurtling headlong after the rogue agent.

It was difficult to see anything in the soupy fog, but, even with his remarkable mechanical enhancements, Ashford was no match for the speed of the steam-powered tricycle. He'd managed to gain considerable ground, but if he were intent on losing Newbury's tail, he showed no signs of it. He remained in plain sight, hurtling along the main thoroughfare. At any point he could have ducked down one of the other alleyways or side passages and lost himself in the confusing patchwork of back streets that Newbury had seen from the rooftops above. But he seemed to be heading somewhere with intent, and Newbury wondered whether his pursuit had even registered as anything above an annoyance. Regardless, he swung the vehicle in behind the man, undeterred. All of these questions could be answered later, once Ashford was safely contained in a cell.

Newbury shot along the road in pursuit, wavering wildly from side to side as he attempted to maintain control of the steering mechanism. It was an awkward, unwieldy device: the two brass knobs on the dashboard appeared to be rigged to a complex pulley system that changed the direction of the front wheel. The driver manipulated the knobs, twisting one to turn right and the other to turn left. If he let them go, the vehicle would right itself once more, travelling directly forward in whichever direction the contraption was pointed. It was hardly elegant, but it was relatively effective, and Newbury soon had a measure of how to keep the vehicle from turning over.

He continued to barrel along after Ashford, gaining on him with every passing moment. The back wheels of the tricycle were spinning at an incredible speed, bouncing on the uneven road and lifting the vehicle physically into the air, so that Newbury had to maintain a tight grip on the controls and jam his feet under the dashboard to prevent himself being thrown from the driver's pit with every movement.

Ashford had gathered a powerful momentum, and was now knocking people bodily out of the way as he charged through the crowds, trying his best to outpace Newbury's borrowed transportation. Newbury had to swerve to avoid hitting the innocent bystanders that Ashford sent sprawling to the ground, and it slowed him down, causing him to concentrate more on the road than his quarry. He supposed that was Ashford's intention.

He considered his next move. He could try to mow Ashford down, but after seeing the man leap from the roof of a four-storey building, only to climb to his feet and walk away unharmed, he had doubts that the tricycle would be strong enough to even knock Ashford from his feet, let alone incapacitate him whilst Newbury sent for help. Instead, as he drew closer, Newbury released both steering knobs on the vehicle, wedged the acceleration lever into its fully open position, and scrambled up into a standing position inside the driver's pit. Then, taking the steering knobs again, he fought to manoeuvre the vehicle alongside the sprinting Ashford.

Surprised, Ashford turned to glare at Newbury as he ran, and Newbury caught his first real glimpse of the man's face. It was an appalling sight. Ashford's flesh was grey and necrotic, peeling away around the dark pits of his eye sockets, into which two bizarre, mechanical devices had been inserted to replace his eyes. These were not makeshift instruments akin to that of Aldous Renwick's, but appeared to be smaller, more precision-made devices. They bore the hallmark of Dr. Fabian.

Ashford's jawbone was exposed at the base of his right cheek, where a hunk of skin had been ripped away, either during a ferocious encounter, or simply due to the fact that it had rotted and sloughed away. The rest of his skin was pitted and raw, and pink fluid seeped from open sores around his nose. Newbury was aghast. The sight of Ashford's face reminded him of the revenant creatures that still prowled the dark corners of the city: victims of an Indian plague that had terrorised the slums since before Christmas. Ashford's rotting, cadaverous face was the mirror image of these horrifying monsters – half alive, half dead – yet his steely grimace betrayed a sense of purpose that was lacking in the revenants. Inside there, behind those cold, glowing eyes, a cool intelligence still lurked, and the thought of it made Newbury shudder. Then there was the smell; even here, standing shakily in the driver's pit of a moving tricycle, the stench of the man was near unbearable.

Newbury was almost caught unawares when Ashford made a lunge for him, swinging out widely with a powerful right hook as he ran. Newbury attempted to duck the blow, causing the vehicle to swerve wildly. He fought to get it under control. Luckily, the other man's fist landed squarely on his shoulder, missing its intended target: his chin. The power behind the punch was phenomenal, intended to finish the matter, and Newbury wondered, as his shoulder alighted with pain, what devices buried within the once-human form of William Ashford had manufactured such a blow.

Releasing his grip on the steering knobs of the tricycle once again, Newbury brought his left arm up to protect his face and jabbed out with his right, raining a series of blows into the side of Ashford's head. Ashford barely seemed to notice. He was still running, still keeping pace with the unusual vehicle, and Newbury, bouncing along the uneven road, had to stoop to regain control of the steering mechanism before the tricycle swerved from its course and he lost control altogether. His options were running out. He could pounce on the running man, trying to bring him down, but the risks were far too great. If he missed, not only would he lose Ashford, probably for good, but he risked ending his own life. The speed at which he was now travelling was such that he would be dashed against the cobbles unless he pitched his move with the utmost precision. Given the circumstances, that seemed unlikely. Instead, he grabbed for the left-hand steering knob, twisting it sharply and causing the vehicle to slew dramatically to the left. He pitched forward as the tricycle slammed into Ashford's legs.

Remarkably, Ashford did not topple over as anticipated. The tricycle rebounded, tipping to one side and almost spilling Newbury out into the street. He clutched desperately for the steering knobs and tried to right the contraption as it skittered off to one side. He fought frantically with the mechanism, balancing the front wheel as best he could and causing a newspaper salesman to throw himself to the ground as his stand collapsed, the tricycle sending plumes of paper into the air as it glanced off the salesman's wooden table. It was all the opportunity that Ashford needed. He veered off sharply to the left, mounting the pavement and darting towards the entrance to Portland Road Underground Station. He hurtled down the steps towards the platforms below.

"Damn it!" Newbury gave a howl of frustration, swinging the tricycle round in pursuit. He jammed the acceleration lever down, opening the valve to its limit and building up a head of steam. The vehicle shot forward, bouncing crazily over the kerb and up onto the footpath. He made a beeline towards the entrance to the Underground station. He couldn't let Ashford get away. He'd come too far.

Newbury closed his eyes and pointed the tricycle at the top of the stairwell. He shot forward. The vehicle breezed over the top of the stairs, soaring into the air as its momentum carried it forward, in a long arc down towards the darkness of the station below. Newbury realised he was holding his breath, waiting for the impact that seemed to take forever to arrive. He was shaking, adrenaline coursing through his system.

The trajectory of the small vehicle was such that Newbury was never going to make it clear of the bottom steps. The undercarriage of the tricycle collided brutally with the stone steps, cracking open with an enormous jolt. For a moment, Newbury honestly believed he was going to die. He opened his eyes to see one of the back wheels spinning away, and realised with horror that the furnace had cracked open, spilling burning coals in a hot trail behind him, as the vehicle continued to skid down the stairs. Water, too, was gushing out of the tank, slopping across the steps and causing the hot coals to fizz noisily as they were doused. He clutched uselessly at the controls, finally realising that, if he were to survive, he had to get out of the skidding vehicle quickly. The wreckage reached the bottom of the stairs, but continued to slide forward across the tiled floor of the station, leaving devastation in its wake.

The frame of the tricycle was buckled, now, and Newbury was practically hanging out of one side, his shoulder only a couple of feet from the ground, as the remnants of the machine continued its long slide across the floor. People were screaming. Wriggling his legs free, Newbury allowed gravity to take its course. He fell out of the ruined tricycle, his shoulder jarring painfully against the hard tiles. He slid to a stop, watching the wreckage of the machine slide away from him towards a nearby wall. His legs had come out of the machine twisted, but intact. He straightened himself out on the floor, surprised that he hadn't been seriously mangled in the crash. Around him, scattered coals still glowed with amber warmth.

A woman rushed forward to help him to his feet, murmuring platitudes. He accepted her arm, scrabbling to his feet and looking around for Ashford. She looked confused when he failed to acknowledge her words, but he had no choice: Ashford was getting away. The man moved fast, faster than Newbury could possibly conceive, but along one of the tunnels Newbury could see his black cloak fluttering as he barged his way through the crowd of passengers; hear also the clanging footsteps of his heavy boots, ringing out in the confined space.

Ignoring the burning pain in his shoulder, Newbury flexed his back, smiled at the young blonde woman who had helped him to his feet, and took off after Ashford. He hurtled along the white-tiled tunnel, pushing his way past rows of blank-faced civilians, who stared at him, dumbfounded, as he forced a path through their ranks, following the hulking giant in the black cloak. Once more, Newbury had his prey in his sights. There was nowhere left for Ashford to run. He would end it here.

Newbury charged along behind the rogue agent, skipping down a series of tiled steps towards the platform. His face was set with grim determination, but nevertheless, he almost laughed out loud when he saw a faded, sepia-coloured bill pasted on the tunnel wall, advertising the miraculous stage show of "The Mysterious Alfonso". He swept past it, driving onwards.

Newbury burst out onto the platform a moment later, only to see, bewildered, the other man leap down onto the train tracks and dart towards the dark mouth of the Underground tunnel at the end of the platform. Newbury ran to the edge of the platform and threw himself forward, jumping high into the air and coming down hard on Ashford's shoulders. Ashford twisted, stumbling on the steel tracks and tottering over under the weight and momentum of the Crown detective. He banged his head, hard, against the curved tunnel wall, and it rang out with the sound of metal striking stone. There were shouts of alarm from the passengers waiting on the platform edge. Newbury heard a whistle blow. The police were on their way. Far from being concerned, Newbury was relieved. If he could only detain Ashford for long enough, perhaps the bobbies would be able to help him restrain the man.

The metal runners of the track were hard against Newbury's back. He was growing weary now, but Ashford, seemingly indestructible, was already climbing to his feet. Newbury mustered his remaining strength. He jumped to his feet, punching out at the rogue agent. His fist connected with the other man's chin, slamming his head backwards, but the blow was almost enough to incapacitate Newbury, for his hand felt as if he had driven it into a lump of solid iron. He glanced at his knuckles. They were shredded, bleeding and sore.

Unperturbed, Ashford lurched forward, using the flat of his hand to slap Newbury hard in the chest. The blow was enough to immediately knock him from his feet. He called out as he scrabbled on the ground. "Ashford! What's the matter with you, man? Have you lost all sense? Give it up!"

Ashford's voice, when he spoke, was a grating, metallic whine. Every word was like a fragment of song, and Newbury had the sense that, somehow, it was being artificially induced. It sounded as if it were being squeezed from a clutch of miniature organ pipes in his throat, like a chorus of a hundred people all speaking the same words at once. But there was no emotion in it, no sense of the person Ashford had once been. The sound seemed to echo from a wheezing vent in his chest. It was cold and inhuman, just like the man himself. "Cease and desist, Sir Maurice. I don't want to hurt you." He stepped cautiously over the train tracks to loom over the prone Newbury. During the tussle, however, Ashford's long cloak had become tangled in the steel runners. In stepping forward, the cloak tore open, exposing, momentarily, the horrifying figure it harboured underneath.

Newbury gasped in shock. "My God! What did they do to you?" The words seemed to catch in his throat. Newbury knew, now, the origin of that detestable stench. Ashford was less than half the man he had once been; less than half the *human being* he had once been. His body had been ravaged, reassembled from a shocking assortment of flesh and brass, like a patchwork monster made real, a nightmare marriage of metal and blood. What flesh there still was, clinging to his brass exoskeleton, was rotten, decaying, sloughing away in great hunks. In places, large patches of leather had been stitched indelicately to this remaining flesh in an attempt to give some semblance of skin, but had succeeded only in exacerbating the monstrous appearance of the man. Newbury had no idea whether this was a part of Dr.

Fabian's original design, or whether Ashford had attempted to repair himself during his five-year exile in St. Petersburg. It mattered not. The result was grotesque.

The man's torso was perhaps the most disturbing aspect of all. The exposed skin of his chest was puckered and pustulant around a large glass porthole that filled the space where his ribcage had once resided. In the murky depths it revealed, Newbury could see the grey muscle of the man's heart, beating in time with a flickering electrical charge that shocked it repeatedly at intervals, like the precise ticking of a clock. Fluid burbled and bubbled along four clear pipes that sprouted, like giant follicles, from his shoulders, curling around the back of his head and disappearing into the depths of his skull. The brown, murky liquid appeared to be pumped around his brain cavity by a further device buried deep inside his chest. His face was just as alarming. The tiny lenses of his eyes flicked back and forth over Newbury's prone body, the red lights glowing in the darkness. When he opened his mouth, Newbury saw that his teeth had decayed to black stumps. What hair was left was hung in long, straggling clumps, and the flesh of his scalp was torn, revealing the horrific juxtaposition of yellowed bone and metal plating underneath.

Newbury shuddered. So this was the disgusting genius of Dr. Fabian, taken to its extreme. He could hardly believe this had been sanctioned by the Crown. He pitied the man, despite himself. Newbury had no idea how Ashford could go on living like this. It was a form of waking torture, that every minute his intellect should be housed in this wreckage of a frame, this parody of a human body. No wonder the man had been driven insane. Newbury was amazed it had not happened sooner. Indeed, he felt a kind of sickening sympathy for the man, an understanding of the desperation that had led him to this point. Science had betrayed him, and so had the Crown. His life had been extended beyond the point of death, certainly, but Newbury doubted it was a life worth living; the pain and hardship he must have suffered since his resurrection would have driven any man insane. And now Ashford had turned to the occult, hoping to find a means to restore himself, to reclaim the life that was once his. It was tragic, and Newbury was repulsed, not only by what the man had become, but the means by which he had become it. Nevertheless, regardless of circumstances, Ashford had committed two murders, and whatever happened there in the train tunnel he needed to be brought to justice.

Newbury inched backwards, shuffling along the tracks, trying to put some distance between himself and the strange, mechanical man. Ashford stooped low in response, as if reaching for Newbury's ankle. The detective rolled, using his momentum to spring up onto his hands and knees and then twisting into a standing position. He fired out a blind kick in Ashford's general direction, in an attempt to keep the other man at bay whilst he found his bearings. To his surprise, his foot hit home, although it seemed to have little effect other than to give Newbury some extra leverage to right himself. Again, Ashford attempted to slap at Newbury with the palm of his hand, swatting at him as if he were a buzzing insect, but Newbury was able to skip away, watchful that his feet did not become entangled in the rails. He could not work out what Ashford was trying to achieve with such bizarre tactics. Surely a trained agent, a man who had lived rough in a foreign territory for over five years, would have developed more comprehensive combat manoeuvres? Especially a man with such power. If he were able to plant even one successful blow to Newbury's head or gut, Newbury knew it would be the end of him. He'd fought machines before, but this was an entirely different proposition. No, it was almost as if, with these flat-handed attacks, Ashford was genuinely attempting not to wound him, instead choosing to parry Newbury's ineffective blows and disable him with the least amount of effort. Perhaps he was telling the truth? Perhaps he really didn't want to hurt him?

Confused, Newbury backed away. By now, people were shrieking loudly on the platform, but the combatants paid them no heed. Newbury wiped his sleeve across his brow. "Ashford... you have to come in with me. They'll hunt you down. *I'll* hunt you down, unless you stop me. Put an end to this now."

The half-human, half-machine rounded on him. Newbury found it difficult to get a measure of the man's facial expression, all subtlety lost beneath the layers of peeling flesh. His voice chimed in its strange, metallic tones. "I cannot."

Newbury sighed. "Then I fear I must detain you myself."

Launching himself from the tunnel wall with a kick of his foot, Newbury pounced towards Ashford. To his horror, he registered, too late, the nature of the screams from the platform. People were shouting a warning. A train was coming. It was hurtling into the platform, heading directly for the mouth of the tunnel where Newbury and Ashford were now locked in combat.

Newbury landed on the other man, chopping down at his neck. Ashford, however, was ready for this, and instead of fending off Newbury's attack, he grappled with him, grabbing him firmly around the waist. Newbury fought frantically against his captor, but Ashford was too strong, and held him, pinned, as the train hurtled into the station. There was no way either of them could now escape the roar of the oncoming engine.

Ashford moved like lightning. He lurched to one side, bodily heaving Newbury up and into the air, spinning the Crown investigator up onto the platform, where he landed with a painful thump. It was just in time. The engine's brakes squealed loudly as the driver caught sight of the figure in its path, but it was too late for Ashford. The train slammed into him, lifting him off the ground with a sickening thud. His body was flung around the curved prow of the engine, trapping him between the side of the tank and the tunnel wall. Newbury watched in shock as Ashford's elbows scraped against the dirty tiles, setting a shower of sparks flying as his metal bones were dragged across the hard ceramic. The train screeched to a halt. Ashford, now partially obscured by the shadows of the tunnel, turned to regard Newbury, his red eyes flashing. Then, without saying another word, he eased himself out from between the engine and the tunnel wall, clambered around the front of the train, and dropped to the ground. Now out of sight, Newbury heard his footsteps padding away into the distance, further away into the depths of the Underground.

Newbury collapsed onto his back, breathing heavily. Ashford had saved his life. There was no doubt. The man had purposefully placed Newbury out of the path of the oncoming train, at great risk to himself. It was only due to Dr. Fabian's enhancements that Ashford had managed to survive the encounter at all. If survive was the right word.

Sighing, exhausted, Newbury took in his situation. The civilians on the platform had formed a large circle around him, their faces gleaming with expressions that ranged from horror to admiration and everything in between. Newbury couldn't help but laugh out loud when, a moment later, a startled-looking Purefoy pushed his way through the press of people, rushing to Newbury's side. The boy looked dishevelled, tired and anxious. "What happened to him? Where is he?"

"He got away."

"What... I..." Purefoy looked devastated. He glanced down at the ruination of his bloody hands, as if refusing to believe that everything he had been through that evening had been in vain, that all of their efforts had led to nothing but failure.

Newbury felt quite the opposite. "I should add at this point, Purefoy, that I'm beginning to think I may have been wrong all along." Newbury glanced in the direction of the tunnel mouth, where Ashford had disappeared into the murky darkness. "He saved my life." He looked up at the quizzical face of the young reporter. "Perhaps Ashford isn't our killer, after all."

Chapter Seventeen

Veronica stirred to wakefulness.

Her eyelids were heavy and she had the bizarre notion that she was floundering underwater, her senses dimmed, her breathing thick and uncomfortable. She gasped at the air, striking out with her hands, encountering only hard, rough panels in all directions. Her heart was racing in her chest. Probing her lips with her tongue, she found that they were dry and sore. She'd clearly been asleep for some time. She wrinkled her nose. There was a cloying scent in the air, a heady aroma of flowers. The smell seemed somehow familiar, somehow comforting. It made her feel as if she wanted to curl up and go back to sleep, to lose herself in its floral embrace. She fought the urge, knowing, somewhere in the back of her mind, that it would be dangerous to allow herself to slip away again. She had no idea how long she had been unconscious, or where she was, now that she had woken. She tried to get her bearings, but her mind was slow and glacial. There was a light breeze brushing against her left cheek and she turned towards it, allowing it to play over her face. The fresh air was cool and sobering.

Slowly, unsure what to expect, Veronica peeled open her eyes. *Darkness.* Nothing but black, impenetrable darkness. She tried to remember where she was, what had happened to her that she might find herself in this bizarre, uncomfortable place. The memories came to her in stuttering bursts of images and colour. *Alfonso. The trapdoor. The box.* She scrabbled with a start. She was still trapped in the wooden casket under the stage! Thankfully, she was still alive. But where was the magician? Why had he left her here for so long?

Veronica felt around with her hands. She realised she was no longer standing, but lying on her back; the fibrous, untreated wood rasped against her skin, even through the substantial fabric of her clothes. The casket was resting at an angle. She tried to sit up, but there was not enough room, and she caught her head with a painful knock. Bracing herself, she lifted her arms above her head, pushing at the roughly hewn panel above her head. There was no give. Shuffling a little, she tried instead with her feet, stamping down at the floor beneath the bundled rags. To her surprise, the panel creaked slightly ajar under the pressure. Frantically, she kicked down with her heels, forcing the wooden floor to snap open on stiff metal hinges. The rags spilled out beneath her, and the dim impression of light seeped in. She shuffled out, using her legs and hips to writhe free, her hands pressed against the sides of the casket to stop her from sliding downwards too quickly. The angle was awkward, but soon her feet struck hard, stone tiles, and a moment later she had spilled out of the box. She sprawled on the cold floor and filled her lungs with the clean air, attempting to clear the stench of the chloroform from her nostrils. Her mind was still woozy, her reactions slow. She sat up, and the room swam. Somewhere, during the battle with Alfonso, she had lost her hat. Her long brunette hair had come unpinned, cascading down across her face. She brushed it to one side, tucking it behind her ear.

Veronica glanced around to get a measure of the room. She was deep underground, in a basement or cellar. Flickering gas jets danced in a series of glass bowls mounted at intervals around the walls. The walls themselves were bare, constructed from blocks of ancient grey stone, and the floor was composed of red clay tiles, laid down in a neat herringbone pattern. They were cold and damp beneath her, and she shifted slightly, swaying from side to side as she almost lost her balance. The drug had affected her more than she had initially imagined.

Near to where she was sitting, a long wooden workbench had been laid out, filling much of the room. It was covered in a scattering of papers and other unusual ephemera. Beyond that, against the far wall, was a strange-looking chair, covered in a spidery assortment of brass arms and surgical instruments. She tried to focus on it, but her eyes betrayed her, and she closed them for a moment, almost slipping back to unconsciousness. She snapped them open again with a start. Nervously, she glanced from side to side. She appeared to be alone.

Hauling herself into a more upright position, she turned back to examine the wooden casket she had tumbled from. This was clearly the room in which the "disappeared" girls were deposited during the show, after Alfonso had triggered the mechanism on the stage, causing them to fall into the box. It was ingenious. The girl was carefully selected from the audience by Alfonso to ensure the correct size and shape, and when her weight was introduced to the casket it was enough to cause the device to begin rolling down an incline beneath the stage, on rails or metal castors. The girl was trapped, of course, but her cries would be muffled by the shouts of the audience, and soon the rags soaked in chloroform would be enough to sedate her, putting her to sleep for – potentially – a number of hours. Until, Veronica supposed, either Alfonso or some secret aide could collect her from the casket and rouse her, or worse. The girls who were set free would be so confused by the drug that they would never be able to accurately recall what had happened to them, and their theatre-going companions would undoubtedly coax them into forgetting the matter, with talk of their bravery and the mysterious nature of their disappearance. The woman would briefly become the talk of her social circle, and for that alone, she would make a point of dismissing any temporary discomfort she may have suffered. After all, she had come to no discernible harm.

That wasn't the case, of course, for all of the girls. Veronica still had no notion of what fate Alfonso had in store for those young women he decided not to set free. Perhaps this room would reveal the truth.

Shakily, Veronica climbed to her feet and approached the workbench, resting her palms upon it whilst she waited for a momentary spell of dizziness to pass. Clearly, because there was no show that evening, there had been no one waiting to receive Veronica upon her impromptu arrival in the room. She wondered what had become of Alfonso. The man had had every opportunity to finish her off whilst she lay there drugged and incapacitated. Perhaps he had lost his nerve, or else he had assumed the chloroform would keep her sedated for longer and was busy elsewhere in the building. Whatever the case, she was grateful to be alive.

She glanced down at the workbench. It was littered with bizarre paraphernalia. Large sheaves of paper, covered in an elaborate scrawl she did not recognise; vials full of a thin brown fluid, stoppered with bulbous corks; medical equipment; scalpels; a pair of tan-coloured, elbow-length leather gloves; pencils, and an assortment of small, Ancient Egyptian artefacts. She gasped in surprise. *Ancient Egyptian.* She swept up one of a number of little statuettes. It was an effigy of a mummified Pharaoh, made of clay and impressed with three neat rows of hieratic script, of which she had no understanding. It was certainly original, of that much she was sure. She dropped it to the table. Nearby, another, similar statuette had been broken in half. She leaned closer. The two pieces lay side by side, and it was clear that the idol had once been hollow. She supposed that whoever had broken the ancient artefact had removed something from inside.

"My goodness," she whispered under her breath, realisation dawning on her. She was certain this could be no coincidence. This had to have something to do with Sir Maurice's investigation of the murder of Lord Winthrop. Did Alfonso have a hand in that, too?

She edged around the table, studying the other artefacts on the workbench. There were a number of similar ushabti figures, each of them broken, their hidden contents now removed. Someone – Alfonso, she presumed – had been conducting a detailed study of the objects, for many of the papers contained scrawling that deciphered the inscriptions, as well as strange mathematical drawings: stars within circles and other pictograms that reminded her of the contents of Sir Maurice's Chelsea library. She drew a deep breath and wiped her brow. She shook her head, trying to clear the drug-induced fug. It occurred to her, then, belatedly, to check for any escape routes from the room, any means by which she could quit the theatre and get away. She needed to find Sir Maurice.

She glanced around. Her vision was still hazy. Across from her, on the other side of the room, was a door. She began edging around the table towards it, and then stopped in horror. There, in the corner, a few feet to the left of the door, was one of the most ghastly sights she had ever encountered: a pile of female corpses, cast against the wall and left to rot.

The women had been piled up haphazardly like discarded marionettes. Flies buzzed chaotically around their slack-jawed faces. Veronica felt bile rising in her gullet. There were five, perhaps six corpses. She'd had no idea the situation was this severe. Only two women had been reported missing in the area, to date, but Alfonso had clearly been much busier down here in his secret slaughterhouse. She was appalled by the sheer magnitude of his perversion. What had he done to the women? How could he continue to work down here with their dead, unseeing eyes fixed on his every movement? And the smell!

Veronica fished around in her jacket pocket for a handkerchief. Finding one, she held it over her mouth and nose, and hesitantly stepped towards the sickening heap of bodies. She could not believe the lack of respect with which the women had been treated, even in death. They remained fully clothed, at least, although whatever *had* been done to them had clearly been appalling. What she could see of their faces showed the frigid signs of terror. These women had stared death directly in the face.

Veronica crouched low beside the nearest corpse. The girl was young – twenty, possibly – with pretty long curls of strawberry blonde, and full, pink lips. Her eyes had once been blue, but were now a grotesque shade of milky grey. She was on her front, partially buried beneath the corpse of an older, brunette woman. One of her arms was dangling free. Veronica grimaced as she turned the head slowly from side to side. A line of dry, dark blood ran from the girl's forehead down the side of her nose. Veronica followed the line of this bloody trail, finding, with dismay, the origin was a small hole that had been burrowed in the girl's forehead. Flinching, she probed it with the end of her finger. It was about the size of a pen nib and was located at the very centre of the woman's forehead. Veronica frowned, checking another of the girls. The marking was exactly the same. A neat bore-hole drilled for an unknown purpose, directly through the bone and deep into the skull cavity itself. Clearly, Alfonso had been intent on extracting something from inside the women's heads.

Veronica moved around the pile of corpses. She was glad that the heady scent of the chloroform was still affecting her sense of smell. Some of the bodies were days old – weeks, possibly – and had begun to decompose. Their waxen flesh had become bloated and saggy, their eyes putrefying in their open, staring sockets. Their terrified, bloodied faces were an alarming juxtaposition against the gaudiness of their colourful evening clothes. Veronica felt an intense burst of sadness for these young women, for how their lives had been so drastically shortened, snuffed out in such a foul manner. She felt anger, too, anger and a need for retribution. She had to stop this. She had to stop it before one more girl fell into the clutches of this terrible man. She knew, now, that the image of these dead girls would be forever burned into her memory, their silent mouths crying out for justice. She knew also of her own predicament, and the fact that – still dazed from the chloroform – she remained in terrible danger. Nevertheless, she felt a need to understand why: the meaning behind the shocking death of these women.

Veronica examined another of the bore-holes, this time in the skull of a brunette. What was their purpose? There was clearly nothing sexual about the deaths; the manner in which the women had been discarded, carelessly, suggested that Alfonso was in no way objectifying the girls. He didn't appear to *desire* their deaths, to treat them with any reverence or passion. No, it was as if he considered them as animals, there to be experimented upon in his laboratory. The bodies were purely carcasses, immaterial, and he had left them there to rot whilst he went about his business, having extracted whatever it was he needed from inside their heads. Veronica knew she risked jumping to conclusions, but she was convinced her reading of the situation was accurate. She'd learned a lot of Newbury's methods in the last few months; now, finally, she had an opportunity to apply them.

Standing, Veronica strode across the room to where the bizarre chair-like device stood against the wall. She needed to focus on something else, to blot out the horror of the dead girls. She fought another wave of dizziness, holding on to the edge of the workbench for support. *The chair.* She needed to concentrate.

The chair was an odd contraption. Its frame was wooden and roughly hewn, with locking iron bands where a person's wrists and ankles could be fixed. Likewise, an adjustable band was attached to the backrest, perfectly placed for clasping a person's head. At the centre of this band was a small opening, and Veronica realised with a shudder that this was the guide mark through which the holes were bored into the women's skulls. Rust-coloured stains around its edges confirmed that blood had been spilled on the metalwork.

Above the chair, rising from the back of it, was a large, multi-jointed brass arm, which curved up and over the seat like a scorpion's tail, terminating in a fine drill bit. It gleamed in the low light of the gas jets. The mechanism had two handles: rods with rubber grips, attached part way along its length, so that a person standing before the chair could easily manipulate the direction of the drill bit, moving it back and forth and adjusting the height and alignment. The drill itself appeared to be powered pneumatically; cables stretched from the drill housing along the length of the brass arm, disappearing around the back of the machine, where they snaked towards a large, grey cylinder of compressed air. Beside this, a glass bell sat atop a chamber containing two brass pistons, which were currently at rest. Tubing curled from two bungs at the top of this glass dome, connecting with two further, smaller mechanical arms, one holding a long-bladed scalpel, the other some bizarre kind of suction device.

It was a terrifying machine. It looked to Veronica like an engine designed solely for the torture of others, but she knew it had to have an even more sinister purpose.

Beside the chair was a low wooden trolley which held a number of metal trays. One of these was covered in a scattered array of glass syringes, another with a series of small vials, each of them filled with the same brown fluid she had seen earlier, in the vials on the workbench. She realised that this liquid – whatever it was – had to be the end product of whatever terrible process Alfonso was conducting down there beneath the theatre: the reason for the entire set up. Some chemical or substance extracted from within the skulls of the dead girls. Veronica felt sick to her stomach. She found it hard to reconcile the understanding she had developed of Alfonso's character with the concept of this monstrous laboratory. Yes, he was a thuggish brute, and egotistical too, but this? Did he really have the gumption and the knowledge to pull off an operation such as this? And what of the links to Lord Winthrop and the Ancient Egyptian artefacts? Surely Sir Maurice would have made the connection by now if it were obvious. She glanced once again around the room. No, this was the work of a scientist, not an illusionist. For the first time she considered the fact that Alfonso may have only been part of the story. Perhaps he was working with an accomplice. Perhaps –

There was a sharp pain at the back of her skull as she was coshed, definitively, from behind. Instantly she crumpled to the floor, the metallic taste of fear on her tongue, and once again she slipped away into darkness.

Chapter Eighteen

Newbury ached with every fibre of his being. He'd taken a number of serious knocks during his pursuit of Ashford, particularly when he'd driven the tricycle down the stairwell to the Underground station, and he knew he was lucky to be alive. His knuckles were bleeding and he had a painful red burn on his left forearm, where a hot coal from the tricycle wreckage had scorched his flesh during the crash. He suspected other minor injuries, too, but he wouldn't have time to examine himself in the cheval glass for some hours.

And yet, for all that, he had failed to capture Ashford once again. He lambasted himself for the fact that the chase had resulted in nothing substantial. He supposed he was able to take some solace from the fact that he now had a better understanding of the man, even if it had left him feeling more confused than ever. The certainty he had felt earlier, the sinister character of Ashford that he had constructed in his mind, all of that had now dispersed, become disassociated with reality. Now, they were playing a different game altogether, and Ashford had shown his hand. Firstly, the rogue agent had refused to strike him during their battle on the tracks; aware, perhaps, of his own incredible strength, he had refused to risk Newbury's life with a direct blow. Secondly, at great risk to himself, he had thrown Newbury out of the path of the moving train. If it were not for that, Newbury would certainly be dead. It seemed to the Crown detective that Bainbridge had been right all along; that Ashford was not the killer that Newbury had earlier presumed him to be. He had much to consider.

"Help me up there, lad." Newbury smiled gratefully as Purefoy offered his arm, enabling him to heave himself to his feet. His back creaked. He straightened up, groaning at his protesting muscles. "What kept you?" he said, grinning.

Purefoy was still trying to catch his breath. He shook his head at the other man's jibe. "I understand now, Sir Maurice, a little more of what you intimated at Lord Winthrop's house."

Newbury gave a curt nod. "Indeed." He brushed his unruly hair back from his face. "And I believe, Purefoy, that you could be a great deal of help in bringing this situation to a happy conclusion. Can I count on you?"

Purefoy's lips curled in a wry smile. "Absolutely."

Newbury glanced along the platform at the gathered crowd of people. Passengers were now disembarking from the stationary train, which was sighing loudly at the platform. The driver had climbed down from the engine and was on the tracks, examining the scorch marks on the tunnel wall, where Ashford's brass skeleton had been dragged across the tiles. He looked confused and not a little shaken by his experience. He couldn't seem to understand why there was no sign of a body on the rails.

Newbury knew that he needed to lose himself in the crowds, before people began to identify him to the authorities and it became too difficult to fade out of sight. He didn't have the time nor the inclination to answer the raft of irrelevant questions that would be put to him before he was able to prove his identity or call in the aid of Sir Charles. He clasped the reporter on the shoulder. "Right, Purefoy. Let's get out of here."

They set off, forcing their way through the press of people. Newbury had a determined look on his face as he tried to ignore the flashes of pain from his sore limbs.

Mounting the stairs, they soon found their way out of the Underground station, passing the wreckage of the tricycle, which was now swarming with police constables and transport officials in neat, black suits. They were holding back the crowd of onlookers who had gathered around the wreckage, and talking to witnesses in hushed tones. Newbury recognised the woman who had helped him to his feet after the crash, and turned away, surreptitiously shielding his face from view.

Above the station, the street was dark and foreboding. Shapes hulked in the thick miasma, causing them to take on new roles; an avenue of trees became a row of forlorn soldiers standing to attention; a solitary flower-seller became an ethereal ghost, haunting the abandoned streets in search of fellow spirits. Newbury drew his jacket closer around himself, coughing a little on the syrupy vapour. He turned to the young reporter, who was loitering anxiously beside him, awaiting instruction. "Purefoy. I need you to fetch the police. Go directly to Scotland Yard and tell them that Sir Maurice Newbury has sent you to speak with Sir Charles Bainbridge. Charles is a good man. Fill him in. Give him all the details of what has occurred here this evening, and then have him send his men round to Arbury House. They need to secure Blake's apartment."

Purefoy smiled. "Of course." He hesitated for a moment. "Surely you're not going after Ashford again?"

Newbury grinned. He took his pocket watch from his jacket pocket and held it for a moment in the palm of his hand, studying the elaborate face. It was approaching seven o'clock. "Me? No, I have an appointment with a beautiful young woman."

Purefoy laughed. "Then may I suggest, Sir Maurice, that you first of all find an opportunity to change your attire."

Newbury glanced down to see that his suit was now torn and filthy, spattered with mud, grit and oil. His green eyes twinkled. "I think, my young friend, you make an excellent point."

†

Purefoy's advice, however, whilst perceptive, proved not to be timely. Newbury knew that if he were to take a cab to Chelsea he would miss his appointment at Kensington with Miss Hobbes. He was not prepared to leave her waiting for him once again. So instead, bedraggled as he was, Newbury had seen Purefoy into a cab, before hailing his own hansom and instructing the driver to ferry him directly to Miss Hobbes's apartments. She'd seen him in worse states than this, after all.

The hansom clattered on through the effluvium-laden streets towards Kensington. The fog had descended swiftly, and looked set to entrench. Newbury watched through the window as figures flitted past, ghostly shapes in the hazy yellow-grey, like spirits attempting to escape the miasma of the afterlife. Every building, every corner, the mouth of every alleyway; suddenly, in the sickly whitewash, they became the haunt of otherworldly things. Newbury imagined shapes in the fog, just as he had since he'd been a boy. Only these were no longer the lucid imaginings of a child. Newbury knew that out there, in the pale darkness, there were real monsters, both human and otherwise. He had the scars to prove it.

Newbury sighed, and leaned back against the soft leather of the seat. He hoped the fog would lift. If not, he was sure that Mrs. Bradshaw's respiratory condition would return. It had affected her badly throughout the winter months, and he was concerned for her wellbeing. Besides, he knew he couldn't live without the woman. She was a miracle. Unfazed, undaunted, she catered to his every whim. And she approved of Miss Hobbes. She hadn't stated it explicitly, but her affection for Veronica was clear for all to see. If nothing else, it gave Newbury hope for the future.

Newbury glanced again at his pocket watch. It was now ten past the hour. He imagined Veronica in her Kensington rooms, sat before the fire, awaiting his arrival. He suspected that, even now, she would be cursing him, in her own gentle way, for his tardiness. He would attend to her directly, and hoped to take a moment to relax a little before going on. He needed a brandy. He needed *more* than a brandy, but for now, a dose of alcohol would help to quell his burning desire for the poppy.

Tonight, he would give himself over to his assistant, enjoy the pleasure of her company and attend to the details of her own case, regarding the missing girls and the magician. After a drink and a wash, they would repair to another carriage, take the short journey to his Chelsea lodgings – where he would change into his evening wear – and together they would enjoy a fine meal at a restaurant on the Strand. He needed that.

Newbury's mind was still a whirlwind, as he considered the Ashford affair. He didn't fancy Purefoy for the crimes, and was now more resolute than ever that he should take the young man under his wing. He'd arranged to call for the reporter in the morning, with Miss Hobbes in tow. In the meantime, Newbury hoped that Charles wasn't being too hard on the young man.

He must have dozed off in the back of the cab, for what seemed like only a moment later, he was awoken by the brisk knock of the driver on the roof of the cab. He rubbed blearily at his eyes and sat forward, glancing out of the window. The hansom had come to rest outside Miss Hobbes's apartment. Newbury clambered out of the cab, paid the driver, and realised for the first time that he must have lost his hat somewhere during the excitement of the afternoon. Shrugging, he followed the path to the house and rapped loudly three times on Veronica's front door. Moments later he heard footsteps creaking on the loose floorboards of the hall. The door creaked open, enough for the slightest sliver of light, and the eye of Mrs. Grant, Veronica's housekeeper, appeared in the opening. It took a moment for her to recognise Newbury in such a dishevelled state. When she did, the door was flung open widely and she was ushering him in, offering him platitudes.

"Oh my poor dear. Come on in. You look like you could use a pot of that Earl Grey you're always asking for. I keep some out the back for when you call."

Newbury smiled. Mrs. Grant was typically the most stoic of housekeepers, rarely finding the occasion to even smile or raise her eyes to greet Miss Hobbes's visitors. Something about the state of his apparel that evening had moved her, however. Either that, or there was already something more significant amiss. He smiled warmly. "Now, Mrs. Grant, fear not. I am quite well, really. But I *am* running rather late for an appointment with Miss Hobbes, who I gather had plans to meet me here this evening. Will I find her in the sitting room?"

Mrs. Grant frowned. She placed her hands on her hips, shaking her head in an exaggerated fashion. "Indeed not, Sir Maurice. Indeed not. Miss Hobbes has yet to return from the museum. I had hoped, upon seeing you, that you would be in a position to put my mind at rest regarding her good health." She looked him up and down once again. "I expected her over two hours ago, but I fear there has been no word."

Newbury nodded, thoughtful. "Hmmm. Well, I should not presume to fear too heartily, Mrs. Grant. It's not a long time to be missing. Perhaps she has simply been delayed in this dastardly weather."

Mrs. Grant did not appear to be pacified by this remark. She nodded, but it was clear she was not persuaded. "I take it you plan to wait for Miss Hobbes, in that case, Sir Maurice?" She looked hopeful. He nodded absently, and then followed her into the sitting room, where she bid him to take a seat. "I'll just go and pop that kettle on the stove." She disappeared through a side door to the kitchen.

Newbury paced the room. What had become of Veronica? He recalled their conversation of earlier that day, during which she had informed him of her intention to visit the family of the most recent missing girl. But that had been hours ago. Surely, she must have returned to the office at the museum following her interview? He frowned. He feared he knew all too well what may have become of his assistant. Whilst he had appealed to her sense of duty and asked for her commitment that she would not venture to the Archibald Theatre alone to confront Alfonso, he had every suspicion that she had done exactly that. Whilst he was occupied chasing Ashford across the rooftops of Regent's Park, Veronica had most likely taken matters into her own hands. Why else would she not be here to meet with him? Newbury knew she had been waiting to speak with him regarding the matter, and she would not have been late for some trivial reason. Indeed, more likely she would have sent word ahead if she had found herself delayed.

Perhaps his night of relaxation would have to wait. He quit the sitting room, walked the length of the hallway until he reached a door that he presumed led to the kitchen, and then called for Mrs. Grant. After a minute, she appeared at the door, looking a little perplexed.

"The tea will be with you presently, sir."

"Ah, no, thank you, Mrs. Grant. I have a sudden notion of where I might find Miss Hobbes." The housekeeper's face lit up. "If I dare put a stop to your tea-making, I'll take my leave, see if I can't track her down and put your mind at rest."

Mrs. Grant smiled gratefully. "Thank you, sir."

Newbury bid her good evening, leaving instruction that, should Miss Hobbes return home in his absence, he would call for her the following morning at the office. Then, buttoning the front of his mud-streaked jacket, he left the house and went in search of transportation to Soho and the Archibald Theatre, where he hoped that Miss Hobbes had not put herself unduly in the path of danger.

†

The theatre was shrouded in darkness when Newbury hopped down from the cab a short while later. Upon seeing the bills pasted in the windows, announcing that the show had been cancelled, Newbury almost stopped the cab driver as he trundled off down the road, thinking that perhaps his intuition had been proved wrong on this occasion. Then, knowing that he would be unable to rest without first establishing Miss Hobbes's safety, he decided to investigate further. A cancelled show would not have been enough to halt his headstrong assistant.

He tried a door and found it locked. Then, upon trying another, he was surprised to find it open. Evidently someone had been neglectful of their duties, or else the theatre was indeed inhabited that evening. Newbury crossed the large foyer in the dark, looking for signs that Veronica may have passed that way. There was nothing. The place was deserted.

Mounting a short flight of steps, Newbury pushed aside the curtain and entered the auditorium proper. Here, things were very different indeed. The only light was coming from a bright electric lamp on the stage, illuminating a grisly diorama, of a type that, unfortunately, he was finding himself growing increasingly accustomed to. The body of a man – Alfonso, no less – was spread-eagled on the stage, one of his own sabres protruding rudely from his chest. Beside him, a small round table had been overturned, spilling its contents, and a top hat lay discarded nearby. Surrounding the body was all the assorted paraphernalia of the show, most of it undisturbed. He had no idea what had occurred here, but he sincerely doubted Veronica could be responsible for such a brutal act. As passionate as she was about discovering what had happened to the missing girls, she would never lower herself to this. If she had come here, it would have been to apprehend the man, not to murder him in cold blood.

Hesitantly, taking care to ensure there was no one watching from the shadows, Newbury passed down the long flight of wooden steps between two rows of seats and made his way slowly towards the stage. He hopped up and crossed to where the body lay waiting. It was an appalling scene. The man's face was struck with terror, frozen in the throes of death. He looked battered and bruised, as if he'd put up some resistance. There was little blood, but Newbury assumed the blade had struck right through the man's chest, piercing his back, so that the blood would have seeped out beneath him, probably dripping through the cracks between the floorboards. He tested the hilt of the weapon. It was stuck fast. Alfonso had been run through with such vehemence that the tip of the sword was buried deep in the wooden stage below. It was clearly a sadistic death, executed with great pomp. It was as if the theatrical nature of the setting had informed the manner of the death; the body had been left here on display, for show. Nevertheless, there was reason behind it, too. Whoever had done this had been anxious to ensure the magician would not be getting up again.

Newbury glanced around, squinting in the harsh electric glare of the stage lamp. It was clear there had been a scuffle of some kind, from the way the table had been overturned, but it didn't look as if Alfonso had been given much opportunity to defend himself. Newbury noted with interest that a small hatch lay open on the stage, just near to where the table now rested. He moved closer to take a look.

Two hinged flaps had dropped aside, giving way to a fair drop. He looked around for any trigger that may have caused the hatch to spring open. Perhaps the body was resting upon a pressure plate of some kind? He peered into the opening. There was clearly a large space beneath the stage, which he realised had been purposefully built to accommodate it. It occurred to him, with a grim smile, that this was how the magician had effected the disappearing act. Bizarrely, in death, Alfonso was finally giving away his secrets. If Veronica had seen this, then perhaps she had followed the mechanism underground. That would be as good a place as any to make a start.

Intrigued, and not a little disturbed by the sight of yet another body, Newbury set out to search for his wayward assistant.

Chapter Nineteen

When Veronica came round again, she felt sick with dizziness. The pain at the back of her head was like a hot lance inside her skull. She groaned and tried to move, realising with horror that her ankles and wrists had been bound. She opened her eyes and blinked, blearily as they adjusted once again to the dim light. She was slumped with her back to the wall, facing the door and the pile of corpses across the other side of the room. A figure was standing by the central table, hurriedly collecting up the scattered ephemera that lay upon it and throwing it untidily into a medicine bag. The man had his back to her. He was dressed in an immaculate grey suit with a crisp white collar. His hair was well kept and was beginning to turn a startling silver-grey, still spotted with freckles of light brown. He was tall and thin, just a little less than six feet.

The man turned to face her when he heard her shuffling. He had a handsome face with an aquiline nose, although it was marred by a deep, puckered scar that ran from his forehead, just above the left eyebrow, down across his left cheek, blighting his eye. The eye was milky and blind, the colour of London fog, although a series of tiny red lights around the cornea suggested the work of a master craftsman: the restoration work of Dr. Fabian, or one of his protégés. Otherwise, his skin was pale and unblemished, like a white mask. His fingers were long and bony. Veronica realised with shock that she recognised the man.

"Aubrey Knox," she croaked.

The man smiled almost imperceptibly. "That's *Doctor* Aubrey Knox to you, Miss Hobbes." His voice was like silk; smooth and warm and full of grace. He was impeccably well spoken, and every word had the ring of perfection. She knew he was an Eton man, and had once been the most charming of gentlemen. He clearly retained this affectation.

Veronica tried to sit up, but her bonds prevented her from gaining purchase on the tiles. She glowered at the villain who had trussed her up in such a manner. "So it was you. All along, it was you." Knox inclined his head in acknowledgement, a smile curling his lips. Veronica glanced at the pile of bodies in the corner. How cold must he be, how dead inside, that he could continue to work in the same room, even stand there smiling, now, all the while aware that he was responsible for those women's deaths? She could find no empathy for the man, no understanding of what might have driven him to this terrible series of acts.

She met his gaze. He appeared to be watching her with amusement. "What do you need them for? What is it you're trying to do?"

Knox's face changed, his mood darkening. He crossed the room to where she was bound and raised his arm, slapping her hard across the face with the back of his hand. Despite herself, Veronica cried out. She could feel tears welling in her eyes, and her cheek smarted painfully. She forced herself to look him in the eye, her expression defiant.

"Miss Hobbes, I'd have thought you'd know better than that. This is not some ridiculous penny dreadful that we're playing out. I'm not about to reveal all of my carefully laid plans to you, now that you're finally here and close to death. Suffice to say, that you will exit this world as ignorant as you are now, and I shall take some measure of satisfaction in that." Grinning, he turned, crossed the room to the long table and continued silently with his work. Watching him, Veronica realised that he was not indiscriminately taking everything from the workbench as she had at first assumed, but rather a selection of choice items, including the little vials of brown fluid and the ancient scrolls of papyrus.

Veronica bit her lower lip, searching for a reserve of strength. She twisted her wrists, trying to wriggle free, but the binds had been expertly tied. Likewise her ankles. She was deeply afraid of what the renegade doctor might do to her. It was unlikely, from what she knew of the man, that he would grant her a clean and simple death. She doubted that would be enough of an amusement for him.

Veronica had been warned about Knox, of course, in her briefings about Newbury, when Her Majesty and her closest aides had been at pain to describe the horrors that the man had committed in the name of progress, and their need to ensure that Newbury did not follow a similar path. Knox had become obsessed with the occult and a desire to achieve extended life, and he pursued the cause with little concern for morality or human suffering. He saw himself as a progressive, the man who would finally learn to wed science with the arcane. That path had led him away from the Empire, and despite the best efforts of Her Majesty and her extended network of agents, he had not been seen for over two years. He was a danger – yes – but he was also an embarrassment, a worm that had turned, a betrayer, deep in the bosom of the Empire. Victoria wished to make an example of him.

Veronica watched him warily. Knox had almost finished gathering up the scattered artefacts and papers into his bag. He glanced over his shoulder at Veronica, a wry smile on the curve of his lips. "So, tell me of Sir Maurice. I understand he's quite the dashing man about town?" Veronica remained silent. Knox laughed. "I understand also that his taste for narcotics is dwarfed only by his taste for occult literature. I should dearly like to meet the fellow." This was a taste of the charming Knox again, the gentleman. Veronica understood that he lived by a code. But unlike Newbury it was a code of his own devising, and not one instilled by an innate sense of right and wrong. It was a code driven by insanity and a desire for self-perpetuation. Watching him now, Veronica could hardly believe the stunning outburst of violence he had demonstrated just a short while before. Her cheek, however, was a stinging reminder. She glared at him.

"Sir Maurice is twice the man you ever were, and twice the agent too."

Knox laughed. "What loyalty the man inspires! How interesting. One imagines he keeps you by his side like a pet dog, there to compliment his ego with doe-eyed looks and pretty frocks. Personally, I imagine you to be far prettier on the inside." He paused. "I should enjoy examining your brain." Knox moved around the table to place his medicine bag by the door. "I'm sure it would pain Sir Maurice terribly to know of your current predicament, my dear Miss Hobbes. Indeed, if I had more time, perhaps I could have made more of the circumstances. A shame." He gave a small, polite cough into his fist. "I must admit that, in the end, I'm disappointed, Miss Hobbes. I'd heard great tales of your derring-do, of your fiery passion. I'd been led to believe that you were perhaps even a worthy opponent. Regrettably, I find you full of righteous indignation. You are nothing but another insipid young woman, a prim and proper society girl, who finds herself afraid and out of her depth. What has become of the young woman who aided in the retrieval of the Persian Teardrop from Milan? Who brought an end to the killing spree of the Liverpool Witch? Pushing papers behind a desk in a museum? What would your sister Amelia say of your decline?" He shook his head. "Victoria used to know better."

Veronica attempted to lurch forward, but succeeded only in toppling onto her side, prone on the floor. "Do not speak of my sister." The words were weighted with vehemence.

Knox was laughing now. "Idle threats, Miss Hobbes. Idle threats. It surprises me that Amelia did not find it appropriate to warn you of this little encounter. Does she not speak to you of the future?"

Veronica's eyes widened. How did this man, this terrible man, know so much about her and her sister? She watched him as he crossed the room, collecting the elbow-length leather gloves from where they rested on the workbench. His eyes flashed, and Veronica knew that her time was almost up. With all her might she struggled against the bonds that held her. But she knew it was useless. Knox had her now, and before long, she would be consigned to the sorry heap in the corner with the other dead girls. She wondered whether she, too, would have a small hole burrowed through the centre of her forehead. The thought made her shudder. She was close to panic, her soundless lips frozen wide with fear.

Knox pulled one of the gloves over his wrist and wriggled his fingers dramatically. Just as he was about to follow suit with the other hand, there was a loud crash from somewhere above them.

Knox looked up, as if he somehow expected to be able to see through the ceiling to whatever it was that had made the noise above. Veronica assumed it must have been Alfonso, treading on the creaking boards of the stage. Knox, however, became suddenly flustered. He peeled the glove from his fingers and threw it instead on the table, a frustrated look on his face. There was another bang and a muffled shout. Veronica was unable to identify the words, or the voice. But something about the situation had startled Knox. His plans had changed.

Knox snatched up a dirty rag from amongst his belongings and approached her. His expression remained fixed. He intended to gag her. Veronica forced her jaw shut and turned her head away from him. But to Knox, evidently an old hand, it was a matter of moments before he was able to force his fingers roughly inside her cheeks and prise her mouth open long enough to shove the rag inside. She did her best to spit it out, to push it out with her tongue, but it was no use. She choked back on its oily, dirty fibres.

Knox offered her one last, sneering look, his milky-grey eye flicking over her face, then turned and stepped through the door, disappearing into the passageway beyond.

Chapter Twenty

Newbury dropped to one knee, running his hands around the edges of the open hatch in the stage. It was dark below, and there were no moveable lamps with which he could examine the trapdoor more closely. Nevertheless, he could see inside that the drop was around eight feet deep, and terminated in two metal runners that appeared to slope away to the right, dipping under the stage to disappear further underground. Clearly, during the disappearing act, Alfonso would position the girl over the hatch and then foot the paddle, dropping her swiftly into the hole beneath. Newbury guessed the victim would land in some kind of padded cart or box, which would then roll away on the tracks beneath, depositing the girl somewhere else in the building.

It was ingenious – a masterpiece of engineering – and having seen the illusion performed first-hand, Newbury knew just how effective it appeared to the onlooker. He rubbed a hand thoughtfully over his chin. The strange thing was that the trap had been triggered at all. The weight of Alfonso's body had opened the hatch – clearly – but what intrigued Newbury was the fact that the cart itself was missing from beneath the stage. The mechanism had been used, but had not yet been reset. A body had been dropped into the missing cart. It could, of course, have been a simple case of tardiness, but in the back of his mind, Newbury feared that if Veronica had come to this dismal place, she may have discovered first-hand exactly how the girls were being whisked away.

Newbury paused, suddenly alert. Somewhere in the shadows, off to the other side of the stage, he thought he had heard a footstep. He waited.

Nothing.

He got to his feet. There! Not a footstep, but something else. The rasping sound of a sword being drawn carefully from a scabbard. Newbury felt himself stiffen. There was someone there, watching him, in the shadows. Someone bearing a weapon. He looked around for something he could use to defend himself. The rack of Alfonso's swords was off to one side, near to the source of the sound. There was the blade sticking out of the magician's rigid corpse, but Newbury knew that it would take him a moment to tug it free, and in doing so he would alert whoever was lurking in the shadows to the fact that he was aware of their presence. That could leave him dangerously exposed. He considered jumping into the hatch, but with the mechanism already triggered he did not know what to expect at the other end, and did not want to find himself trapped in an underground shaft with no means of escape. His options were limited. Reluctantly, he decided to call his opponent out. Unarmed, it was a dangerous course of action, but nevertheless, he wanted whoever it was lurking off stage in plain view.

"If you're going to remain there in the shadows, I'll feel compelled to carry on with my investigation. I don't have time to stand around waiting for you." His voice echoed out around the empty auditorium. He heard a man chuckling in the darkness. And then a figure emerged, drifting out of the shadows like a ghost suddenly adopting corporeal form. The man strolled boldly forward, his sword held, unusually, in his left hand. The blade glinted in the harsh electric light.

"Bravo! Bravo! I admire your panache." The man stopped as he entered the circle of light thrown down by the electric lamp. "So, you're Newbury. How I've wanted to meet my successor."

Newbury blanched. His successor? Then this was the much-maligned Dr. Aubrey Knox. How did he fit into the picture? Was he the one behind the missing girls? And what else? It seemed too significant a coincidence that both he and Ashford should surface in London at the same time. There had to be a connection. Perhaps Ashford really was looking for revenge. Perhaps that's why he was here, after all this time. But now was not the time to ponder on it. Newbury met his opponent's gaze. "Dr. Aubrey Knox. I can't say it's a pleasure to make your acquaintance."

Knox laughed. "We're not so different, you and I. Not so different at all. You shouldn't listen to everything that others tell you, Newbury. Perhaps it is only your misguided sense of duty that sets us apart."

Newbury shook his head. "No, we are not alike. I am nothing like you at all." He was curious to see how the situation would play out. He knew very little of his predecessor, little more than he'd learned in the last few days. He wondered if the man would live up to his fearsome reputation.

Knox came forward, further into the light. "You sound like Charles. How is the old boy?"

Newbury glanced across the stage at the rack of swords. His response was terse. "Well enough."

Knox grinned. "Yes, I always thought the job would wear him down. Still, I suspect he'll hold on until the bitter end. Wouldn't be like Charles to throw in the towel." He paused, smiling. "Oh, and Miss Hobbes sends her regards."

Newbury's curiosity about the man ignited into rage. Knox was taunting him. He clearly knew what had become of Veronica; more than likely had a hand in it, also. Newbury sprang into action. He rushed forward, catching Knox off guard so that he could batter the other man's sword arm easily to one side and bring his elbow up sharply into the pale man's face. Carrying forward with his momentum whilst Knox was dazed, Newbury darted towards the rack of swords, grasped one by the hilt and swept it out from its wooden notch. He spun around, presenting the point of the weapon to Knox.

There was little more than three feet between them. Knox allowed his sword arm to idle casually by his side. He was laughing, spitting blood. "So, perhaps she *is* more than a pet, after all."

Newbury decided that enough was enough. He could not allow this man to slight Veronica in such a manner. He would wound him, force him to reveal what he had done with Veronica, and then take him in. Or, if it came to it, he would run him through. He lurched forward, the point of his sabre singing out towards the other man's breast.

Knox moved like lightning. One minute, he was standing nonchalantly eyeing Newbury, jesting with him; the next his arm had flashed up in a blindingly quick parry, and he was facing the Crown detective, his wiry body poised, ready for the interplay of the two weapons. He was still laughing as Newbury thrust again, and once more was parried. Newbury had fenced in his youth, but Knox, it seemed, was an expert. He sent Newbury's thrusts wide each time, with only the smallest flick of his wrist. He barely seemed to draw breath whilst doing so. Newbury recognised the tactic. Knox was attempting to tire him out. He could not let that happen. Ceasing his series of ineffectual thrusts, he drew back, his sword at the ready.

"Oh, come, come, Sir Maurice. Haven't you the stomach for a good fight? I was quite enjoying our little tête-à-tête." He shifted again, reaching forward with his blade, his foot stamping the floor as he threw his weight behind the movement. Newbury felt a flash of pain on his right cheek. Knox recovered his poise, and Newbury realised that blood was flowing freely from a cut on his face. He hadn't even had chance to react. He was clearly outclassed.

Knox smiled. He had a superior air about him, as if he were enjoying the encounter, knowing full well that of the two men, he currently had the upper hand. When he spoke it was almost genial, as if he and Newbury were nothing but two old acquaintances, sharing a conversation at a gentlemen's club. "Fight me, Newbury! I can see the fire behind your eyes. You want to know what I've done with her, don't you?"

Newbury, composing himself, rocked forward onto the balls of his feet. He kept his blade low, ready, waiting. He would not rise to the other man's taunts. "Tell me where she is, Knox, and I shall let you live." His voice was a low growl.

"Hmmm. Quite a dilemma. I didn't have you down as the sort of chap to make idle threats, Newbury. That's a crashing disappointment." He was sneering now, his words dripping with sarcasm. Newbury hoped he was coming to the end of his game. If Knox had no time for idle threats, Newbury had no time for cat and mouse. He may not have been able to demonstrate such finesse with a blade, but what he lacked in theatrics, he gained in brute force and spirit.

"There is nothing idle about the threat, Knox."

Knox whipped out his blade, aiming high, but Newbury caught it easily, their swords ringing out as they clattered, tick, tick, tick, whilst the two men thrust and parried frenetically. Searching for a means to gain the upper hand, Newbury eyed the stage behind the doctor. The hatch was still open. If he could manoeuvre the fight just a few feet closer towards that narrow opening, he reasoned he'd be able to send Knox crashing backwards into it. The difficulty came in circumnavigating the body of Alfonso, spread-eagled on the boards between the two fighting men and the hole.

Newbury met Knox's gaze as their swords crossed, staring deep into the other man's eyes. He repressed a shudder. The man was cold and seemed to extract a discernible relish from the thrill of the fight, from the danger. Newbury recognised himself in that, and it repulsed him. It was like looking into a mirror and seeing his twisted reflection glare back at him, all sense of his humanity removed. He understood Charles's words, now, and they angered him. His path was not pre-determined. He would not allow himself to become a monster like the odious wretch he now faced. Newbury knew not to cross the line. Knox appeared to relish the opportunity to do so.

Knox's left eye twinkled, and Newbury watched the tiny red pinpricks of light describe a circle, as whatever device had been buried inside the blinded organ turned, tightening Knox's focus. Such stunning artifice could only be the work of one man: Dr. Lucius Fabian.

The two men broke apart, dancing, carefully, around the corpse of the dead magician. Newbury made a concerted effort to drive the other man back. Knox stepped backwards over Alfonso's legs, placing the body between them. Their swords hovered above the unseeing corpse. "So, what of your accomplice, Knox? Did he offend you in some way?" Newbury glanced briefly at the dead man.

Knox shrugged. "He'd outlived his usefulness. Besides, he was always a conniving toad."

"But he sourced the girls for you through his stage act? And you cherry-picked the ones you wanted. For what purpose?"

Knox's lips curled in amusement. "Newbury, if you want to

discuss it we can down our blades and smoke a cigarette together like gentlemen. Otherwise, let us put an end to this encounter. It's becoming tedious." The man's flippancy was astonishing, but it provided Newbury with the opening he needed. He slashed out with his blade, causing Knox to lurch backwards to avoid having his chest opened in a streak from right to left. The tip of the sword tore through his jacket and shirt, opening a wide smile in the fabric. As Newbury reached the end of the movement, however, he flicked the blade upwards, using the tip of his sword to catch the hilt of Knox's sword and whipping it clean out of his hand. The weapon sailed across the stage, clattering loudly to the boards.

To Knox's credit, he barely allowed the situation to faze him. Whilst Newbury was recovering from his swing, Knox reached for the blade that he had left buried in Alfonso's chest, and with a powerful tug to free the tip from the stage below, he pulled it clear of the corpse. Blood sprayed in a shower as he brought the weapon to bear. Alfonso, then, had not been dead for long.

Blood was still trickling down Knox's chin where Newbury had caught him earlier with his elbow. Yet he seemed to be enjoying the encounter, the rush of the battle, the opportunity to taunt the man who was currently living his earlier life. Newbury's face, in turn, was set with grim determination. With every second that passed, with every one of Knox's arrogant remarks, he grew more and more anxious for Veronica's safety.

Knox was now only a few feet away from the open hatch in the stage. Newbury pressed on with a series of deft, forceful strikes. He thrust relentlessly at Knox, not attempting to strike the man, but to drive him backwards, forcing him to parry, constantly, and to distract him from where his feet were taking him. Newbury knew he was leaving himself open to a counter-attack, but at the same time, he was succeeding in forcing the other man back towards the hole. Clambering over Alfonso's body, trying desperately not to lose his footing, he pushed forward.

The two men fell into a smooth rhythm: thrust, parry; thrust, parry. The steel blades clanged noisily. Slowly, they inched towards the open hatch. Newbury was growing hot and tired. The rooftop dash and the fight on the Underground had taken it out of him, and he knew his endurance would soon reach its limit. And the need for laudanum was a persistent itch, growing in intensity with every moment that passed.

As Knox neared the lip of the hole, Newbury took his chance. Using the flat of his blade to batter Knox's sword wide, he leapt into the air, kicking out, his foot connecting hard with Knox's breastbone. But the man had been expecting as much. Pivoting around on his left foot, he swung himself out of danger, narrowly missing the hole. He came to rest at a right angle to Newbury, his back to the empty auditorium. He was chuckling. "Really, Newbury, if you'd expected to—"

Knox's words were lost as Newbury's fist thundered into his face. His head snapped to the side and Newbury stepped closer, dropping his weapon so that he could rain blow after blow into the other man with both fists. Knox sputtered and tried to raise his sword, but Newbury beat him back, providing no opportunities for him to retaliate. Spittle and blood flew into the air as Newbury pounded Knox's face. He knew he did not have the finesse of a swordsman, but at Oxford he had taken to the ring and he was quick with his fists. Knox staggered backwards, heading towards the edge of the stage. Newbury saw his opportunity. He stepped in close again and aimed a powerful hook at Knox's kidney. As Knox bent forward with a rasping gasp, Newbury shoved him over the edge.

Knox tumbled backwards, crying out as he struck the ground. Newbury dashed forward to see. Knox was attempting to gather himself. He shuffled backwards on his hands and feet, still clutching the sabre tightly in his fist like a talisman. He looked dazed, and his face was raw and puffy from the battering. His good eye darted from left to right, as if he were trying to work out from which direction his assailant would come next.

Newbury could find no sympathy for the man. He wanted only to know what had become of Veronica, and to bring the criminal to justice. At the back of his mind, however, he recognised that he also needed to prove, to himself and to Charles and the others, that he and Knox were not as alike as they had imagined. He hopped down from the stage, standing over the rogue agent as Knox pulled his head and shoulders up against the front row of seats. He lay there panting for breath.

Newbury stepped closer. He needed to bind the man, to stop him from escaping. But first he needed some answers.

Knox had not given up, however. As Newbury leaned over to reach for Knox's collar, Knox flicked out his left hand, stabbing at Newbury with the point of his sword. Newbury was ready for him, though, and leaned back, grasping the hilt of the sword and following Knox's move through, so that the sword swept in a tight arc in front of him. He forced the blade down, hard, driving the point of the weapon through the outstretched palm of Knox's right hand, spearing him to the back of the nearest seat. Knox howled in agony as Newbury pushed the sword deeper, pinning the doctor in place.

Twisting Knox's other hand free from the hilt of the sword, Newbury looked down at him in disgust, and slapped him hard across the face. "Where is she?" Knox was still laughing, blood bubbling from the corner of his mouth. Newbury struck him again and repeated his question. "Where is she?"

Knox looked up at him, his strange, milky eye regarding the Crown investigator with something approaching admiration. "In the basement. She's still alive."

Newbury straightened. Grasping at his own collar, he pulled his necktie free. He stooped, using it to bind Knox's free hand to a post between two other chairs. In this state, the man had no chance of escaping. Newbury would come back for him. He needed to find Veronica.

Wiping his brow on the sleeve of his jacket, Newbury crossed to the stage. He staggered up the wooden stairs. Backstage, he would find the route to the network of underground rooms beneath the theatre, and from there, hopefully, Veronica.

Glancing once more over his shoulder at the pitiful figure of Aubrey Knox – who lay there with his arms outstretched, the sword blade pinning his hand to a seat, his body propped awkwardly against the front row – Newbury knew that he would soon have more answers. But one thing was certain. Knox was not the fearsome monster that Charles had claimed him to be. For that he was more than grateful.

Sighing, Newbury slipped into the shadows behind the curtains.

Chapter Twenty-One

Veronica fought ineffectually against her bonds. The gag was dry and choking, and tasted stale with oil and grime. She tried her best to spit it out, but to no avail; she could gain no purchase on it with her tongue. Knox had known what he was doing when he'd forced it so deep into her throat. She wondered where he had gone. Perhaps to confront Alfonso.

Veronica tried to move into a more comfortable position, taking the weight off her shoulder. Beneath her, the cellar floor was cold and damp with condensation. It was clear the laboratory was a makeshift operation, a temporary workshop, and that Knox did not spend a great deal of time inhabiting it. From what she'd observed, she assumed he was now clearing out: the cancelled show, the hurry to collect up his work into the medicine bag. Either he had what he needed, or else he had discovered that she and Newbury were on his trail.

Veronica glanced at the door, but her eyes kept flitting back to the disturbing heap of corpses just beside it. She couldn't take her eyes off the faces of the dead girls. She thought it was perhaps the worst sight she had ever seen, worse even than all of those burnt, twisted cadavers she'd discovered on the wreck of *The Lady Armitage*, or the drained, desiccated corpses that she and Newbury had encountered at Huntington Manor. No, it was the heartlessness that disturbed her most, the careless manner in which the bodies had been tossed, used, into the corner, like commodities, like discarded meat. She hated the thought that a human being could be reduced to that. It was this, more than anything else, which offered her insight into Knox's cold, calculating mind. He was truly a monster. He would do anything for his own ends.

Veronica kicked at the ground in frustration. Knox knew what he was doing, that much was clear. The bonds with which she'd been tied were unbreakable. She could see no means of escape.

She heard footsteps from the passageway outside, and flinched. Knox was returning. It was likely she did not have long left to live. The footsteps approached the door. It creaked open. She found it hard to see the figure in the gloom of the passageway. A man in a suit. Yes, Knox. He stepped forward into the room.

Her heart leapt. Sir Maurice! It was Newbury. She tried to call out, but was able only to offer up a muffled squeal. Newbury turned at the sound and saw her there, sprawled on the floor. He rushed over to her side. Lifting her head, he reached inside her mouth and gently extracted the gag. Veronica gasped for breath. "Sir Maurice! How?"

Newbury smiled softly, the relief evident on his face. "Well, Miss Hobbes, of late it seems I have provided you with ample opportunity to save my life, and you have done so on more occasions than I care to count. I felt this would be the appropriate opportunity to redress that balance."

"Oh, you foolish, brilliant man." Veronica smiled, warmly, and Newbury swept her up in his arms, cradling her to him. He held her there for what seemed like an age. She could feel his heart hammering hard in his chest, his breath becoming shallow. He brushed her hair tenderly away from her eyes where it spilled loose over her face.

"I thought I'd lost you."

Veronica gave the briefest of nods. "Me too." She expected him to chastise her, but he only held her close, trying to make her feel safe once again. She wanted to sink into that embrace, to be away from this place, this horrible place with its stench of death and decay. Newbury knew her so well, knew where to find her in a crisis, knew everything about her... except...

She had to put it out of mind. There was still work to be done.

Newbury held her for a moment longer, before placing her gently back on the ground so that he could attend to her bonds. She looked up at him, noticing the state of his suit. "What –"

"Later. First we have to free you from these damnable knots." He reached into his pocket, searching for a penknife.

"What of Knox?" Her voice was hesitant.

Newbury indicated with his head. "Up there. He won't be going anywhere for a while. Except a cell, and then, perhaps, a hangman's noose."

"And Alfonso?"

"Dead."

"What! You...?"

Newbury shook his head. "No, Knox."

Veronica looked thoughtful, as Newbury gently held her ankles and cut the cord that bound her with a sharp flick of his wrist, slicing easily through the thin silken rope. He did the same to the tightly knotted cord around her wrists.

"He must be clearing out. He was finished down here." Veronica felt suddenly tired.

Newbury slipped the penknife back into his pocket and got to his feet, dusting off his hands. He glanced around at the room. He stopped, in startled horror, when he saw the pile of female corpses in the corner. "What the devil?"

"The devil is right. Knox is dangerous: cold, calculating and murderous. He'll stop at nothing to get what he wants. He's always been the same."

Newbury nodded absently. He paused for a moment, moving over to stoop over the nearest corpse. "What's this? Holes in their heads?" His face wrinkled in disgust.

"Yes." Newbury grasped the girl's head and turned it slowly from side to side, examining the bizarre wound. "He's obviously used this device, here, to bore a hole in their skulls. I think he's been extracting a secretion or hormone from their brains." Newbury straightened and turned to glance at the chair that Veronica was indicating. He marched over to it, grasping one of the large mechanical arms and swinging it round so that he could see the deadly drill bit. He ran his fingers over the tiny pistons that controlled the movement of the arm itself, seeming to admire the craftsmanship. Then, with his fingertips, he followed the trailing cable that ran from the end of the arm in a wide loop around the back of the device. A moment later he re-emerged from the rear of the chair, a small glass vial clutched in his hand. It was filled with a brown, brackish fluid. He held it up for Veronica to see.

"Hmmm." Newbury looked confused. "But what exactly was he extracting? And more importantly, why?" He looked at the bottle in disgust. "Let's see if we can have this analysed." He checked the stopper and then slipped the small glass bottle into his jacket pocket.

He crossed to the workbench, where a smattering of artefacts was still in situ: a few drawings, some scraps of paper covered in scrawled hieroglyphs and the broken shells of three ushabti figurines. Newbury's eyes widened as he recognised the items. He stared at the table for a while, before picking up the remnants of one of the statues. "This is one of the pieces I saw at Lord Winthrop's house, at Albion House! Have you seen them? They've been broken in two. Knox was after the contents. My God." His voice was a low growl. "It was Knox all along." He cast the broken idol back on the tabletop. "The Osiris Ritual. That's why he's here, in London." He turned to her. "Miss Hobbes, that mummy, the screaming mummy that Winthrop found in Thebes. It's the remains of an ancient priest, a priest who was mummified alive and cursed by the Pharaoh for attempting to extend his life in the physical world. I'll wager these idols contained the secrets of his discoveries, that these poor girls gave their lives to provide some sort of ingredient for the ritual." He slammed his fist on the workbench. "And here I was chasing Ashford halfway across London. Ashford would most likely have led me to Knox, given half a chance. It all makes sense now. Ashford saved my life earlier today. He may be rogue, but he's not a killer. He's out for revenge. He wants Knox."

Veronica sighed. "I should have realised. If I'd helped you... if I'd been there. Knox was always your man, Sir Maurice. He was always obsessed with extending his life. It's the motivation that drives him, that gives him purpose. Alfonso was just a cover, a means of obtaining the girls. Knox is the key to all of this, to Winthrop, the mummy, and to the girls." She indicated the other gruesome occupants of the room with a wave of her hand.

Newbury, however, was wearing a mystified expression, and seemed unable to take his eyes off her. She realised, in a panic, that she had said too much. Did he know? Had she given it away? Had she said it on purpose? She wanted so much to tell Newbury the truth, had she revealed the information about Knox as a means of setting him on the right trail? No. She had done it because the information was fundamental to the case. Newbury needed to know that Knox was responsible for the deaths, and that Ashford – presumably the missing agent that Newbury had been following – was not. She had done it for the good of the Empire. Or so she wanted so much to believe. But somehow she still felt hollow inside.

Unsure what else to do, she joined Newbury at the table and began sifting through the remaining papers, looking for anything that might help her to explain her outburst. She felt her cheeks flush hot and red, and silently cursed herself for her actions. Newbury appeared to accept this without comment. He moved around the table, continuing to sort through the remaining pieces of ushabti.

Veronica was struck by a sudden flash of inspiration. "The bag!"

"What bag?"

"The bag by the door. The medicine bag. Knox was sorting through the items on the table here, stuffing them into his bag: vials full of liquid, papers, artefacts. Clearly the results of his experiments. He must have what he needed."

Newbury turned, looking for the bag. "What – where is this bag?"

"There, by the door. I saw him set it down before he left." Veronica turned to see there was no bag. She shrugged. "He must have taken it with him when he left."

"Hmmm. We'll find it up there, by the stage, no doubt. It'll be all the evidence we need to link Knox to the murders." He studied Veronica intently. "Can you walk?"

"Yes, yes, I'm quite well."

"Are you sure?"

"Sir Maurice..." Her voice was stern. Newbury met her gaze. He nodded once, and then extended his arm. She took it gratefully.

"Come on. Let's find that bag and go and fetch the police. It's time to get Charles here." They left the dank cellar, stepping out into the passageway, along which Newbury guided Veronica carefully, allowing her to lean on him as he edged his way through the warren. It was long and narrow and must have wound halfway under the theatre. Veronica had no real notion of where they were in relation to the auditorium above.

After a short while, their feet scuffing on the rough stone floor, Newbury dipped his head under a stone archway and took a left turn, leading her to a wooden door. He had obviously come this way earlier. "Through here." He ushered her through to the wooden stairwell beyond. She mounted the bottom step.

Newbury cleared his throat, causing her to pause and look back. "Veronica," – she noted the use of her first name – "can you face him? After all of this, I mean."

"Who, Knox?"

"Yes. He's quite incapacitated, of course. But if you'd rather leave by another exit, I wouldn't think anything less of you." He looked concerned. "I could see you to a carriage?"

"Sir Maurice, I appreciate that, very much. But it won't be necessary. I'm quite ready to face him again."

"As you say."

The stairs creaked as they made their way slowly towards the light. A moment later they emerged, squinting, from a small wooden trapdoor just off to one side of the stage. Veronica blinked, blearily, as her eyes adjusted to the sharp electric light, after hours spent in the gloomy depths of the basement. She righted herself on the stage, and then turned to watch Newbury pulling himself out of the opening. She offered him a hand as he steadied himself. She could see where a large red carpet had been rolled away to reveal the secret trapdoor. The cellar in which Knox had set up his temporary workshop had once been a storage room for props, she supposed, or else a space for the actors to rest or effect a quick change of costume as they traversed the tunnel beneath the stage, quitting the boards at stage right, only to reappear a short while later at stage left. Now, she shuddered as she considered the sinister purpose to which Aubrey Knox had put it to use.

Newbury strode forward onto the stage, stopping to sweep up one of the swords from Alfonso's rack. Clearly, he was not underestimating the resourcefulness of the rogue doctor. A little further across the stage, near to the hatch into which Veronica had tumbled a few hours earlier, Alfonso the magician lay dead. His arms and legs were both outstretched, describing a bizarre star shape, and his chest was covered in a dark crimson stain. His jaw was open, slackly, and his eyes were staring at the rafters.

"Oh God," was all she could murmur. She had seen so much death that day already. Despite Alfonso's terrible role in Knox's plot, despite what he had done to her, she could not feel relief at the sight of his rigid corpse. That was too much. She averted her eyes.

"Veronica! Here!" She turned to see Newbury throw the sword down upon the stage in frustration.

She ran to his side. "What is it?"

"Knox. He's gone." He indicated the row of seats just to the left of the stage. "I left him here, pinned to the chair, a blade driven through his hand. I trussed his other with my neck tie. How the devil did he get away?"

Veronica glanced around, looking for any indication that the man may still be in the theatre.

"He's long gone. And no doubt his medicine bag has gone with him." He turned to Veronica, and she could see the anger burning behind his eyes. "You were right. He's clearing out. He has what he wanted, and now he'll disappear, just like he did all those years ago. I underestimated him. I'm a ruddy fool."

Veronica sighed. She couldn't bear to see Newbury torturing himself in such a manner. "You saved my life. That has to count for something."

His face softened. "Miss Hobbes, it counts for everything. But it doesn't alter the fact that I allowed him to escape."

Veronica put her hand on his arm. "Let's check the rear exit."

Newbury nodded. It was clear he did not expect to find anything. He followed behind Veronica, alert, as she crossed the stage and took the steps down to the main auditorium, two at a time. They passed close by the seat to which Knox, until recently, had been bound. Veronica could see where the blade had pierced the seat back, shredding the fabric and staining it with dark blood. Now, both man and sword had gone. Newbury's black tie lay discarded on the floor, still knotted. He didn't pick it up.

Together, they hurried around the side of the stage and pushed their way through the double doors that led to the actors' enclosure, where they had first met Alfonso, lounging idly in his dressing room. At the end of the long corridor, the door to the street was hanging open, banging noisily against the wall in the breeze. The hinges creaked and groaned with the strain. Outside, it was dark, and the swirling fog gave everything a murky, hazy appearance. Veronica ran to the threshold, peering out into the night. There was no sign of Knox, or the medicine bag.

Newbury was right. Somehow, the doctor had escaped.

Chapter Twenty-Two

Newbury slammed awake with a start. He was momentarily disorientated; he had no idea where he was. Slowly, the room began to resolve around him. A bookcase. A writing desk. A fireplace with a low flame, guttering in the grate. He felt dazed. He was in his drawing room.

After a moment, he realised there was someone standing beside him, calling his name. He looked round. It was Mrs. Bradshaw, her hands on her hips. He had the sense that she had been there for some time. "Good morning, Sir Maurice. Will you be taking breakfast today?" she asked in her dulcet, Scottish tones, when she noticed he was finally paying attention. She looked him up and down. "Whatever have you been up to for your suit to be in such a condition?" She said this with a weariness born of familiarity, of one accustomed to her employer's more bizarre pursuits. She expected no answer. If she were concerned for his health, she showed no signs of it.

Newbury took stock of the situation. He was lounging in a Chesterfield, still wearing yesterday's suit, which was torn at the knees and covered in grime from rolling around in alleyways, factory roofs and an Underground station. His elbows were scuffed, and his jacket was sliced across the front from the swipe of a sword blade. He had not yet attended to his toilet, either, meaning his face was still crusty with blood and oil. He realised he must have looked a pretty sight to his housekeeper.

There was a heavy weight on his chest. He looked down. A book. Meyer's *Treatise on Futurism*. Beside his chair, on an occasional table, was a near-empty glass of red wine. He knew what else had been in that glass, too. Sighing, Newbury looked up into the impenetrable face of Mrs. Bradshaw. "What time do you make it, Mrs. Bradshaw?"

She glanced at the clock on the mantelpiece. "Time for breakfast, I should say, sir."

Newbury grinned. "Very well. I shall make haste to my rooms where I shall endeavour to make myself presentable. My thanks to you, Mrs. Bradshaw. I suspect I might have slept all day if it had not been for your timely interruption."

The housekeeper smiled without saying another word, and quit the room. Newbury listened to the tread of her feet as she descended the stairs to the kitchen below. Then, heaving himself out of his chair, his bones creaking after hours spent in a less-than-ideal posture, he repaired to his rooms to wash and dress.

†

After washing and cleaning his wounds – which, Newbury was surprised to discover, were more plentiful than he had imagined – he had partaken of Mrs. Bradshaw's excellent breakfast, before heading out to meet Miss Hobbes at the museum as they had arranged the previous evening.

As he trundled along in a hansom, Newbury considered the events of the theatre. After discovering that Knox had somehow managed to slip his bonds and escape the venue, Newbury, exasperated, had escorted Miss Hobbes to her Kensington home, where, after he had filled her in regarding the situation with Ashford, he had insisted she took the opportunity to gain an evening's rest. There was very little else that could have been achieved that night, and not being aware of the full extent of Knox's plans, they were unable to predict his movements.

What was clear to Newbury was the fact that Knox had been hunting for the key to the Osiris Ritual. Winthrop's and Blake's deaths had been inconsequential to Knox; they were killed by virtue of the fact that they were in his way, regardless of the fact that they had been the ones to recover the artefacts he desired. That much was obvious. But had Knox been waiting for them to return from Egypt? Did he already have a notion of what the ritual involved? The girls had been going missing for weeks, if not months, before Winthrop's death. Newbury could only assume that they were somehow central to the execution of the ritual, that the secretion or hormone Knox had been extracting from their brains was an ingredient of the process. But Knox had the contents of the ushabti figures, the outline for the ritual. Everything was supposition until Newbury could study those contents himself.

All of this had led Newbury to two conclusions. Firstly, that Knox was planning to enact the ritual, and soon, in the hope of artificially extending his own life. Secondly, that Knox was entirely insane. Neither revelation filled him with comfort. Newbury knew that he had to stop him. He doubted very much whether Knox would have anything left to offer the Empire, even in captivity, but he also knew it was his duty to bring him in alive. There were questions that needed answering.

Newbury considered their encounter at the theatre. The experience of meeting his predecessor had shaken him, more than he cared to admit. The man was cold and calculating, yet there was a cool intelligence there, too, an understanding of the world and the way that it worked. He was charming, resourceful, a master manipulator. He knew how to twist things to his own ends. Newbury knew that he had allowed the rogue doctor to get under his skin.

And where did that leave Ashford? The man was still rogue, too, still loose in the city and working to his own set of directives, ignoring the imperatives of the Crown. Newbury's mission had not changed, then. Ashford still needed to be brought in, even if he wasn't the vicious murderer that Newbury had originally mistaken him for.

That only left Miss Hobbes. What had she been trying to tell him down in that dank cellar? He thought he knew, of course, thought he understood the implication of her words. She knew Knox. At least, she knew *of* Knox. There could be very few ways in which she had come across that information, and she had divulged far more than she could have possibly learned from the man himself in such a short space of time. He felt torn. What had she been keeping from him? And for how long? The notion tied a knot in the pit of his stomach. If he couldn't trust Veronica...

Yet, how could he doubt her integrity? She had saved his life on numerous occasions. She knew everything about him. And besides, she was more to him than simply an assistant. She was... *important* to him. Yet he could not still the sharp sense of disquiet that had settled upon him, and throughout his breakfast he had replayed the events of the previous evening, over and over in his mind, trying to recall the exact look on her face, the precise tone of her voice. There was definitely more to it than a slip of the tongue. But what? He was not yet sure.

Whatever the case, he feared causing an imbalance in their relationship. He resolved to manage the situation carefully. He would not confront her outright. That, he thought, could bring about only disaster. He needed more time to ponder on the consequences of what she had said.

First, though, he needed to act on the information she had given him. He needed to find Aubrey Knox. Knox was the key.

And Newbury had no idea where to start.

†

Around two hours later, a smartly dressed Newbury, clean-shaven and bright with energy, opened the door to his office at the British Museum and stepped inside. He filled his lungs with the familiar smell of the place. For all of his adventuring, Newbury enjoyed the calm respite he found here, the sense of stillness in a world so usually filled with chaos. He glanced around. Both Miss Hobbes and Miss Coulthard were sitting at their desks, studiously engrossed in their work.

"Good morning, ladies." Newbury removed his hat. "Do I smell a fresh pot of Earl Grey brewing in the pot?" He beamed at Miss Coulthard, who was quick to acknowledge his request, shuffling off towards the stove to fetch him a drink. Newbury crossed the room without removing his coat, and stepped through the partition to the smaller office where Veronica was working. "Miss Hobbes. Are you quite well?"

Veronica looked up at him, pushing her papers to one side. "I am quite well, Sir Maurice."

Newbury lowered his voice, glancing back at Miss Coulthard, who was still busying herself at the stove. "It's only... after yesterday's ordeal, I questioned –"

"– There is no question." Veronica interjected. "Really, I am quite well."

"I am most pleased to hear it. Then we shall fortify ourselves with Miss Coulthard's excellent brew, before setting out in search of our villain."

Veronica furrowed her brow. "Have you a notion, then, of where to begin our search for Knox?" She was toying absently with her left wrist, where a red mark belied the fact that, just a few hours earlier, she had been viciously bound.

Newbury nodded, slowly. "Perhaps. I still believe that Ashford could hold the answer. But first, there's someone I'd like you to meet." He looked round to see Miss Coulthard approaching, clutching a large silver tray. "Thank you, Miss Coulthard. If you would be so kind as to set that down on my desk." He began unbuttoning the front of his topcoat.

Miss Coulthard placed the tray on the rather cluttered desk as directed. Then, turning to Newbury, she reached into the pocket of her blouse and withdrew a small, neatly folded piece of paper, which she held out to him. "The information you requested, sir."

Newbury's emerald eyes flashed in recognition. "Ah, marvellous! My thanks to you, Miss Coulthard." He took the note and slipped it carefully into his trouser pocket without unfolding it.

"You're most welcome, sir. I also have a message from Sir Charles. He requests that you pay him a visit at Scotland Yard at your first convenience."

"I shall take it under advisement, Miss Coulthard. Thank you."

"Very good, sir." Miss Coulthard returned to her desk, and before Newbury had finished removing his winter layers, she was already back to work.

Grinning, Newbury draped his coat across his desk and placed his hat beside it. Then, reaching for the steaming teapot, he turned to Veronica. "Tea?"

✝

George Purefoy's apartment was above a tailor's shop in Ladbroke Grove, which boasted two large bay windows, each filled with displays of exquisite dinner suits, hats, gloves and canes. Newbury knew the reputation of the place. All of the assorted paraphernalia desired by a society gentleman could be found inside. Newbury usually took his business to Bond Street, but he was sure that Charles had recommended this particular establishment on more than one occasion. The legend above the door read: J. SIMPSON ESQ., GENTLEMEN'S OUTFITTERS.

The city was still buried beneath a thick blanket of yellow fog, which showed no sign of abating during the coming morning. Nevertheless, a light was on inside the shop, and through the window, Newbury could see the dark shapes of figures shifting around, going about their daily business. To the left of the shop's frontage was a nondescript green door. This, Newbury fathomed, would likely be the door to Purefoy's apartment.

Despite Veronica's protestations, Newbury had insisted upon taking a steam-powered carriage across town, keen to ensure that no further time was lost. She had taken the opportunity to make a sly comment about tea, suggesting that perhaps, if he were so anxious for them to be on their way, they might have forgone the morning brew, but Newbury had only laughed dismissively and hailed the cab. Ritual was important to him. It gave him time to think.

After helping Veronica down from the carriage, at which she glared in disdain as she dismounted, wrinkling her nose at the smell of the throbbing engine, Newbury approached the door. He removed his glove and rapped loudly with the brass knocker. Beside him,

Veronica shivered in the cold.

A few moments passed in silence. There was no answer from the apartment above. Newbury knocked again, and then stepped back into the street, glancing up at the windows. Still nothing. No call from inside, no sign of movement at the windows. With a growing sense of unease, Newbury tried the handle, and found that the door was unlocked. It swung open to reveal a steep, carpeted staircase leading up to the apartment above.

Newbury crossed to the foot of the stairs. "Purefoy? Are you there, Purefoy?"

Then, with a look of horror, Newbury noticed something on the bottom step. He dropped into a squat, examining the tread. "Oh no..."

Veronica stepped forward, trying to make out what he'd seen. "What is it?"

"Blood. A footprint." Newbury's voice was barely a whisper. Feeling sick to the stomach, and praying that what he had feared had not suddenly become a reality, Newbury bounded up the stairs two at a time. There were more footprints in evidence further up the stairwell; a man's shoe, caked in blood, had passed this way only a handful of hours before. The imprints were still wet and sticky on the pale green carpet.

At the top of the stairs Newbury found himself presented with three white, panelled doors. He chose the one to the right, judging this one would lead him to Purefoy's sitting room. He turned the handle, pushing his way inside. The sight that greeted him was enough to make him cry out in anguish and fall to his knees. He hung his head. He was too late.

Purefoy's corpse had been laid out on the sitting room floor to form the shape of a human star. Around him, his butcher had drawn a series of large, concentric circles, each of them divided into precise intervals. Within these intervals he had carefully drawn a series of inscriptions, diagrams and runes, each of them bearing its own dark, esoteric meaning. It was incredibly elaborate.

Purefoy himself had been stripped naked. His belly had been rent open with a long, deep gash, and his bowels and intestines had been spilled out onto the floorboards. His intestines had been stretched out around him and pinned within the circles to form a horrific spider's web of flesh, a web in which Purefoy himself had been caught, trapped at its centre like a fly awaiting its inevitable fate. Inside the abdominal cavity of the dead man, Newbury could see that the killer had placed a series of small tributes: a holly leaf, the broken remnants of an ushabti figurine, a small, rolled fragment of linen inscribed with some archaic scripture, and a single tarot card, bearing the image of a goblet, overflowing with water: the ace of cups.

The look on the boy's face was one of wonder, as if he had not yet come to terms with what had been about to happen to him, as if his reporter's instincts had remained engaged until the last, his curiosity somehow outweighing his fear.

It was immediately obvious to Newbury what had occurred. Aubrey Knox had attempted to divine the future in the reporter's guts.

Newbury heard Veronica's footsteps on the landing behind him, and he turned to try to stop her from entering the room. But he was too late. She saw everything. He saw her gag reflexively and turn away from the scene.

There was blood everywhere, of course; thick and cloying. It filled Newbury's nostrils, seeming to penetrate everything. But under it all there was another smell, the familiar stench of rotting flesh. Ashford had been here too.

Newbury felt a fury welling up inside of him, a burning rage deep in the pit of his belly. Knox would pay for this. He would pay dearly for it. There was one thing that Knox cared for above all else, one thing that drove him onwards, the very core of his being: his own life. Newbury would take that from him. He realised this as he rested there on the threshold of Purefoy's sitting room, eyeing the devastation before him. The boy was dead, killed only for being in the wrong place at the wrong time, for being on the periphery of something that he didn't even understand. All of that potential, all of that enthusiasm, had gone, stolen in a moment for nothing but Knox's wicked gratification.

Dark thoughts bubbled into Newbury's head. He would see justice done. Even if it meant that he had to become like Knox to do it. He would find Knox. And then Purefoy would be avenged.

Standing, Newbury looked back at Veronica on the landing. "He's toying with us."

Veronica coughed. "Knox, you mean?"

"Yes. What threat could Purefoy have *possibly* proved to the man?"

Veronica shook her head. She swallowed. "No, Sir Maurice. The pattern is the same as before. He's tidying up loose ends, leaving no stone unturned. He must have been aware of Purefoy's involvement."

Newbury nodded but didn't say a word. He stepped into the room, closer to the body. He looked down, his eyes limned with sadness.

"What does it all mean?" Veronica called from over his shoulder. She was hovering in the doorway, unwilling – or unable – to enter the room.

Newbury hesitated. "He... he was attempting to divine the future. Many of the ancient rituals involve disembowelling cats, dogs, or flightless birds. He chose to use Purefoy."

"My God..." Veronica's voice was full of pity.

"He must have been disturbed. By Ashford, I mean. Otherwise I can see no reason why he would have left these items in such a way."

"Why? Do they tell you something?"

"Perhaps." Newbury studied the objects that were resting inside the carcass of his young friend.

Veronica shook her head. "We're running out of time. His next move will be to disappear, to go to ground."

Newbury shook his head. Stooping, he gingerly removed the tarot card from the bloody mess on the floor. "No, Miss Hobbes. He's not going to ground. It seems old habits die hard. He's going to water."

Veronica stared at him, wide-eyed. "What, the docks?"

Newbury nodded. "The ace of cups. Water. That's where they found Ashford's body last time, isn't it? By interrupting Knox, Ashford has done us more of a favour than he could possibly imagine." His eyes flashed with steely resolve. "We have Knox's trail."

Veronica straightened her back. "Shall I fetch the police?"

Newbury was studying Purefoy's face. His head snapped up at Veronica's words. His voice was forceful. "No. No police. Not even Charles. We finish this alone." He saw Veronica shudder at the cold timbre of his voice. She looked at the horrifying remnants of Knox's ritual.

"Will it work?"

"What, the divination? No."

Veronica shook her head. "No, not that. The Osiris Ritual. Will it work?"

Newbury sighed. "There are more things in this world of ours than I can possibly explain, Miss Hobbes. But it didn't help Khemosiri, and I doubt it will help Knox."

"All the same..." Veronica let her sentence trail off.

Newbury offered her a weak smile. "All the same..." He dropped the tarot card to the floor beside the corpse, and then turned and disappeared further into the apartment, returning a moment later with a large white sheet he had clearly stripped from Purefoy's bed. He knelt beside the body, laying the makeshift shroud neatly over the dead man to hide the ruination. Lastly, before covering Purefoy's face, he used the tips of his fingers to draw the reporter's eyelids closed.

Then, resolute, Newbury took Veronica by the arm and marched her out of the apartment, with only one goal in mind: revenge.

Chapter Twenty-Three

Veronica bobbed up and down in her seat, lightly, as the hansom cab bowled onwards across the city. Newbury watched her from the other side of the cabin. Her head was turned away from him, looking out of the window, and he admired her profile. There was no mistaking her beauty. What was more, she had flowered in the few months since he'd known her, growing in confidence. He followed the line of her jaw, admired the way in which her glossy brunette hair curled behind one ear. To Newbury, she was a near-perfect example of womanhood. He watched her strain to see through the fog, blinking, as if the action would help to shift the cloying grey vapour within which they were travelling.

Yet, for all that, Newbury had never felt so far removed from her. Their relationship seemed somehow fractured, distant. Her actions towards him had not altered, of course. But he knew more, now, knew that she was holding something back from him, something fundamental. His fury at Purefoy's death had not abated – if anything, it was growing more and more forceful with every passing minute – but neither could he shake the horrible sense of betrayal in the pit of his stomach, even for Purefoy. Unwelcome questions raised themselves in his mind. If she had acted sooner, if she had warned him about Knox, would Purefoy still be dead? Could she have saved him? Had she known about Ashford all along? Where had she got the information about Knox? All of these questions needed answers, but the very act of asking them was at odds with how he felt about the woman. In questioning her, he risked losing her altogether. And for now, he felt he knew which of the two options represented the lesser evil.

Veronica turned towards him, snapping him out of his reverie. "Sir Maurice, I thought we were heading to the London Docks?"

Newbury nodded, slowly. "We are. But first, I must make a brief stop." Veronica frowned. "I believe I know where to find Ashford. I must talk with him."

Veronica nodded, sagely. "Very well." The moment stretched, and they stared at each other in silence, neither one of them wishing to be the first to look away. After a while, Newbury turned to glance out of the window. He had the terrible, dawning sense that everything was unravelling around him.

Presently, the hansom trundled to a stop in the foggy wilderness of Bethnal Green. Newbury rose to his feet. "You wait here, Miss Hobbes. I shall return momentarily." He clicked open the door and stepped down into the quiet street beyond. It was still early, and this peaceful residential street had not yet fully awoken to the morning. Newbury took a small, cream-coloured card from inside his jacket pocket and unfolded it, revealing an address written in Miss Coulthard's neat copperplate. He checked the address against the house in front of him. It was similar, in many ways, to Newbury's own residence: a small end-terrace house, with two prominent bay windows, one on either of the two floors; a small front yard, filled with potted plants; and a panelled front door, painted in a royal blue. A waist-high railing ran around the front and side of the yard. The mouth of a dimly lit alleyway separated the house from the next long terrace about six feet to the right.

It seemed to Newbury like rather an affluent dwelling for a widow on an agency pension. Nevertheless, this was clearly the address that Miss Coulthard had discovered for him. Slowly, Newbury approached the building. For a moment he stood before the door, considering whether to rap the brass knocker. Then, changing his mind, he edged round to stand before the window, peering into the living room beyond. The room was lit brightly by a gas-lamp and was well stocked with furnishings: a sideboard, two armchairs and a daybed. A large fireplace dominated the room, although its grate was cold and unlit. On the floor, a pretty woman in her late twenties, with strawberry blonde hair, was sitting with two children, playing a game with counters. A boy, of around eight years, and a girl, slightly younger, who were clearly brother and sister, and Newbury smiled as he watched their faces light up whilst they laughed and carolled with their mother. He didn't turn his head as, in a low voice, he began to speak. "You'll have to give yourself up soon, Ashford. All of this running around is doing neither of us any good. I'm supposed to take you in myself, but I'm too busy with this blasted Knox business. I'm about to head to the London Docks to find him before he disappears again." He turned his head slightly, to watch Ashford emerge from the shadows around the side of the building. The other man's red eyes were piercing in the gloom. "I know you'll do the right thing."

Ashford lowered his hood, and once again, Newbury was appalled by the yellowed, rotting pallor of his skin and the disfigurements that Dr. Fabian's machinery had inflicted upon him. His black cloak was now shredded and hanging loose around his shoulders, exposing the mechanical pump in his chest, and Newbury could see where his encounter with the train in the Underground had scorched the flesh at his elbows, revealing the brass joints underneath. The tubing that curled between his head and chest flexed as he moved.

Newbury pitied Ashford, then, not for what had become of him, but rather for the impact it had had on his life; left out in the cold, Ashford was separated from his wife and children by only a thin pane of glass. But that pane of glass represented a yawning chasm, a barrier that Ashford was forever unable to cross. It must have been torture, to stand watching his wife and children and be prevented from reaching out for them, from holding them, from being a husband and a father to them. But Newbury knew that, to those children, their father was dead, and this *thing* would stand before them only as a monster, a creature drawn from their darkest nightmares. Ashford knew it too. He had spared them that horror.

The former agent turned to regard the joyful scene inside the house. Newbury was unable to read any emotion on his grim visage, but he was now sure that, somewhere, it still resided deep inside the man. "Thank you, Newbury." Ashford's voice chimed out in his grating, metallic tone. "I will do the right thing."

Newbury gave a curt nod, and then turned, making his way along the short path towards the waiting carriage, leaving Ashford alone to contemplate his nightmare. Just as he reached the railing, however, Newbury heard Ashford call out behind him. "Newbury." A brief pause. "Methuselah."

Newbury turned, a quizzical expression on his face, but Ashford had already gone, melted away into the foggy morning.

†

Newbury coughed, absently, as he helped Miss Hobbes to dismount from the hansom a short while later at the London Docks. The sun had done its work and burned away much of the morning fog, transforming it into thin wreaths of mist that still clung, determinedly, to the masts of the innumerable vessels that cluttered the harbour. The docks were teeming with boats of all shapes and sizes, from steamships, to yachts, to schooners, and the quayside, in turn, was bustling with life.

Veronica wrinkled her nose. The docks had a distinctive aroma that was all their own. Laughing, Newbury paid the cabbie his fare and sent him on his way. He held his arm out for Veronica. "I suggest, my dear Miss Hobbes, that we begin with the major shipping lines. See if we can't discover the intended destination of the doctor."

The offices of the shipping companies were, as one, small and pokey; dimly lit, and without substantial furnishings. The Crown investigators were forced to wait in line whilst merchants, businessmen and explorers all arranged passage to a vast array of destinations, exotic locales from China to the Continent, from India to Africa, booking berths on the large steamers that were due to sail that week. Hours passed, and innumerable interviews with office clerks – who were each so alike that Newbury considered they could have been stamped out of the same mould – yielded nothing. There was no trail. No person matching Knox's name or description had booked passage on a vessel sailing that day, or indeed any day that week. Newbury, frustrated, feared they had already lost Knox, that perhaps his assumption back at Purefoy's apartment had been incorrect, or worse, that Knox had fooled him, leaving a false trail to throw him off the scent. Had the ace of cups meant something else entirely? He was wracked with doubt.

Together, Newbury and Veronica agreed to walk the quayside in search of inspiration. Newbury was not hopeful that he would find it. That sense of impending chaos was still bearing down on him, still growing in force and magnitude. He had the notion that he was at the centre of a vast maelstrom, standing in the eye of the storm, looking out as everything went to pieces around him. Purefoy was dead, and Knox was free. Perhaps he needed help from Charles after all.

They strolled along the water's edge, avoiding crates of stinking fish, fine silks from the East, spices, tobacco and any number of other goods being unloaded from the vessels that had moored along the quayside. Newbury scanned the faces in the crowds as they walked, until those faces became nothing but an indistinct human blur. *So many people.* If Knox had come here, Newbury understood why he had chosen the place. It would be easy to lose oneself amongst this vast cornucopia of nationalities and noise. Easy to adopt a false identity or to slip down a side street, or even to stow away aboard one of the great ships that towered over the harbour like behemoths in the morning light.

His only clue, now, was that last, cryptic word that Ashford had muttered to him, before he'd slipped away into the darkness. *Methuselah.* Newbury turned it over and over in his mind. *Methuselah.* He knew the relevance of the word, the implication. He had studied the biblical texts as a schoolboy. It was clearly a reference to Knox, to Knox's plans. Methuselah was a watchword for longevity. He was the son of Enoch, who had lived for countless years in the early days of the Christian myth, his life supernaturally extended by the will of God. Newbury was not a religious man, and did not consider the Bible as literal truth, yet he knew there were more things in this world than those he could see, hear or touch, had even witnessed them himself on occasion. The supernatural realm was hidden only by a thin veil. Or so experience suggested. The line between science and the occult was thin and intangible. "Methuselah." He mouthed the word, speaking it aloud, trying to wring the meaning from it. He had come to a stop before a small, makeshift stall, behind which a burly man was selling cockles by the jar.

Veronica, who had been staring out across the water, turned when she heard him speak. "Methuselah?"

Newbury nodded. "Yes, yes." He sighed. "The last word that Ashford spoke to me before we parted company."

Veronica's eyes widened. "Methuselah... Ashford said that to you?"

"Indeed. Clearly he was referring to Knox."

"Yes! Sir Maurice, I believe he was. But look!" He followed the line of her finger towards a small boat, bobbing gently with the lap of the water against the harbour wall. It was a bizarre craft, a submersible, capable, Newbury assumed, of spending extended periods beneath the water. It had the look of a small ironclad about it: all metal plates and reinforced glass portholes, with a tall funnel that would remain above water when the vessel dived, providing a source of air for the inhabitants. There was a wooden deck, surrounded by a short rail, and a sealable hatch for climbing down into the habitable space below. An extendable periscope jutted rudely from the deck. Submersibles such as this were rare, and Newbury had only seen one or two of them in his lifetime. Presently, this one sat afloat in the harbour, sandwiched between two larger boats, and was tied to a mooring post on the quayside nearby. On the side of the vessel, in small, black letters was the legend: METHUSELAH.

Newbury turned to Veronica. "You don't think..."

Veronica nodded. "It makes sense. It must be Knox's ship."

Newbury couldn't prevent himself from grinning. "So that's how he intends to get away. Underwater. Come on!" He ran along the harbour edge, careful not to trip or lose his footing. Veronica followed close on his heels.

The prow of the vessel was around three feet from the edge of the harbour. Murky river water sloshed in the space between. Glancing back over his shoulder to ensure Veronica was still following behind, Newbury readied himself and then sprang from the edge of the harbour towards the small deck of the *Methuselah*. He landed with a dull thud. Turning, he held his arms out towards Veronica, willing her to jump. "Come on! That bang may have alerted him. We need to move quickly."

Veronica regarded the jump with trepidation. Then, shrugging, she fixed her eyes on Newbury, bent her knees and leapt forward. In her haste she nearly overshot, but Newbury was able to catch her firmly, staggering back a few paces before setting her down beside him. Their faces were only inches apart. He could hear her ragged breath. "Are you ready?"

"I'm ready."

There was a choking sound from deep beneath them, followed by a long, mechanical purr. The *Methuselah* began to gently vibrate. Newbury's and Veronica's eyes met. "He's started the engines. He must have heard us. We need to move, fast. If he dives, we're done for. We need to get inside." Newbury moved quickly. He shot around the deck, searching out the hatch that would allow them both access to the decks below. It was nothing but a round hole in the decking, covered by a thick metal lip and a rubber seal. Crouching, Newbury ran his fingers around the edge of it until he had located the catch. He pulled it free, and the metal plate eased open on a creaking hinge, revealing a steel ladder that disappeared into the shadowy depths below.

Veronica stepped forward. "I'll go first."

Newbury shook his head. "No, Miss Hobbes. I'll go first." His voice was firm.

Swinging himself down, his feet catching on the metal rungs, he began his swift descent of the ladder. Moments later, Veronica followed suit, pulling the hatch closed behind her. Their feet echoed in the confined space as they climbed.

Below, they found themselves in a small antechamber, which branched off in three different directions. The decor was functional, at best; the walls and doorways consisted of grey, featureless steel. Everything was quiet, aside from the gentle slapping of the water against the sides of the boat. There was a light, pleasant aroma, such as that of burning incense, lavender and rosemary.

Newbury looked around for something he could use as a weapon, but could find nothing. Giving up on that idea, he decided to follow his instincts. "This way." He whispered to Veronica, nodding towards the prow of the vessel. Cautiously, they edged their way through the small opening, careful to ensure that their footsteps did not immediately give away their position. Newbury kept his back to the wall. They crept further into the depths of the ship.

The small passageway terminated in an open doorway. Newbury peered through the opening. On the other side of the bulkhead was the main cabin. It was a relatively small space, with a single bunk, a square table fixed to one wall, and another open hatchway, which he supposed led through to the control pit. The room was sparsely furnished, but nevertheless cluttered with books, jars and strange artefacts, in much the same manner as Newbury's Chelsea study, but filled also with the paraphernalia of normal life: clothes, a top hat, a pocket watch laid out on the table. The bedclothes were ruffled, slept in. This place, this boat – not only was it Knox's means of escape, it appeared also to be his home.

The scene on the floor told an even more bizarre tale. A large pentagram had been marked out with string, pinned to the floor within a large circle. Between each of the five points of the star lay a curled, aged fragment of papyrus, each of them covered in an inky black scrawl. These, Newbury presumed, were the contents of the ushabti figures that Knox had fought so hard to obtain. The last words of Khemosiri. The instructions for how to perform the Osiris Ritual.

At the centre of the pentagram were arranged three tall, glass phials, filled once again with the brown, brackish fluid that Knox had extracted from the brains of the women he had killed. Aside from this there was a jar of thick, gelatinous blood, the clay effigy of a man, rudely formed, and a leather-bound book which lay open to reveal bright, illuminated pages. There was no sign of Knox.

Gesturing silently to Veronica to follow, Newbury stepped carefully over the threshold, dipping his head carefully to avoid banging it on the bulkhead. He heard Veronica steal in behind him. "What now?" she whispered.

"Now, my dear Miss Hobbes, you listen to me." The voice was a familiar, sensuous purr. As if on cue, Aubrey Knox appeared in the doorway of the submersible's control pit. He was dressed in an immaculate black dinner suit and was wearing a scabbarded sword on his left hip. In his left hand, he bore a pistol, and his scarred left eye twinkled as he regarded the two investigators. His right hand was bandaged where Newbury had run it through at the theatre. He was about to launch into another oratory, when Newbury launched himself forward, carelessly trampling the delicately arranged ritual on the floor. He charged towards Knox with wild abandon, driven by a fiery passion for revenge. Grasping Knox's gun arm at the wrist, he twisted the weapon away from him whilst bringing his other fist down hard against the side of Knox's head. Knox had not expected such a bold move, and he floundered under the impact of the blow, his finger twitching, firing off a shot over his shoulder, which pinged off the toughened glass of the *Methuselah*'s viewing port, causing a spidery crack to open in the glass.

"Fool!" Knox shouted as he kicked out at Newbury, catching him hard in the calf and causing his leg to buckle. Newbury stuttered backwards and Knox swung the gun round in a fierce arc, cracking the butt of the weapon into Newbury's temple. Pain ignited in Newbury's skull. Lights danced before his eyes. He tumbled to the ground, disorientated, unable to prevent his fall. Knox kicked him once more, this time hard in the gut, and then turned the pistol on Veronica. He pulled the trigger.

There was a loud report, that seemed to echo throughout the entire ship, and Newbury rolled to the side in horror to see blood spray in a wide arc from Veronica's back, spattering the wall as she screamed in pain, the front of her jacket stained by a spreading blot of crimson. She collapsed in a heap, whimpering with pain.

Numb with shock, Newbury turned to find himself staring down the barrel of Knox's gun. The rogue doctor was grinning. He didn't need to say anything; the look in his eyes did the gloating for him. Newbury knew he couldn't move in time. Knox's finger squeezed the trigger. The chamber clicked round in its housing...

...and stopped. It must have jammed.

Newbury tried to scramble to his feet, but Knox struck out again, whacking him hard across the back of the head with the gun, before tossing it, frustrated, into the control pit. By this time the vessel was beginning its slow dive, and water was lapping at the bottom of the portholes. The crack, caused by the errant shot, was beginning to groan. Soon the water pressure would cause it to give in altogether, flooding the vessel with river water. It would sink like a stone.

Newbury needed to get to Veronica. All he could think about was helping Veronica. But stars were still dancing before his eyes. He shook his head. He heard footsteps. Knox was standing over him. "What a terrible disappointment." The former agent spat at him in disgust. Then more footsteps, followed by the sound of Knox mounting the ladder in the antechamber. *Let the bastard get away.* There would be more opportunities in the future. For now, he needed to get Veronica to safety before she bled to death or drowned. He pushed himself up onto his hands and knees, his head spinning. He got to his feet, shakily, and crossed the cabin. Veronica lay unconscious, a dark pool of blood forming all around her. He hoped he wasn't already too late.

Chapter Twenty-Four

Groggily, Newbury stumbled across the lurching vessel towards Veronica. She was a mess. There was blood everywhere, staining her clothes, spattered over her face, pooling on the deck beneath her. He stooped over her and she stirred, semi-conscious. He dropped to his knees, scooping her up and cradling her in his arms. "Oh, Veronica..." He held her like that for a moment, his heart breaking. Then, suddenly realising that he needed to act, he stood, carrying her across to the daybed, where he propped her upright, trying to keep her wound higher than her heart. Cautiously, he examined her injury. The bullet seemed to have torn directly through her shoulder, leaving a ragged, open exit wound from which blood was gushing freely. "Hold on. Hold on, Veronica. You're going to be all right." He grabbed the lapels of her mauve jacket and wrenched it open, popping the buttons. He took up a fistful of her blouse and used both hands to tear off a long strip, exposing the alabaster-coloured skin of her midriff. He wrapped the strip of fabric around her shoulder and bound it tight, trying to compress the wound. She cried out in pain as he applied pressure, and her eyes blinked open, searching for him frantically.

"I'm here. I'm here, Veronica."

The shock, the pain and the loss of blood were evident in her eyes. She was unable to focus. "Newbury..." was all she could manage, her voice weak, tiny bubbles of blood forming on her lips as she mouthed the word.

Newbury tried to fight the rising sense of panic that was gripping him, making it harder to breathe. He had recovered a little from the blows he'd received to the head and adrenaline was coursing riotously through his veins, causing his hands to shake. He glanced over his shoulder, trying to get a measure of their situation. Knox had fled. Newbury had heard him scramble up the ladder and out onto the deck a few moments earlier, ditching the sinking vessel. The remnants of the Osiris Ritual were scattered across the floor, disturbed in the scuffle, but the vials of brown liquid were gone. The boat's engines were still roaring. He heard a splintering crack. In the control pit, the fractured glass of the viewing port was splitting open under the pressure of the water. Newbury realised with shock that the *Methuselah* was nearly completely submerged. The glass would give way soon, allowing the river water to flood in. Not only that, but he guessed that Knox would have left the hatch open as he fled. If the upper deck of the vessel were to dip beneath the surface, there would be no stopping the onslaught of water, and their only route of escape would be blocked.

Newbury put his hand on Veronica's cheek. She was icy cold. "Stay with me, Veronica. Hold on."

Jumping to his feet, Newbury dashed towards the control pit. The vessel's control system made no sense to him whatsoever. Dials, levers, knobs; he had no idea where to start. He grabbed the nearest thing at hand, a lever that had been cranked forward and which he hoped controlled the speed of the dive. He needed to reverse the direction of the ship. He pulled it back, fully, and felt the *Methuselah* judder as the engines whined, shifting into reverse. Triumphantly, he stepped back from the controls, only to see his relief dashed almost immediately. The crack in the glass had now extended across the whole of the viewing port, a vast spider's web with a small impact crater at its epicentre, where the stray bullet had struck home. Tiny beads of water were beginning to form along the fracture lines. Beyond, he could see nothing but dirty, swirling river water.

He had to get out of there, had to get Veronica out of there. He dashed back into the main cabin. "Veronica? Miss Hobbes!" He knelt, turning her head from side to side, but it lolled pathetically. "Veronica!" It was no use. She was fading fast. He was going to have to carry her. He bent low and placed his hands under her arms, heaving her up onto his shoulder, careful not to exacerbate her wound. She gave a low moan. The makeshift bandage was holding, but blood was still seeping through, pattering to the floor. He realised his hands were covered in it. He had to get her to a surgeon, quickly. He couldn't lose her. Not Veronica.

There was a loud bang from somewhere up above, the sound of metal striking metal, as something heavy landed on the upper deck of the vessel. The whole ship shook, rocking from side to side with the impact. He heard Knox cry out in dismay, although the words themselves were lost, swallowed by the incessant roar of the engines. The reply was unmistakable, however: the dry, metallic croak of William Ashford, calling the name of his eternal opponent. "Knox!"

So, Knox hadn't yet been able to get away. Newbury had lost all sense of time.

He steadied himself with a deep breath. His burden safely secured on his shoulder, Newbury rushed to the ladder in the antechamber. The space was small, and he had to be sure not to knock Veronica's head against the wall as he mounted the first rung of the ladder. He began to climb, using one hand to haul himself upwards, the other hand wrapped safely around the waist of his unconscious assistant. The going was tough, but he made steady progress, driven on by the sounds of the scuffle from above: a sword striking metal and the grunting of the two men, locked in deadly combat.

Below, the glass pane finally gave way with a splintering crack, and water began to gush into the main cabin. He didn't have long. Newbury knew that. Soon the weight of the water would overwhelm the power of the engines and the *Methuselah* would resume its slow, ponderous course towards the bottom of the river. He was resolute, however. He would get Veronica to safety. This ship would not become their tomb. He pressed on.

Newbury emerged from the open hatch to find himself grasping at water. It was lapping at the lip of the hatch, about to start streaming over the side, into the vessel itself. The *Methuselah* had almost completely submerged, its upper deck sloshing in water as it listed from side to side, its paddle engines straining against the sheer weight of the water that was flooding into the main cabin below. Gasping as the cold water slapped him in the face, Newbury struggled to pull himself and Veronica out of the hatch and onto the unstable deck above. He knew he was exposed, but a quick glance reassured him that Knox was already occupied. The doctor had drawn his sabre and was facing off against the hulking figure of Ashford, who had now abandoned his torn, tattered cloak and had his arms outstretched, taking sweeping blows at the other man. The remains of his discarded cloak drifted away lazily with the gentle current of the river, like a puddle of spilt ink.

Knox was grinning foolishly, his once-blind eye twinkling with glee. He was parrying deftly with his blade – and Newbury, stumbling onto the deck and falling to his knees, Veronica still clutched tightly in his arms – winced at the sound of metal striking metal. Rotten flesh, flayed from Ashford's forearms by the constant thrashing of the sabre, spun away in great clods, exposing more of the bizarre, brass skeleton beneath. Ashford barely seemed to register the blows. If he felt any pain, it was lost in the snarl of rage that Newbury could see writ on his face. This was why Ashford had come back. It had all been for this moment. He would have his revenge on Knox, for separating him from his family, for being the catalyst that caused him to be turned into a monster. Newbury thought he caught a glimpse of something else in that expression, too. Sadness. Ashford had reached the end. He didn't want to live any longer, not the abject half-life he'd been forced to endure for the last five years. He was set on a path of self destruction, and he fully intended to take Knox down with him when he fell.

The huge, recreated man staggered forward, almost losing his footing near the prow as the *Methuselah* dipped into the water. He swung at Knox, his feet causing water to spray into the air as he stomped across the half-submerged deck. The fight between the two men was far less elegant than Newbury's earlier encounter with Knox, but in many ways more effective. It was clear that Ashford had the upper hand, if by nothing other than virtue of the fact that he seemed unconcerned by the shower of blows he was allowing Knox to rain down on him as he pushed forward, relentlessly, focused on his goal.

Newbury could hear the ship's engines choking now, and he knew it wouldn't be long until they were all pitched into the cold water. He looked down at Veronica. Her face was pale from loss of blood. Hastily, he tested the tourniquet he had placed around her shoulder. It was still holding, but she needed surgery, and soon. He needed to get her to the Fixer. But there was no way off the boat, other than the river. He dared not risk plunging into the cold river with

Veronica already so weak. He feared she wouldn't survive the shock. He needed to get past Knox and Ashford. Perhaps then he'd be able to make a jump for the quayside.

As if reading his thoughts, Ashford took decisive action. Ploughing forward, he raised his arms and grabbed for Knox, ignoring the sharp downward swing of the other man's sword, which bit hard into the coil of tubing that stretched from Ashford's chest to the back of his skull. Blood and chemicals sprayed into the air, describing a wide arc, but Ashford paid them no heed. He chopped down hard at Knox's wrist, causing the doctor to lose his grip on the sabre. It spiralled away, clattering to the wooden boards, the weight of it causing it to slide across the uneven deck of the listing ship. Newbury watched it slip away into the water, disappearing into the murky depths of the Thames. Ashford was about to finish it.

Standing, Newbury held Veronica tightly to his chest as Ashford grasped hold of Knox, wrapping his huge, sinewy arms around the other man's chest and lifting him bodily into the air. Mechanical servos squealed as Ashford applied crushing pressure, his feet planted firmly on the deck, water lapping at his knees.

Knox wailed and spluttered, wheezing as the air was forced out of his lungs by his slowly collapsing ribcage. His legs kicked uselessly, his arms pinned to his sides, as his body was constricted by his former victim. His head turned, his eyes fixing on Newbury. Newbury could see the panic there, the desperation behind those eyes. His mouth opened and closed. He was mouthing something. Newbury stepped closer.

"Help... me..." Knox gasped. But all Newbury could see were the faces of the dead girls in the cellar beneath the Archibald Theatre, Veronica's face as the bullet ripped through her shoulder, and Purefoy's disembowelled corpse, spread out on the floor like an anatomical doll. He remained steadfast, unmoved by the doctor's plight. His jaw was set firm. There would be no redemption for this man. The hate burned within Newbury like a furnace. Knox was everything that Newbury was not. Charles was wrong. The similarities were superficial. Perhaps they were two extremes on the same scale, but they were poles apart. He needed to believe that.

Knox gave a spasm, his neck jerking back, blood spouting from his lips, his eyes rolling back in his sockets, as, with one, last, sudden movement, Ashford squeezed the last of the life out of him. The doctor's head lolled to one side.

After a moment, Ashford released the corpse, which flopped like a child's toy to the deck of the boat and then slid, ungraciously, into the river. A moment later there was nothing but a few escaping air bubbles to mark the departure of Dr. Aubrey Knox.

The *Methuselah* shook violently as its engines began to fail. Ashford stood, watching the water for a moment, as if anxious to ensure that Knox would not suddenly resurface, and then turned and staggered towards Newbury. The pump in his chest was still pushing fluid through the severed pipe, but it now become a pathetic trickle, dribbling down the side of Ashford's head. The man himself had begun to tremble. With great difficulty, he raised his feet above the sloshing water and jerked himself over to where Newbury was still cradling the unconscious Veronica to his chest. River water was now pouring into the open hatch by Newbury's feet, and he knew he had only minutes to get Veronica to safety.

Before he could reach Newbury, Ashford collapsed to his knees. The red lights of his eyes were flickering, unsteady and dim. Newbury realised that without the preserving chemicals his brain must have been drying out, starved of moisture and oxygen. He was near death. He looked up at Newbury, who met his gaze with a smile. "You did it, Ashford. You did it."

Ashford's ventilator was wheezing heavily, rasping as he dragged air into his artificial lungs. He seemed to be struggling to open his mouth. When he did, the tinny, metallic sound of his voice lacked its usual bass timbre. "Thank Charles for me, Newbury." And then he convulsed, froze, and dropped to the sinking deck of the ship, the red lights of his eyes fading to a pinprick of light, and then disappearing to a steady black. His head dipped below the water line.

Newbury lurched into action. Veronica's breathing was shallow. She'd lost a lot of blood, but the wound was clean, straight through. He only hoped he could get her to a surgeon in time.

Cautiously, he walked to the rear of the boat, his feet sloshing in the water. There was no way he could make the jump to the harbour, not with Veronica in his arms. He'd have to swim. He hoped Veronica could survive it. But there was no other option.

Cursing, he glanced up and down the quayside, looking for a means by which he could scale the harbour wall. His best option was to get to one of the other nearby boats, and from there, to safety. Hesitantly, he lowered himself into a sitting position on the side of the ship and then pitched himself forward into the water, careful to buoy Veronica so that her head remained above the surface. It didn't seem that long since he was last in the Thames, since Veronica was dragging him from the belly of a sinking airship, and he would have laughed aloud at the irony, had it not been for the gravity of his current situation.

Long, powerful strokes soon propelled him towards the nearest vessel: a large, white yacht, bobbing on the water about a hundred yards from the sinking submersible. The owners were nowhere to be seen. It wasn't difficult for Newbury to haul himself and his precious cargo up the small ladder to the safety of the deck.

Shivering with cold, his head pounding from the earlier blows, he didn't wait to catch his breath. Instead, he took a running jump over the small gap to the dock, from where he knew he could carry Veronica to a hansom, and from there on, swiftly, to safety.

Chapter Twenty-Five

"So, what did Her Majesty have to say about it all?" Sir Charles Bainbridge took a large gulp from his glass of claret and leaned heavily on the dinner table, regarding Newbury. The two men had only recently finished their meal and Mrs. Bradshaw had yet to return to clear away the evening's debris.

Newbury shrugged. "Nothing, as yet. I'm seeing her tomorrow."

Bainbridge raised a knowing eyebrow. "Tomorrow? It's been, what, three days?"

"A day or two won't change anything, Charles. Her Majesty knows that." Newbury smiled.

Bainbridge sighed. "You'd do well to remember that it's not our place to take the law into our own hands, Newbury. I mean, why didn't you call me, man?" Bainbridge was adamant. "You went and put yourself, and Miss Hobbes, in great danger. I could have helped."

Newbury shook his head. "No, Charles. The Yard would have only got in the way. This was not an occasion for the police. It had to be handled differently. You must recognise that sometimes, we need to act *outside* the law."

"But Newbury, you're forgetting. I'm not only a policeman."

Newbury grinned, a twinkle in his eye. "You can take the man out of the Yard, Charles, but you can't take the Yard out of the man.

You'd do well to remember *that*."

"Well, yes. Perhaps you're right." Bainbridge chuckled. "Dastardly affair, though. Do you believe that's the last we'll see of Aubrey Knox?"

Newbury's expression grew serious. He picked at the remnants of his pudding. "I believe so. I *hope* so. He looked quite dead when Ashford dropped him into the water."

"Quite... quite. But they're saying they haven't been able to find the body, as yet."

"Charles, I'd be amazed if anyone could find anything in that dock, let alone a man's corpse. For all we know, it was caught up in the propeller of some passing steamship or other, dashed into a thousand pieces."

"Yes. I suppose you might have it, there." Bainbridge placed his glass on the table before him, and shifted position, leaning back in his chair. "But what about this... Isis Ritual? What would have become of Knox if he'd managed to complete his machinations?"

Newbury shrugged, dropping his serviette onto the table and leaning forward to regard his friend. "The Osiris Ritual, you mean? Charles, I don't believe for one moment that it would have had any effect at all. That's what makes the whole episode even more grotesque. What he did to all those young women. He was extracting a hormone from their pituitary glands. But that, coupled with some esoteric ritual from Ancient Egypt? No. I believe it would have singularly failed to help him achieve his aim."

"Ah yes, his quest for extended life."

"I don't believe there's an answer, Charles. Knox was driven by an innate desire to live forever, and in doing so he surrendered what time he did have to this folly. What a waste. We should use our time on this earth wisely, Charles. Ashford knew that."

"Indeed he did." Bainbridge looked momentarily forlorn. "So what of Miss Hobbes? I understand it was a grave injury she endured."

"Quite so. Have you been to see her?"

Bainbridge nodded. "Of course. She seems to be convalescing well. No doubt she'll be back on her feet within a week or so. She has a strong will, that one."

"That she does." Newbury felt tired. He studied the empty plate before him. "I feared for her, Charles. I feared for what might become of her, for the danger that my gallivanting has put her in. This whole affair..." He sighed. "I don't know. I just had the sense that I was losing control."

Bainbridge nodded sagely, but didn't respond. After a moment, Newbury reached for his glass of wine and downed its contents in one long pull. He set it down again neatly before him. "Shall we retire to the drawing room, Charles? I'm feeling a need for my pipe."

Bainbridge grinned. "Excellent idea, old chap, excellent idea."

The two men abandoned the remains of their dinner and made their way through the large set of double doors into the drawing room. Newbury's clockwork owl sat on a perch in one corner, clicking its wings excitedly as they entered the room. A fire was burning low in the grate. Newbury felt immediately better. He strode over to the mantelpiece, collecting his battered old tobacco pouch and pipe. "Pour us a drink, Charles."

Bainbridge approached the worn, mahogany drinks cabinet, from which he produced two tumblers and a decanter of the finest brandy. Removing the glass stopper, he sloshed a generous measure into each glass and then turned and handed one to Newbury, who accepted it gratefully.

Standing by the fire, his sharp features cast in relief, he looked almost statuesque, a picture of nobility. His proud, hawk-like nose, his olive eyes, his finely chiselled jaw line: they were as distinctive and unmistakable as any man in London. Yet there were dark lines beneath his eyes, dark lines that told of another life.

"You look tired, Newbury."

"I feel it, Charles."

"You need to go to her."

Newbury looked perplexed. "Who, the Queen?"

"Miss Hobbes."

Newbury placed his tumbler on the marble mantelpiece with a chink, and began stuffing the bowl of his pipe with his usual fine, aromatic shag. He didn't raise his eyes to look at his friend. "Perhaps I do." He blinked, and then buried the storm of emotions he could feel welling up inside of him. He needed to avoid that particular conversation. "So, Charles. It seems you were right about Ashford. Tell me, what connection is there between you, and Mrs. William Ashford? I know about the house."

Bainbridge sighed and downed his brandy in one long draw. He reached into his pocket for his cigar case. "It's nothing untoward, Newbury. It's not what you might imagine."

Newbury shrugged. He looked up, meeting his friend's gaze. "I hadn't imagined anything, Charles. I'm in no place to judge..."

Bainbridge smiled; a world-weary smile. "Well, I don't believe that for a moment." He used his cutter to snip the end off his fat, brown cigar. "You see, things were different in those days. We all knew one another, like you and I. Now, I think myself lucky if I can spot another agent in the same room. Her Majesty keeps us all at arm's length. But in those days... Well, suffice it to say that I knew Ashford well, and I knew Catherine too. She used to get on well with Isobel." Newbury nodded. It was rare that his old friend spoke of his late wife. "I think I told you that I was the one sent to talk to her after Ashford died. Or rather, as it transpires, after Ashford died for the *first* time. I could hardly bear it, Newbury. It was the first time. The first time I'd lost a friend like that, a friend in service. Yes, we'd lost policemen, and Catherine wasn't the first widow I'd had to break the bad news to. But this was different. Catherine was a friend. She cried on my shoulder, the entire night. She wanted me to help her tell the children."

Newbury could see that even the simple act of recounting the story was a painful exercise for his friend.

"I spent much of the night comforting her, and then managed a few hours of fitful sleep in the spare room. The next morning, I helped her to break the news to the boy. He was only three years old, Newbury. It broke my heart." Bainbridge paused, rasping a match across the rough strip on the back of the matchbook and bringing the flame up to the end of his cigar. He shook it out with a wave of his hand, taking a moment to puff on the acrid smoke. "It wasn't until afterwards that I became aware of their situation. She was destitute, and a Crown pension would be hardly enough to live on. She had two children, Newbury, two beautiful young children, and her husband had given his life in the service of the Empire. What was I to do? I couldn't see her cast out or sent to the workhouse."

Newbury sucked thoughtfully on his pipe, still standing by the fire, leaning on the mantelpiece with one arm. "So you took on the house in Bethnal Green. You paid the rent, and moved her in there with her family."

"I did. I'm not ashamed of it, Newbury. She's a good woman, and I never asked for anything in return. You should see her with those children."

"I did see her. So did Ashford. He knew, Charles. He knew what you had done for him. On his death bed he told me to thank you."

Bainbridge smiled. His voice was filled with sadness. "I should have liked to have said goodbye."

"Better that you didn't, Charles. I'm not sure you would have liked what he'd become."

Bainbridge plumed smoke through his nostrils. He regarded Newbury with a severe expression. "I'm not sure any of us like what we've become."

Newbury nodded. He recognised the truth in the other man's words. He turned and retrieved his glass from the mantelpiece, taking a long, slow drink.

Bainbridge stood, collecting his empty glass from the arm of his chair. He returned to the decanter. Beside it, on the lacquered surface of the drinks cabinet, was a tall, ornate object, made of glass and bone, with a small brazier on top, and a curling pipe that terminated in a matching bone mouthpiece, carved like the head of a dragon. "What is this, Newbury?"

Newbury looked sheepish. "A pipe, Charles. A new pipe."

Bainbridge caught his meaning. "For God's sake, Newbury! Haven't you realised that stuff is killing you? I'll not allow a friend of mine to succumb to a slow death by narcotics, least of all you."

"It helps me think, is all, Charles. There's nothing more to it."

"Like hell!" Bainbridge was red in the face. "You tell yourself that, Newbury, but in truth you're just like any of us, looking for a means of escape, something to hide behind. You've simply decided that this is your particular poison. And it is poison. You're killing yourself."

Newbury looked him in the eye. "Perhaps you're right. Perhaps I am looking for an escape. Then why is it you judge me so harshly?"

Bainbridge poured himself another large measure of brandy.

"Because I don't want to be the one to put you six feet under. Because I know what it is you're doing, and I have no time for it. Why the hell should *you* be allowed to hide behind a veil of narcotics whilst the rest of us have to suffer regardless? We all have demons, Newbury." He placed the decanter back on the drinks cabinet. "For Heaven's sake, Miss Hobbes deserves better than that."

Newbury sighed. "You're right. Of course you're right. She deserves far better." It pained Newbury that he was the one who always put Veronica in harm's way. But she, in turn, was playing a game of her own, a game which he had yet to fully understand. But what he did know is that he could not allow her to become like Catherine: widowed young, abandoned. He understood why Bainbridge felt the need to protect that woman, to save her and her children from the workhouse, to offer her a better life. He was giving her the life that Ashford could not, but he was also giving her the life that he *wanted*. That was what Bainbridge was hiding behind. He craved normality. He longed for ignorance. The life of an agent was lonely, and it was lonely for a reason. He would do what he could for Miss Hobbes, but the kindest thing, he knew, was to do nothing. Charles was right. She deserved more than he could give her.

Newbury's pipe had gone out. He looked around, catching sight of a small carriage clock on a bookcase, surrounded by heaps of notebooks and journals. The night was still young. "I say, Charles. We're terribly maudlin this evening. What do you say to a trip to the White Friar's? A game of billiards and some banter."

Bainbridge smiled, his whiskers twitching amicably. "You know what, Newbury, that's the best idea I've heard in days."

"Come on then, old man." Newbury placed his pipe carefully on the mantelpiece. "Let's forget about the past for a while, and the future. Let's revel in the present."

Bainbridge nodded. "But first," he raised his glass, "the brandy."

Newbury chuckled and did the same. "Yes, indeed. The brandy."

Chapter Twenty-Six

Newbury stood by the window, holding back the netting and peering out onto the sprawling view of Kensington High Street below. It already seemed like a lifetime had passed since the incident on Knox's submersible, but in truth it had only been a matter of days. The fog had lifted during the intervening days, leaving behind only a few thin fingers that still clung obstinately to the street lamps, or lurked in the quieter parts of the city.

Below, the street was a hive of activity. He watched a ground train rolling by, the passengers inside bobbing easily with the motion of the vehicle. Hansom cabs sent pedestrians scattering as they bowled along the cobbled road, and children ran circles around each other, frolicking in the morning sunshine.

This was the third time that Newbury had called on his assistant since she had been discharged from the hospital, and on each occasion he had found her sleeping, unable to receive visitors. As she had on both previous occasions, Mrs. Grant had tried to send him away with assurances that her mistress was recovering well – no doubt concerned that his presence would in some way disturb that recovery – but today he had resolved to not take no for an answer. So, instead, he found himself waiting in the drawing room as Veronica dozed peacefully nearby.

He turned to her, leaving the constant drone of the traffic behind him. She was resting on a chaise longue, her head and shoulders propped up, covered by a blanket that had been neatly embroidered with the design of a willow tree. Her shoulder was strapped to protect her wound. She stirred, and he crossed the room, stepping closer so that she might see him when she woke. Her eyes opened. She looked momentarily dazed, and then her eyes fixed on Newbury, a pretty smile lighting her face. "How are you, Miss Hobbes?"

Veronica moistened her lips, and then looked around for a drink. Newbury fetched the jug from the bedside table and poured her a glass of water. She drank from it thirstily. After a moment, she handed it back to Newbury and gave a small cough. She looked up at him. "I'm well enough, Sir Maurice. It takes more than a bullet to incapacitate me."

Newbury smiled. "I'm delighted to hear it. I've been... concerned."

Veronica's eyes were shining. "Yes, I'd rather hoped you might." She paused whilst he tried to make sense of her statement. "But really, I'm recovering well. The doctor was able to repair the wound, so now it's just a matter of time. Although I admit I find this convalescing business most tiresome. There is so much to be done."

Newbury laughed. "Yes, well. You'll recall how often you berated me for attending the office last December when I should have been at home, resting. I fear I set a rather bad example. I've never been the best at sitting still."

Veronica glanced at the door, as if to be sure that her housekeeper, Mrs Grant, was nowhere in the vicinity of the room. "It's a good thing you were wrong about Ashford, isn't it?"

"How so?" asked Newbury, an impish expression on his face.

Veronica shrugged, and then winced as the gesture obviously caused her shoulder to spasm in pain. "He said he would turn himself in after you'd seen him at the house, just before we set off for the docks."

Newbury offered her a wry grin. "No, Miss Hobbes. I said that I was confident he would do the right thing."

Veronica frowned. "Precisely... Oh... you mean..."

Newbury glanced away. His expression darkened. "I fear I used the poor man, Miss Hobbes. I used his anger, his desire for revenge. I used him as a weapon against Aubrey Knox. In truth, I suppose I engineered his death. I must take responsibility for that, just as I must take responsibility for poor Mr. Purefoy, and for your injury. I could hardly bear the fact that you were hurt."

Veronica shook her head emphatically. "No. Sir Maurice, the responsibility is wholly mine. I went after those girls. I knew the danger I was opening myself up to. And as for Ashford – he was dead long before you ever got to him. He was just a ghost in a machine, the remnants of a man, bound to steel and brass. If you offered him anything, you offered him a resolution, an end to his nightmare. You offered him a chance at peace."

Newbury took her hand and held it gently in his own. "You're too kind, Miss Hobbes. I don't deserve that. But I thank you for it all the same."

Veronica squeezed his hand. "You deserve more than you allow yourself room to imagine." They regarded each other in silence.

After a moment, Newbury brightened. "There is something I've been meaning to say." He looked her in the eye. "But I haven't been able to find the right time."

Veronica's response was almost breathless. "Yes."

Newbury could see something in her eyes, in her expression. The weight of expectation. Hope. In turn, something inside him snapped. He could barely look at her. "It's about Amelia."

"Oh."

"No, it's good news!"

Veronica offered him a weak smile. Clearly, she'd hoped for something more. But he couldn't give her that, couldn't put her through it. Couldn't put *himself* through it. He'd seen what had become of Charles and Isobel, of Ashford and Catherine. The risks were too great.

Veronica, of course, was brave enough to put it to one side, to hide her disappointment. She toyed, absently, with the edge of her blanket. "Go on."

"I've spoken with Her Majesty. She's in agreement. Amelia is to be moved to a private establishment, the Grayling Institute, under the care of her personal team of physicians."

Veronica's eyes widened. "Oh, Maurice." She tried to sit up, but it was clearly too much. Newbury waved her still.

"I believe it is a sign of Her Majesty's gratitude towards you. For all your work on her behalf, and for your help with the Chapman & Villiers case. Evidently, you're highly regarded."

Veronica sighed, as though a weight had been lifted from her shoulders. "That's quite wonderful news. Please extend my gratitude to Her Majesty."

"I will." He put his hand on her arm. "Just as soon as you're well, I'll take you to see her – Amelia, that is – in her new home. I'm convinced things will work out for the best."

Veronica smiled, warmly. "More than that, Sir Maurice, I'm convinced this intervention will save her life. Or at least prolong it for some time." She glanced out of the window, as if seeing something that wasn't there. "I shall have to inform my parents."

"No need. The matter has already been taken in hand. Your parents have signed the relevant documents. Amelia is being transferred on Friday."

Veronica touched her damaged shoulder with an unconscious gesture. "I don't know how to thank you."

"By getting better. There's nothing more important now." Newbury paced back to the window.

"So what did Her Majesty have to say about the deaths of Knox and Ashford?"

Newbury shrugged. "I saw her this morning. She was sanguine. She gave little away. I suspect it draws a line under a long and complicated story, a story that I'm only now beginning to understand."

Veronica nodded. "I suppose it does." Newbury studied her expression. What was it that she wasn't telling him? For now, he knew, he had to forgo all such thoughts. What was important was that she recovered, as quickly as possible. "So, what next?" she asked, inquisitively.

"Next? Next we do what we always do. We return to our sedentary lives, to fine wine and cigars, to meals with Sir Charles, and to an office at the British Museum. To filing papers and writing dry academic treatise, as we await further instruction. It doesn't sound so bad, when you put it like that, does it?"

Veronica looked longingly out of the window, and sighed. "I'm not so terribly good at waiting."

Newbury's face cracked in a wide grin. "Nor am I, my dear Miss Hobbes," he crossed to where his coat was draped on the back of a chair, preparing to leave her to rest, "nor am I." He studied her from across the room. His eyes twinkled. "I'm sure it won't be long before something comes our way. Besides, it's nearly spring. It wouldn't do to miss the fine weather, stuck indoors behind a musty old desk." He located his hat, and placed it on his head with a flourish.

"You're leaving, then?"

"For now. I've had word that an old friend of mine is in town. It's high time I paid him a visit. In the meantime, you need to rest. I'll return on Friday with news of your sister."

Veronica allowed herself to sink back into the cushions of the chaise longue. "Be sure to do just that. Friday seems like an eternity away."

Newbury offered her a dramatic bow. "Until then, Miss Hobbes."

"Until then, Sir Maurice."

And without further ado, he was gone.

Chapter Twenty-Seven

Amelia Hobbes rocked back in the carriage seat, brushing the window drape aside with her hand. She stared out at the city beyond. The streets rushed by like a series of still, blinking images; grey, unfamiliar. It had been so long since she had left the grounds of the sanatorium, she'd lost all sense of time. Was it months? Years, even?

Sighing, she allowed the drape to fall back into place, casting her once more in darkness. She felt tired and weak, yet filled with a new sense of optimism. She had yet to see that optimism reflected in the eyes of others, however. Dr. Mason had been kind, as always, seeing her off at the sanatorium gates, even suggesting that – time permitting – he would consider making the long trip to the Grayling Institute to pay her a visit. But Amelia could see what was really reflected in his eyes: he did not think that she was long for this world. Perhaps he was right... but perhaps not.

She knew little of the mysterious Dr. Fabian, but Veronica spoke highly of his reputation, and Amelia was well aware of his status as the personal physician to the Queen. She could hardly be bestowed with a greater honour. She had much reason to thank the enigmatic Sir Maurice Newbury, although she didn't doubt that his motives had been less than altruistic, more to do with winning the affections of her sister than with truly aiding Amelia in her plight. But that was by-the-by. Whatever his motive, Sir Maurice had given her hope: hope that Dr. Fabian might see her visions as more than just a facet of her supposed insanity; hope that in doing so, he might help her to find a way to control those visions and prevent her body from descending further into wrack and ruin. Not that there was much of her body left, she thought bitterly, glancing down at her bony knees, clearly protruding through the thin fabric of her dress.

Amelia had once been pretty, as pretty, at least, as her sister. But now, emaciated, subjected to a harsh life in the sanatorium, and covered with scars from wounds she had earned during her numerous "episodes", she looked older, worn out. There were lines on her face, dark rings beneath her eyes. And she was disgusted by her own fatigue. Above all else, she hoped that Dr. Fabian could help her to restore her energy, her enthusiasm for life, her desire to want to get out of bed in the morning. Dare she consider that Dr. Fabian might even find a cure for her? No, that was too much of a fantasy. But nevertheless, she felt the little germ of hope seed itself in the back of her mind. If she chose not to acknowledge it, perhaps it could grow unimpeded.

Tired, Amelia rested her head against the cool leather of the seat back, and closed her eyes. She would sleep now. Soon, she would have much to remain awake for.

†

Amelia came to as the carriage juddered to a brisk stop. She sat forward, urgently scrabbling for the window drapes. The carriage had come to rest at the far end of a long, gravelled driveway, and through the window she could see the corner of a grey, stone mansion. They were here. She felt her heartbeat quicken. This was it. Her new home. The Grayling Institute.

Amelia clasped her hands on her lap, letting the curtains fall back into place. It wouldn't do to display her impatience. She waited. Unbearable minutes ticked by, although in truth she had no way of judging how much time had actually passed. After what seemed like an eternity, she heard footsteps crunching on the gravel outside. Someone called up to the driver, but the words were lost in the breeze. The footsteps approached the cab. She realised she was holding her breath, as the handle turned slowly and the door of the cab was pulled open. Light flooded in through the open doorway, stinging her eyes. She blinked away tears, momentarily bringing her hand up to her face to shield her eyes from the glare. She had spent too long in darkened rooms at the sanatorium.

Framed in the doorway was a diminutive man, no taller than five foot four, balding, with trailing wisps of dark hair still clinging, resolutely, to his temples. He blinked up at her through the small, wire-rimmed spectacles that were perched on the end of his nose. He was dressed in a smart brown suit, with a white collar and black tie. His face split in a wide grin. "Good morning, Miss Hobbes. It's a pleasure to make your acquaintance. My name is Dr. Lucius Fabian."

Amelia smiled, edging forward in her seat. "Good morning. Dr. Fabian. It truly is an honour. I –"

He cut her off with a wave of his hand. "No need, Miss Hobbes." He looked her up and down. "I'm sure you are tired after your long journey. I think it best that we see you to your new rooms inside the Institute, where you can take some time to rest and recuperate. Then, later, we can talk of how we intend to manage your... affliction." He grinned. "Come now. Are you able to walk?"

Amelia sighed. "A little, perhaps. I fear that, these days, I am rather weak."

Dr. Fabian searched her face with beady eyes. "Yes. We'll have to see what we can do about that. Now, if you can manage to climb down from the carriage, there, we have a wheelchair at hand to assist you to your rooms."

Amelia nodded. With a huge effort, she lifted herself up from her seat, clutching at the sides of the cab to lend her support. Dr. Fabian stepped up onto the footplate and offered her his hand. She took it gratefully, noting that his fingers were fat and soft and well kept. Hesitantly, leaning on the doctor for support, Amelia stepped down from the cab onto the driveway below. She glanced up at the building as she dusted herself down. The Grayling Institute was an enormous country house, probably two or three hundred years old, once the domain of princes and kings, but now given over to science and more practical pursuits. This was Dr. Fabian's private establishment, managed on behalf of Her Majesty the Queen. This is where he did his great work, where members of the Royal Family themselves were brought for treatment, whether it be a dose of syphilis or a case of the "family sickness". She'd learned all this from Veronica, and consequently, she found herself in awe of the place, of the doctor and of her wondrous surroundings. To live in a palace! Already she felt her spirits lifting. How could she not recover here? Just the look of the place was enough to imbue her with energy.

Dr. Fabian adjusted his glasses. Amelia wondered if it was a nervous tic – it was the third time she'd noticed him do it in as many minutes. He glanced at the open doorway of the institute, which sat behind four Corinthian pillars at the top of a long slope. Amelia suspected that there had once been a set of stone steps, but these had now been replaced by a ramp to improve access for the infirm. Dr.

Fabian's reedy voice echoed out in the empty courtyard. "We're ready now, Mr. Calverton."

Amelia sensed movement in the shadow of the doorway. She watched intently. Sure enough, a moment later, a figure appeared, brandishing a small wicker wheelchair, which she assumed would be used to escort her into the premises. But as the figure emerged from the shadows of the doorway, Amelia felt her breath catch in her throat. *The man with no face!* The figure she had seen in her visions. She felt suddenly gripped with panic. The man pushing the wheelchair barely had the look of a man about him at all. His face was entirely hidden behind a featureless, porcelain mask, designed to give the impression of a blank human face. Two slits allowed his startling blue eyes to peer out from behind the mask, and his head was closely shaved, covered in a fuzz of auburn stubble. His upper torso was still human, and he was wearing a smart black jacket and a cravat. Beneath the waist, however, Mr. Calverton was more machine than man. His legs had been replaced by gleaming brass contraptions that parodied their biological counterparts, pistons spitting furiously in the thighs, servos grinding in the knees.

Mr. Calverton cocked his head as if to acknowledge Amelia, but otherwise remained mute. There was a long, silent pause, before he edged forward with the wheelchair, his pointed metal feet scraping on the flagstones. The servos squealed and whined as he slowly descended the ramp. When he reached the gravel path, he rolled the wheelchair forward, as if gesturing for Amelia to take a seat. She noticed he was wearing white gloves.

Amelia felt a shiver run along her spine. There was something about the man, something she'd seen in her visions, but was not yet able to place. He had a story. A story that had not yet come to an end. She wasn't sure if she wanted to know what that end might be.

Dr. Fabian seemed to notice Amelia's alarm, and put a steadying arm around her shoulders. "Come now, Miss Hobbes. There is no need to be afraid. Mr. Calverton will see to your every need."

Trying not to grimace, Amelia allowed herself to be led forward towards the entrance. Mr. Calverton came forward to greet her. She studied his blank expression, realising that it was this, more than anything, which had inspired her sense of unease. She was unable to read his face. She had no idea if, behind that plain, porcelain visage, the man was smiling or frowning at her. His eyes seemed vacant. Dead. Suddenly, she felt a longing for her old room, back at the sanatorium. She closed her eyes and tried to suppress her fears.

Dr. Fabian gently placed his hands on her arms and lowered her into the wheelchair. Amelia gave him a brisk nod of acknowledgement, and then together, the small party wound its way slowly inside the stark edifice of the Grayling Institute.

Inside, the reception hall retained many of its original features: the bold, galleried staircase, the glassy marble floor and the high, decorative ceiling. Rooms and passageways branched off from the hallway all manner of illogical directions, like arteries winding away from a heart. It was quite different from the sanatorium, and briefly, Amelia allowed herself a smile. Perhaps she had been hasty. Perhaps her earlier hopes had been right. This was a place to heal.

Dr. Fabian led them away down a small passageway to the left of the staircase. The space had obviously been converted from old servants' quarters, and now, Amelia realised, the rooms that stemmed off from the main corridor had been remodelled as apartments for the patients. The wheelchair creaked as they rolled on along the corridor, the sound of Mr. Calverton's clicking feet a constant distraction.

Presently, Dr. Fabian came to a stop. He gestured through an open doorway on the right-hand side of the corridor. Mr. Calverton brought the wheelchair to a stop. Dr. Fabian coughed into his fist. "These shall be your rooms, Miss Hobbes, for the duration of your stay. I hope you find them to your liking." He stepped to one side, allowing her a clearer view. Amelia gasped. The apartment consisted of two rooms, linked by an internal door, with tall sash windows that looked out upon the perfectly manicured gardens at the rear of the old mansion. Topiary sculptures described creatures from ancient mythology, and birds wheeled in the sky above a glittering lake. The rooms themselves were panelled in dark oak and well furnished. A four-poster bed filled the antechamber, and in the large drawing room an ornate marble fire surround dominated one wall, a low fire crackling in the grate. Two armchairs, a chaise longue and a sideboard completed the arrangements, and an ancient portrait hung on the far wall, showing a regal-looking fellow in plate armour, standing beside an immense globe.

Amelia began to climb out of her wheelchair, but Dr. Fabian waved her to remain seated, instead ushering Mr. Calverton to wheel her forward into the room. "Really? This is really where I shall stay?"

Dr. Fabian's lips curled. "Indeed it is, Miss Hobbes. I am sure you will be comfortable. Now," he stepped back, as if suddenly galvanised into action, "we shall take our leave. No doubt you're tired after your long journey. Perhaps this evening we could dine together, and I could tell you a little more of our work here at the Institute?"

Amelia nodded. "I'd like that very much."

"Excellent! I shall return to escort you to dinner at seven o'clock. In the meantime, your belongings will be delivered shortly. Good day to you, Miss Hobbes."

"Good day to you, Dr. Fabian." She glanced, warily, at the other man, who stood to one side, regarding her, unblinking. "And to you, Mr. Calverton." The masked man remained silent, turning to stomp unceremoniously from the room. Dr. Fabian gave a curt bow, and then also took his leave, pulling the door shut behind him.

Amelia gazed longingly out of the window. Then, surprised, she turned back to regard the door as she heard a key pushed into the lock and bolts slide shut in the doorframe. The doctor had locked the door behind him. Why should he do that? She wheeled herself over to the door and tested the handle. It was locked firm. She was trapped.

Frustrated, Amelia considered her situation. The lavishly furnished room, then, was nothing but a lavishly furnished cell. What was this place? It certainly didn't seem like a hospital. And what of Mr. Calverton? What affliction had he endured to wind up in such a way? Amelia gave an involuntary shudder. Perhaps, with him wandering the premises, it was better that the door to her room was locked after all.

Easing herself out of the chair, Amelia crossed to the chaise longue and took up a position at the foot of the window. She watched the birds dancing in the sky above the lake, and hoped it would not be long before her sister, Veronica, was able to pay her a visit.

Epilogue

The morning was crisp and chill, and the sun had yet to poke its way through the hazy layer of yellow fog that still clung to the tree-tops and surrounding buildings, cloaking everything in a fine, gossamer web.

Newbury watched his breath plume in the frigid air. The cold was penetrating, bone deep, and he longed for the comfort of his Chelsea drawing room and the roar of an open fire. It was early – too early – and he had not slept. In truth he'd been unable to sleep properly for a week, not since the events in the Archibald Theatre and his conversation with Veronica in Knox's makeshift laboratory. He'd managed to lose himself in laudanum-inspired dreams, draped on the daybed in his study, but sleep – real sleep – had continued to elude him. Instead, he'd been reduced to lying on his bed, staring not at the ceiling but at an elaborate reconstruction of events, as conjured by his mind's eye. He kept replaying their conversation, over and over, attempting to tease meaning out of half-remembered looks and hastily spoken words. What had Veronica been trying to tell him? He thought he knew, now. The evidence was incontrovertible: her knowledge of Knox had helped to bring a swift conclusion to the case. But if he was right, why on earth would she reveal the truth to him in such an opaque fashion? What else was there that he still did not know? There had to be another dimension to it, something that was staring him in the face.

Newbury hated the thought that he was working in the dark, and also that he was forced to resort to such clandestine activities as loitering outside her apartments and following her across town. The emotional conflict was enough to make his stomach churn. But he needed to know if he could trust her.

Still, he had little time to consider the implications now. He'd been following Veronica for over an hour, first by hansom cab, and then, for the last mile, on foot, ever since she'd abandoned her transport and taken instead to the footpath. He watched her slight figure sway from side to side with every footstep as he kept pace, careful to remain out of sight. It was clear she was still suffering with her damaged shoulder; her gait was a little awkward and she held her upper body stiffly, like a soldier, erect and alert. He knew if he asked her, later, she would tell him she had remained at home, convalescing under doctor's orders.

Ahead of them loomed the splendour of Buckingham Palace, towering out of the mist like a grey monolith. There could be no mistaking her destination.

Hanging back, Newbury watched Veronica approach the gates. To his surprise, she was acknowledged immediately by the guard, who pulled the iron portal open and admitted her to the Palace grounds without a word. Newbury crossed the road and followed her progress through the tall railings, catching glimpse after stuttering glimpse as she strode, purposefully, across the courtyard. Newbury could see she was heading around the side of the building. He stopped in the shadow of an ash tree, watching, waiting, his heart in his mouth.

Moments later, he watched as she stopped before a familiar door and rapped loudly, three times. He heard the wooden panel slide open, and imagined Sandford, the agents' butler, peering out.

A second later the panel clicked shut and the door swung open. Veronica disappeared inside.

And there he had it.

Veronica Hobbes: agent to the Queen.

Newbury felt a growing sense of tightness in his chest, like a dead weight had been laid upon him, forcing the air out of his lungs. So he'd been right. Veronica worked for the Queen. The duplicity made his head spin. To what end had it been kept from him? Did Charles know? He'd suspected it since their conversation in the cellar, but to have it confirmed... He was surprised by the bizarre sense of vertigo he felt, standing there in the cold morning in the shadow of a tree.

Newbury didn't want to acknowledge what he knew in his heart to be true. Veronica had been employed by the Queen to spy on him, to monitor his actions and report back to the Palace. Even now, he could hear Charles's words, echoing around inside his head. "The Queen is worried... Even the best of men are fallible."

Victoria was concerned he would turn out like Knox. He cursed under his breath. He didn't know where this left him, with the Queen, with Veronica. The feelings she'd intimated... had they even been real? A ruse to draw him closer? The implication was too awful to bear.

Sighing, Newbury turned and walked away into the hazy morning. He could be at Johnny Chang's place within the hour, chasing the dragon, losing himself in the sickly-sweet vapours. The pull of it was like lightning in his veins.

Gathering speed, he allowed himself to be swept up in his cravings. He was tired, and after all, he had a great deal to consider.

What Lies Beneath

A Maurice Newbury Investigation

Dear Alice

Soon! Soon we will be together again. It seems like centuries have passed since I was last able to drink in your sweet scent, to caress your pale cheek, to gaze upon your pretty face. I miss watching you dance in the gardens in that delicate floral gown; miss seeing your tousled hair tumble loosely over your shoulder; miss your beaming smile. How much it pains me to be apart from you! Yet we must take care not to arouse suspicion. Our secret must remain safe. We share it, a burden, together. I will come to you soon, and we can be together again, if only for the shortest of times.

How I long for the day when we do not have to consider the thoughts of others. I live for it. My heart thumps in my chest even now, as I think of that day, so loud that I wonder Felicity cannot hear it in the next room!

Poor Felicity. How little she knows. Often I sit here, at my desk, and wonder whether it would be kinder to tell her the truth. It amazes me that she does not yet know. Under her own roof! She glides through her days in blissful ignorance, unaware of the love that has blossomed between her husband and another. She is no sort of wife to me, but I pity her still. I console myself with the knowledge that she will know soon enough. When the time is right, she will know.

Now, my dearest Alice, I must go. An old friend is coming to visit us. Sir Charles Bainbridge, a policeman from Scotland Yard. Think what he would say if he knew! But do not fear, my love. Soon I will hold you again. Soon.

Isambard

Dear Alice

I fear our liaison must be once more delayed. Much to my surprise, Sir Charles has arrived with another visitor in tow – Sir Maurice Newbury – an anthropologist from the British Museum.

The man is neither wanted, nor welcome. I know you shall think harshly of me for such words, Alice, but I admit I find Sir Maurice difficult to palette. He has a certain manner about him; overbearing, direct; arrogant, even. Still, it gives me a feeling of secret glee to know that neither he nor Sir Charles are aware of our secret. Nor shall they be, for I shall take great care not to let it slip, even though I feel a burning desire to shout about it from the highest rooftops.

Sir Maurice is unwell. I do not know the cause of his illness, but he starts and shivers and has dark rings beneath his eyes. He barely ate at dinner last night, but guzzled brandy readily enough, until he was clearly inebriated. Sir Charles then saw him off to his room. I wonder if he drinks to forget?

Felicity, of course, fawns over him like a pet. It's disgusting to watch. She fetches him brandy and walks around the gardens with him as if he is the most interesting man alive. Little does she pay me, her husband, such attention! (Still, my dear, I have you. That means more to me than you could possibly imagine. I do not want or need her attention any longer).

Sir Charles says that Sir Maurice is in need of a rest, that he has imposed his friend upon me in an effort to get him away from the city for a few days. Clearly there is more to the matter than that, but it remains unspoken. Of course, I have smiled graciously and welcomed them both with open arms, as any worthy gentleman should. But in truth I cannot wait for them to leave so that I may pay you a visit. I live in torment, awaiting the time when I can see you next.

Now, I must away to dinner.

Be patient, my love.

Isambard

Dear Alice

Questions, questions. Incessant questions! Newbury knows nothing but questions.

Today, my dear, I took the men shooting on the grounds. The pickings were lean, and we returned with only a handful of mangy rabbits. Needless to say, Newbury was near useless. It was all I could do to still my hand from aiming my shotgun at the odious academic. He proved relentless with his conversation, worming his way into our lives, probing for clues; digging, digging, digging. A constant torrent of questions, right up until we broke to change for dinner.

I think he may suspect something. Does he know of our secret? Does he imagine our trysts? I tried to test him with clever questions – eking out a little information and gauging his response – but he is clever, that one, and did not give himself away. I thought I saw a little smile on his lips, however – a secret, knowing smile – and I'll be watching him. Watching his every movement, listening to his every word. I have a measure of the man, dear Alice, and he shall not be allowed to discover our secret. I promise you. He shall die before he knows the truth.

I shall leave this note for you tonight, my love, but shall not risk discovery by lingering for too long in the hope of seeing you. Surely they must leave soon! I need so much to hold you in my arms.

Isambard

Dear Alice

Today I almost let it slip! Tonight at dinner, Sir Charles and I we were talking of his late wife, and I said your name when I meant to speak of Felicity. Thankfully no one appeared to notice, save for a sly look from Newbury. More and more I wonder if he has somehow discovered the truth about us, and worse, that he secretly wants you for himself. You would never leave me, would you, my dearest Alice? Not for him. Not for that secretive, conniving academic. No, I know you too well for that. Of course you would not. You made me a promise, and you are mine forever more. Such is my promise to you.

Nevertheless, it gave me something of a thrill to speak of you in public, to let your sweet name form on my lips. I wish I could talk of you to Sir Charles. We were at school together, the two of us, and I long to confide in him. I am sure he would understand. But I dare not. I cannot risk it. What if he brought it up with Newbury? What if he were unable to keep it to himself, to share in the secret, just as you and I do? Then they would be free to spirit you away from me, and I would lose you forever. I could not bear that.

I must get rid of them, and soon. Sir Charles seems insistent on overstaying his welcome. Two days already! The longer they remain, the longer it will be before we can be together.

Your love

Isambard

Dear Alice

Newbury is incorrigible! Today I found him skulking around the entrance hall, examining things, looking for answers, for hidden clues. He'll never work it out, the damn fool. He claimed to be simply admiring the portraits, but I know his words for the lies they are. He is looking for evidence. He plans to expose us.

If he and Sir Charles do not leave after breakfast tomorrow I will have to take action. Newbury is already ill. I will introduce a poison to his meal. I have some hidden in the potting shed. A slow, deadly poison that will offer up all the symptoms of a heart complaint. He will be dead by late afternoon, and no one will suspect a thing. I know you will think me clever and brave for taking such decisive measures.

Tomorrow night, we will be together!

Isambard

Dear Alice

He knows! I can see it in his eyes! That damnable Newbury. He knows our secret!

He is a sly one, I'll give him that. He did not join us for lunch. After all of my efforts! I had taken great care to create an opportunity to be alone with his food. I dosed his soup with the poison, and took my place at the table just in time for Sir Charles and Felicity to arrive together (after doing heaven knows what, alone, in the gardens!).

Newbury, however, sent his apologies, claiming he was feeling unwell and would retire to his room for the remainder of the afternoon. Throughout the meal I could do nothing but imagine him creeping around upstairs whilst I was trapped in the dining room with the others. He was searching for you, Alice, rummaging around where he's not wanted, trying to expose our secret. To take you for himself.

Well, tonight I draw a line. I'm coming for you, dearest. Tonight I shall make my move. I can wait no longer. We shall flee this place, together. I shall make the preparations. Be ready, my love!

Isambard

Dear Alice

I can barely bring myself to write a word. All is lost. Newbury and Sir Charles are conspiring in the drawing room. I overheard them talking this afternoon. Newbury has seeded insidious thoughts in Sir Charles's mind. He uses words such as 'erratic behaviour' and 'unhinged'. He makes out that I have lost my mind!

I have no doubt, now, my dear. They're coming for me. I have such little time left. We shall not get away.

Hold on, my love. Our secret is exposed. I'm coming now to bid you farewell before they tear you from my arms. Newbury will not have you! I will die before I give you up.

Know this, my sweetest Alice: I have always loved you!

Isambard

Miss Veronica Hobbes placed the sheaf of letters on the low table beside the chaise longue. Her shoulder was still strapped from the bullet wound she had received two weeks earlier, during her encounter with the rogue agent, Dr Aubrey Knox. She winced as she moved, turning to regard the man standing over by the window. She was wearing a serious expression on her pretty face. "These letters are clearly the work of a madman, Sir Charles. What the devil is going on?"

Sir Charles Bainbridge offered her a heartfelt shrug. His bushy grey moustaches twitched as he spoke. "The world is going to pieces, is what, Miss Hobbes. Dr. Isambard Ward was a good man. I spent many of my formative years in his company. It's a damnable affair. I can hardly believe it myself."

Veronica looked lost. "Believe what? What exactly occurred? And what of Sir Maurice?"

Bainbridge edged over to where Veronica was resting on the chaise longue. He looked at the pile of letters. "It was meant to be a relaxing break. I believed I was taking Newbury to a place of sanctuary, a place where he could cast off his dependence on that wicked poppy." He sighed heavily. "Little did I imagine that an attempt would be made on his life, nor that I was planting him directly in the middle of another mystery."

"So, what, Dr. Ward had lost his mind, and fixated on Sir Maurice, believing him to be a villain? But who is Alice? And what did Newbury want with her?"

Bainbridge smiled, a sad smile "Alice was once a maid in Ward's employ. What's clear now is that he developed an obsession with her, a deep passion that I'd venture she did not reciprocate. I believe it was this unrequited love that drove him to commit the most heinous of crimes. He became unhinged. He poisoned Alice and hid her corpse beneath the floorboards in one of the disused guest rooms. He rubbed salves into her dead flesh in an attempt to preserve her body, and paid her visits on a regular basis, fantasising that they were having an affair." He shuddered, clearly disturbed by the memory of what he had seen. "He wrote her love letters – such as these – and posted them to her through a crack in the floorboards. He couldn't have her in life, so he made sure she couldn't leave him in death. His wife, Felicity, had no notion of what was going on. She was simply told that Alice had left their employ to take up a position as a governess in another nearby household."

Veronica shook her head, clearly dismayed. "I'm so sorry, Sir Charles. It must have been a terrible shock, to discover an old friend had committed such a terrible act. How did it come to light?"

"Newbury. From the time we arrived Newbury knew that something wasn't right with the chap. I knew he was right, but put it down to stress or anxiety. I suppose I was more forgiving of an old friend's eccentricities. But it didn't sit right with Newbury. Not one bit of it. He said that he'd seen the signs before. He thought that Ward was hiding something, and he was right."

"So Ward was right, too. In the letters, I mean. Newbury really was on his trail."

"In a manner of speaking. Newbury suspected that something was amiss, but in no way had he fathomed just how depraved and shocking that something would prove to be. And whilst he was certainly monitoring Ward's behaviour, he really was unwell, and assures me that at no point did he actually spend time snooping around the house as Ward suggests in his letters. Those are just the ravings of a paranoid mind, I fear."

"So what did occur?"

"It was Ward himself who gave it away. After writing that last letter, the bundle of which we discovered only after the Yard had been in to clear up the whole damn mess, Ward decided that we were on to him. In a last, desperate attempt to get away, he rushed to the guest room where he'd hidden the girl's body and began ripping up the floorboards. I think he'd intended to steal away with the corpse. Needless to say, all that banging and shouting alerted us downstairs, and we all went rushing up to discover him cradling the dead woman's body like a baby. The stench was near unbearable. Thankfully, Newbury was able to spare Mrs Ward the shock of seeing her husband reduced to such a state. I was able to prise Ward free of that grim embrace, and we sent for the Yard immediately. Ward confessed the whole thing to me, later, after we'd taken him back to London and thrown him in a cell."

"I expect he'll hang for his crime?"

"Without a doubt."

Veronica reached for a glass of water that was perched on the table beside her. She took a long drink. Bainbridge stood by, watching her, wordless. The silence between them was enough to convey everything that they were both thinking.

"It's Mrs Ward that concerns me." Bainbridge turned to gaze out of the window once again, the sunlight dappling the front of his jacket. Veronica watched the dust motes dance lazily in the air. "She doted on Isambard. Hung on his every word. She'll never be the same again, poor woman. How could you go on living after discovering a secret like that, about someone you loved?"

Veronica couldn't look at him. "People keep secrets from one another, Sir Charles. Sometimes for the best of reasons."

"Pah. Poppycock. There's never a good reason for keeping something from the people you love. Secrets are never anything but destructive. Believe me. I was married once." He turned to meet her gaze, a warm smile on his lips. "Anyway, I didn't come to regale you with stories of murder and insanity. I came to find out how you were recovering from your injury."

Veronica grinned. "In that case, Sir Charles, I do believe we should have Mrs Grant put the kettle on. Would you mind terribly if I asked you to search her out and have her fetch the tea?"

"Of course not. It would be my pleasure." He turned and quit the room, calling out for Veronica's housekeeper as he made his way along the landing to the top of the stairs.

Veronica lay back on the cushions and sighed. He was right. Of course he was right. Secrets would be the end of them all. Secrets were the foundation upon which she had built her entire life, what lay beneath the thin veneer of her existence. Secrets were her burden, too, and she knew how they had driven Isambard Ward towards insanity.

Veronica placed the empty glass on the table and turned to see Bainbridge open the door and step into the room. Her heart sank. Secrets would be the end of her friendship with this man, and perhaps the end of her relationship with Newbury, too. She only hoped it wasn't too late. She feared it probably was.

Only time would tell. Time, and the truth, and she feared the latter more than she had feared anything else in her entire life.

The Shattered Teacup

A Maurice Newbury Investigation

London, December 1901

"**N**ewbury! Thank God you're here."

Sir Maurice Newbury swept into the hallway, his overcoat billowing open behind him as he marched across the marble floor towards his friend. His expression was serious. "Don't thank God, Charles. Thank the cabbie who agreed to take my fare this close to Christmas." His face was ruddy from the biting cold and his breath was shallow with exertion. He began removing his black leather gloves, one finger at a time, eyeing the older man for any clue as to why he'd been called from his bed at such an early hour of the morning.

Sir Charles Bainbridge, his grey moustache twitching with irritation, glanced over Newbury's shoulder as if he were expecting someone else. "Miss Hobbes?" He looked flustered.

Newbury shot his friend a stern look. "Charles. It's Christmas Eve!"

Bainbridge nodded in acknowledgement, as if the date had only just dawned on the Chief Inspector. He glanced at his pocket watch. "Quite so, old man. Quite so." He shook his head. "Well, Christmas or not, I'm afraid the situation here is rather grave."

Newbury nodded. He was a young-looking man approaching his fortieth year, with jet black hair and a hawkish nose. His eyes were a startling, emerald green. He glanced into the open doorway behind Bainbridge. "Lord Carruthers?"

"In there. Dead."

Newbury raised an eyebrow. "Indeed?" He shrugged out of his overcoat and scarf and handed them both to the Chief Inspector, who accepted them with a begrudging sigh. Newbury paused for a moment to examine the burst lock and splintered frame where the door had been forced, and then stepped over the threshold into the dimly-lit room beyond. He cast his eyes around. "The drawing room, then."

"Yes. Not the most auspicious place to die."

Newbury frowned, glancing round at the dusty stacks of books and trophies. "Oh, I don't know..." Then he caught sight of Carruthers's corpse, sprawled out on the floor before the desk and contorted into a shape that it was never meant to achieve in life. He turned to Bainbridge. "Ah. Well perhaps not."

He paced further into the room, taking in his surroundings. The room was panelled in dark oak, giving it a gloomy cast, despite the large sash window in the south wall that looked out over an expanse of lawned garden. There was a large wooden writing desk, a bookcase full of austere biographies and Dickens novels, and a chair in one corner, a newspaper draped haphazardly over one arm. There was a small occasional table beside the chair, a well-loved pipe and an empty white saucer resting on its surface. The room had a musty smell about it, of old books and stale air. It reminded Newbury of his study back in Chelsea, only lacking the specimen jars and other, more arcane trinkets.

Something trilled in the corner of the room behind the chair. Newbury glanced at Charles.

"One of Carruthers's little toys. We haven't been able to work out how to shut the thing up."

Intrigued, Newbury approached the chair. The noise sounded again, a kind of 'tee, tee', accompanied by a quiet mechanical whirr. Leaning over the back of the chair, Newbury peered into the shadowy corner. A strange brass object was moving about on the floorboards, its metal feet clacking against the smooth lacquer. It was about the size of a human head, but crafted to resemble a barn owl. Its metallic feathers shimmered in the low light of the gas lamps. Newbury watched it for a moment as it paced about, just like a real bird, its head twitching from side to side as it walked. After a few seconds, it turned its head as if to regard him, gears grinding as its glittering, beady eyes adjusted their focus, turning slowly to settle on his face. Then its brass wings clacked and fluttered noisily, and it began to trill again, shuffling off to hide beneath the chair.

Newbury looked across the room at Bainbridge. "What a marvellous little device. Seems almost as if it's alive."

"Hmmm."

Newbury grinned at his friend's disdain. The older man looked tired and exasperated, and was clearly in need of a rest. He decided to press on. "So, before I examine the body, what can you tell me of the circumstances?" He indicated Carruthers's cadaver with a wave of his hand. "How did you come to find him like this?"

Bainbridge moved over to stand beside Newbury. He kept his eyes on the corpse whilst he talked, as if the dead man were somehow likely to move if he so much as dared to look in the other direction. "Well, it seems to me that he's suffered a massive failure of the heart. The door was locked from the inside when the valet found him this morning. He's been here since some time last night. Alone."

Newbury nodded, urging the other man to continue. "Go on."

Bainbridge cleared his throat. He frowned. "I'll admit it doesn't sit right with me, Newbury. He was a healthy man, in the prime of his life. He was only thirty-six, for Heaven's sake. What should cause him to drop down dead in such a way?" He rubbed his hands over his face, sighing. "And then there's the note."

"The half-scrawled note on the desk, you mean?"

Bainbridge raised an eyebrow. "Yes, I thought you would have spotted it." He sighed, as if in recognition of the fact that his observations were likely to be redundant in the presence of the other man. "Over here." He led Newbury over to Carruthers's desk, stepping around the contorted body, which lay heaped on a Turkish rug, a wooden chair overturned just beside it. He pointed to a sheet of crisp, vellum paper that was resting on the surface of the desk. "He must have been trying to write it as he died."

Newbury stooped over to examine it. Bainbridge was right – it did look as if the note had been prematurely curtailed. The letters B, R, O had been scrawled untidily in black ink, printed hastily in capital letters with a shaky hand. This half-formed word was followed by a smudged black line that trailed off the page and across the desk, terminating at the lip of the desk as if the pen had been dragged violently across the surface. He noted that the leather writing surface had been severely scored where the nib of the pen had bitten into it, opening a large rent.

Newbury crouched, searching out the missing pen. It lay on the floor a few inches from Carruthers's right hand. He reached for it, turning it over in his fingers. It was a fine specimen, crafted in Switzerland about a decade before. He touched the tip against the back of his hand. The nib was dry. The note had been written hours ago.

He glanced under the desk. There was a heap of shredded paper, bits of torn envelope, cream-coloured writing paper, and newspaper. It seemed almost as if the strange clockwork owl had been trying to build a nest.

Newbury turned his attention to the body, noting that the dead man's fingers were stained with black ink. It was clear that Carruthers had been trying to scrawl a message on his notepad when whatever had killed him had caused him to convulse to the floor, leaving the message unfinished. He was still dressed for dinner, although he had obviously retired to the drawing room in his shirtsleeves, as his jacket was absent from the scene. His hair was blonde and clipped short. His eyes had once been blue, but had now taken on a milky glaze. His skin, too, had developed a waxy sheen, and his face was twisted in a disturbing, rictus grin. He had clearly been dead for some hours.

Bainbridge cleared his throat. "What do you make of it?"

Newbury, still crouching beside the body, looked thoughtful. "The note? Nothing, as yet." He studied the corpse for a moment longer, before glancing up at Bainbridge, distracted. "What is it that you're not telling me, Charles?"

Bainbridge smiled, caught out. "I believe I have a measure of what that note could mean. Carruthers's valet. His name is Brownlow. I've had him detained in the dining room for questioning. I supposed that Carruthers could have been attempting to identify his killer, if indeed it proves to be anything other than a natural death. The letters, see: 'BRO'. The beginning of the name: Brownlow."

Newbury stood. "Very clever, Charles." He placed the pen carefully on the desk beside the note. "And it was certainly murder. Whatever made him convulse like that...his heart may have stopped, but it wasn't the cause of his death."

Bainbridge glanced down at the body. "Strangulation? I didn't see any bruising to the throat."

Newbury shook his head. "Poison."

Bainbridge studied his friend for a moment in silence. It was the last thing he needed to hear on Christmas Eve.

The clockwork owl trilled again from the corner of the room. 'Tee, Tee.'

The moment stretched. Finally, the Chief Inspector sighed, rubbing a hand over his face. He smiled at Newbury, a wordless appreciation for the other man's help. "Brownlow, then?"

Newbury nodded. "Brownlow."

Together the two men left the drawing room – and the corpse – behind them, making their way towards the dining room, where Carruthers's valet, Brownlow, was waiting patiently to be questioned.

†

The dining room was long and grandiose, with a dominating marble fireplace, exquisitely moulded cornicing, a large, austere portrait of Lord Carruthers on one wall, and a glittering glass chandelier that hung low over the table. By the door, a uniformed Bobbie was standing watch, his hands tucked neatly behind his back. He stood to attention as Bainbridge and Newbury entered the room.

At one end of the table sat an aged man in a black suit. He looked haggard and drawn, his skin pale, his eyes rheumy and tired. He was wringing his hands nervously, glancing from side to side as if he expected someone to sneak up on him from behind. Newbury would have placed him in his mid-sixties, although, judging by his wisp of white hair and his leathery, liver-spotted skin, he could have been much older. He had evidently been worn down by many years of continual service.

"Mr. Brownlow?" Bainbridge asked, his tone authoritative, as the two investigators approached the seated man.

The other man looked up. "Yes."

"We've come to ask you some questions. About the death of Lord Carruthers. My name is Sir Charles Bainbridge, of Scotland Yard."

"Yes." Brownlow glanced down at his hands.

Bainbridge pulled out a chair and lowered himself to sit opposite the man. Newbury stood off to one side, observing.

"So, Mr. Brownlow. You are Lord Carruthers's valet?"

"Indeed. I've been with the family for many, many years." His voice was reedy and high pitched. He was clearly distraught. "I was with Lord Carruthers's father before he died. I've lived in this house all of my adult life."

Bainbridge nodded. "I can see this has all been a grave shock to you. Who else was in the house last night, besides yourself and Lord Carruthers?"

"Just Mrs. Richards, the Housekeeper, and Mr. MacKinnon, the Butler. Many of the others servants have been dismissed for Christmas."

Bainbridge stroked his moustache. "Can you tell us what occurred when you found your master's body?"

Brownlow looked down at his fingers, and then moved his hands underneath the table, as if suddenly conscious of his own nervousness. "It wasn't until this morning that I discovered anything was awry. Lord Carruthers is −" he caught himself, "was an early riser by habit. Consequently, I have grown accustomed to retiring early, so to be ready to rise before my master each morning. Last night he dismissed me after dinner, around eight o'clock, and I went immediately to my room. I spent some time reading before taking to my bed around half past nine." He cleared his throat, glancing at Newbury, who was studying the man intently. "When I woke this morning I completed my usual round of preparations for the day, before looking in on the master at precisely eight o'clock. That was when I discovered his bed had not been slept in."

Bainbridge leaned back in his chair, looking thoughtful. "What was your first reaction?"

"I know my master's habits well. This was highly irregular. I spoke with Mrs. Richards and she informed me that the last she had seen of the master was the previous evening, in the drawing room. I went immediately to the door to that room and found it locked from the inside. I knocked three times but did not elicit a response. I tried my key but found the master's key was still in the lock from the other side. Fearing the worst, I shouldered the door from its hinges and found the master dead on the floor before his desk. I sent for the police immediately."

Newbury stepped forward. "Did you touch anything in the room, Mr. Brownlow? This is very important. Did you move anything other than Lord Carruthers's body?"

Brownlow shook his head. He looked perplexed. "No. I'm sure of it. I didn't touch a thing."

"Then thank you, Mr. Brownlow. I believe you are free to go about your business." Newbury looked to Bainbridge, who frowned, confused, but nodded his approval, trusting Newbury's instincts.

The valet got to his feet and shuffled slowly towards the door. Newbury pulled out a chair beside Bainbridge and lowered himself into it. Then, as if it were an afterthought, he turned around in his seat and called after the valet. "Mr. Brownlow? Could you please see if Mrs. Richards is available for interview?"

The valet nodded. "Of course. I'll ask her to attend to you immediately." He disappeared into the hall.

Bainbridge turned to Newbury, a question in his eyes. Newbury shook his head. "Bear with me Charles."

The Chief Inspector sighed, loudly.

Newbury stared thoughtfully into the fireplace, where the flames were licking hungrily at the yuletide logs.

✝

Mrs. Richards was stout woman in her fifties, with dark brown hair scraped back into a tight bun, and a warm face that showed what Newbury deemed to be genuine shock and sadness at the death of her employer. She sat at the end of the table facing the two investigators, her hands folded neatly on her lap. She was wearing a long, blue, flower-print dress beneath a plum-coloured apron.

Newbury leaned forward, looking her in the eye. "So tell me, Mrs. Richards. Who stands to benefit from the death of Lord Carruthers?"

The woman looked taken aback by the directness of the question. "To be honest with you, sir, I have little to no idea. As you know, the master was not yet married, and his father was buried just a year ago this last spring. There was a younger sibling, once, a boy named Harry, but he and his mother died shortly after childbirth and the former Lord Carruthers never remarried. I expect there is a cousin or an uncle who will benefit from the estate." She shook her head. "I also expect my husband and I will be turned out before too long, once the answer to that question has been successfully ascertained."

Newbury looked thoughtful. "When was the last time you saw Lord Carruthers alive, Mrs. Richards?"

"Last night. It was just before ten o'clock. I was on my way to bed, when I happened across Mr. MacKinnon, the Butler, who was taking the master a tray of tea. I offered to deliver it on my way."

Newbury smiled. "And how did you find Lord Carruthers when you knocked on the door to the drawing room?"

Mrs. Richards thought for a moment. "Relieved, I should say. I recall thinking he must have been very much looking forward to the refreshment, given the look on his face."

"But aside from that. No sense that he was feeling unwell, or troubled in any way?"

"Not unwell, no. But it was unusual for him still to be up and about at that hour. He seemed animated, certainly. Vexed, even. But he was polite enough, and when I asked him if he needed anything else he was kind to me as usual and sent me on my way."

"And what of the tray of tea?"

"I poured him a cup and removed the tray and teapot to the hall. I collected them this morning before I began making preparations for breakfast."

"Excellent!" Newbury stood and began pacing before the fireplace, lost in thought. The Housekeeper watched him with cautious eyes. After a moment, Newbury paused behind Mrs. Richards's chair. "You may take your leave now, Mrs. Richards. I'd appreciate it very much if you could send Mr. MacKinnon along to talk with us."

Mrs. Richards got to her feet, clearly relieved. "I'll do so right away, sir."

The two men watched her as she crossed the room and disappeared through the doorway. Bainbridge glanced at Newbury, raising an eyebrow at his friend. "I know. I won't even ask."

†

Douglas MacKinnon was a smart-looking man in his early thirties. He was wearing an immaculate black suit and tie, and his hair was blonde and worn in a side parting. His eyes were a piercing, electric blue. He spoke with a gentle Scottish lilt that Newbury placed as an Edinburgh accent, and his voice itself was soft and even.

Bainbridge was first to start with the questions. "So tell me, Mr. MacKinnon. How long have you been with Lord Carruthers's household?"

The man smiled. "Only this last six months, Chief Inspector. Before then I was engaged as a butler in Edinburgh, to the Collins family."

"And how have you found Lord Carruthers?"

"An excellent man in many regards. He treated his staff well, and I was made very welcome in his household."

"And the rest of the staff. Did they accept you readily?"

MacKinnon shrugged. "They did. It was obviously a difficult time for many of them. They had lost the former Lord Carruthers only six months before my arrival, and they were still recovering from the loss of the previous butler, who had been with the family for many years. But they accepted me readily enough."

Bainbridge cleared his throat. "So when did you last see your former master alive?"

Newbury watched the butler's reaction. He remained steadfastly unemotional. "Last night. Just before ten o'clock. He rang the bell for tea."

Newbury leaned forward. "And did you deliver that tea?"

"No, sir." The butler paused. "After hearing the bell I called on the master in the drawing room to enquire as to his needs. Then I repaired to the kitchen to organise the tea. However, I met Mrs. Richards in the passageway outside of the kitchen, and since she was already heading in the direction of the drawing room, she offered to deliver the tray on my behalf."

"So can you explain why Lord Carruthers may have been showing signs of vexation when she knocked on his door just a few minutes later with that very same tray?"

"I cannot."

Newbury drew a deep breath. "You can stop pretending now, Harry. I understand that none of this has been easy."

The butler's eyes opened wide in shock, and he glanced at the door, as if making ready to run. The Bobby stiffened and stepped into the opening, blocking his escape route. Bainbridge stood, nearly knocking his chair over as he did. He glared at the butler.

"Harry? Harry Carruthers?"

Newbury nodded. "That's right, isn't it, Mr. MacKinnon? That's your real name, although no one would know it. The Scottish accent is an excellent disguise."

The man glowered at Newbury across the table. "It's no disguise. I spent my childhood rotting in an orphanage in the north, abandoned by my father after my mother's death. He couldn't bear to give up his precious Alastair, of course – my dear brother was his pride and joy – but he blamed me for my mother's death and cast me out, telling the world I had died alongside my mother. I was just an infant. I didn't discover this until years later, of course, and by then I'd already been to hell and back. But a few months ago, when my father died, I finally discovered the truth. I was visited by one of the women who had taken me in at the orphanage. She said that she couldn't live with the secret any longer."

"So you decided to get close to the family. The death of the previous butler was the perfect opportunity, I gather?"

"I was already working as a servant at the Collins house,

although my position was that of an underling. But I couldn't let the opportunity pass. I moved to the nearby village and took a cheap room at the inn. I courted one of the maids who worked at the house, and soon enough she put a word in for me with Mr. Brownlow. He was quick to take me on when I listed my credentials. By that time they were much in need of another pair of hands."

"And of course, the Scottish accent and the years of harsh living ensured that no one would recognise you. Not least your brother, who had no reason to even suspect a resemblance. For years he'd been labouring under the impression that you were dead."

"And I might as well have been, for all the difference it made when I confronted him after dinner last night. He refused to believe me. He claimed that I was dredging up his family's past in the hope of extorting his father's fortune from him. He told me to get out of his house and to never come back."

Newbury nodded. "So you decided to enact your revenge. You went directly to the kitchen, found the bottle of strychnine you had secured there for just this occasion, and prepared a deadly brew for your sibling. The clever part is how you tricked poor Mrs. Richards into delivering the poisoned cup on your behalf, so that you were never anywhere near the room whilst your brother was struggling for his life. Did you plan to come forward later to claim the inheritance?"

"Perhaps. I would have asked for what was rightfully mine."

Bainbridge banged his fist on the table. "You're a despicable wretch." He turned to the bobby, who had been standing patiently by the door, awaiting instructions. "Get him out of here. Throw him in a cell. He can spend Christmas where he belongs."

He slumped back into his chair beside Newbury, and the two of them watched as the young man was led away, his hands cuffed firmly behind his back.

"How the devil did you work it out, Newbury?" The Chief Inspector looked bemused. He tugged on his moustache, pondering the flames that still danced in the grate.

Newbury laughed. "It was the clockwork owl that gave it away."

Bainbridge turned to look at his friend, his brow furrowed. "How so?"

"It was trying to tell us all along. Those sounds it was making. 'Tee, tee'. I think it was telling us how the murder was effected. We assumed all along that there were no actual witnesses to the murder. But we were wrong. That automaton saw everything. And that's why it was making that infernal racket. It wasn't just programmed to make those sounds. It was repeating the same word over and over to put us on the right trail. 'Tea, tea'."

"My God! Are you sure?"

"I'll wager if we were to go back to the drawing room now and shift that chair we'd find all the pieces of that shattered teacup hidden under there, collected up by the owl during the night. That was the first thing I noticed when I walked into the room this morning. There was a saucer on the table, but no matching cup. Carruthers must have dropped it when he'd fallen, and the owl had saved the pieces as evidence, just like the nest it had built from scraps of paper under Carruthers's desk. The Scotsman hadn't counted on that. He was nowhere near the room when the cup was smashed, so he had no reason to look for the debris when the valet found Carruthers the next morning. He probably didn't even consider it. But the missing cup was enough to put me on his trail."

Bainbridge shook his head. "Remarkable. But what about the note? It seemed to be pointing to Brownlow."

Newbury grinned. "No, Charles, although you were on the right track. If the note had been intended to implicate Brownlow, why wouldn't he have destroyed it or removed it when he broke the door down and found Carruthers this morning, before calling the police?"

"What was it then?"

"B, R, O. He was spelling the word 'BROTHER'. He must have realised that MacKinnon had been telling him the truth, and was trying to leave us a note. One more letter and we might have got it sooner."

Bainbridge shrugged. "Well, it wouldn't have helped poor old Carruthers. We were already too late for him." He glanced at his pocket watch. "We should make haste. It'll soon be Christmas. I'll take you home in my carriage."

Newbury eyed his old friend. "Do you have plans for Christmas dinner, Charles? Mrs. Bradshaw makes a passable plum pudding, and I've no doubt the goose is big enough for the three of us."

Bainbridge smiled. "Well, now you come to mention it..."

"Come on then, old man. Let's retire to Chelsea for a brandy. We can put this whole affair out of mind and attempt to enjoy what's left of the season's festivities. Douglas MacKinnon – or rather Harry Carruthers – can wait until Boxing Day."

Bainbridge nodded, getting to his feet. "Thank you, Newbury. If you hadn't put your finger on it so quickly I'd be spending my Christmas here, interviewing the staff."

"Think nothing of it, old man. Think nothing of it. But I do ask one thing of you."

"What's that?"

"Keep an eye on what happens to that marvellous bird. If you find it needs a home..."

"It's yours, Newbury." He clapped a hand on Newbury's shoulder, laughing out loud. "Happy Christmas."

"Happy Christmas, Charles."

The two men collected their coats from the stand in the hallway and set out into the fog-laden night, in search of brandy, cigars and Mrs. Bradshaw's excellent plum pudding.

CHAPTER ONE FROM THE FORTHCOMING

GHOSTS OF MANHATTAN

BY GEORGE MANN

I have no name.

I am the judgement that lives in the darkness, the spirit of the city wrought flesh and blood.

I was born of vengeance and I have no past. I am both protector and executioner. I represent the lives of the helpless; those who will not or cannot help themselves. I show no mercy.

I exist only in the shadows. The alleyways and the rooftops are my domain. I feel the heartbeat of the city, like a slow, restless pulse; I flow unimpeded through its street map of veins.

I live to keep the city clean, to search out the impurities and deliver retribution.

I am Life and Death, Yin and Yang.

I have no name...

And I know where to find you.

CHAPTER ONE

DOWNTOWN MANHATTAN, NOVEMBER 1926

Something stirred in the shadows.

'Fat Ollie' Day flicked the stub of his cigarette towards the gutter, watching it spiral through the air like a tumbling star. It landed in a puddle of brackish rainwater and fizzed out with a gentle hiss. Nervously, he rested his sweaty palm on the butt of his pistol and edged forward, trying to see what had made the noise. It was too dark to see anything other than the heaps of trash piled up against the walls of the alleyway, illuminated by the silvery beams of the car headlamps. The air was damp. Ollie thought it was going to rain.

Behind him, the car engine purred with a low growl. He'd left it running, ready for a quick getaway. Ollie had stoked it himself a few minutes earlier, shovelling black coal from the hopper into the small furnace at the rear of the vehicle, superheating the fluid in the water tank to build up a head of steam. It was a sleek model – one of the newer types – and Ollie couldn't help grinning every time he ran his hands over its sweeping curves. Who said crime didn't pay?

Now, his smart grey suit was covered in coal dust and soot, but he knew after they'd finished with the job they were doing, he could buy himself another. Heck, he could buy himself a whole wardrobe full if he had the inclination. The boss would see him right. The Roman knew how to look after his guys.

Inside the tall bank building to his left, the four men he'd ferried downtown in the motor car were carrying out a heist – their third in a week – and once again he'd been left outside to guard the doors. It suited Ollie just fine; he'd never had a stomach for the dirty stuff. Being on the periphery didn't worry him – as long as he still got his share of the proceeds.

There was another scuffing sound from up ahead, like a booted foot crunching on stone. Ollie felt the hairs on the back of his neck prickle with anxiety. The pressure valve on the vehicle gave an expectant whistle, as if in empathy, calling out a shrill warning to its driver. Ollie glanced back, but the car was just as he'd left it, the side doors hanging open like clam shells, waiting for the others to finish the job inside.

"Who's there?" He slid his pistol from its holster, easing it into his palm. "I'm warning you. Don't you mess with Ollie Day."

There was a sudden, jerky movement as a nearby heap of trash was disturbed, causing cardboard boxes to tumble noisily to the ground. Ollie swung his pistol round in a wide arc. His hand was shaking. He couldn't see anything in the gloom. Then more movement, to his right. Something crossed the beam of the headlamps. He spun on the spot, his finger almost squeezing the trigger of his pistol...

...and saw a black cat dart across the alleyway, scuttling away from the pile of boxes. Ollie let out a long, wheezing sigh of relief.

"Hey, cat. You got Ollie all jumpy for a minute there." He slipped his pistol back into his holster, grinning to himself. "Man, I gotta learn to take it easy." He looked up.

Two pinpricks of red light had appeared, thirty feet further down the alleyway, hovering in the air at head height. Ollie stood silent for a moment, trying to figure out what was going on. For a minute he thought he was seeing things, and made to rub his eyes, but then the lights began to move, sweeping towards him through the gloom.

Footsteps running. Ragged breath. Ollie fumbled for his weapon, but he was already too late.

The man sprang at him from nearly ten feet away, hurtling through the air towards him like panther, body coiled for an attack. Ollie caught only glimpses of his assailant as the man was crisscrossed in the headlamp beams; dressed fully in black, a long cape or trench coat whipping up around him, a fedora on his head. And those glowing red eyes, piercing in the darkness. Ollie thought they might bore right into him, then and there.

He got the gun loose just as his attacker came down on him, hard, causing the weapon to fly from his hand and skitter across the ground towards the car. It clattered to a stop somewhere out of sight. The man was fast, and Ollie was hardly able to bring his hands up in defence before he was punched painfully in the gut, causing him to double over, all of the air driven out of his lungs. The man grabbed a fistful of Ollie's collar and heaved him bodily into the air. Ollie tried desperately to kick out, or to cry for help, but was able only to offer an ineffectual whimper.

Before he knew what was happening, Ollie felt himself being flung backwards. He sailed through the air, his limbs wheeling, and slammed down across the bonnet of the car. He felt the thin metal give way beneath his bulk. But he had no time to lament the damage to his precious vehicle. Pain blossomed in his shoulder. He realised that his arm had been crushed and was hanging limply by his side. The back of his head, too, felt like it was on fire, and he could sense a warm liquid – blood? – running down the side of his face. He emitted a heartfelt wail, just in time to see the grim face of his attacker looming over him.

The man was unshaven and raw. His eyes – his real eyes – were obscured by a pair of glowing goggles, strange red lights shining bright behind the lenses, transfixing the mob driver as he struggled to inch backwards on the car bonnet, to get away from this terrifying apparition of the night. He had nowhere to go. He was going to die. He squeezed his eyes shut, waiting for the fatal blow. Seconds passed. He peeled his eyelids open again.

The man was still hovering over him. After a moment, he spoke. His voice was gruff and filled with ire. "In there?" He gestured towards the set of double doors that the others were planning to use as their escape route from the bank.

Ollie nodded. He knew he was likely signing his own death warrant by giving them away, but all he could think about was getting free from this maniac, this...vigilante. He could taste blood. If the car would still drive...

The stranger grabbed the front of Ollie's jacket with both fists and hauled him into the air again. "Oh no. No, no, no..."

Turning, the man charged at the double doors, swinging Ollie in front of himself like a battering ram. Ollie's shoulder connected painfully with the heavy wooden doors as they burst through, causing the hinges to splinter and the doors to cave inwards with a huge crash.

Stars bloomed in his field of vision. His head spun. He couldn't remember what it was like to not feel numb with pain. He felt as if he was going to die, and realised that he probably was.

They were standing in the main lobby of the bank. The scene inside was one of utter chaos. Around thirty or forty civilians were scattered over the polished marble floor, laying prone on their bellies, their hands behind their heads, their distraught faces pressed to the ground. Another of The Roman's men was standing over them with a gun, keeping guard. Two further men were standing by the bank tellers as they stuffed cloth bags full of paper bills, and a fourth was up on the gallery overhead, surveying the scene below, a Tommy gun clutched tightly in his hands.

A huge holographic statue of Pegasus dominated the lobby space, flickering ghostly blue as it reared up on its hind legs, its immense wings unfurled over the swathe of terrified civilians below. Above that, an enormous chandelier shimmered in the bright light.

Silence spread through the lobby as everyone turned at once to see who had burst through the doors in such a violent fashion. A woman screamed. The four mobsters offered Ollie and the other man a silent appraisal before raising their weapons.

Ollie was struggling to catch his breath. He couldn't feel his left arm anymore, and he didn't know if this was troubling or a blessed relief. He didn't have time to consider it any further before he found himself unceremoniously dumped against the wall.

"Stay there."

The man in black stepped forward, glancing from side to side. Ollie could see now that his billowing trench coat concealed a number of small contraptions, including what looked like the long barrel of a weapon under his right arm. Dazed, he watched the chaos erupt again before his eyes.

His attacker spread his arms wide, facing the rest of The Roman's men. "Time's up, gentlemen."

One of the mobsters opened fire. There was a series of loud reports as he emptied his chamber, yelling at the others to take the newcomer down. The man in black seemed unconcerned by the spray of bullets, however, waiting as they thundered into the wall behind him, failing even to flinch as the mobster went wide with his shots, too hasty to take proper aim. Ollie watched in dismayed awe as the man gave a discreet flick of his right arm, causing the long, brass barrel of the concealed weapon to spin up on a ratchet and click into place along the length of his forearm. It made a sound like a steel chain being dragged across a metal drum.

The man swung his arm around towards the crook that had fired on him and squeezed something in his palm. There was a quiet hiss of escaping air, and then he gave his reply. A storm of tiny, steel flechettes burst out from the end of the strange weapon, a rain of silver death, hailing down on the crook and shredding him as they impacted, bursting organs and flensing flesh from bone. It was over in a matter of seconds. The shattered body crumpled to the floor, gore and fragments of human matter pattering down around it in a wide arc. The teller who'd been standing beside the felon dropped to the floor in a dead faint, the pile of cash in his hands billowing out to scatter all around him as he fell.

The vigilante didn't wait for the stutter of another gun. He rolled forward and left, moving with ghost-like precision. He came up beside the holographic statue, his weapon at the ready. Another hail of flechettes dropped the man on the gallery above, sending him tumbling over the rail, his face a mess of blood and broken bone fragments. He crashed to the marble with a sickening crunch, his limbs splayed at awkward angles.

The mobster guarding the civilians – who Ollie knew as Bobby Hendriks – wasn't taking any chances. He leapt forward, grappling with one of the women on the floor and dragging her to her feet. Looking panicked, the heavily-set man pressed a knife to her throat, which gleamed in the bright electric light as he turned the blade back and forth, threatening to pull it across her soft, exposed flesh. The woman – a pretty blonde in a blue dress – looked terrified, and froze rigid, trying not to move in case she somehow made the situation worse.

"I'll kill her! I'll kill her!" His voice was a gravelly bark.

The man in black flicked a glance at Hendriks, and then back at the other mobster guarding the tellers, who were still furiously emptying the cash drawers. He stepped towards Hendriks and the hostage.

Hendriks stepped back, mirroring the movement. He pressed the blade firmly against the woman's throat, drawing a tiny bead of blood. She wailed in pain and terror.

A shot went off. The man in black flinched as a bullet stroked his upper arm, tearing a rent in his clothing and drawing a line of bright blood on his skin. He flinched, and then turned on the gunman, but Ollie realised he wasn't able to draw a clear bead due to the tellers. Instead, the man reached inside his trench coat and gave a sharp tug on a hidden cord.

There was a roaring sound, like the deep rumble of a distant explosion. Bright yellow flames shot out of two metal canisters strapped to the back of the man's boots, scorching the floor. Ollie stared on, bewildered, as the stranger lifted entirely into the air, propelled by the bizarre jets, and shot across the lobby at speed, flitting over the prone civilians and swinging out over the mobster's head. He didn't even need to fire his weapon. Bringing his feet around in a sweeping movement, he introduced the searing flames to the face of the gunman, who gave a gut-wrenching wail as his face bubbled and peeled in the intense heat. He dropped on the spot, still clutching his gun, hungry flames licking around his ears and collar.

The man in black reached inside his coat and pulled another cord. The flames spat and guttered out. He crashed to the floor, landing on one knee. All eyes were on him. He climbed slowly to his feet and stood, regarding the last of the felons.

"I'll kill her! I'll kill her!" Hendriks was swinging the girl around as he looked for an escape route, edging away from this terrifying man who had come out of nowhere and murdered his companions.

"I'll kill her! I'll kill her!"

When he spoke, the vigilante's voice was drenched in sorrow. "You already have."

Hendriks looked down at the girl in his arms. Sudden recognition flashed on his face. His knife was half buried in the woman's throat, blood seeping down to drench the front of her dress, matting the fine hairs on his forearm. Shocked, he stumbled backwards, allowing the dead woman to slide to the floor, the knife still buried in her flesh. "Oh crap. Oh crap. I didn't mean to do it. Hey, mister, I didn't mean it! I just –"

There was a quiet snick. Something bright and metal flashed through the air. Hendriks's head toppled from his shoulders, the stump spouting blood in a dark, crimson fountain. The body pitched forward, dropping to the floor. The head rolled off to one side. Ollie glanced round to see a metal disc buried in the wall behind the body. He started to scramble to his feet.

All around, people were screaming, getting up off the floor and rushing towards the exits. The massacre was over. Or at least Ollie hoped it was over. He needed to get to his car, fast.

The man in black stooped low over the body of the dead hostage. He seemed to be whispering an apology, but Ollie wasn't quite able to hear over the noise of the crowd.

Ollie backed up, edging towards the burst double doors. His arm was hanging limp and useless by his side, he was sure his ribcage had been shattered and he was still bleeding from the back of his skull. Even if he made it out of there alive, he'd never be the same again.

He saw the red eyes of the stranger lift and fix on him from across the lobby. He didn't know what to do, didn't dare turn and run or take his eyes off the stranger for a second. The man watched him for a moment, unmoving. Then in three or four graceful strides, he was on top of him. He grasped Ollie by the collar. The fat man whimpered as the vigilante leaned in close. He could feel the hot breath on his face, smell the coffee and whisky it carried. Ollie's heart was hammering hard in his chest. Was this how it was going to end?

"Today, you get to live."

Ollie nearly fainted with relief. "I... I..."

"But you take a message to The Roman for me."

Ollie nodded enthusiastically, and nearly swooned from the movement.

"You tell him he's not welcome in this town anymore."

The stranger dropped Ollie in a heap on the ground, and then stepped over him, making slowly for the exit, his boots clicking loudly on the marble floor.

Ollie's mouth was gritty with blood. He called after the mysterious figure. "Who... who are you?"

The man shrugged and kept on walking. "Death," he said, without bothering to look back.